BEL=AMI

Guy De Maupassant.

The works of Guy de Maupassant

BEL·AMI

Newly translated into English
by
MARJORIE LAURIE

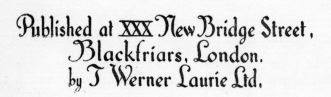

Published at XXX New Bridge Street,
Blackfriars, London.
by T Werner Laurie Ltd.

Printed in Great Britain by Wyman & Sons Ltd., London, Reading and Fakenham.

PART I

I

WHEN the woman at the cash-desk had given him the change
out of his five-franc piece, George Duroy left the restaurant.

To his naturally fine bearing, he added an affectation of
the manner of his former rank of non-commissioned officer.
He threw back his shoulders, and with a soldierly trick of
twirling his moustache, he swept the lingering guests with a
swift glance, such a glance as from the gay eyes of youth
finds its mark as surely as the swoop of a hawk.

All the women in the room looked up at him.   There
were three little working girls ; a music-mistress of doubtful
age, unkempt and untidy, who wore a hat that was never
free from dust and a dress that always hung awry ; and two
middle-class women with their husbands, all of them habitual
frequenters of this fixed-price eating-house.

Once on the pavement he stood still a moment debating
what to do next.   It was the 28th of June, and to last him
until the end of the month he had exactly three francs forty
centimes in his pocket.   This sum was the equivalent of
two dinners without luncheons, or two luncheons without
dinners, whichever he preferred.   A midday meal, he
reflected, would cost him one franc ten centimes, whereas
dinner would be one franc fifty, and if he restricted himself
to luncheons only, he would have a balance of one franc
twenty, the price of two meals of bread and sausage, not to
mention two glasses of beer on the Boulevard.   This last

was his chief extravagance and his principal amusement of an evening.

He began to stroll down the Rue Notre-Dame-de-Lorette. He walked with the same gait as in the days when he wore Hussar uniform—his chest thrown out, his legs a little straddled as if he had just dismounted from horse-back—and he swaggered along the crowded street, jostling and pushing people out of his way. Tilted slightly over one ear he wore a silk hat that had lost its first freshness. His heel struck the pavement crisply. Towards things in general, the passers by, the houses, the whole city, he wore an air of perpetual challenge appropriate to the dashing soldier who has relapsed into a mere civilian.

Although he now wore a ready-made suit costing sixty francs, he had a certain showy smartness, a little vulgar but none-the-less genuine. Tall, well-made, fair, he had a downy moustache with turned-up ends, light blue eyes with very small pupils, chestnut hair with a hint of red, curling naturally and parted in the middle, and his appearance strongly suggested the scapegrace of popular romance.

It was one of those summer evenings when there is no air in Paris. The city, hot as a vapour bath, seemed to sweat in the suffocating night. From the apertures of drainage channels issued noisome exhalations, and from the sunk windows of basement kitchens rose revolting fumes of dishwater and stale sauces.

Hall porters in their shirt-sleeves, seated astride straw-bottomed chairs, were smoking their pipes in the courtyard gateways, and the passers by moved with leaden footsteps, bareheaded, carrying their hats in their hands.

On reaching the Boulevard, George Duroy, still undecided as to what to do next, came again to a halt. He now thought of making his way to the Champs Elysées and the Avenue of the Bois de Boulogne for the sake of the cool air under the trees. But he was actuated too by a second longing, a longing for some amorous adventure.

In what form would this present itself? Of this he had no idea, though he had been waiting for it day and night for three months. Sometimes, indeed, thanks to his good looks and the gallantry of his bearing, he had snatched here and there a casual gratification, but he never lost hope of something more complete and satisfactory.

Though his pockets were empty, his blood was in a ferment, and his senses were kindled by his encounters with the women who haunt the street corners and murmur, " Will you come home with me, my dear ? " But having no money to give them, he dared not follow them. Moreover what he was seeking was something different, endearments of another sort, less promiscuous.

He was none-the-less attracted by the haunts which these young women of the pavement frequent in swarms, their dances, their cafés, their promenades. He enjoyed rubbing shoulders with them, talking to them familiarly, catching a whiff of their crude perfumes, and realising his proximity to them. When all was said and done, these people were women, women whose business was love. He had for them none of the inborn contempt felt for them by the domesticated man.

He turned towards the Madeleine, following the stream of heat-oppressed people. The great crowded cafés overflowed on to the pavements, making a parade of their customers, in the dazzling glare of their frontage. On the little round or square tables in front of the guests stood glasses containing liquids of all shades of red, yellow, green, brown, and in the decanters sparkled solid transparent cylinders of ice, chilling the exquisite clear water.

Duroy had slackened his pace. His throat was parched with his craving for a drink. He was afflicted with a burning thirst, a summer evening thirst, and he kept thinking of the delicious sensation of cold liquids trickling into his mouth. But even if he were to drink no more than two glasses of beer that evening, it meant farewell to to-morrow's meagre supper, and he was only too familiar with those hunger-stricken hours at the end of the month.

He said to himself, " I must carry on till ten o'clock and then I will have my glass of beer at the American Café. But good Lord ! what a thirst I've got ! "

And his eyes swept all those men seated there drinking, men who could quench their thirst at their pleasure. He walked past the cafés with an air of jauntiness and high spirits, and with quick glances at demeanour or dress he estimated the amount of money each customer was likely to have about him.   And he felt a gust of anger at the sight of these people seated there at their ease.   If their pockets were searched, gold, silver and copper would be found there. On an average each man must have at least two louis, and there were certainly a hundred people in the café, and a hundred times two louis came to four thousand francs !

" Pigs ! " he muttered, but he never lost his nonchalant bearing.   If he could have held one of them up at a street corner in a nice dark place, he would have wrung his neck, by Jove ! without turning a hair, just as he used to do with the peasants' fowls, out on manœuvres.

And he called to mind his two years in Africa and how he used to fleece the Arabs in the little outposts in the South. And a smile of cruel amusement passed over his face at the memory of an escapade which had cost the lives of three men of the Ouled-Alane tribe, but to his comrades and himself had been worth a score of fowls, a couple of sheep, some money, and a joke that had lasted them six months.

The culprits had never been discovered, nor indeed, had there been any attempt to do so, Arabs being considered more or less as the soldiers' natural prey.

Paris, however, was another matter.   In Paris there was no possibility of this pleasant freebooting with sabre at side and revolver in fist, far removed from civil justice, safe from interference.   His heart thrilled to all the instincts of the troop sergeant let loose in a conquered country.   How he regretted his two years in the desert.   What a pity he had not stayed there !   But there it was ; he had looked for something better at home.   And now ! what a time he was having to be sure !

With his tongue he made a little clucking sound, to attest the dryness of his palate.

Around him the crowd moved with slow and enervated steps, and he kept thinking :

" What a lot of brutes !   All these imbeciles have got money in their pockets."

4

He jostled people and softly whistled a cheerful tune. Men whom he had hustled, turned and growled at him ; women exclaimed, " Clumsy brute ! "

He passed the Vaudeville and came to a halt opposite the Café Américain, and debated whether he should not have his glass of beer at once, his thirst was such a torture to him. Before making up his mind he looked at the illuminated clock in the middle of the roadway. It was a quarter past nine. But he knew his own weakness. As soon as the glass of beer was set before him he would swallow it down. And then what would he do till eleven o'clock ?

He walked on.

" I shall go as far as the Madeleine," he said, " and walk slowly back."

At the corner of the Place de l'Opera he ran across a stout young man whose face he vaguely remembered to have seen before.

He went after him, racking his memory, saying half aloud :

" Where the deuce have I met that fellow ? "

He ransacked his mind without success. Then suddenly, by a curious freak of memory, the man came back to him, slighter, younger, and in Hussar uniform.

He exclaimed aloud :

" Forestier, of course ! "

He lengthened his stride and tapped him on the shoulder. The other man turned round, looked at him and said :

" What do you want with me, sir ? "

Duroy began to laugh.

" Don't you remember me ? "

" No."

" George Duroy of the VI Hussars."

Forestier held out both his hands.

" My dear old fellow. How are you ? "

" Very well, and you ? "

" I ? Only middling. You'd hardly believe it, but I've a chest like paper pulp now. I have a cough six months out of twelve and all through an attack of bronchitis which

5

I caught at Bougival the year I came back to Paris. It's four years now."

" You don't say so. You look fairly robust for all that."

Forestier took his old comrade's arm, spoke to him of his malady, and told him all about the doctors' consultations, opinions and advice, and how difficult it was for a man in his position to carry out their orders. He had been advised to spend the winter in the south, but how was that possible for a married man and a journalist of good standing ?

" On the *Vie Française* I am political editor ; for the *Salut* I do the Senate, for the *Planète* I occasionally write articles. You see I have got on."

Duroy looked at him in surprise. He had changed greatly and had matured. He now had the manner, the deportment, the clothes of a man in an assured position, certain of himself ; his figure was that of one who dines well. In the old days he had been slender and supple, careless, boisterous, noisy and always in high spirits. Three years of Paris had made him a different being ; he was stout, composed, and had a sprinkling of grey on the temples, although he was not more than twenty-seven.

" Where are you going ? " he asked.

" Nowhere in particular," replied Duroy. " I am taking a stroll before going home."

" Well, will you come with me to the *Vie Française ?* I have some proofs to correct there. Then we will go and have a glass of beer."

" I'm with you."

And they walked away arm in arm with the easy familiarity which exists between school-fellows and comrades in arms.

" What are you doing in Paris ? " asked Forestier.

Duroy shrugged his shoulders.

" Starving, neither more nor less. When my time was up, my idea was to come here to make my fortune, or rather to live in Paris. For the last six months I have been working in the office of the Nord Railway, on a salary of fifteen hundred francs a year—not a sou more."

" You won't get fat on that," Forestier murmured.

" You are right there, but how am I to get out of it ?

I am all by myself. I don't know a soul. I can't get a footing anywhere. It's not the will that's lacking, it's the means."

His comrade looked him up and down with the air of a practical man who is taking a person's measure. Then he gave his opinion in a tone of conviction.

" Listen, my boy. Here in Paris everything depends on being able to carry it off. It is easier for a man with some adroitness to become a minister of state than a permanent official. You must assert yourself and not beg favours. How the deuce haven't you managed to find something better than a clerkship at the Nord ? "

" I've hunted everywhere," Duroy replied, " and I can find nothing. But at the present moment I have something in view. I have been offered a post as riding-master at Pellerin's. That would be worth at least three thousand to me."

Forestier stopped short.

" Don't do that. It would be idiotic when you ought to be earning ten thousand. You would ruin your prospects at one blow. In your office you are at least out of sight. No one knows you. If you have the grit, you have a chance of getting out of it and making your way. But once a riding-master, it is all up with you. It would be like being head waiter in an establishment where all the right people dine. Once you have given riding lessons to men of that sort or to their sons they will never get used to looking upon you as an equal."

He fell silent, thought for a few moments, and then asked :
" Have you taken your degree ? "
" No. I failed twice."
" That doesn't matter, as long as you have done the work for it. If people mention Cicero or Tiberius, you know more or less what they mean."
" Yes, more or less."
" Good, nobody knows any more than that, except a score or so of imbeciles who hadn't the sense to get out of it. It's easy enough to pass for clever ; the only thing that matters is not to let yourself be caught out in any obvious

blunder. You change your tactics, use a little adroitness, get round the obstacle, stop other people's mouths with a dictionary. They all are as stupid as geese and as ignorant as mudfish."

He talked with the genial composure of one who knows life, and as he looked at the passing crowd he smiled. But suddenly he was seized with a fit of coughing, and he stood still until the attack was over. Then he resumed in a tone of depression :

" Isn't it maddening not to be able to get over this bronchitis ? And this is midsummer. I shall certainly go to Mentone this winter and get cured. The rest can go hang. Health comes first."

In the Boulevard Poissonnière they came to a big glazed door, at the back of which was pasted up an open newspaper. Three people were standing there, reading it.

Above the door, to attract attention, the words *La Vie Française* were displayed in huge flaming letters formed by gas jets, and the passers-by, entering suddenly into the space lighted by these three fiery words, were all at once revealed in the bright illumination as clearly and distinctly as at midday ; then they plunged again back into shadow.

Forestier pushed open the door.

" Come in," he said.

Duroy entered and ascended an imposing but ill-kept staircase, visible to the whole street ; thence he passed into an ante-room where two office boys said " good evening " respectfully, and finally he stopped in a kind of waiting-room, dusty and shabby, hung with imitation velvet of a greenish colour, bespattered with stains, and eaten away in parts, as if it had been gnawed by mice.

" Sit down," said Forestier, " I shall be back in five minutes."

And he disappeared through one of the three doors leading out of the little room.

The strange, indescribable odour, characteristic of newspaper premises, hovered about this place. Duroy remained motionless, somewhat overawed, and not a little surprised. Every now and then men passed him, running in at one door and out at the other, before he had time to take them in. Some of them were young, very young indeed, and appeared to be very busy ; they held in their hands sheets of paper which fluttered as they ran. Others were compositors wearing inkstained cotton overalls, clean white shirt collars, and trousers of good material. They carried carefully strips of printed paper, proofs damp from the press. Sometimes a small dandified gentleman would enter, dressed with an elegance a little too conspicuous, his frockcoat too closely moulded to his figure, his legs too well defined under the material of his trousers, his feet confined in shoes excessively pointed. These men were society reporters bringing in the evening gossip. Others were continually arriving, solemn, full of importance, and all wore tall hats with flat brims, as though by this fashion to distinguish themselves from the outside world.

Forestier reappeared, holding by the arm a tall, thin man, between thirty and forty years of age, wearing a black coat and a white tie. He was of very dark complexion ; the ends of his moustache were twisted to sharp points, and he had an insolent and self-satisfied air.

Forestier said to him :

" Good-bye, my dear sir."

The other shook hands with him :

" Good-bye, my dear fellow," and he descended the stairs whistling, with his walking-stick under his arm.

" Who is that ? " asked Duroy.

" That is the celebrated Jacques Rival, the journalist who is always fighting duels. He has just been correcting proofs. For getting at the facts and handling them well he and Carin and Montel are the three best men in Paris. We pay him thirty thousand francs a year for two articles a week."

As they left the building they met a small, stout, long-haired man, of unwashed appearance, who breathed heavily as he climbed the stairs. Forestier made him a low bow.

" Norbert de Varenne, the poet," he said, " author of *Dead Suns*. Another of the high-priced ones. Every story he gives us costs us three hundred francs and the longest of them is under two hundred lines. But let's go along to the Café Napolitain ; I am dying of thirst."

When they were seated at a table in the café Forestier called for two glasses of beer, and swallowed his own at a draught. Duroy, on the other hand, sipped his beer slowly, with leisurely and careful appreciation, as if it were something rare and precious.

His companion seemed to be busy with his own reflections and kept silence. But suddenly he broke out :

" Why not try journalism ? "

Duroy looked at him in surprise.

" Yes, but the difficulty is that I've never written anything."

" Nonsense. Everything has a beginning. You could do some work for me, picking up information, doing the preliminaries, and going to see people. To begin with you would have two hundred and fifty francs a month and your cab fares. Would you like me to speak to the Director about it ? "

" Of course I should like it immensely."

" Well, to begin with, come and dine with me to-morrow. I am having just five or six people, the proprietor, Monsieur Walter, his wife, Jacques Rival, and Norbert de Varenne, whom you have just seen, and a friend of my wife's. You'll come ? "

Blushing and perplexed, Duroy hesitated. At last he said shamefacedly :

" I'm afraid——I haven't any proper clothes."

Forestier was horrified.

" You haven't a dress suit ? My dear fellow, it's an absolute necessity. I assure you in Paris you had better be without a bed than without a dress suit."

Then without a moment's delay, he felt in his waistcoat pocket, brought out some gold coins between thumb and finger, took two louis and laid them down in front of his old comrade. Then in a cordial and friendly tone he said :

" Pay me back when you can. You must hire, or buy by monthly instalments, what clothes you require. Do what is necessary, in short, and come to dinner at my house, 17, Rue Fontaine, to-morrow at half-past seven."

Duroy, in confusion, picked up the money and stammered :

" It's much too good of you. I can't thank you enough. I assure you I shan't forget."

The other interrupted him.

" That's all right. Another glass of beer, don't you think ? "

And he called for two more glasses.

When they had finished them, Forestier said :

" Would you care to stroll about with me for an hour or so ? "

" Yes, certainly."

They set out again in the direction of the Madeleine.

" How shall we put in our time ? " asked Forestier, " People tell you that there is plenty for an idle man to do in Paris, but it is not true. When I want to amuse myself of an evening I never know where to go. A turn in the Bois is only amusing when you have a woman with you, and you can't always lay your hand on one. Variety shows may be amusing enough for apothecaries and their wives, but not for me. So what is there to do ? Nothing. There ought to be an open-air place like the Parc Monceau for summer evenings, for listening to the best music, with cold drinks under the trees. I don't mean a place of entertainment, but somewhere to loaf about. To attract the pretty ladies the price of admission would be kept high. You could take a stroll along the gravelled walks, which would be lighted by electricity, and sit down and listen to the music from any distance you liked. We used to have something of the sort at Musard's. But there was a certain cheapness and rowdiness about it, too much dance music, not enough space and shade and darkness. It would have to be a very fine garden with plenty of room. That would be delightful. Well, where would you like to go ? "

Duroy was perplexed and did not know what to say. But at last he made up his mind.

" I have never been to the Folies-Bergère. I should like to look in there."

" The Folies-Bergère," exclaimed his companion, " it will be like an oven. Never mind. It's always amusing."

And they turned on their heels in the direction of the Rue Faubourg-Montmartre. The music hall stood at the junction of four streets, along which the brilliantly illuminated façade cast a bright light.

A string of carriages was awaiting the end of the performance.

Forestier was walking straight in when Duroy stopped him.

" We haven't paid."

" We don't," replied Forestier consequentially.

The three officials at the ticket barrier received him politely, and the one in the middle shook hands with him.

" Have you a nice box for me ? " Forestier asked.

" Yes, certainly, Monsieur Forestier."

Forestier took the slips of paper that were offered him, pushed open the padded, leather-bordered double doors, and they found themselves in the hall. The stage and the remoter parts of the hall were veiled in a thin mist of tobacco smoke, a mist which streamed ever upwards from cigar and cigarette, accumulated in the ceiling and formed a cloudy canopy beneath the great dome, around the chandelier, and above the crowded balcony.

In the wide entrance corridor leading to the circular promenade, with its bedizened troops of young women and its crowd of soberly dressed men, a group of women was standing waiting for new arrivals in front of the three bars, each of which was presided over by a siren, a trafficker in love and drink, rouged and no longer youthful.

The tall mirrors behind them reflected their backs and the faces of the passers-by.

Forestier moved quickly forward through the throng with the manner of one entitled to special consideration. He went up to an attendant.

" Box No. 17 ? " he said.

" This way, sir."

They were shut into a little compartment open at the top. It had red hangings and contained four chairs of the same colour, set so close together that it was almost impossible to pass between them. The two friends sat down. On either side, in a long curve reaching as far as the stage, there was a row of boxes similar to their own, containing people seated like themselves, with only their heads and shoulders visible. On the stage three young men in tights, one tall, one of medium height, the third small, were performing on a trapeze in turns. The tall young man was the first to come forward, advancing with short, quick steps. He smiled and made a gesture, as if kissing his hand to the audience.

The muscles of his arms and legs stood out under his fleshings. He swelled out his chest in order to make less conspicuous his somewhat prominent stomach. The careful parting which divided his hair equally along the precise centre line of the crown gave him the look of a barber's assistant. With a graceful bound he caught the trapeze, and hanging by his hands he swung round and round like a revolving wheel. Again with stiff arms and taut body, he held himself motionless and horizontal in space, supporting himself on the bar of the trapeze merely by the force of his wrists.

Then he leaped to the ground, acknowledged with a smile the applause of the pit, and went and leaned up against the scenery, taking care at every step to show off the muscular development of his legs.

The second acrobat, shorter and more thickset, came forward in turn and went through the same performance, and the third repeated it yet again, with the special approbation of the public.

But Duroy paid little attention to the performance. His head was turned away and he gazed unceasingly at the great promenade behind him full of men and prostitutes.

Forestier said to him :

"Look at the body of the house, nothing there but middle-class people with their wives and children, decent stupid creatures who have come to watch the show. In the boxes are men about town, artists, a few ladies of the *demi-monde*, and at the back there the queerest mixture in all Paris. What do you make of them all ! Just look at them.

All sorts and conditions of men, and the common bond is some form of depravity. There are bank clerks, store clerks, government clerks, reporters, bullies, officers in mufti, swells in evening dress, who have been dining at a restaurant and have just come out of the Opera, and are going on to the Italians, not to mention a whole crowd of suspicious characters who don't fall into any class. As for the women they are all tarred with the same stick, the lady who sups at the Café Américain, or the girl whose price is one or two louis, though she does the foreigner out of five, and who lets her regular clients know when she is free. Year after year the same lot turns up. Every evening, the whole year through, you meet them at the same places, except when they are having a little rest at St. Lazare or Lourcine."

Duroy was no longer listening. One of these women was leaning her elbows on the box and looking at him. She was a big, dark girl, her skin whitened with cosmetics. Her black eyes, lengthened and underlined with crayon, were shadowed by exaggerated, painted eyebrows. Her over-developed bosom strained the dark silk of her gown, and her painted lips, red as an open wound, invested her with something bestial, ardent, fantastic, but provocative none the less.

She made a sign with her head to one of her friends, a fair girl, red haired and, like herself, fat, and she said to her, loud enough to be overheard :

" I say, here's a good-looking fellow. If he wants ten louis' worth of me, I shan't say no."

Forestier turned round and smiled and tapped him on the leg.

" That's meant for you. You've made a hit, my boy. I congratulate you."

Duroy had blushed. He kept mechanically fingering the two gold coins in his waistcoat pocket. The curtain was lowered and the orchestra was now playing a waltz.

" Suppose," said Duroy, " we take a turn in the gallery."

" Certainly."

They left the box and were forthwith swept away by the moving throng.

Crowded, jostled, crushed, pushed here and there, they were borne along, with a sea of hats before their eyes. And the young women moved about, two and two, through this crowd of men, making their way with ease, gliding in between elbows, chests and backs as if they were perfectly at home, perfectly at ease, like fish in the water, in the midst of this swaying sea of males. Duroy gave himself up to his enjoyment. With exhilaration he breathed in the air polluted by tobacco smoke, the general odour of humanity, and the special perfumes of the courtesans. But Forestier sweated, panted and coughed.

" Let's go into the garden," he said.

And turning to the left they entered a kind of covered garden, kept cool by two badly designed fountains under yews and evergreens in tubs. People of both sexes sat drinking at zinc tables.

" Another glass of beer," suggested Forestier.

" Yes, thank you."

They seated themselves and watched the people passing by.

Occasionally one of the women who were prowling about would stop and ask with a set smile :

" Won't you stand me a drink ? " And as Forestier invariably answered, " Yes, a glass of water from the fountain," she would move away murmuring, " O shut up, you silly ass."

But the stout, dark woman, who had been leaning against the back of the box that the two friends had occupied, reappeared, walking along with an arrogant air, her arm in that of the stout, fair woman. And a pretty pair they made, the two of them.

She smiled when she caught sight of Duroy, as if their eyes had already told each other intimate and secret things. Taking a chair she calmly seated herself opposite to him and made her friend sit down too. Then in a loud voice she called out, " Waiter, two grenadines."

" You make yourself at home," exclaimed Forestier in astonishment.

She replied, " It's your friend who attracts me. Isn't

15

he good looking ? I believe I'd make a fool of myself for him."

Duroy was embarrassed and had nothing to say. With a foolish smile he twisted the ends of his moustache. The waiter brought the grenadines and the women tossed them off. Then they rose and the dark one, with a friendly nod, tapped Duroy on the arm with her fan and said :

" Thank you, my dear. You haven't much to say for yourself."

And they walked away, swinging their hips.

Forestier began to laugh.

" I say, my dear fellow, do you know that you have a way with women ? That's worth cultivating. It may carry you far."

He was silent a moment, then resumed with the abstracted air of a person thinking aloud :

" After all, it's the women who get you there quickest."

As Duroy continued to smile without answering, he said :

" Are you staying any longer ? I'm going home. I have had enough."

His friend replied, " Yes, I shall stay a little longer. It isn't late."

Forestier rose to go.

" Well, then, good-bye. See you to-morrow. Don't forget, 17 Rue Fontaine at half-past seven."

" You can depend on me. To-morrow then. And thank you."

They shook hands and Forestier moved away.

When he was out of sight Duroy had a feeling of freedom, and again he joyfully fingered the two gold coins in his pocket. Then he left his chair, and began to search the crowd with eager eyes.

He soon caught sight of the two women, the one fair and the other dark, who kept moving with the demeanour of truculent beggars, to and fro in that crowd of men.

He went straight towards them, but when he was quite near his courage deserted him.

The dark one said to him :

" Have you found your tongue again ? "

" Upon my soul," he stammered, and could not manage to bring out another word.

All three came to a halt, blocking the movement of the promenade, which eddied around them.

Then without further preface, she put a question :

" Will you come home with me ? "

And Duroy, trembling with eager desire, replied with equal frankness :

" Yes, but I have only one louis in my pocket."

She smiled with indifference.

" That doesn't matter."

And she took his arm as a sign of ownership.

As they went out, he reflected that with the second louis he could easily hire his evening dress for the following day.

II

"Where does Monsieur Forestier live, please?"

"Third floor on your left."

The hall porter had made his reply in amiable tones that indicated a favourable opinion of his tenant. George Duroy ascended the staircase.

He felt somewhat awkward, timid, and embarrassed. For the first time in his life he was wearing evening dress and he was uneasy about his general appearance. He was conscious that every detail was imperfect, from his shoes, which were not of patent leather, though for the matter of that neat enough, as Duroy was particular about his feet, to his shirt which he had purchased that very morning at the Louvre for four francs fifty, and of which the front was so flimsy that it was already giving way. His everyday shirts were all more or less the worse for wear so that even the best of them was hardly presentable. The trousers, which were a little too loose for him, did not fit his legs well and seemed to flap about his calves, and had that crumpled look which second-hand garments have on the limbs which they fortuitously clothe. The coat, however, looked fairly well, and was a moderately good fit.

He went slowly up the stairs. His heart was beating, and his mind was full of anxiety. What especially disquieted him was his fear of being ridiculous. Suddenly he came face to face with a gentleman in full evening dress, who looked at him. They were so near to each other that Duroy took a step backwards and then halted in stupefaction. It was himself he was looking at, his own image reflected in a tall pier glass on the first floor landing, which gave the illusion of a vista resembling a long gallery. A thrill of joy passed through him ; he looked so much more presentable than he would ever have believed.

Having only a small pocket mirror at home he had not been able to obtain a complete view of himself, and as he had only gained a very imperfect idea of the various parts of his improvised attire, he had exaggerated the defects and had been in an agony at the idea of being grotesque.

And now suddenly confronted with his image in the mirror he actually had not recognised himself ; he had taken himself for another person, some man of fashion, who had immediately impressed him as being thoroughly well turned out. Examining himself carefully he came to the conclusion that the general effect was quite satisfactory.

Then he began to study himself as actors do in preparing their parts. He smiled at himself, held out his hand, made gestures, assumed expressions of surprise, pleasure, approbation, and made trial of various smiles and signs and significant glances such as serve to make an impression upon ladies, and intimate to them that they have inspired admiration and desire.

A door on the staircase was opened. He was afraid of being taken by surprise and started running upstairs very quickly, his mind full of the fear of having been seen posturing by some fellow guest.

On the second landing he saw another mirror. As he passed, he slackened his pace to look at himself and he was struck by the elegance of his appearance. He walked well. And he felt himself overflowing with boundless self-confidence. Of a certainty, he could not but succeed with a face like his, with the ambition and the determination of which he was conscious, and his independence of spirit. A desire seized him to run and leap up the stairs of the last story. In front of the third mirror he halted again, and twirled his moustache with the gesture so familiar to him, took off his hat in order to smooth his hair, and murmured half aloud as he often did :

"What an excellent idea this is ! "

Then he stretched out his hand to the bell and rang it.

The door was opened at once and he found himself confronted by a manservant in black, solemn, clean-shaven and so well turned out that Duroy was again perturbed, without realising the source of his vague emotion. It sprang perhaps from an unconscious comparison between the cut of their clothes. The servant, who was wearing patent leather shoes, took the overcoat which Duroy had been carrying over his arm, for fear of displaying the spots on it.

"What name, sir ? " he asked.

From the looped-back curtain at the door of the drawing-room which Duroy was about to enter he announced his name. Duroy's self-possession suddenly deserted him ; he felt paralysed and breathless with fear. He was about to take his first step into the life to which he had looked forward and of which he had dreamed. He advanced into the room. A young, fair-haired woman stood waiting for him all alone in a large well-lighted room, which was full of plants like a greenhouse.

He stopped short, quite taken aback. Who was the lady who was smiling ? Then he remembered that Forestier was married, and the thought that this pretty and graceful young woman must be his friend's wife completed his consternation. He stammered :

" Madam, I am——"

She held out her hand.

" I know all about you. Charles told me about your meeting yesterday evening and I am very glad he had the happy thought of asking you to dine with us to-day."

He blushed up to the ears, not knowing what to say, and he was conscious that he was examined and inspected from head to foot, and weighed and judged. He felt a desire to make excuses, to apologise for the defects of his dress, but he could think of nothing to say and did not venture to touch on that difficult subject.

He sat down in an arm-chair that she had indicated to him, and when he felt the soft, springy velvet yielding under him, when he felt himself sinking into, sustained, embraced by this caressing piece of furniture, gently supported by its padded back and arms, it seemed to him that he was entering upon a new and delightful existence, that he was taking possession of something delicious, that he was no longer a nobody, that his chance had come. And he looked at Madame Forestier, whose eyes had never left him.

She wore a gown of pale blue cashmere, which moulded her slender figure and plump bosom. Her bodice and short sleeves were trimmed with filmy white lace which left her arms and neck bare, and her hair, which was dressed on the top of her head, broke into little curls on the nape of the neck, like a soft cloud of light-coloured down.

Duroy recovered confidence under her gaze, and it reminded him, he did not know why, of the young woman he had met the night before at the Folies Bergère. She had eyes of grey, a blue-grey that gave them a curious expression, a small fine nose, strong lips, a somewhat full chin. Her features were irregular but attractive, and her face full of grace and archness. It was one of those women's faces of which each lineament reveals a special charm and possesses its own significance, and whose every play of feature is a mystery or a revelation.

She broke the short silence by asking him, " Have you been long in Paris ? "

Gradually regaining his composure he replied :

" Only a few months. I have a post in the railways, but Monsieur Forestier has allowed me to hope that thanks to him I might gain a footing in journalism."

Her smile became more pronounced, more friendly, and lowering her voice she murmured :

" Yes, I know."

The bell had rung again. The servant announced :

" Madame de Marelle."

The new-comer was small and dark, the type one describes as brunette. She entered with an alert air. The contours of her figure were moulded from head to foot by a perfectly simple black gown.

A single red rose in her black hair challenged the eye and gave a sort of distinction to her countenance, accentuating its special character and conferring on it the requisite note of brisk vivacity.

A little girl in a short frock followed her. Madame Forestier darted forward :

" Good evening, Clotilde."

" Good evening, Madeleine."

They kissed each other. Then the child offered her forehead with the assurance of a grown-up person and said :

" Good evening, cousin."

Madame Forestier kissed her, and then made the necessary introductions.

" Monsieur George Duroy, an old friend of Charles's— Madame de Marelle, my friend and my distant relation. You know," she went on, " we don't stand on ceremony in this house ; there's no formality or pretence. That's understood, isn't it ? "

Duroy bowed.

The door opened again, and a stout gentleman, squat and rotund of figure, entered ; on his arm a handsome woman, taller and much younger than he, of distinguished manners and grave demeanour. These two were Monsieur Walter, Deputy, financier, wealthy business man, Jew from the south of France, director of the *Vie Française*, and his wife, who was the daughter of Basile Ravalau, the banker.

Then, one on the heels of the other, came Jacques Rival, perfectly dressed, and Norbert de Varenne, whose coat-collar was shining from the friction of his long hair, which reached to his shoulders and scattered over them a sprinkling of white dust. His carelessly knotted tie seemed to have done service before. He came forward with the air of an old beau, and taking Madame Forestier's hand imprinted a kiss on her wrist. As he bent down his long hair fell forward like a cascade on his hostess's bare arm.

Forestier then entered with apologies for being late. He had been detained at the office by the Morel affair. Monsieur Morel, a radical Deputy, had just addressed a question to the Ministry on a vote of credit relative to the colonisation of Algeria.

The servant announced that dinner was ready and they went into the dining-room.

Duroy found himself seated between Madame de Marelle

and her daughter. His embarrassment returned ; he was afraid of making some mistake in the conventional use of forks, spoons or glasses. He had four glasses and one of them was tinted a faint blue. What was one supposed to drink out of that ?

Nothing was said during soup ; then Norbert de Varenne asked :

" Have you read the Gauthier case ? What an odd affair ! "

Then they discussed this case of adultery complicated by blackmail. They did not talk of it as one talks in the bosom of one's family of events one has read about in the newspapers, but rather after the fashion of doctors discussing a case, or greengrocers, vegetables. They showed neither indignation nor surprise ; they investigated the deep and hidden causes with professional curiosity and with utter indifference towards the crime itself. They endeavoured to explain clearly the origin of these acts, to define all the phenomena of the brain that had resulted in the drama, which was the logical consequence of a particular mental condition. The women, too, were passionately interested in this work of investigation and dissection. Other recent events were analysed, commented upon, regarded from every point of view, estimated at their proper value, and with the practised glance and the special way of regarding things which is peculiar to the purveyors of news, who sell the comedy of humanity by the line, after the manner of tradesmen examining, turning over and weighing the goods they are about to deliver to the public.

Mention was made of a duel, and the word was now with Jacques Rival. This was his province, and no one else was permitted to deal with the subject.

Duroy did not venture to utter a word. Occasionally he glanced at his neighbour, whose rounded bosom allured him. A diamond on a gold thread was hanging from the lobe of her ear like a drop of water that had glided there. Now and then she made a remark which always evoked a general smile. She had a quaint, pleasing, unexpected wit, the wit of a tomboy with experience of life, who regards things unconcernedly and judges them with a kindly scepticism.

Duroy racked his brain in vain for a pretty speech, but as he could think of nothing, he turned his attention to her daughter, filled her glass, handed her dishes, looked after her. More reserved than her mother the child thanked him gravely with slight inclinations of her head.

" You are very kind."

And she listened to what the grown-up people were saying with a little meditative air.

It was a very good dinner and every one was in raptures. Monsieur Walter devoured his food like an ogre, hardly spoke at all, and contemplated the dishes offered to him with sidelong glances from beneath his eyeglasses. Norbert de Varenne kept pace with him and occasionally spilt some drops of gravy on his shirt front.

Forestier, smiling gravely, his eye on everything, exchanged glances of intelligence with his wife in the manner of confederates engaged on a difficult task which is progressing satisfactorily.

Faces were flushed, voices raised. And the servant, at short intervals, murmured in the ears of the guests :

" Corton—Chateau-Laroze ? "

Duroy had found the burgundy to his taste, and each time he allowed his glass to be filled. A delicious sensation of gaiety stole over him, a genial gaiety rising from his stomach to his head, racing through his limbs and pervading his whole system. He felt himself invaded by a sense of perfect well-being, a well-being of life and thought, of body and soul, and he wanted to talk, to attract notice, to be listened to and appreciated like the men whose slightest utterance is relished.

But the conversation which had flowed on without a break, now linking one idea with another, now leaping from subject to subject at a word or the merest hint, after making the round of all the topics of the day and touching by the way upon a thousand questions, reverted to Monsieur Morel's great interpellation concerning the colonisation of Algeria.

Monsieur Walter, who had a coarse and sceptic wit, made some jesting remarks between two courses. Forestier ran through his next day's article. Jacques Rival demanded a military government, with land grants to be issued to all officers after thirty years of colonial service.

" In this way." he said, " you will form a flourishing community of men who have long ago learnt to know and to love the country, who are well acquainted with the language and are in touch with all those important local questions which new-comers are always coming to grief over."

Norbert de Varenne interrupted him :

" Yes, they will know about everything except agriculture. They will be able to speak Arabic, but they won't know how to transplant beetroot or how to sow corn. They may be very strong with the foils, but they will be very weak on fertilisers. No, the right thing to do is to throw open this new country to every one. The intelligent people will get on ; the others will go under. That's the law of society."

There was a short silence. Smiles were exchanged.

George Duroy opened his mouth and made a statement ; he was as much surprised at the sound of his own voice as if he had never before heard himself speak.

" What is most lacking over there is good soil. The really fertile estates are as expensive to buy as in France, and have been purchased, as investments, by wealthy people in Paris. The colonists proper, who are poor people, driven into exile by hunger, are thrown back upon the desert where nothing will grow because of the want of water."

Every one looked at him. He felt himself blushing.

" You know Algeria, Monsieur Duroy ? " asked Monsieur Walter.

" Yes," he answered, " I was there two years and four months and was stationed in all three provinces."

And suddenly forgetting all about the subject of Morel, Norbert de Varenne questioned him about some detail of manners and customs of which he had been informed by an officer. It dealt with the Mzab, that strange little Arab republic, sprung up in the midst of the Sahara, in the driest zone of that burning region.

Duroy had paid two visits to the Mzab, and he told stories of the customs of that curious country, where drops of water have the value of gold, and every inhabitant is bound to perform all public duties, and where commercial honesty attains a higher standard than among civilised nations.

He talked with a certain braggadocio, excited by the wine and by his anxiety to please. He narrated anecdotes of his regiment, characteristics of Arab life, incidents of warfare. He even found some vivid words to describe those lands that lie bare and yellow, for ever desolate under the devouring heat of the sun. All the women kept their eyes on him. Madame Walter murmured in her slow way of speaking :

" Your recollections would make a charming series of articles."

Monsieur Walter contemplated the young man over the top of his spectacles, as he always did when he wanted to study a face. Dishes he would look at under his glasses.

Forestier seized his opportunity.

" My dear sir, I spoke to you just now about Monsieur George Duroy, asking you to let me have him for the purpose of obtaining information on political matters. Since Marambot left us I have no one to send out to secure urgent and confidential reports, and the paper suffers in consequence."

Old Monsieur Walter grew serious and pushed his spectacles right up, in order to look Duroy full in the face. Then he said :

" It is clear that Monsieur Duroy has an original mind. If he will be good enough to come and have a talk with me to-morrow at three o'clock, we will arrange matters."

After a silence, and addressing himself entirely to the young man, he continued :

" But do us a series of fanciful little sketches about Algeria at once. You can tell this story of your recollections, and introduce into it the question of colonisation as you did just now. It's the genuine thing, absolutely genuine, and I am sure our readers would like it very much. But you must be quick. I must have the first article for to-morrow or the day after to catch the public while the discussion is going on in the Chamber."

With a certain gracious seriousness, which characterised all her actions and lent an air of kindly condescension to her words, Madame Walter added :

" And you will have a charming title ' Recollections of an African Light Horseman.' Don't you think so, Monsieur Norbert ? "

The old poet, to whom fame had come late in life, detested and feared new-comers. He answered dryly :

" Excellent, as long as the series strikes the right note. That's where the great difficulty lies. The right note, what you would call the key in music."

Madame Forestier enveloped Duroy with a smiling, protective glance, the glance of an expert, which seemed to say :

" You are all right ; you will get there."

Madame de Marelle had turned towards him repeatedly, and the diamond in her ear trembled unceasingly, as if the tiny drop of water were about to detach itself and fall. The little girl remained motionless and solemn, her head bent over her plate. The servant went the round of the table, pouring Johannisberg into the blue glasses, and Forestier, bowing to Monsieur Walter, proposed a toast

" Long life and prosperity to the *Vie Française !* "

Every one bowed to the director, who smiled, and Duroy, intoxicated with his triumph, drained his glass. It seemed to him that, with the same ease, he could have tossed off a whole barrel, devoured an ox, strangled a lion. He felt in his limbs superhuman strength and in his mind invincible resolution and boundless hope. He was at his ease now in the midst of these people ; he had secured his position among them and won for himself a place. His eyes swept their faces with newly acquired assurance, and for the first time he ventured to address his neighbour.

" You have the prettiest ear-rings I have ever seen."

She turned towards him with a smile.

" It is my own idea to string diamonds like this, singly on the end of a thread of gold. You would take them for dew-drops, wouldn't you ? "

Abashed at his own audacity and trembling lest he should be going too far, he murmured :

" It is charming, but the ear itself gives value to the diamond."

She thanked him with a glance, one of those bright glances from a woman's eyes that strike home to the heart.

And when he turned his head to meet Madame Forestier's eyes, they were friendly still, but to his mind they now sparkled with a livelier gaiety, archness and encouragement.

The men were now all talking at the same time, gesticulating and raising their voices. They were discussing the great scheme for the Metropolitan Railway. The subject was not exhausted till dessert was over, every one having a great deal to say about the slowness of communications in Paris. the shortcomings of trams, the tediousness of omnibuses and the insolence of cab-drivers.

Then they left the dining-room to have coffee. Duroy, in joke, offered his arm to the little girl. She thanked him gravely and raised herself on tiptoe so that she could place her hand in the crook of his arm.

On entering the drawing-room, he had again the impression of stepping into a greenhouse. In all four corners of the room tall palms unfolded their graceful leaves. They reached up to the ceiling, and there they spread themselves out like jets of water.

On either side of the fire-place were indiarubber plants, with columnar stems and tiers of long dark green leaves. On the piano stood two small trees of a kind unknown to him. They were round in shape, the one covered with pink, the other with white blossoms. They had a look of artificiality, of improbability, as if too pretty to be real.

The air was cool and pervaded with a vague and pleasant perfume, which could neither be defined nor named. More self-possessed now, Duroy surveyed the room attentively. It was not large ; except the plants, there was nothing in it to attract the eye ; no striking note of brilliant colour. But one felt at one's ease there, tranquil, soothed. Its atmosphere gently enveloped and charmed, embracing one as with a caress.

The walls were hung with an old fabric of faded violet strewn with small yellow silk flowers about the size of flies.

The doors were draped with curtains of blue-grey uniform cloth, on which carnations were embroidered in red silk. The chairs, which were of all shapes and sizes and distributed haphazard through the room—long chairs, arm-chairs, large and small, ottomans and foot-stools—were covered with Louis XVI silk or handsome Utrecht velvet, with a crimson pattern on a cream ground.

" Will you take coffee, Monsieur Duroy ? "

And Madame Forestier handed him a cup of coffee with the friendly smile that never left her lips.

He took the cup, and as he was painfully bending down to extract a lump of sugar with the silver tongs from the sugar bowl that the little girl was carrying, his hostess said to him in an undertone :

" You had better go and pay your respects to Madame Walter."

Then she withdrew before he could say one word in reply.

First of all he drank his coffee, as he was afraid of spilling it on the carpet. Then, his mind more at ease, he sought for some pretext for approaching the wife of his new director and entering into conversation with her.

Suddenly he noticed that she was holding an empty cup in her hand, and that, as there was no table near her, she did not know what to do with it. He sprang to her side.

" Permit me."

" Thank you, Monsieur Duroy."

He took away the cup and then returned to her.

" I wish I could tell you, Madame Walter, what pleasant moments I owed to *La Vie Française* when I was in the desert out there. It is really the only newspaper that is worth reading when one is away from France ; it is the most literary, the most intellectual and the least monotonous of all. There is a little of everything in it."

She smiled with amiable indifference and answered gravely :

" My husband has taken great pains to create a journal of this type, in response to a new demand."

They began to converse. Duroy had an easy flow of small-talk, a charming voice, a very pleasing expression, and a moustache which was irresistibly fascinating. Curly, wavy, attractive, it grew crisply on his lip. It was fair with a hint of red, and the pointed ends were of a lighter shade.

They talked about Paris and its surroundings, the banks of the Seine, watering places, the pleasures of summer, all the current topics which one can discuss indefinitely without tiring one's brain.

When Norbert de Varenne approached with a glass of liqueur in his hand Duroy discreetly retired.

Madame de Marelle, who had been talking to Madame Forestier, called to him :

"Well, Monsieur Duroy," she said abruptly, "so you want to try your luck at journalism?"

He spoke in vague terms of his plans, and then recapitulated the conversation which he had just been carrying on with Madame Walter. But as he was now more at home in his subject, he acquitted himself better and repeated things that he had heard, as if they were his own. And he never ceased to gaze into his companion's eyes as if to invest what he was saying with deep meaning.

In her turn she told him anecdotes with the easy animation of a woman who is aware of her intelligence and aims at being always amusing. With an assumption of familiarity she laid her hand on his arm, saying trivial things in lowered tones that lent them an air of intimacy. He was inwardly elated at the gentle contact with this young woman, who was interesting herself in him. He longed to devote himself to her at once, to protect her, and show his mettle, and the delay with which he answered her bore witness to the preoccupation of his thoughts.

But suddenly, for no apparent reason, Madame de Marelle called out :

"Laurine," and the little girl came to her.

"Sit down there, my child. You will be cold near the window."

Duroy was seized with a passionate desire to embrace the little girl, as if something of his kiss could be transmitted to the mother.

He asked in a tone at once courtly and paternal :

"Will you allow me to kiss you, Miss Laurine?"

The child looked at him with an air of surprise.

Madame de Marelle said laughingly :

"Say to him, ' Yes, you may to-day, but I shan't always let you.' "

Seating himself Duroy took Laurine on his knee and touched the child's soft wavy hair with his lips.

The mother expressed astonishment.

"Dear me, she didn't run away ; that's amazing. As a rule she allows only women to kiss her. You are irresistible, Monsieur Duroy."

He blushed, but did not reply, and he rocked the little girl gently to and fro on his knee. Madame Forestier approached them uttering a cry of astonishment :

"Look, he has tamed Laurine. What a miracle !"

Jacques Rival joined them, with a cigar in his mouth, and Duroy rose to take leave, fearing to spoil by some awkward remark the task that he had accomplished, the first step in his work of conquest.

He bowed, gently pressed the ladies' friendly little hands and shook those of the men vigorously. He noticed that Jacques Rival's hand was dry and warm, and responded cordially to the pressure of his own ; that of Norbert de Varenne was clammy and escaped from his grasp, slipping through his fingers. Old Monsieur Walter's hand was cold and flaccid, without energy or expression ; that of Forestier plump and cool. His friend said to him in an undertone :

"Don't forget to-morrow at three o'clock."

"O ! no, you can depend on me."

Once more on the stairs, Duroy felt an impulse to take them at a run, such was the exuberance of his joy, and he bounded down them, two steps at a time. But suddenly in the large mirror on the second floor he caught sight of a gentleman who came skipping to meet him and he stopped short in confusion as if he had been surprised in some misdemeanour.

He took a long look, amazed to find himself such a presentable fellow ; he smiled on himself complacently ; then taking leave of his reflection, he bowed to himself very low, and ceremoniously, as one bows to important personages.

III

Once more in the street, George Duroy debated what he should do. His impulse was now to run, now to dream, now to wander along thinking of the future, and breathing in the mild night air. But he was haunted by the thought of the series of articles for which old Monsieur Walter had asked him, and he decided to return home and set to work at once.

He strode rapidly along, reached the outer Boulevard and followed it as far as the Rue Boursault where he lived. The house, six stories high, was inhabited by some twenty small families of the working and lower middle-classes. As he climbed the stairs, lighting with wax matches his way up the filthy steps, which were littered with scraps of paper, cigarette ends, and kitchen refuse, he felt a nauseating sensation of disgust and an urgent need to make his escape and to live as the rich do in well-kept houses with carpeted floors. The place was pervaded from top to bottom with a heavy odour of food, cesspools, humanity, a stagnant odour of accumulated dirt and old masonry, an odour which would have defied ventilation to dislodge it.

The room on the fifth floor occupied by Duroy, looked out, as over a deep abyss, on the huge cutting of the Railway de l'Ouest just above the end of the tunnel and near the Batignolles station. Duroy opened his window and leaned his elbows on the rusty iron bar.

Beneath him, in the depths of the dark chasm, he saw three red signal lights, motionless, and like the great eyes of animals. Farther away he saw other lights and others again still farther away. Every moment, the shriek of engine whistles, prolonged or brief, was borne to him on the night air. Sometimes the sound was close at hand, sometimes it was barely audible, coming from a distance, from the direction of Asnières. These sounds sank and swelled like human voices raised in appeal. One of them came nearer, its plaintive and continuous wail increasing each moment in volume, and soon a great yellow light shone out, and a loud clanking of wheels was heard. Duroy watched the long string of waggons being swallowed up by the tunnel.

Then he said to himself :

" Come, I must get to work."

He placed the light on his table, but just as he was setting to work he found that he had nothing to write on except a quire of letter paper. That was a drawback, but he could make use of the sheets by opening them out to their full extent. He dipped his pen in the ink and wrote at the top of the page in his best hand :

" Recollections of an African Light Horseman."

Then he searched his brain for an introductory sentence.

He remained with his forehead propped on his hand, and his eyes fixed on the square of white paper spread out in front of him.

What was he to say ? Of all that he had related a little while since he could now remember nothing—not a single anecdote or fact, absolutely nothing. Suddenly it occurred to him that he must begin with his departure from France.

And he wrote :

" It was in 1874, about the 15th of May, when France, exhausted, was resting after the catastrophes of the terrible year——"

Then he broke off, not knowing how to lead up to what was to follow, his embarkation, the voyage, his first emotions. After ten minutes of reflection he decided to postpone the introductory page till the following day and to proceed at once to a description of Algiers. So he wrote down the words :

" Algiers is an entirely white town." But he failed to produce anything further. In his mind's eye he beheld again the bright attractive city, sweeping down in a cascade of flat-roofed houses from its mountain tops to the sea, but he could no longer hit upon a single word to express what he had seen and what he had felt.

After a mighty effort, he added :

" It is partly inhabited by Arabs——"

Then he threw down his pen and rose from his chair.

On his narrow iron bedstead, hollowed by the weight of his body, he saw his everyday clothes lying limp and repulsive, like those you see at the Morgue. On a straw-bottomed chair was his silk hat, his one and only hat, standing on its crown, as if gaping in the expectation of alms.

The wall-paper, grey, with blue posies, had as many stains as flowers, stains ancient and suspicious which defied analysis, crushed remains of insects, drops of oil, smudges of fingers greasy with pomade, splashes of soap-suds from the wash-hand basin. All this was redolent of humiliating squalor, the squalor of furnished lodgings in Paris, and the sordidness of it roused his anger. He must get out of this place, without a day's delay, he declared, and be done with this hand-to-mouth existence.

The fever for work suddenly possessed him anew, and he seated himself once more at his table and began to rack his brains for phrases which should adequately describe the strange and charming aspect of Algiers, that antechamber to unfathomable, mysterious Africa, the Africa of Arab nomads and negroes, of unknown tribes, unexplored and alluring Africa, whose improbable-looking fauna we some-times gaze at in Zoological Gardens, animals, seemingly, created for fairy tales, ostriches, those gallinaceous freaks, gazelles, those exquisite goats, giraffes, surprising and grotesque, solemn camels, monstrous hippopotami, shapeless rhinoceroses, and gorillas, those terrifying brothers of man.

He was vaguely aware of ideas flitting through his mind ; he might perhaps have uttered them in speech, but he could by no means embody them in written words. Exasperated to a fever by his incapacity, he again rose from his chair, his hands moist with sweat and the blood throbbing in his temples. He happened to catch sight of his laundress's bill which the hall porter had brought up that evening and he was all at once plunged into the depths of despair. In a moment all his joy had vanished, and with it his confidence in himself and his faith in the future. It was over ; everything was over ; he would accomplish nothing ; he would never be anything. He felt barren, incapable, futile, rejected.

He turned again to the window and leaned out just as a train emerged from the tunnel with a sudden roar. It was setting out on a long journey across field and plain, towards the sea. And into Duroy's heart entered memories of his parents. This train would pass quite near them, a few leagues only from their home. He saw again the little house on the outskirts of the village of Canteleu, on the top of the hill, overlooking Rouen and the wide valley of the Seine.

His father and mother kept a little drinking shop, a tavern where the middle-class people from the suburbs of Rouen used to go for luncheon on Sundays. " A la Belle-Vue," it was called. They had wished to make a gentleman of their son and had sent him to college. When he had finished his studies and had failed to take his degree, he had left to go into the army, with the intention of becoming an officer, a Colonel, a General. But disgusted with military life long before the end of his five years, he had dreamed of making his fortune in Paris.

To Paris then he betook himself at the end of his term of service, in spite of the pleadings of his father and mother, who, now that their first visions had fled, were anxious to keep him with them. It was now his turn to cherish hopes of the future. He looked forward to a triumph through circumstances as yet indefinite but which he would assuredly succeed in bringing to pass and in turning to account.

While with the regiment he had had successes of the usual garrison type, easy conquests ; and he had even had some adventures in a higher grade of society, having seduced a tax collector's daughter who would have left everything to follow him, and a solicitor's wife who had attempted to drown herself in her despair at being abandoned.

His comrades said of him :

" He's all there ; he's a cool hand, a slippery customer. He will always manage to wriggle out of a tight corner."

And he had vowed to himself that he would really be a cool hand and a slippery customer.

His inborn Norman conscience had had the edges rubbed off by the daily usages of garrison life, and had been rendered elastic by the marauding that went on in Africa, the cases of illicit profiting, of suspected frauds ; on the other hand it had been excited by the ideas of honour current in the army, by military bravado, patriotic sentiments, stories of magnanimous deeds told in the sergeants' mess and by professional vainglory, until it had become a sort of conjurer's box with a little of everything in it. But the desire to succeed was the dominating element.

Unconsciously he had relapsed again into the restless dreams in which he indulged every evening. He imagined himself the hero of some magnificent romance, by means of which he would attain at one bound the fulfilment of his hopes. He pictured himself marrying the daughter of a banker, or of some great personage, after a chance meeting in the street, when he had made a conquest of her at first sight. He was aroused from his dream by the piercing shriek of a locomotive which issued from the tunnel, like a giant rabbit from its burrow, and raced at full steam along the line, making for its resting place the engine-house.

Captured anew by the vague and joyful hope which never ceased to haunt his mind, he threw a kiss at random into the night, a kiss of love for the vision of the woman he awaited, a kiss of desire for the fortune he coveted. Then he closed his window and began to undress, murmuring :

" Pooh, I shall be more disposed for it to-morrow. My mind is too much occupied to-night. Besides I may have had rather too much to drink. One can't work well in these conditions."

He went to bed, blew out his light, and fell asleep almost at once.

He awoke early, as one wakes on days of vivid hope or anxiety, and jumping out of bed he threw open his window for a mouthful of fresh air, as he put it.

In the Rue de Rome, on the opposite side of the wide
railway cutting, the houses were irradiated by the light of
sunrise and looked as if coated with a luminous whiteness.
Far away to the right, the hills of Argenteuil, the heights
of Sannois and the windmills of Orgemont were visible
through a faint bluish haze which floated over the horizon
like a thin, transparent veil.

Duroy remained some minutes contemplating the distant
landscape, and he said to himself :

" How jolly it would be over there on a day like this."

Then he remembered that he must set to work, and that
without delay, and the hall-porter's son must be given ten
sous to go to the railway office and say that he was ill. He
seated himself at his table, dipped his pen in the ink, and
resumed the search for ideas. All in vain. Nothing came
to him.

None the less he did not lose heart.

" Pooh ! " he reflected, " I haven't got into the way of
it yet. It's a trade that has to be learnt like any other. I
must get help for the first attempt. I'll look up Forestier,
and he will get my article going in ten minutes."

So he dressed.

Once in the street, he decided that it was still too early
to present himself at his friend's house. Doubtless Forestier
would sleep late. So he took a quiet stroll beneath the trees
of the outer Boulevard.

It was scarcely nine o'clock when he entered the Parc
Monceau, which had just been watered and was deliciously
cool. Seating himself on a bench he again gave himself up
to his dreams. There was a very well-dressed young man
walking up and down in front of him, doubtless waiting for
some woman. Presently she appeared on the scene. Her
veil was down, she walked hurriedly. After a brief hand-
clasp she took the young man's arm and they moved away.

A tumultuous yearning for love entered Duroy's heart,
a yearning for love that should have about it a distinction, a
perfume, an exquisiteness. He rose from the bench and
went on his way, thinking of Forestier. What luck that
fellow had !

He arrived at Forestier's door just as his friend was coming out.

"What ! you here at this hour ! What on earth do you want me for ?"

Disconcerted by the suddenness of the meeting, Duroy stammered :

"The fact is—the fact is, I simply can't manage that article of mine, the one on Algeria that Monsieur Walter asked me for. It's not very surprising considering that I've never written anything before. One must have practice at it, just like anything else. I shall soon get into the way of it, I'm quite sure, but just at first I don't know how to set about it. I have ideas all right, plenty of them, only I can't manage to express them."

He stopped, hesitating still, and Forestier smiled ironically.

"Don't I know it ?"

"Yes," replied Duroy. "It must be a common enough experience at the beginning. Very well, then, I came—I came to ask you to lend me a helping hand. You could get me going in ten minutes ; you could show me how to get it into shape and give me a lesson in style. Without your help I don't see how I can pull it off at all."

With the same amused smile, Forestier tapped Duroy on the arm.

"Go along and see my wife," he said, "she'll get you out of your difficulty as well as I could. I have trained her to this sort of work. Personally, I haven't time this morning ; otherwise I should have been delighted to help you."

Duroy's courage suddenly deserted him.

"But surely I can't intrude upon her at this hour of the day ?"

"Yes, of course you can. She is up. You will find her in my study, busy arranging some notes for me."

But Duroy refused to go up to the flat.

"No, it's out of the question."

Forestier took him by the shoulders, spun him round on his heels and pushed him towards the stairs.

"Why on earth don't you go when I tell you to, you duffer ? You surely don't want to force me to scramble back up my three flights of stairs, so as to introduce you and explain your difficulties ? "

Duroy made up his mind.

" Thanks, I'll go. I'll tell her that you forced me, absolutely forced me."

" Do. Make your mind easy. She won't eat you. And whatever you do, don't forget your appointment at three o'clock."

" O ! don't worry about that."

Forestier walked off as if in a hurry, while Duroy climbed the stairs slowly, step by step, making up his mind what he should say and ill at ease as to the reception that awaited him.

The manservant opened the door to him. He was wearing a blue apron and had a broom in his hand.

" The master is out," he said without waiting to be asked. Duroy persisted.

" Ask Madame Forestier if she can receive me, and tell her that I have come from Monsieur Forestier whom I met in the street."

He waited. The servant returned, opened a door on the right and said :

" Madame Forestier will see you, sir."

Madame Forestier was seated in an office arm-chair in a small room whose walls were completely hidden by books carefully arranged on shelves of black wood. The bindings, in various shades of red, yellow, green, violet and blue, brightened with a note of colour the monotony of these rows of volumes.

She turned to him with a smile on her lips. She was wearing a white lace-trimmed morning gown, and as she held out her hand the wide sleeves revealed her bare arm.

" So early ? " she said. Then she continued, " That's not a reproach. It's simply a question."

He faltered.

" O ! Madame Forestier, I didn't mean to come up. But I met your husband downstairs and he made me. I am so confused that I haven't the courage to tell you what has brought me."

She pointed to a chair.

" Sit down and tell me about it."

She was twirling a quill briskly between finger and thumb ; in front of her lay a large sheet of paper, half covered with writing, which had been interrupted by Duroy's arrival.

She seemed as much at home at a writing-table as if she had been engaged in commonplace tasks in her drawing-room. A faint perfume hung about her morning gown, the fresh perfume of a recent toilet. And Duroy sought to divine, and persuaded himself he could trace, the lines of her white young body, plump and warm, seductively concealed under the soft fabric of her gown.

As he did not reply, she continued :

" Tell me what is the matter."

He murmured hesitatingly :

" Yes—but to tell you the truth—I can't summon up courage. The fact is, I worked very late last night—and very early this morning—at that article on Algeria Monsieur Walter asked me to do for him—and I can't get on with it at all. I have torn up all my attempts. The truth is that I'm not used to this sort of work, and I was coming to ask Forestier to help me for once——"

Pleased, delighted and flattered, she interrupted him with a hearty laugh.

" And he told you to come to me. What a charming idea ! "

" Yes, Madame Forestier. He said that you would be better able to help me out of my difficulty than he. But I did not dare ; I was unwilling. You understand ? "

She rose from her chair.

" It will be delightful to collaborate like that. I am enchanted with your idea. But you must sit here in my place ; you see, they know my writing at the office. Now we'll turn you out something that will make a hit."

He seated himself, took up a pen, spread a sheet of paper in front of him and waited.

Madame Forestier remained standing, and watched his preparations. Then she took a cigarette from the mantelpiece and lighted it.

" I can't work unless I'm smoking," she remarked. " Now what are you going to say ? "

He turned his head towards her in surprise.

"But I don't know; that's exactly what I've come to you to discover."

"Yes," she replied, "I'll manage that. I'll mix the sauce, but you must supply the ingredients."

He preserved an embarrassed silence; at last he said hesitatingly :

"I thought of telling the story of my journey right from the beginning."

She seated herself opposite him on the other side of the big table and looked him in the eyes.

"Very well. First of all tell me about it, simply for my benefit, you know, quite quietly and without any omissions. And then I will select what is wanted."

But as he could not make up his mind where to begin, she set to work to question him like a priest in the confessional. By her precise inquiries she recalled to his mind forgotten details, persons he had met, faces of which he had merely caught a glimpse. After he had been induced to talk in this way for about a quarter of an hour, she suddenly interrupted him :

"Now we can begin. First of all let us assume that you are describing your impressions in a letter to a friend. That will leave us free to say all sorts of absurd things and make remarks of every description and to be natural and amusing if we can. Begin :

"My dear Henry,

"You wanted to know what Algeria is like, and so you shall. As there is nothing whatever to do in this little hut of dried clay which serves me for dwelling I will send you a sort of diary of my life, day by day, hour by hour. It may be somewhat startling at times, but that can't be helped; there is no necessity for you to show it to the ladies of your acquaintance."

She broke off to relight her cigarette which had gone out, and the creak of the quill on the paper ceased simultaneously.

"To continue," she said.

"Algeria is a large French colony, bounded by those

vast, unexplored regions known as the desert, the Sahara, Central Africa, etc.

" Algiers is the gateway, the white and alluring gateway, that leads to this strange continent.

" But first of all you have to get there, which is not such a rosy business for every one. I am, as you are aware, an excellent horseman, considering that I train the Colonel's horses, but a man can be a good rider and a bad sailor. That is the case with me.

" Do you remember Major Simbretas, whom we used to call Dr. Ipecac ? Whenever we considered ourselves ripe for twenty-four hours in the infirmary, that happy land, we would present ourselves for medical inspection.

" He was invariably seated in his chair, his fat red-trousered legs spread well apart, his hands on his knees, his arms bent, his elbows turned out, and he would roll his large round eyes, and nibble his white moustache. You remember his prescription.

" ' This soldier's stomach is out of order. Administer emetic No. 3 according to my formula ; after that twelve hours rest. He will be all right.'

" It was a sovereign remedy, that emetic, sovereign and irresistible. You swallowed it, because you had to. After you had got over Dr. Ipecac's formula, you enjoyed twelve hours of well-earned repose.

" Well, my dear fellow, to reach Africa you have to submit for forty hours to another kind of emetic, equally irresistible, according to the formula of the Transatlantic Company."

She rubbed her hands, charmed with her idea. Then she rose from her chair and after lighting another cigarette began to walk up and down. As she continued to dictate, little puffs of tobacco smoke issued from her pouted lips, and then spread out and vanished, leaving here and there in the air grey trails of transparent mist, filmy threads like gossamer.

Sometimes with her open hand she would efface the most persistent of these airy traces ; sometimes she would bisect them with a trenchant movement of her forefinger and then with serious attention watch the two segments of intangible vapour slowly fade away.

Duroy followed with raised eyes every gesture and attitude, every movement of her limbs and features in her absent-minded pursuit of this aimless pastime.

Next she set herself to picturing the incidents of the voyage. Out of her own fancy she invented travelling companions, and she sketched a love affair with the wife of a captain of infantry on her way to rejoin her husband. Then, seating herself, she questioned Duroy on the topography of Algeria, of which she was completely ignorant. In ten minutes she knew as much as he, and she introduced a short dissertation on political and colonial geography, to enable the reader to understand the serious questions which would be raised in later articles. This she followed up with a trip into the province of Oran, a fanciful digression, treating mainly of women, Moorish, Jewish and Spanish.

"Nothing else really interests people," she said.

She concluded with a visit to Saida, at the foot of the lofty tablelands, and with a charming little intrigue between troop-sergeant George Duroy and a Spanish workgirl, engaged in the Alfa factory at Ain-el-Hadjar. She described their meetings at night on the bare and rocky uplands where jackals, hyenas and Arab dogs clamoured, barked and howled among the crags.

Then gleefully she exclaimed :

"To be continued in our next."

Rising from her chair.

"That's the way to write an article, my dear sir. Sign it, if you please."

He hesitated.

"Of course you must sign it."

Then he burst out laughing and wrote at the foot of the page,

"George Duroy."

She went on smoking as she walked up and down, and he continued to gaze at her, finding no words with which to thank her, happy to be near her, overflowing with gratitude and the sensuous pleasure of this dawning intimacy. It

D

seemed to him as if everything that surrounded her were part of her, even to the walls covered with books. The chairs, the furniture, the air, in which the scent of tobacco lingered, had something characteristic about them, something good, kind and charming, emanating from herself.

" What do you think of my friend, Madame Marelle ? " she asked abruptly.

He was taken aback.

" Why, I think—I think she's very charming."

" Yes, isn't she ? "

" Yes, certainly."

He would have liked to add :

" But not so charming as you," but did not dare.

" If you only knew," she continued, " how amusing, original and intelligent she is ! Now there's a Bohemian for you, a real Bohemian. And that's why her husband doesn't care for her. He sees only her defects and has no appreciation at all of her qualities."

Duroy was dumbfounded at hearing that Madame de Marelle was married. And yet it was perfectly natural that she should be.

" Dear me," he said. " is she married ? What does her husband do ? "

Madame Forestier shrugged her shoulders and at the same time raised her eyebrows slightly, the two gestures together having a significance that he could not fathom.

" Oh, he's an Inspector on the Nord Railway. He spends one week a month in Paris, a period that his wife refers to as ' compulsory service,' or ' fatigue duty,' or ' Holy Week.' When you know her better you will discover how quick-witted and charming she is. Why don't you go and call on her one of these days ? "

Duroy no longer thought of taking his departure. He felt as if he were going to remain there always, as if he were at home.

But the door opened noiselessly, and a tall gentleman entered, unannounced.

He stopped short on seeing Duroy. For a moment Madame Forestier showed signs of embarrassment ; then although a slight flush had risen from her bosom to her cheeks, she said in her natural voice :

" Do come in, dear friend. Let me introduce to you an old comrade of Charles's, Monsieur George Duroy, a budding journalist."

Then, in a different tone of voice she announced :

" Our best and most intimate friend, Count de Vaudrec."

The two men bowed and looked each other straight in the face. Immediately afterwards Duroy took his leave.

No attempt was made to detain him. He stammered out some words of thanks, pressed Madame Forestier's outstretched hand, bowed again to the new-comer, whose face still wore the cold, grave expression of a man of social distinction, and he left the house with the discomforting sensation of having made a fool of himself.

Once in the street, he felt depressed, uneasy, obsessed by a vague consciousness of some obscure annoyance. He dawdled along asking himself why this sudden mood of melancholy had come over him. He could discover no reason for it. But his mind was unceasingly haunted by the severe countenance of Count de Vaudrec, a man no longer young, grey-haired, with the calm insolent manner of a person who is very rich and very sure of himself.

Then he realised that the arrival of this stranger, interrupting a delightful *tête-à-tête* in which he was already beginning to feel at ease, aroused in him that sense of discouragement with which an overheard word, a hint of trouble, a mere trifle, sometimes suffices to afflict us. It seemed to him, too, that, for some obscure reason, the man had been displeased at finding him there.

He had nothing to do until three o'clock, and it was not yet noon. He had six francs fifty left in his pocket, so he lunched at Duval's. Then he strolled about the Boulevard, and on the stroke of three he ascended the show staircase of the *Vie Française.*

The office boys were seated on a bench waiting with folded arms, while at a little desk like a lecturer's, a porter sorted out the post which had just arrived. Everything was staged admirably in order to impress visitors. Every one there had the presence, bearing, dignity, and smartness, that befitted the antechamber of a great daily journal.

" I wish to see Monsieur Walter, please," said Duroy.

" The director has a conference," replied the porter, " will you be so good as to wait a little ? "

And he showed Duroy into the waiting-room, which was already full of people.

Among them were men of importance with serious faces, and wearing the ribbons of orders. Others had a neglected appearance, their linen was hidden from sight ; and their frock coats, buttoned up to the collar, displayed on the breast stains resembling outlines of continents and oceans upon a chart. There were three women. One of them was pretty, smiling, showily dressed, and seemed to invite approach. Her neighbour had the wrinkled face of a tragic mask. In a sober fashion her dress, too, was conspicuous, and there hung about her that suggestion of frippery and artificiality which clings to old actresses, a kind of spurious, vapid juvenility, like the stale aroma of an extinct love affair.

The third woman, who was dressed in mourning, remained in a corner of the room, and had the demeanour of a widow in affliction. Duroy conjectured that she had come to ask for alms. Time went on ; nobody was summoned to the farther room, and more than twenty minutes had slipped away.

An idea occurred to Duroy. He returned to the vestibule and spoke to the porter.

" Monsieur Walter made an appointment with me for three o'clock. Perhaps you could find out whether my friend Monsieur Forestier is here."

He was conducted down a long corridor into a large room where four gentlemen sat writing round a big table with a green cover.

Forestier was standing in front of the fire-place, smoking a cigarette and playing at cup-and-ball. He was very skilful at this game, and never missed catching the large ball of yellow boxwood on the small wooden point. He was counting his score.

" Twenty-two, twenty-three, twenty-four, twenty-five. Oh, there you are—yesterday I made fifty-seven catches running. Saint-Potin is the only one here who can beat me. Have you seen the director ? It's the funniest thing imaginable to watch that old idiot Norbert playing cup-and-ball. He opens his mouth as if he meant to swallow the ball."

One of the editors turned his head towards him :

" I say, Forestier, I know of a beauty for sale, in West India wood. It is said to have belonged to the Queen of Spain. The price is sixty francs. That's not dear."

" Where's it to be found ? " asked Forestier.

Having missed his thirty-seventh shot, he opened a cupboard, where Duroy saw about twenty fine sets of cup-and-ball, arrayed and numbered like curiosities in a collection. When he had put his plaything away, Forestier repeated his question.

" Where's this toy of yours to be found ? "

" A man who sells tickets at the Vaudeville has got it," replied the editor, " I'll bring you the thing to-morrow if you like."

" Yes, do. If it's really a fine specimen I'll buy it. You can't have too many sets of cup-and-ball."

Then he turned to Duroy.

" Come along with me," he said, " I'll take you in to see the director. Otherwise you might stay kicking your heels here till seven o'clock in the evening."

They passed again through the waiting-room in which were the same people, grouped as before. At Forestier's appearance, the young woman and the old actress both sprang from their seats and went up to him. He led each in turn into the window recess, and although they were careful to lower their voices, Duroy noticed that he addressed both of them in terms of familiarity.

Having passed through two padded doors, Forestier and Duroy entered the director's private room.

The conference, which had already lasted an hour, proved to be a *partie* of écarté with some of the gentlemen of the flat brimmed hats, whom Duroy had noticed the previous evening. Monsieur Walter handled his cards with wary concentration, while his opponent manipulated the thin, coloured pasteboards with the facility, skill and grace of the practised player.

Norbert de Varenne was seated in the director's arm-chair, writing an article, while on the divan, stretched out at full length and with closed eyes lay Jacques Rival, smoking a cigar. The room had a mingled smell of closeness, leather furniture, stale tobacco and printer's ink and that odour peculiar to newspaper offices, and familiar to every pressman.

The table of black wood inlaid with copper was littered with incredible accumulations of papers, letters, cards, journals, reviews, tradesmen's bills, and printed matter of every description.

Forestier shook hands with the men who were standing behind the players and betting on the hands. Then, without a word, he began to watch the game. As soon as old Monsieur Walter had won, Forestier presented his companion.

" Here is my friend Duroy."

The director subjected the young man to a brief scrutiny, glancing at him in his usual manner over the rim of his spectacles.

" Have you brought me my article ? " he asked ; " it would fit in very well to-day, with the Morel debate."

Duroy drew from his pocket the sheets of paper folded in four.

" Here it is, sir."

The director appeared delighted.

" Excellent, excellent. You are a man of your word. We had better have it revised, Forestier."

But Forestier hastened to reply :

" Quite unnecessary, sir. I did the article with him to teach him his work. It's very good."

The director, to whom a hand was now being dealt by a tall thin gentleman, a Deputy of the Left Centre, added in an indifferent tone :

" That's all right then."

Forestier, however, would not let him begin his new game. He stooped and whispered to him :

" You know you promised to engage Duroy in Maram-bot's place. Shall I take him on on the same terms ? "

" Yes, certainly."

Taking his friend's arm Forestier hurried him away, while Monsieur Walter resumed his game.

Norbert de Varenne had never raised his head. He appeared not to have seen, or at least not to have recognised Duroy. Jacques Rival, on the contrary, had shaken hands with an energy indicating good fellowship, which could be counted upon in case of need.

Once more they passed through the waiting-room, and as every one looked up, Forestier said to the youngest of the women, loud enough to be heard by her fellow-sufferers :

" The director will see you immediately. For the moment he is engaged with two members of the Budget Committee."

Then he moved briskly away, with an air of importance and haste, as if he had to compose an article at once on a matter of the utmost importance.

As soon as they had returned to the editor's room Forestier immediately resumed his cup-and-ball, and while he played he would break off in the middle of a sentence to count his score.

" Now listen," he said to Duroy. " You will come here every afternoon at three o'clock and I will tell you what rounds and visits have to be made, either during the day, or in the evening, or the next morning. One— ! First of all I shall give you a letter of introduction to the superinten-dent of the head office of the prefecture of police—two—who will put you in touch with one of his men. You will arrange with him to get all the important news—three—official and demi-official. For all details you will apply to Saint-Potin, who is well up in such matters—four—you will see him presently, or else to-morrow. Your principal business is to get into the way of pumping people whom I send you to see. Worm your way in everywhere. Never mind closed doors—six—. For this you will get a salary of two hundred francs a month, and besides that two sous a line for any interesting paragraphs you pick up ; also two sous a line for articles written to order."

Then he paid no further attention to anything except his game, and he continued to count slowly—nine, ten, eleven, twelve, thirteen. When he missed the fourteenth, he swore.

"Confound that thirteen. That brute of a number always brings me bad luck. I shall certainly die on the thirteenth."

One of the editors who had finished work took another cup-and-ball from the cupboard. He was a very small man who looked like a child, although he was thirty-five years of age. Several other journalists entered the room, and, one by one, each went to fetch his own particular plaything. Soon there were six of them side by side, their backs against the wall, all tossing away with balls of red, yellow, or black wood. And a match having been arranged, the two editors who were still at work rose from their chairs to judge the strokes.

Forestier won by eleven points. Then the small man with the childlike manner, who had lost, rang for the office boy and ordered nine glasses of beer. They resumed their play while waiting for the beer.

Duroy drank a glass of beer with his new associates, and then asked his friend:

"What is there for me to do?"

"I have nothing for you to-day," replied Forestier, "you can go away if you like."

"And our—our article. Will it go in to-night?"

"Yes, but don't bother about that; I'll correct the proofs. Write the continuation for to-morrow, and come here at three o'clock, as you did to-day."

After shaking the hands of all these men of whom he did not even know the names, Duroy made his way with a joyful mind down the imposing staircase.

IV

GEORGE DUROY slept badly; he was too much excited by the prospect of seeing his article in print. He was up by daybreak and was roaming the streets long before the newspaper runners had made their tour of the kiosks.

He made his way to the Saint-Lazare station, knowing that the *Vie Française* would be delivered there before it would reach his own quarter of the town. But even there he was too early and had to wander about the pavement.

He watched the saleswoman arrive and open her glass-sided shop; then he caught sight of a man carrying on his head a pile of large folded papers. He pounced down upon him; there were the *Figaro*, *Gil-Blas*, the *Gaulois*, the *Evènement* and two or three other morning papers, but the *Vie Française* was not among them.

He was seized with apprehension. Suppose the "Recollections of an African Light Horseman" had been held over to the following day, or that at the last moment old Walter had not been pleased with the thing !

Turning back to the kiosk, he perceived that the *Vie Française* was on sale there without his having seen it arrive. He swooped down on it, threw down his three sous, unfolded it and cast his eye over the headings on the front page. Nothing there. His heart began to beat. He opened the sheet, and with a thrill of emotion he read at the foot of a column the words, George Duroy, in heavy type.

It was really there ! What rapture ! With his head in a whirl, he began walking along, the paper in his hand and his hat on one side. He longed to stop the passers-by and to say to them :

"You must buy this; you must buy this. There's an article of mine in it."

He would have liked to shout with the full force of his lungs, like the newsvendors on the boulevards of an evening :

" Read the *Vie Française*, read the article by George Duroy, ' Recollections of an African Light Horseman.' "

Then suddenly he was seized with a desire to read the article himself, to read it in a public place, in a café, in full view of every one. He looked about for some establishment with guests already in it. He had to go a long way, but at last he took a chair in front of a kind of wine shop where several guests were already seated, and regardless of the earliness of the hour he called for rum. He would have been just as likely to order an absinthe.

Then he called the waiter and a man in a white apron came running.

" Waiter, bring me the *Vie Française*."

" We haven't got it, sir, we only take in the *Rappel*, the *Siècle*, the *Lanterne*, and the *Petit Parisien*."

" You call this a restaurant ! " exclaimed Duroy in a tone of fury and indignation. " Get me a *Vie Française* at once."

The waiter ran out for it and returned with a copy.

Duroy began to read his article, and several times he exclaimed aloud, " Very good, very good ! " in order to attract the attention of his neighbours and to inspire in them a desire to know what there was in that paper. As he was going away he left it lying on the table. The owner of the wine shop noticed it and called him back.

" Sir, sir, you are forgetting your newspaper."

" I'll leave it here," replied Duroy, " I've read it. By the way, there's a very interesting article in it to-day."

He did not point out the article, but as he took his departure, he saw one of his neighbours pick up the *Vie Française* from the table where he had left it.

" What shall I do now ? " he wondered.

He decided to go to the railway office, draw his month's pay and hand in his resignation. He felt a thrill of pleased anticipation at the thought of the amazement of the head of his office and his fellow-clerks. The idea of the shock his employer would receive enraptured him most of all.

As the cashier's office did not open till ten o'clock, he walked slowly so as not to arrive before half-past nine. His office was a large gloomy room where the gas had to be kept burning nearly all day long in the wintertime. It looked out upon a narrow courtyard, with other offices opposite. There were eight clerks in it as well as a senior clerk, who was hidden in a corner behind a screen.

First of all Duroy went to draw his hundred and eighteen francs, twenty-five centimes, enclosed in a yellow envelope and deposited in the drawer of the pay clerk ; then with the air of a conqueror he entered the large office where he had already spent so many days.

As soon as he arrived, the senior clerk, Monsieur Potel, called out to him :

" O ! there you are, Monsieur Duroy. The head has been asking for you several times. You are aware that he does not accept an excuse of ill-health on two consecutive days without a doctor's certificate."

Duroy, who for greater effect had remained standing in the middle of the room, replied in a loud voice :

" I don't care a hang if he doesn't."

There was a movement of consternation among the clerks, and the startled face of Monsieur Potel appeared above the screen which enclosed him like a box.

He barricaded himself inside this screen for fear of draughts, because he suffered from rheumatism. He had, however, made two small holes through which he could keep an eye on the staff.

One could have heard a pin drop.

At last Monsieur Potel asked in a hesitating voice :

" What did you say ? "

" I said that I didn't care a hang. I have merely called in to hand in my resignation. I have joined the staff of the *Vie Française* as editor with a salary of five hundred francs a month with extra payment for contributions. I have in fact made my first appearance in print this morning."

It had been his intention to prolong his enjoyment, but he had been unable to resist the temptation to burst out with his news all at once. The effect, to be sure, was complete. Not a soul stirred.

"I will go and inform Monsieur Perthuis," announced Duroy, "and then I'll come back and say good-bye."

He left the room for his interview with the head of the office, who exclaimed as soon as he saw him :

"O ! there you are. You know that I won't have——"

Duroy cut him short.

"You needn't trouble to roar at me like that."

Monsieur Perthuis, a stout man, with a face as red as a cock's comb, choked with surprise.

"I've had enough of your shop," Duroy continued. "I have taken my first step in journalism this morning and have been given an excellent appointment. I have the honour to bid you good day."

And he went out. He had had his revenge.

He went and shook hands with his former associates, who hardly ventured to say a word to him for fear of compromising themselves, for through the open door they had overheard his conversation with the chief.

He found himself in the street again with his salary in his pocket. He treated himself to an excellent luncheon in a good cheap restaurant. After buying another copy of the *Vie Française* and leaving it on the table at which he had lunched, he entered several shops and made some trifling purchases simply for the pleasure of ordering them to be delivered at his house and stating his name, George Duroy. To this he added, " I am the editor of the *Vie Française.*" Then he would give the name of his street and his number, carefully stipulating that the parcels should be left with the hall porter.

As he still had some time to spare he went to a lithographer who printed visiting cards in full view of the street. He had a hundred struck off then and there, with his name and his new designation.

Then he betook himself to the newspaper office.

Forestier received him condescendingly, as one receives a subordinate.

"O ! there you are. Very good. As it happens, I have

several things for you to do. Just wait ten minutes, until I have finished what I am doing."

And he went on with the letter he was writing.

At the other end of the big table a short, fat man sat writing. He had a colourless, puffy face and a bald shining head, and was so excessively short-sighted that his nose almost touched the paper.

"I say, Saint-Potin," said Forestier, "at what time are you going to interview those people?"

"At four o'clock."

"Take young Duroy here along with you and show him the mysteries of the craft."

"Certainly."

Turning to his friend Forestier added:

"Have you brought your instalment on Algeria? The first one made quite a hit."

"No, I thought I should have time this afternoon; I have had heaps of things to do. I really hadn't——"

The other shrugged his shoulders with an air of displeasure.

"If you are not more punctual than that you will certainly spoil your prospects. Old Walter was counting on your copy. I shall have to tell him that it won't be ready till to-morrow. If you think you are going to be paid for doing nothing, you're mistaken."

Then, after a silence, he added:

"You must strike the iron while it is hot."

Saint-Potin rose from his chair.

"I'm ready," he said.

Thereupon Forestier, leaning back in his chair, assumed a pose of great solemnity, and issued his instructions. Turning to Duroy he said:

"Now listen. For the last two days we have had the Chinese General Li-Theng-Fao and the Rajah Taposahib Ramaderao Pali staying in Paris, the one at the Continental, the other at the Bristol. You will go and interview them."

Then addressing himself to Saint-Potin:

"Don't forget the principal points I mentioned to you. Ask the General and the Rajah their opinion of the machinations of England in the Far East, their ideas on her system of colonisation and domination, their hopes relative to intervention in their affairs on the part of Europe, and specially of France."

After a short silence he added, for the benefit of those behind the scenes :

" Could anything interest our readers more than to know what China and India think of the questions that agitate our own public so intensely at this moment ? "

Turning to Duroy he continued :

" Watch how Saint-Potin sets about it. He's a first-rate reporter. Try to learn the ropes and how to turn a man inside out in five minutes."

Then he gravely resumed his writing, with the evident intention of marking the distance between them and of putting his old comrade in his place.

As soon as they had crossed the threshold Saint-Potin burst out laughing.

" Isn't he a humbug ? He tries it on even with us. You might really think he took us for his readers."

Out on the Boulevard, Saint-Potin said to him :

" Will you have a drink ? "

" Yes, thank you. It's very hot."

They entered a café and ordered cool drinks, and Saint-Potin began to talk. He talked about the newspaper and everyone connected with it with a profusion of surprising details.

" The director ! An out-and-out Jew. And you know nothing will ever change the Jews. What a people ! "

And he cited amazing examples of the form of avarice peculiar to the sons of Israel, economies of ten centimes, cheese-paring bargains, discounts shamelessly insisted upon and obtained, with the whole outlook on life of the usurer and the pawnbroker.

" And with it all he's a jovial old ruffian who doesn't believe in anything and imposes on everybody. His newspaper, which is the official mouthpiece of Catholics, Liberals, Republicans, Orleanists, anything you like to pay for, was started simply to back up his operations on the stock exchange and elsewhere. That's where he comes out strong. He makes millions out of companies that haven't twopence of real capital."

He talked away, calling Duroy " my dear fellow."

" And the old hunks says things that might have come out of Balzac. Just imagine. The other day I was in his study with that old idiot Norbert and that Don Quixote Rival, when Montelin, our manager, came in, with his morocco portfolio under his arm, the portfolio known to the whole of Paris. Walter pricked up his ears and said ' Anything new ? '

" Montelin answered innocently :

" ' I have just paid the sixteen thousand francs that we owed the paper maker.'

" The director gave a jump that surprised us.

" ' What did you say ? '

" ' That I had just paid Monsieur Privas.'

" ' But you must be mad.'

" ' Why ? '

" ' Why—Why—Why—— '

" He took off his glasses and rubbed them. Then he smiled that curious smile which always steals over his fat cheeks when he is going to say something shrewd or weighty. And he said sarcastically but with an air of conviction :

" ' Why ? Because we could have got a reduction off our of five thousand francs.'

" ' But, sir,' replied Montelin in astonishment, 'the accounts were all in order ; I had verified them and you had passed them.'

" The director, grown serious again, said :

" ' No one has any business to be so innocent as you. You ought to know, Monsieur Montelin, that you should always let your debts mount up and then make an offer.' "

Saint-Potin added, with an appreciative nod :

" Well, isn't that Balzac all over ? "

Duroy had never read Balzac, but he replied with conviction :

" I should just think so."

Then Saint-Potin spoke of Madame Walter as a great

goose, of Norbert de Varenne as an old miss-fire, of Rival as a pinchbeck Fervacques. Then it was Forestier's turn.

"As for him, he had the luck to marry his wife, that's all."

"What do you really think of his wife?" asked Duroy.

Saint-Potin rubbed his hands.

"Oh, she's a rip, she's a deep one. She's the mistress of an old rake called Vaudrec, Count de Vaudrec, who gave her a dowry and married her off."

Duroy suddenly felt a sensation of chill, a nervous irritation, an impulse to break out upon this chatterer and to box his ears.

But all he did was to change the subject by asking:

"Is Saint-Potin your real name?"

The other replied ingenuously:

"No, my real name is Thomas; Saint-Potin is a nickname they've given me at the office."

As Duroy paid for the drinks, he remarked:

"It seems to me to be getting late. We still have our distinguished strangers to interview."

Saint-Potin burst out laughing.

"You're still very innocent. Do you really think I'm going to ask that Chinaman and that Indian their views on England? As if I didn't know better than they what the readers of the *Vie Française* expect them to think. I have already interviewed five hundred of these Chinamen, Persians, Hindus, Chileans, Japanese and others. According to me they all give the same answers. I have only to look up my article on the last one who was here, and to copy it word for word. The only real changes are in their appearance, their names, their titles, their age, their suites. On those points there must be no mistake, or I should be caught out by the *Figaro* or the *Gaulois*. But on details like that the hall porters at the Bristol and the Continental will put me right in five minutes. We will stroll along there while we smoke a cigar. Total result, five francs cab fare to be recovered from the office. That, my dear sir, is the way a practical man sets about it."

"With the conditions you describe, a reporter's work must bring in a good deal," suggested Duroy.

Saint-Potin replied with an air of mystery :

"Pretty fair. But nothing pays so well as personal paragraphs, on account of the cover they give to advertisements."

They had risen from their seats and were proceeding along the Boulevard in the direction of the Madeleine. All at once Saint-Potin said to his companion :

"You know, if you have anything else to do I can spare you."

Duroy shook hands with him and left him.

He was worried by the idea of the article he had to write that evening, and he began to think about it. As he walked along, he stored up ideas, reflections, opinions, anecdotes. He reached the end of the Champs Elysées Avenue, where only a few people were strolling about, for on those hot days Paris was deserted.

After dining at a wine shop near the Arc de Triomphe he returned home slowly on foot by the outer boulevards, and he sat down at his table to work.

But as soon as the large blank sheet of paper lay before his eyes, every vestige of the material that he had accumulated vanished from his mind, as if his brain had dried up. He endeavoured to recapture and transfix his fragmentary recollections, but the more he sought to grasp them, the more they eluded him. Sometimes, on the other hand, they would come with a rush, pell-mell, and he did not know how to introduce them or dress them up, nor with which one to begin.

After an hour of effort, and when five sheets of paper were scrawled over with opening phrases that led nowhere, he said to himself :

"I am not properly broken in to the trade yet. What I need is another lesson."

And all at once he trembled with desire at the prospect of another morning's work with Madame Forestier, and at the hope of just such another long, intimate, cordial, and delightful *tête-à-tête*. He went straight to bed, half afraid now to apply himself again to his task, lest he should suddenly succeed.

He did not rise till fairly late on the following day, postponing his visit so as to enjoy it in anticipation. It was past ten o'clock when he rang at his friend's door.

" The master is busy with his work," said the servant.

It had not occurred to Duroy that the husband might be there too. Nevertheless he persisted.

" Tell him who it is, and that I have come on urgent business."

After he had been kept waiting for five minutes, he was shown into the study, where he had spent such a pleasant morning.

In the chair that he had occupied, Forestier now sat writing, in dressing gown and slippers, with a small cap of English fashion on his head, while his wife, in the same white morning gown, a cigarette in her mouth, was leaning against the mantelpiece, dictating.

Halting on the threshold, Duroy murmured :

" I must apologise ; I am disturbing you."

His friend, turning towards him a face of fury, growled out :

" What do you want now ? Be quick. We have no time to spare."

Duroy stammered in confusion :

" Oh, it's nothing. I beg your pardon."

But Forestier, losing his temper, exclaimed :

" Oh, confound it, don't waste time. Surely you didn't force my door for the pleasure of wishing us good morning."

Greatly embarrassed, Duroy made up his mind.

" No. The trouble is that—I still can't manage to do my article—that I hoped—that I ventured to come——"

Forestier broke in :

" You're a cool customer, I must say. Do you really imagine that I'm going to do your work, and that all that you have to do is to look up the cashier once a month? A great idea that ! "

Without saying a word, Madame Forestier went on

smoking, and on her lips hovered a smile which was like an amiable mask concealing the irony of her thoughts.

Blushing, Duroy faltered out :

" I beg your pardon. I imagined—I thought——"

Then suddenly he spoke without a tremor in his voice :

" A thousand apologies, Madame Forestier, and once more my warmest thanks for the very delightful sketch you did for me yesterday."

Then he bowed and said to Charles :

" I shall be at the office at three o'clock," and left the room.

He strode home, muttering :

" Very well, then, I shall go and do the thing all by myself, and they shall see——"

Scarcely had he entered his room when, under the stimulus of his anger, he began to write.

He continued the romantic episode which Madame Forestier begun. He strung together incidents like those in newspaper serials, startling events, bombastic descriptions, all in the clumsy style of a schoolboy and the phraseology of a troop sergeant. In an hour he had completed an article which was a chaos of absurdities, and he took it confidently to the office of the *Vie Française*.

The first person he met was Saint-Potin who, shaking his hand with the fervour of a confederate, said :

" Have you read my conversation with the Chinaman and the Hindu ? Quite funny, isn't it ? It amused the whole of Paris. And I never saw so much as the tips of their noses."

Duroy, who had not read any of it, at once took the paper and ran his eyes over a long article entitled, " India and China," while the reporter pointed out and dwelt upon the most interesting passages.

Forestier joined them ; he was out of breath and in a hurry and appeared to be busy.

" Oh, good, I want you both."

He mentioned various political matters on which information was required for that very evening.

Duroy handed him his article.

" Here is the second instalment about Algeria."

" Excellent. Give it to me ; I will take it to the director."

That was all.

Saint-Potin carried off his new comrade. As soon as they were in the corridor he said :

" Have you been to the cashier's office ? "

" What for ? "

" To draw your pay. You see it's just as well always to draw a month's pay in advance. You never know what may happen."

" Why—I should like nothing better."

" I'll introduce you to the cashier. He won't make any difficulties. They pay well here."

Duroy drew his two hundred francs, besides twenty-eight francs for his article of the previous day. Added to the balance of his pay from the railway company, he now had three hundred and forty francs. Never in his life had he had so much money. He considered himself rich for an indefinite period.

Taking Duroy along with him, Saint-Potin went to gossip in the offices of four or five rival newspapers in the hope that the information he had been instructed to collect had already been obtained by others, and that he would succeed in getting it out of them by fluency and adroitness.

In the evening it occurred to Duroy, who had nothing else to do, to go again to the Folies-Bergère. Putting a bold face on it, he presented himself at the box office.

" My name is George Duroy. I am on the staff of the *Vie Française*. I came here the other day with Monsieur Forestier, who promised to ask for a free pass for me. I don't know if he has remembered to do so."

A register was consulted. His name was not there. But the man at the box office, who had very pleasant manners, said :

" Just go in, sir. You can write to the director yourself and he will no doubt attend to the matter."

Duroy entered and almost immediately ran across Rachel, his conquest of the first evening. She came up to him.

" Good evening, my dear. How goes it ? "

" Quite well, thank you, and how are you ? "

" Not so bad. Do you know I've dreamt about you twice, since the other day ? "

Duroy felt flattered. He smiled.

" Well, and what does that mean ? "

" It means that I've taken a fancy to you, you silly boy, and that we'll start off again whenever you please."

" To-day, if you like."

" Yes, certainly."

" Good, but first listen "—he hesitated, a little ashamed of what he intended to do. " The fact is, this time I haven't a sou in my pocket ; I have just been to the club and I was cleared out."

She looked him straight in the eyes. With the instinct and experience of a woman accustomed to the chicanery and the haggling of men, she suspected him of a lie.

" Humbug ! " she said. " You know it's not nice of you to treat me like that."

He smiled in embarrassment.

" If ten francs is any use to you, it's all I've got left."

She murmured with the casualness of a courtesan indulging a whim :

" Anything you like, my dear. All I care about is you."

And fixing her fascinated eyes on the young man's moustache, she took his arm and leaned on it lovingly.

" First, a grenadine. And then we will take a stroll together. I should like to go to the Opera with you, just like this, to show you off. And then let's go home early."

He slept late at her house. It was daylight when he came away. His first thought was to buy the *Vie Française*. He opened the paper with feverish hand. His article was not there, and he remained standing on the pavement, anxiously scanning the columns of print in the hope of finding at last what he was seeking. His heart felt suddenly oppressed as by some heavy weight, for after his late night, this disappointment, supervening upon his weariness, had all the force of a disaster.

He returned to his room and fell asleep on his bed, fully dressed.

Some hours later he entered the office and presented himself before Monsieur Walter.

" I was much surprised this morning, sir, not to see my second article on Algeria in the paper."

The director looked up and said dryly :

" I gave it to your friend Forestier and asked him to read it ; he did not think it good enough. It will have to be done over again."

Duroy left the room in a rage without a word of reply, and abruptly entering his friend's office, exclaimed :

" Why didn't you let my article appear this morning ? "

Forestier was smoking a cigarette, with his back in the depths of his arm-chair, his feet on the table, his muddy boots on an article that he had begun. He enunciated his words slowly in a listless, far-away voice, as if he were speaking from the bottom of a pit.

" Walter didn't like it. He told me to hand it back to you to do over again. Look, there it is."

He pointed to some open sheets of manuscript under a paperweight.

Dumbfounded, Duroy could think of nothing to say, and as he put his composition in his pocket Forestier continued :

" To-day you will go first of all to the préfecture——"

And he detailed a number of calls to be made and items of news to be collected.

Duroy went away without having hit upon the cutting retort he wished to make.

He brought back his article on the following day. It was again returned to him. After he had re-written it a third time and it had again been rejected, he realised that he was going ahead too fast, and that Forestier's hand alone could help him on his way.

Accordingly he made no further reference to his " Recollections of an African Light Horseman." But since it was essential, he resolved to become adaptable and resourceful, and that while he was waiting for something better, he would devote himself to his reporter's work.

He gained a footing behind the scenes of theatrical and political life ; in the lobbies and vestibules of statesmen's houses and of the Chamber of Deputies. He grew familiar with the complacent faces of private secretaries and the scowling countenances of sleepy doorkeepers.

He was in constant touch with ministers, hall-porters, generals, police agents, princes, bullies, courtesans, ambassadors, bishops, adventurers, men of the world, cab-drivers, waiters at cafés, and many others. He took an impartial and friendly interest in all these people, measuring them by the same standards, judging them with an unprejudiced eye, by dint of meeting them daily and hourly, and of preserving the same attitude towards all. All his discussions with them were carried on entirely from a journalistic point of view. He compared himself to a man tasting one kind of wine after another, and soon becoming unable to distinguish Château-Margaux from Argenteuil.

In a short time he became a first-rate reporter, trustworthy, resourceful, quick, subtle, of real value to the newspaper, as old Monsieur Walter said, who knew all there was to know about reporters.

None the less, as he was still paid at the rate of only ten centimes a line, and his salary remained fixed at two hundred francs, and as the life of boulevards, cafés and restaurants is expensive, he never had a sou in his pocket and he chafed at his poverty.

"There is some dodge about it," he reflected, observing his companions with their pockets full of money, and unable to discover the secret devices through which they doubtless secured this affluence. Enviously he suspected them of underhand and equivocal transactions, services that they rendered, a whole system of unwarranted trafficking, connived at and condoned. It was his business to penetrate the mystery, to become a member of that tacit confederacy, to push his way into that group of comrades, who were dividing the spoils without him. And often of an evening, as he stood at his window watching the trains go by, he wondered by what steps he could attain this result.

V

Two months had elapsed. It was close on September, and the rapid fortune for which Duroy had hoped seemed to him very slow in coming. It was the social mediocrity of his position that chiefly mortified him, and he could not discover how to scale the heights where esteem and wealth are to be found.

He felt himself confined to his humble calling of reporter, immured without possibility of escape. He was appreciated but he was kept in his place. Even Forestier, to whom he rendered a thousand services, no longer invited him to dinner, but treated him in every respect as a subordinate, although he still addressed him familiarly.

From time to time, Duroy seized his opportunity and had a short article accepted. By his practice in personal paragraphs he had acquired the tact, the flexibility of pen which were lacking when he wrote his second article on Algeria, and he ran no risk of seeing his present contributions rejected. But the gulf between that and writing articles according to his own ideas or treating of political matters as an authority, was as great as the difference between driving in the avenues of the Bois as coachman and driving in them as master.

Especially humiliating was his consciousness that the doors of society were closed to him, that he had no circle of acquaintances whom he could meet on an equal footing, and that he was never admitted to intimate terms with women, although at times more than one well-known actress had received him with a not disinterested familiarity.

Yet experience had made him aware that one and all, society women or inferior actresses, felt him singularly attractive, instantaneously sympathetic, and at the thought that he was debarred from knowing those on whom his future might depend, he became as impatient as a hobbled horse.

He had often thought of calling on Madame Forestier, but the humiliating recollection of their last encounter checked him ; besides he was waiting for an invitation from Forestier. Then the memory of Madame de Marelle came to his mind, and recollecting her invitation to come and see her, he called on her one afternoon, when he had nothing to do.

"I am always at home till three o'clock," she had said.

She lived in the Rue de Verneuil, on the fourth floor. He rang at her door at half-past two. The bell was answered by a maid with untidy hair, who was tying on her cap.

"The mistress is at home," she said, "but I don't know if she is up yet."

She pushed open the drawing-room door, which was ajar. Duroy went in. The room was fairly big, but was scantily furnished and had a neglected appearance. Old and shabby arm-chairs stood in a row along the wall, just as the servant had arranged them. There were no signs of the exquisite care that a woman bestows on the home she loves. Four wretched daubs, representing respectively a boat on a river, a ship on the sea, a windmill in a plain, and a wood-cutter in a forest, were suspended in the centre of the four panels of the walls, on cords of uneven length, and all four were hung crooked. It was obvious that they had long remained thus awry under the heedless eyes of a person who did not care.

Duroy seated himself and waited. He waited a long time. Then a door opened and Madame de Marelle tripped in, dressed in a pink silk kimono embroidered with gold landscapes, blue flowers and white birds.

"Just imagine, I was still in bed," she exclaimed. "How nice of you to come and see me. I had made up my mnd that you had forgotten me."

She held out both her hands to him with a gesture of delight, and Duroy, set at ease by the commonplace appearance of the room, took them and kissed one as he had seen Norbert de Varenne do.

She invited him to sit down ; then, scanning him from head to foot :

" How you have changed ! You have quite an air now. Paris is doing you good. Come, tell me all your news."

And immediately they began to chatter away like old acquaintances, conscious of a sudden feeling of familiarity, of one of those bursts of confidence, intimacy and affection that in five minutes create friendship between individuals of similar character and race.

All at once Madame de Marelle exclaimed in surprise :

" It is odd how well I get on with you. I feel as if I had known you for ten years. We are sure to become good friends. What do you think ? "

" Yes, certainly," he replied, with a smile which said more than his words.

He thought her most captivating in her bright-coloured, silky kimono, less refined than Madame Forestier in her white morning gown, less charming, less exquisite, but on the other hand more exciting, more piquant. When he felt Madame Forestier near him with her unchanging and gracious smile, which allured and yet kept at a distance, as though to say, " I like you," but at the same time, " Beware ! " that smile whose true meaning could not be fathomed, he longed to be at her feet or to kiss the fine lace on her bodice and slowly to inhale the warm fragrance of her bosom. In the presence of Madame de Marelle he was conscious of a more fierce, brutal, definite desire, a desire which made his hands tremble at the nearness of the swelling contours beneath the light silk. She went on talking, seasoning each phrase with the facile wit of which she had caught the trick, like a workman who has mastered the necessary dexterity for some task of supposed difficulty, to the astonishment of his fellows. As he listened to her, he thought to himself :

" All this is worth remembering. What charming articles one could write about Paris, by getting her to chatter about the events of the day."

There was a soft, a very soft, tap at the door through which Madame de Marelle had entered. She called out : " Come in, darling."

Her little girl appeared, went straight up to Duroy, and gave him her hand. Her mother murmured in surprise :

"Why, you've made a real conquest. I simply don't recognise her."

Duroy kissed the child and made her sit beside him, and with a serious air he questioned her politely about what she had been doing since their last meeting. She replied to his questions in her soft flute-like voice, and in her solemn, grown-up manner.

The clock struck three—Duroy rose.

"Come often," Madame de Marcelle pressed him. "We must have some more chats like to-day's, and I shall always be pleased to see you. But why are you never to be met at the Forestiers ? "

"Oh for no special reason," he answered, " I have had a good deal to do. I hope we shall meet there again one of these days."

He left the house, his heart full of hope, he knew not why. He did not mention his visit to Forestier. But the memory of it remained with him during the succeeding days, and more than the memory, a sense of this woman's unsubstantial and haunting presence. Something of her he seemed to have retained, in his eyes the image of her outward form ; in his heart the essence of her personality. He remained obsessed by her image as is sometimes the case when one has spent delightful hours with a person. One is subjected as it were to a kind of possession, strange, intimate, vague, distracting, and exquisite because of its mystery.

A few days later he paid her another visit.

The maid showed him into the drawing-room and immediately afterwards Laurine appeared. She offered him not her hand, but her forehead.

"Mamma told me to ask you to wait for her. She will be busy for another quarter of an hour, because she isn't dressed. I will keep you company."

Amused by the little girl's ceremonious manner, Duroy replied :

" That will be delightful, Miss Laurine. I shall be charmed to spend the time with you, but I must warn you that I am not at all a serious-minded person ; I simply play all day long. So I suggest a game of catch-who-catch-can."

The little thing was taken aback ; then, somewhat shocked as well as surprised at the idea, she smiled as a grown-up woman might have done.

" Flats aren't made to be played in."

" I don't care," he replied, " I just play anywhere. Come and catch me."

He began to circle round the table, egging her on to chase him, and she followed, still smiling with a kind of polite condescension and sometimes stretching out her hand to touch him, but never letting herself go sufficiently to run.

He stopped short, stooped down, and when she came near him with her little hesitating steps, he jumped up in the air like a jack-in-the-box. Then with one stride he bounded to the other side of the room. This struck her as funny, and she ended by bursting out laughing, and, roused at last, she began to trot after him, uttering timid little cries of delight when she thought she had caught him. He disarranged the chairs, using them as obstacles, he made her revolve round the same one for a whole minute ; then deserted it for another. Laurine was running now and had entered completely into the delights of this new game. With rosy face and the impetuosity of an ecstatic child she made a rush at each new flight, ruse, and feint of her companion.

Suddenly, just as she thought she had caught him, he seized her in his arms and lifting her up to the ceiling, cried out :

" I've got you."

The little girl wriggled in her efforts to escape and laughed with all her heart.

Madame de Marelle entered, and exclaimed in astonishment :

" What ? Is that Laurine, Laurine actually playing ? You're a magician, Monsieur Duroy."

He set the child down, kissed the mother's hand and they seated themselves with the little girl between them. They wanted to talk, but Laurine, usually so silent, was wild with excitement and chattered all the time until she had to be sent to her room. She obeyed without a word, but with tears in her eyes.

As soon as they were alone Madame de Marelle lowered her voice.

" Do you know, I have a great scheme and I have thought of you. Just listen. As I dine every week with the Forestiers, in return I sometimes ask them to dinner at a restaurant. Personally, I don't like entertaining in my own house ; it isn't adapted for it. Besides I know nothing about housekeeping, nothing about cooking, nothing about anything. I like living anyhow. So occasionally I invite them to a restaurant, but when we are only three, it isn't amusing, and my own friends don't hit it off with them. I am telling you this to explain a somewhat unconventional invitation. You understand, don't you, that I am asking you to join our party on Saturday at half-past seven at the Café Riche. You know the place ? "

He accepted joyfully.

" There will be only the four of us," she continued, " a real *partie carrée*. These little entertainments are very amusing for us women who are not used to them."

She wore a gown of dark maroon which defined in a provocative, seductive manner her hips, her bosom and her arms, and Duroy felt a vague surprise, almost a sense of discomfort, the cause of which he could not clearly trace, at the contrast between the studied and fastidious elegance of her own person and her obvious indifference towards her dwelling. Everything that clothed her ; everything in close and direct contact with her person, was dainty and exquisite, but she cared nothing for her surroundings.

When he left her he was haunted as before by the illusion of her presence, prolonged in a kind of sensuous hallucination. And he looked forward to the day of the dinner party with growing impatience.

His means had not yet permitted him to buy a suit of

evening clothes. For the second time, he hired a tail coat.
He was the first to arrive at the appointed place, a few minutes
before the hour. He was shown into a small dining-room
on the second story. It had red hangings and a single
window, which opened on to the Boulevard.

A square table was laid for four. Its white cloth was so
highly glazed that it appeared to be varnished, and the glasses,
the silver and the chafing dish glittered gaily in the glow of a
dozen tapers set in two tall candelabra. The eye was
caught by a great patch of green outside, the leaves of a tree,
illuminated by the bright light that poured from the windows
of the private rooms.

Duroy seated himself on a low sofa, red like the hangings
on the wall, and with worn out springs that yielded under
his weight and gave him the sensation of sinking into a pit.
Throughout the large building, he heard a confused din,
the babel of sound common to all big restaurants, the clatter-
ing of dishes and cutlery, the waiters' rapid tread, muffled
by the carpets in the corridors, doors opened for a moment
and releasing a clamour of voices from all those narrow rooms
where the guests were cooped up.

Forestier entered and shook hands with him with a cordial
familiarity which he never displayed towards him at the
office of the *Vie Française*.

"The two ladies will be arriving together," he said,
"these little dinners are very pleasant."

Then he surveyed the table. He had a gas jet, no bigger
than a night light, turned out completely, closed one side
of the window for fear of the draught, and chose a sheltered
place for himself.

"I have to be very careful," he observed, "I was better
for a month, but the last day or two I've been worse again.
I must have caught cold on Tuesday coming out of the
theatre."

The door opened and the two ladies appeared, followed
by a waiter. Discreetly veiled and cloaked they had about
them the fascinating air of mystery which they assume in
unconventional places of assignation.

Duroy shook hands with Madame Forestier and she

scolded him severely for not having been to see her again. Smiling at Madame de Marelle, she added :

" It's because you prefer Madame de Marelle. You find plenty of time for her."

They sat down at table, and when the waiter presented the wine list to Monsieur Forestier, Madame de Marelle exclaimed :

" Bring these gentlemen anything they like. Iced champagne for us, the best you have, sweet champagne, and nothing else."

When the man had left the room she exclaimed with an excited laugh :

" I am going to get tipsy. We'll make a night of it, a regular night of it."

Forestier did not appear to have heard her remark.

" Do you mind if I have the window closed ? " he asked. " I have been suffering with my chest the last few days."

" Not in the least."

He closed the side of the window that had remained open and returned to his seat with an expression of relief on his face. His wife said nothing and appeared to be deep in thought. With her eyes on the table, she smiled at the glasses with that vague smile of hers that seemed to make promises that were never kept.

Ostend oysters were served, fat and delicious, like little ears enclosed in shells. They melted between the palate and the tongue like salted bonbons. After the soup came trout, pink as the flesh of a young girl. Conversation began. First of all the party discussed a piece of scandal that was running round the town, the story of a society woman caught by a friend of the husband's supping in a private room with a foreign prince. Forestier laughed heartily at this adventure. The two women declared that the indiscreet tale-bearer was nothing less than a blackguard and a cad. Duroy was of the same opinion and announced emphatically that it was a man's duty to bring to affairs of this kind, be he actor, confidant, or merely a witness, the silence of the tomb. He added :

" How full of charming incidents life would be if we could

count on absolute discretion in one another. What pulls a woman up often, very often, indeed almost invariably, is the fear of her secret being betrayed. Now isn't that true? " he added, smiling. " How many women would surrender themselves to a sudden desire, a violent and momentary impulse, a romance of love, were it not for the fear of having to pay for a fleeting happiness with irrevocable scandal and bitter tears."

He spoke with a conviction that communicated itself to the audience. He was as if pleading a cause, and that cause his own. It was as if he had said :

" But with me there would be no such danger to be feared. Try me and see."

Both women studied him with glances of approval, admitting inwardly that what he had said was reasonable and true, confessing by their sympathetic silence that their inflexible Parisian morality would not have held out long, given a certainty of secrecy.

Forestier, almost full length on the sofa, one leg folded beneath him, his table napkin tucked into his waistcoat to save his clothes, assented with a cynical laugh.

" By Jove, yes, one would make the most of it if one could count on silence. Heaven help the unfortunate husbands."

Then they began to talk about love. Without supposing that love was eternal, Duroy's idea was of something enduring, something that formed a bond of tender friendship and confidence. The union of the senses was merely a seal upon the union of hearts. But he protested against the tormenting jealousies, tragedies and scenes, all the miseries which almost invariably accompany a rupture.

When he ceased Madame de Marelle sighed.

" Yes, it's the only good thing in life and we often spoil it by insisting upon the impossible."

Madame Forestier, who was toying with a knife added :

" Yes, yes. It is good to be loved."

She lingered over her reverie and seemed to be dreaming of things that she dared not utter.

As the first entrée was a long time in coming, they took occasional sips of champagne and nibbled bits of crust. And by slow degrees the idea of love entered into them, gradually intoxicating their souls, as the sparkling wine trickled drop by drop down their throats, heated their blood and confused their ideas.

Lamb cutlets were brought, tender and dainty, served on a heaped up layer of asparagus tips.

" How delicious ! " exclaimed Forestier.

And they ate slowly, appreciating the delicate flavour of the meat and the creamy vegetables.

" As for me," Duroy resumed, " when I love a woman, everything else in the world vanishes."

Elated by the thought of the joys of love, and exhilarated by the pleasures of the table, he said this as if he really believed it.

Madame Forestier murmured with her air of aloofness : " There is no happiness to be compared with the first pressure of the hands, when the one asks, ' Do you love me ? ' and the other replies, ' Yes I do.' "

Madame de Marelle, who had just tossed off a fresh glass of champagne said gaily as she set it down :

" As for me, I am less platonic."

And each of them smiled meaningly at this remark, and their eyes sparkled.

Forestier stretched himself on the sofa, flung out his arms on the cushions, and said in serious tones :

" Your frankness does you honour and proves that you are a practical person. But may one ask what Monsieur de Marelle's views are ? "

She shrugged her shoulders slowly with a prolonged gesture of infinite disdain.

" Monsieur de Marelle has no views on the subject. He practises only—self-denial."

Then the conversation, descending from idealism of love, entered the flowery garden of polite suggestiveness. This was the time for adroit insinuations, veils raised by words as one lifts a petticoat, suggestive language, audacity cleverly disguised, all varieties of immodest hypocrisy, the veiled phrase that reveals unclothed images, swift flashes of things unmentionable, the phrase that yields to the sophisticated a subtle, mysterious form of love, a kind of impure contact of thoughts, through its perturbing and sensual evocation, of all the circumstances of human love.

The roast had been brought, partridges flanked by quails, followed by green peas, a dish of *foie-gras* served with a curly-leaved lettuce, green as moss, in a large deep salad bowl, and they had eaten of everything, unconsciously, without tasting it, solely preoccupied with their topic and steeped in an atmosphere of voluptuousness.

The two women were now saying outrageous things, Madame de Marelle with a natural and provocative audacity, Madame Forestier with an alluring reserve, a modesty of tone, voice, smile, and demeanour, which emphasised, while it appeared to attenuate, the daring utterances that issued from her lips.

Forestier, sprawling at full length on the cushions, laughed, drank, ate unceasingly, and occasionally interjected a word or two, so crude that the two women assumed for form's sake a little air of embarrassment, which lasted two or three seconds. Whenever Forestier had given utterance to some glaring impropriety he would add :

" You are getting on well, my dears. If you continue like this, you will end by making fools of yourselves."

Dessert was brought and then coffee, and the liqueurs increased the feverish confusion of their excited spirits. In accordance with the intention she had announced when she sat down to table, Madame de Marelle was tipsy, and she acknowledged it with the merry, talkative playfulness of a woman exaggerating for the amusement of her companions a degree of intoxication which was real enough.

Madame Forestier was now refraining from speech, perhaps from motives of prudence, and Duroy feeling too much excited to speak with safety, preserved a discreet silence. Cigarettes were lighted, but suddenly Forestier was convulsed with a fit of coughing. With red face and sweat on his forehead, he choked behind his table napkin. When the paroxysm had subsided, he growled with an air of fury.

" I have no use for these stupid dinner parties."

All his good humour had vanished before the haunting fear of his malady.

" Let's go home," he said.

Madame de Marelle rang for the waiter and asked for the bill, which was brought to her immediately. She attempted to read it, but the figures danced before her eyes, and she passed it to Duroy.

" Here, pay this for me. I can't see properly. I'm too drunk."

At the same time she tossed her purse into his hands.

The total amounted to a hundred and thirty francs. Duroy checked the bill, handed over two notes, and took the change, asking in an undertone :

" How much shall I give the waiter ? "

" Anything you like. I don't know."

He laid five francs on the plate, returned the purse to his hostess and said to her :

" Would you like me to see you home ? "

" Certainly. I am quite incapable of finding my house myself."

They shook hands with the Forestiers and Duroy found himself alone with Madame de Marelle in a cab.

He felt her touching him, close against him, cooped up with him in that small dark space, which every now and then was suddenly lighted by the gas jets of the street lamps. Through his sleeve he could feel the warmth of her shoulder, but he could think of nothing to say to her. His mind was paralysed by his imperious desire to clasp her in his arms.

" Suppose I risked it, what would she do ? " he reflected.

The memory of all the whispered improprieties at dinner emboldened him, but at the same time he was restrained by his fear of a scandal.

Motionless, buried in her corner, she, too, remained silent. He would have imagined her sleeping if he had not seen her eyes glitter whenever a ray of light penetrated into the carriage.

Of what was she thinking ?

He felt keenly that he must on no account speak, that one word, one single word breaking the silence, would spoil his chances. But he lacked the audacity necessary for sudden and brutal action.

Suddenly he felt a touch on his foot. She had made a movement, a quick, nervous movement of impatience or perhaps of appeal. At this almost imperceptible gesture, a deep shudder ran over his whole frame from head to foot, and turning suddenly he threw himself upon her, his lips seeking her mouth and his hands her bare skin.

She uttered a cry, a low cry, endeavoured to sit up, to struggle, to repulse him. Then she yielded, as if she had not the strength to resist him longer.

The carriage soon came to a halt before her house and Duroy, taken by surprise had no time to search for passionate words with which to thank her, bless her, express his love and gratitude. But overcome by what had happened, she made no movement. Fearing that the cabman's suspicions might be aroused, Duroy stepped out first and offered her his hand.

At last she emerged from the cab. She walked unsteadily and said not a word. He rang the bell and when the door opened, he asked trembling :

" When can I see you again ? "

So softly that he could scarcely hear her, she whispered :
" Come and lunch with me to-morrow."

And she vanished into the shadow of the vestibule, pushing to the heavy door, which closed with a noise like a gun.

He gave five francs to the cabman and walked away with a rapid, triumphant step, his heart brimming over with joy. At last he possessed a woman, a married woman ! A society woman ! A real Paris society woman ! How easy and unexpected it had been.

Till that moment he had imagined that to approach and conquer one of those beings whom he so ardently desired, would demand infinite pains, interminable efforts, a cunning siege by means of gallantry, words of love, sighs and presents. But now all of a sudden, unresisting, the first one he met abandoned herself to him so readily that he remained dumbfounded.

"She was tipsy," he reflected. "To-morrow it will be another story. There will be tears."

This idea disquieted him, but he said to himself:

"Well, it can't be helped. Now that I've got her I shall take good care to keep her."

In the confused mirage of his vague hopes, his hopes of greatness, success, fame, fortune, love, he had a vision resembling those bevies of fair forms that hover in the celestial atmosphere of an apotheosis. He saw a procession of women, elegant, rich, powerful, who passed by smiling, to disappear one after the other in the golden mist of his dreams.

And his sleep was peopled with visions.

The next day he felt some slight agitation, as he ascended the stairs to Madame de Marelle's flat. How would she receive him? What if she refused to receive him? Supposing she had forbidden him the house? Suppose she had told——? But no, she could say nothing without allowing the whole truth to be divined. So he was master of the situation.

The little maid opened the door. There was nothing unusual in her expression, and this reassured him, as if he had been expecting her to exhibit a face of consternation.

"Is your mistress quite well?" he asked.

"Yes, thank you, sir," she answered, "just as usual."

She showed him into the drawing-room.

He went straight to the mantelpiece to satisfy himself as to the condition of his hair and his dress, and he was straightening his tie before the mirror when he caught the reflection of his hostess who was standing on the threshold looking at him.

He made as if he had not seen her, and they studied each other for several seconds in the mirror, secretly observing and scrutinising each other, before meeting face to face.

He turned round. She had not stirred and seemed to be waiting for him. He sprang towards her, faltering:

"How I love you! How I love you!"

She opened her arms and fell upon his breast, then she turned her face up to his and they kissed each other lingeringly.

" It's easier than I thought," he reflected. " I'm getting on very well."

When their lips drew apart, he smiled without saying a word, endeavouring to express an infinity of love in his glance.

She, too, smiled, a woman's smile, conveying desire, consent, eagerness to surrender.

" We are all alone," she said softly. " I have sent Laurine to lunch with a friend."

He sighed and kissed her wrists.

" Thank you. I adore you."

Then she took his arm, as if he had been her husband, and led him to the sofa where they seated themselves side by side.

He had intended to open the conversation with some clever and charming remark, but as he could think of nothing satisfactory he merely stammered :

" You're not very angry with me."

She laid her hand on his mouth.

" Hush ! " she said.

They sat in silence hand in hand gazing into each other's eyes.

" If you only knew how I wanted you," he said.

" Hush ! " she repeated.

The maid was heard moving plates about in the dining-room the other side of the wall.

He rose.

" I mustn't stay so near you. I should lose my head."

The door opened.

" Luncheon is on the table, madame."

Gravely he offered her his arm.

They lunched sitting opposite to each other, continually exchanging glances and smiles and occupied solely with themselves, enveloped by the exquisite charm of a love affair in its infancy. They did not notice what they were eating. He felt a foot, a little foot, roving about under the table. He caught it between his own and kept it there, pressing it with all his strength.

The maid came and went, bringing in and removing dishes

with an indifferent air and without appearing to notice anything.

When luncheon was over they returned to the drawing-room and resumed their seats on the sofa, side by side. Little by little he pressed closer to her, endeavouring to embrace her. But she repulsed him calmly.

" Be careful. Someone might come in."

" When can I see you really alone," he whispered, " to tell you how I love you ? "

She leaned towards his ear and said very softly :

" I shall come and pay you a little visit one of these days."

He felt himself blushing.

" To tell you the truth—my lodgings are rather humble."

She smiled.

" What does that matter ? I'm coming to see you, not your lodgings."

Then he pressed her to say when she would come. She fixed on a day well on in the following week, but with faltering words and shining eyes he besought her for an earlier date. He held her hands and crushed them ; his face was flushed and fevered with desire, the impetuous desire that follows a *tête-à-tête* repast. It amused her to see him pleading with her so ardently, and now and then she would yield a day.

But he insisted.

" To-morrow ; say to-morrow."

In the end she consented.

" Very well. To-morrow at five o'clock."

He heaved a deep sigh of joy ; and then they conversed calmly, on a footing of intimacy as if they had known each other for twenty years.

The ringing of a bell startled them, and with a single impulse, they drew away from each other.

" That must be Laurine," she murmured.

The child appeared ; stopped short, taken aback ; then she ran to Duroy, clapping her hands in a transport of delight, and called out :

" Oh, Bel-Ami ! "

Madame de Marelle burst out laughing.

" Just listen to that ! Bel-Ami ! Laurine has christened you. It's a charming pet name for you. I shall call you Bel-Ami, too."

He had taken the child on his knees and she made him play all the little games he had taught her.

At twenty minutes to three he rose to go to his office, and at the door of the flat he whispered again :

" To-morrow at five o'clock."

" Yes," replied his hostess with a smile and vanished.

As soon as he had finished his work, he considered how to arrange his room for his mistress's reception and how best to disguise the poverty of the place. The idea occurred to him of pinning up on his walls small Japanese ornaments and he bought five francs worth of crepe paper, knick-knacks, little fans and little hand-screens with which he concealed the too obvious stains on the walls. On the window panes he pasted transparencies representing boats on rivers, flights of birds across red skies, many-coloured groups of ladies on balconies, processions of little dark figures over snow-covered plains. His room, where there was just sufficient space to sleep and to sit down, soon resembled the interior of a Chinese lantern. He thought the effect satisfactory, and he spent the evening gumming to the ceiling birds he had cut out of the coloured papers left over.

Then he went to bed lulled by the whistling locomotives.

Next day he came home early carrying a bag of cakes and a bottle of Madeira bought at the grocer's. He had to go out again to buy two plates and two glasses, and he arranged the collation on the dressing table, after covering its dirty wooden surface with a napkin, and hiding the basin and ewer underneath.

Then he waited.

She arrived about a quarter-past five, and was charmed by the decorations of coloured paper.

" How pretty your room is," she exclaimed. " But what a lot of people there are on the stairs."

He had clasped her in his arms, and was passionately kissing through her veil the hair between her forehead and the rim of her hat.

An hour and a half later he was escorting her to the cabstand in the Rue de Rome. When she had entered the cab he whispered :

" Tuesday, at the same time."

" At the same time on Tuesday," she replied.

And as darkness had fallen, she drew his head inside the window and kissed his lips. Then when the cabman had whipped up his horse, she exclaimed :

" Good-bye, Bel-Ami," and the old vehicle rolled away, drawn by its white horse at a weary trot.

Thus every few days for three weeks Duroy received Madame de Marelle's visits, sometimes in the mornings sometimes in the evening.

One afternoon when he was expecting her, he was drawn to the door by a loud voice on the staircase. A child was screaming. A man's voice, raised in fury, exclaimed :

" What the deuce is the brat howling for now ? "

The screeching, indignant voice of a woman replied :

" That good for nothing hussy who goes to see the journalist on the top floor has knocked Nicholas over on the stairs. Baggages like that, who don't even look out for children on the staircase, oughtn't to be allowed."

Duroy retreated in dismay, for he heard a rapid rustling of skirts and a hasty step mounting the flight of stairs below him.

Soon there was a knock at his door, which he had just closed. He opened it and Madame de Marelle flung herself into his room, breathless, distracted, gasping out :

" Did you hear that ? "

He pretended to be aware of nothing.

" No. What was it ? "

" How they insulted me ? "

" Whom do you mean ? "

" The wretches who live downstairs."

" No. What is the matter ? Tell me."

Unable to utter a word, she burst into sobs.

He had to remove her hat, unlace her, lay her on the bed and dab her forehead with a wet cloth. She gasped for breath. When at last her emotion had somewhat subsided, all her fury and indignation burst forth. She urged him to go down at once, to fight them and kill them.

He replied :

" But they are workmen, mere clodhoppers. Remember that it would mean an affair with the police, that you might be recognised, taken into custody, and ruined. You can't get into rows with people of that sort."

Another idea struck her.

" But what are we to do now ? I can't possibly come here again."

" It's quite simple," he replied, " I shall move."

" Yes, but that will take a long time," she objected.

All at once a plan occurred to her and she was suddenly restored to serenity.

" No, listen. I've thought of a scheme. Leave it to me. Don't trouble about anything. I'll send you a *petit bleu*." She meant the sealed telegrams that are in use in Paris.

She was now all smiles, enchanted with her inspiration, but she refused to say what it was, and she showed her love in a thousand absurd ways. None the less she was very much agitated and on her way downstairs she leaned her whole weight on her lover's arm, because she felt her limbs refuse their support. They did not meet a soul.

As he was a late riser, he was still in bed at eleven o'clock the next morning when the telegraph boy brought him her *petit bleu*.

Duroy opened and read it :

> *To-day five o'clock, Rue de Constantinople,* 127. *Ask for flat engaged by Madame Duroy. Love from Clo.*

At the stroke of five he entered the hall-porter's room in a big house with furnished apartments, and said :

" Is this where Madame Duroy has taken a flat ? "

" Yes, sir."

" Please show it to me."

The man, doubtless accustomed to situations requiring tactful treatment, looked him straight in the face. Then, selecting one from a long row of keys :

"I presume you are Monsieur Duroy?" he asked.
"Yes, certainly."

The porter ushered him into a small two-roomed flat on the ground floor, opposite his lodge.

The drawing-room was hung with a fairly clean, flowered wall-paper, and had a suite of mahogany furniture upholstered in greenish rep with a yellow pattern. The meagre carpet had a design of flowers and was so thin that the foot could feel the boards beneath.

The bedroom was so diminutive that the bed occupied three-quarters of it. It stood in the farther side, entirely filling the space between the two walls—a bulky piece of furniture of the lodging-house variety, hung with heavy blue curtains, likewise of rep, and smothered with a big eiderdown of red silk, spotted with suspicious-looking stains.

Uneasy and displeased, Duroy thought to himself:
"This will run me in for no end of money. I shall have to borrow again. What an idiotic thing for her to do."

The door opened and Clotilde entered like a whirlwind, arms outstretched and skirts rustling. She was in raptures.

"Isn't it charming; tell me, isn't it charming? No stairs to climb. Right on the street, on the ground floor. You can go in and out by the window without the porter seeing you. What an ideal place for two lovers!"

He kissed her coldly, not venturing to ask the question that was on the tip of his tongue.

She had deposited a large parcel on the round table in the middle of the room. Opening it she took out a cake of soap, a bottle of eau de Lubin, a sponge, a box of hair-pins, a button-hook, and a small pair of tongs, for adjusting the locks on her forehead which were always coming out of curl. She played at moving in, finding a place for everything and enjoying herself vastly.

She talked away as she opened the drawers.

"I must bring some underclothes, so that I can change if necessary. It will be very convenient. If I happen to be caught in a shower when I'm out shopping, I shall come here and dry myself. We will each have a key, besides the one in the porter's lodge in case we should forget our own.

I have taken it for three months, in your name of course, as I couldn't give mine."

" You will let me know when the rent is due ? " he asked.

She answered with simplicity :

" But it's already paid, my dear."

" Then I owe the money to you ? " he resumed.

" Certainly not, my pet ; it's nothing to do with you. This is my own little extravagance."

He pretended to be vexed.

" No, that won't do. I can't possibly allow it."

She came to him pleadingly and laid her hands on his shoulders.

" George, I entreat you. It will give me such pleasure, such pleasure to think that it's mine, mine entirely, this little nest of ours. Why should you feel hurt ? Why ? I want this to be my contribution to our love. Tell me that you will let me, my George, tell me that you will."

She besought him with her eyes, her lips, her whole being.

He took a great deal of persuading, and he made his refusals with a semblance of irritation ; in the end he gave way, reflecting that it was only fair after all.

But when she had left him, he rubbed his hands together and murmured :

" Really, she's very sweet."

And he did not search the recesses of his heart to discover from what special source just then he derived this opinion.

A few days later he received another telegram saying :

My husband arrives this evening, after six weeks on inspection duty. So we shall have to take a week off. What a bore.—Clo.

Duroy was dumbfounded. He had quite overlooked the fact that she was married. Here was a man, whose face he wished to see just once, so as to be able to recognise him.

In the meantime he waited patiently for the husband's departure, but he spent two evenings at the Folies-Bergère, ending up at Rachel's.

At last one morning he received a four-word telegram :

Five o'clock to-day.—Clo.

Both arrived at their meeting place before the time. She threw herself into his arms with a great demonstration of affection, covering his face with kisses. Then she said to him :

" Afterwards, if you like, you can take me out to dinner somewhere. I have kept myself free."

It happened to be the beginning of the month and although his salary had long been forestalled, and he was living from day to day on money scraped together from all sides, Duroy chanced to be in funds and he was glad to have an opportunity of spending some money on her.

" Certainly, my love," he replied. " Wherever you like."

Accordingly about seven o'clock they left the flat and proceeded to the outer Boulevard. She leaned heavily on him and whispered in his ear :

" If you only knew how happy I am walking along on your arm, and how I love feeling you close to me ! "

" Would you like to go to Lathuille's ? " he asked her.

" Oh, no, that's too smart," she replied ; " I should prefer something amusing and vulgar, like those restaurants to which shop assistants and working girls go. I simply adore parties in little taverns. Oh, if only we could have got out into the country ! "

As he knew no place of this description in that quarter, they strolled the whole length of the Boulevard, and at last turned into a drinking-shop with an eating-room attached. Through the window she had seen two bareheaded girls sitting with two soldiers. Three cabmen were dining at the end of the long narrow room, and a person impossible to class in any profession, his legs stretched out, his hands in the waistband of his trousers, was smoking his pipe, sprawling in his chair with his head hanging backwards over the rail. His jacket was a museum of spots and in his bulging pockets was a bottle, with neck protruding, a bit of bread, a parcel wrapped in newspaper, and a piece of string with its end hanging out. He had thick, curly, tangled hair, grey with dust, and his cap lay on the ground under his chair.

The entrance of Clotilde in her fashionable clothes

created a sensation. The two couples ceased their whispering, the three cabmen stopped arguing, and the individual who was smoking took his pipe out of his mouth, spat in front of him, and turned his head slightly to look.

"It's very nice," said Madame de Marelle; "we shall do very well here. Another time I shall dress up like a working girl."

Without a sign of embarrassment or disgust she seated herself at a wooden table, shining with grease, washed only with spillings from the glasses, and wiped down with the waiter's napkin. Somewhat embarrassed and ashamed, Duroy looked for a peg on which to hang his silk hat. Finding none, he laid it on a chair.

They had a ragout of mutton, a cut off the joint and a salad.

"I simply adore this," Clotilde repeated; "I have low tastes. This amuses me more than the Café Anglais. If you want to give me a real treat," she continued, "take me to a public dancing place. I know a funny one near this called the *Reine Blanche*."

"Whoever took you there?" asked Duroy in surprise.

He looked at her and saw her blush in some confusion as if his abrupt question had awakened recollections of a delicate nature. After one of those pauses common with women, and so slight as to be hardly noticeable, she replied:

"A friend——" adding, after a silence, "He is dead now."

And her eyes drooped with a very natural sadness.

For the first time Duroy was struck by the thought of all that was unknown to him in this woman's past. She had assuredly had other lovers, but of what description? Of what social standing? A vague jealousy awoke in him, a feeling of hostility towards her, towards everything of which he remained in ignorance, towards whatever in her heart and her existence had not belonged to him. He glanced at her, stung by the mystery hidden within her pretty head, which at that very moment was perhaps thinking with silent regret of that other, of those others.

How he would have loved to peep and rummage in this memory of hers, and get at the heart of all its secrets!

"Will you take me to the *Reine Blanche* ? " she asked
again. "It will just round off the evening."

"Pooh ! " he reflected. "What does the past matter ?
I am a fool to bother my head about it."

And he replied with a smile :

"Certainly, my love."

Once more in the street, she continued in the low, mysterious tone in which confidences are made :

"I didn't venture to ask you before. But you have no
idea how much I enjoy these schoolboy escapades to all
the places where women don't go. In carnival time I
shall dress up as a student. It's the funniest thing you ever
saw, me as a student."

When they entered the dancing hall, she pressed close
up to him, frightened, but happy, viewing with delighted
eyes the young women and their souteneurs. From time to
time, as if to reassure herself against a possible danger, she said
as she caught sight of some imperturbable police officer :

"There's a good solid fellow."

After a quarter of an hour, she had had enough of it and
he took her home.

This was the first of a series of expeditions to all sorts
of doubtful places of entertainment, and Duroy discovered
in his mistress a passion for the random escapades of a student
on the spree.

She would arrive at their flat in a cotton frock and the
vaudeville variety of servant's cap. But however studiously
simple her dress might be, she persisted in wearing her rings
and bracelets and diamond earrings, and when he begged her
to take them off, she protested :

"Pooh. Nobody will take them for real."

She believed herself to be admirably disguised, though her
method was about as effective as that of the ostrich, and she
went into taverns and drinking-dens of the vilest repute.
She had tried to persuade Duroy to wear workman's clothes,
but he refused and retained the correct dress of a man about
town, declining even to change his silk hat for one of soft
felt.

She consoled herself for his obstinacy by arguing :

" People will think that I'm a lady's maid who has caught the fancy of a gentleman."

This all seemed to her an enchanting farce.

They would enter some low-class pot-house and seat themselves on rickety chairs at an old wooden table at the far end of the room, which was pervaded by a cloud of pungent smoke, wherein the odour of the fried fish of the evening meal still lingered. Men in smocks talked at the top of their voices as they drank their liqueurs, and the waiter stared in surprise at this odd couple as he set before them their brandied cherries.

In trembling, terror-stricken ecstasy, she slowly sipped the red fruit juice, casting alert, uneasy glances around her. Every cherry she swallowed gave her a sensation of a sin committed ; every drop of the fiery liquid as it trickled down her throat, thrilled her with keen delight, the joy of an unlawful indulgence.

At last she would say in an undertone :

" Let's go now."

And they would make their way to the door. She would pass down the room with the bent head and short, quick steps of an actress walking off the stage. The men who sat drinking with their elbows on the table would watch her with ill-will and suspicion. When she crossed the threshold she would heave a deep sigh as if she had escaped from some terrible danger.

Sometimes she asked Duroy with a shudder :

" What would you do if somebody insulted me in one of those places ? "

He replied in a blustering voice :

" I should stand up for you, by Jove."

And she squeezed his arm happily, perhaps with a vague desire of being insulted, so that he might have to defend her, and that she might see her lover come to blows even with such men as those, for her sake.

But Duroy began to weary of these jaunts, repeated two or three times a week. Moreover of late he had had great difficulty in procuring the half-louis necessary for the cab and their refreshments.

At this time he could scarcely make both ends meet ; it was worse than when he was a clerk at the Nord. During his first month of journalism he had spent his money lavishly and imprudently in the constant hope of making more in the near future, and now he had reached the end of all his resources present and future.

The simple process of borrowing from the cashier had soon been exhausted, and he already owed the office four months' salary, besides six hundred francs advanced for work not yet done. In addition to this he owed one hundred francs to Forestier, three hundred to the open-handed Rival, and he was harassed by a host of petty, humiliating debts, five francs here, twenty there, and so on.

Saint-Potin, consulted as to the means of raising another hundred francs, could suggest no expedient, although he was a man of resource, and Duroy chafed at his plight, which he felt all the more keenly with his increasing needs.

A dull resentment towards all the world smouldered in him, together with a continual feeling of irritation which manifested itself on the slightest provocation.

Sometimes he asked himself how he had contrived to spend an average of a thousand francs a month without any excess or extravagance. Then he had to admit that if you added an eight-franc luncheon to a twelve-franc dinner at some big restaurant on the Boulevard you arrived at once at a total of one louis. This together with ten francs or so of pocket money, money that runs away nobody knows how, came to a total of thirty francs. Now thirty francs a day amounted to nine hundred at the end of the month, without reckoning the cost of clothes, boots, linen, laundry, and so on. Thus on the fourteenth of December, he found himself without a sou in his pocket and without an idea in his head as to how to lay hands on any ready cash. He did as he had often done in former days, he went without luncheon, and during the afternoon he spent at the office he was peevish and preoccupied.

About four o'clock he received a telegram from Madame de Marelle.

"Shall we dine together, and have some fun afterwards ? "

He replied at once.

" Dinner impossible."

Then he reflected that it would be very foolish to deprive himself of pleasant moments with her and he added, " But I will expect you at nine o'clock at the flat."

He sent one of the office boys with this note to save the cost of a telegram. Then he considered how he might secure an evening meal. By seven o'clock, no plan had occurred to him and a fierce hunger was gnawing his stomach. At last he had recourse to a stratagem of despair. He waited till all the other reporters had, one by one, left the office, and when he was alone, he rang the bell sharply. The director's door-keeper, who remained in charge of the office, appeared.

Duroy stood nervously fumbling in his pockets. He said in an abrupt voice :

" I say, Foucart, I have left my purse at home and I have to go to the Luxembourg to dinner. Can you lend me two francs fifty for my cab ? "

The man drew three francs from his waistcoat pocket.

" Won't you have more than that, sir ? "

" No, no, that will be enough. Thank you very much.'

Pocketing the silver, Duroy ran down the stairs and then went and dined at a cheap eating-house where he used to run to ground when he was hard up.

By nine o'clock he was awaiting Madame de Marelle in the little drawing-room with his feet at the fire.

She came in full of animation and gaiety, stimulated by the cold air of the streets.

" If you like we will go for a stroll," she said, " and come back here at eleven. It's splendid weather for walking."

" Why go out ? " he replied in a sulky voice. " We're very comfortable here."

" You don't know what a lovely moonlight night it is," she rejoined, without removing her hat. " Walking is a real joy this evening."

" Possibly, but I don't happen to want a walk."

His ill-temper was obvious, and she was startled and hurt.

" What is the matter with you ? " she asked. " Why do

you behave like that ? If I wish to go for a stroll, I don't see why that should annoy you."

He rose from his seat in exasperation.

" It doesn't annoy me. It bores me. That's all."

She was one of those women who are irritated by opposition and infuriated by discourtesy. Scornfully, with cold resentment, she exclaimed :

" I am not accustomed to being spoken to like that. Very well, I shall go for a walk by myself. Good-bye."

He understood that matters were serious and hastening towards her he seized her hands and kissed them, faltering :

" Forgive me, darling, forgive me. I am very nervous and irritable this evening. It's because things have been going wrong, you know, and I have been bothered about my work."

Slightly relenting but not entirely appeased, she replied :

" That's no concern of mine and I don't propose to be a target for your bad temper."

He took her in his arms and drew her towards the sofa.

" Listen, pet, I did not mean to hurt you. I was not thinking of what I was saying."

He had obliged her to sit down and he knelt at her feet.

" Have you forgiven me ? Tell me that you have forgiven me."

" Very well," she murmured in a cold voice, " but don't do it again."

Rising to her feet she added :

" Now let's go for a stroll."

He had remained on his knees, clasping her round the hips with both arms.

" Let us stay here, I entreat you," he stammered. " I implore you to grant me this favour. I should love to keep you all to myself this evening, by the fire. Do say yes, I entreat you. Do say yes."

She answered flatly, in a hard voice :

" No. I want to go out and I won't give way to your caprices."

" I implore you," he persisted. " I have a reason, a very serious reason."

Again she replied :

" No, I won't.   And if you don't come out with me I shall go away.   Good-bye."

She had shaken herself free and had reached the door. He ran to her, and caught her in his arms.

" Listen, Clo, my little Clo, listen to me, you might at least do that."

Without speaking she shook her head in refusal, and avoiding his kisses, she endeavoured to escape from his embrace and to go away.

He stammered out :

" Clo, my little Clo, there is a reason."

She stopped short and looked him in the face.

" You aren't speaking the truth.   What is the reason ? "

He blushed, not knowing what to say.   She retorted indignantly :

" You know you're lying to me, you brute."

And with a furious gesture and her eyes full of tears, she broke away from him.

He seized her again by the shoulders, and in despair, ready to avow everything to avoid a rupture, he exclaimed in a distracted voice :

" The reason is that I haven't a sou in the world.   That's all."

She stopped short and looked deep into his eyes to read the truth in them.

" What did you say ? "

He had blushed to the roots of his hair.

" I said that I hadn't a sou.   Can you realise it ?   Not twenty sous, not ten sous, not enough to pay for a ratafia in a café.   You force me to make these humiliating admissions.   But I couldn't possibly go out with you, and, when we were seated at a table with two glasses in front of us, calmly announce that I was unable to pay for them."

She still looked at him searchingly :

" Then it's really true, what you said ? "

In a moment he turned out all his pockets, trouser pockets, waistcoat pockets, coat pockets, and he muttered :

" Look.   Now are you satisfied ? "

Suddenly she flung out her arms with a passionate impulse and fell on his neck, faltering out :

" O ! my poor darling, my poor darling. If I had only known ! How ever did you get into such a fix ? "

She made him sit down and planted herself on his knees with her arms round his neck, and while she continued to imprint kisses on his moustache, his mouth, his eyes, she insisted on his telling her the cause of his predicament.

He invented a moving story. He had been obliged to come to the rescue of his father who was in embarrassed circumstances. He had not only given him all his savings, but he had also incurred heavy debts on his behalf.

" There is nothing for it but short commons for at least six months. I have exhausted all my resources. It can't be helped. Life has its critical moments. After all, money isn't a thing worth bothering about."

She whispered in his ear :

" You will let me lend you some, won't you ? "

He answered with dignity :

" It's very sweet of you, darling. But please don't let's talk of such a thing again. It would hurt my feelings."

She was silent, then throwing her arms round him she murmured :

" You will never know how much I love you."

This evening of love-making was one of the best they had had.

As she was leaving she said with a smile :

" In a situation like yours, it's very jolly to find some money forgotten in a pocket, or a coin that has slipped into the lining."

" I should think so," he replied with conviction.

She insisted on returning home on foot, making the beauty of the moon a pretext and she went into raptures as she looked at it.

It was a cold, calm night of early winter. The passers-by and the horses moved rapidly along, stimulated by the clear frosty air. Heels rang out on the pavement.

As they took leave of each other she said :

" Shall we meet the day after to-morrow ? "

" Yes, certainly."

" At the same time ? "

" At the same time."

" Good-bye, darling."

They kissed each other tenderly.

He strode home at a rapid pace, wondering what plan he could hit upon on the morrow to extricate himself from his difficulties. But as he opened the door and felt in his waist-coat pocket for matches, he was amazed to find a coin under his fingers. As soon as he had a light, he seized the coin and examined it. It was a louis.

He thought he must be mad.

He turned it over and over, wondering by what miracle the money had got there. Certainly it could not have dropped from heaven into his pocket.

Then all at once the truth dawned on him, and he was seized with a fury of indignation. He remembered that Clotilde had said something about coins that slipped into coat linings and were discovered again in one's hours of poverty. It was she who had bestowed upon him these alms. What a humiliation !

" O very well," he vowed to himself, " I shall give her a warm welcome the day after to-morrow. She shall have a pleasant quarter of an hour."

And he went to bed seething with rage and humiliation.

He awoke late. He was hungry. He tried to go to sleep again, so as not to have to get up until two o'clock. Then he said to himself.

" This doesn't get me any further. Sooner or later I simply must raise some money."

He went out, hoping that an idea would occur to him in the street. None, however, came to him, but whenever he passed a restaurant, a fierce desire for food made his mouth water. At noon, as no plan had presented itself, he suddenly made up his mind.

" Pooh, I shall lunch out of Clotilde's louis. That won't prevent me from returning it to her to-morrow."

Accordingly he had a luncheon at two francs fifty. On

entering the office, he returned another three francs to the porter.

" Foucart, here is what you lent me last night for my cab."

He worked till seven o'clock. Then he dined and spent three francs more out of the twenty. His two glasses of beer that evening brought the day's expenditure up to nine francs thirty. But as he was unable either to restore his credit, or to create new resources in twenty-four hours, he borrowed another six francs fifty the next day out of the louis which he had planned to return that very evening. In the end he went to keep his appointment with four francs twenty in his pocket. He was as savage as a mad dog and he vowed to himself that he would place the matter on a proper footing at once. He would say to Clotilde :

" Of course you know I found the louis you put in my pocket the other day. I am not going to give it back to you to-day, because I am still in the same fix, and I haven't had time to set about raising money. But next time I see you I shall return it."

Clotilde arrived all tenderness and eagerness, and full of apprehension. How would he receive her ? She kissed him persistently to avoid too hasty an explanation.

On his part he said to himself :

" There will be plenty of time presently. I shall wait for an opening."

No opening presented itself and he said nothing, reluctant to approach this delicate subject. She did not suggest that they should go out and was charming in every way.

They parted about midnight, and arranged not to meet again till the following Wednesday, Madame de Marelle having several successive engagements to dinner.

The next day, as he was paying for his luncheon, Duroy felt for his remaining four coins, and he found that there were five of them, and one of them was gold. In the first moment he supposed that he had been given a louis in his change by mistake the previous evening. Then he realised the truth and his heart beat fast under the humiliation of this persistent charity. How deeply he regretted his silence ! If only he had expressed himself energetically, this would never have happened. For four days he made efforts as futile as they were numerous to raise five louis. In the meantime he spent Clotilde's second gift. The next time they met, although he said to her angrily :

" Don't play that game you played the last two nights again, or I shall be annoyed," she succeeded in slipping another louis into his trouser pocket.

When he discovered the coin he merely exclaimed, " Well, upon my word ! " and he removed it to his waistcoat pocket, so as to have it handy, for he did not possess a centime of his own. He quieted his conscience by arguing that after all it was only a loan, and he would pay it all back in a lump.

At last the cashier at the office, moved by his despairing appeals, agreed to dole him out five francs a day. It was just enough to live on, but did not bring him any nearer repaying the three louis. Eventually as Clotilde had been seized again by her passion for nocturnal expeditions to all the shady haunts of Paris, he came to feel no very serious irritation when, after these adventurous rambles he found a yellow coin in his pocket. One day there was actually one in his boot, and another time one in his watch case.

Since she had wishes which for the moment he was unable to gratify, what more natural than that she should pay for her caprices herself rather than give them up ?

None the less he kept an account of all that he received from her in this manner, with the intention of returning it to her some day.

One evening she said to him.

" Would you believe it, I have never been to the Folies-Bergère ? Will you take me there ? "

He hesitated, afraid of meeting Rachel. Then he reflected :

" Pooh, after all it's not as if I were a married man. If Rachel sees me, she'll understand the situation and won't talk to me. Besides we shall have a box."

Another reason influenced him. He was very glad of the opportunity of offering Madame de Marelle a box at a theatre, without having to pay for it. It would be some slight compensation.

When they arrived at the theatre he left Clotilde in the cab, while he went for his pass, so that she should not see that it was presented to him free. Then he came back for her and they entered and were received politely by the man at the door.

The promenade was packed. With difficulty they made their way through the crowd of men and women. At last they reached their box, midway between the orchestra and the restless throng in the gallery. But Madame de Marelle did not cast a single glance at the stage ; her whole attention was attracted by the women who were roaming about behind her, and she turned round continually to watch them. She wanted to touch them, to feel their clothes, their faces, their hair, to discover what those creatures were made of.

" There's a stout dark woman," she said suddenly, " who keeps on looking at us. I thought just now that she was going to speak to us. Did you see her ? "

" No," he replied, " you must be mistaken."

But he had noticed her long before.

It was Rachel who was prowling round them angrily, with violent words on the tip of her tongue.

Duroy had brushed against her just as they were making their way through the throng, and she had said, " Good evening," in a low voice, and with a wink of understanding. But he had not replied to this civility for fear of being seen by Clotilde ; he had passed her by coldly, his head held high, and a disdainful expression on his face. Stung by unconscious jealousy, Rachel retraced her steps, and once more brushed up against him, exclaiming in louder tones, " Good evening, George."

He still made no reply. Then she determined to force him to recognise her and greet her, and she kept returning to the back of the box, waiting for a favourable opportunity.

When she noticed Madame de Marelle looking at her, she touched George's shoulder with the tip of her finger.

" Good evening. How are you ? "

But he did not turn round.

" Well," she continued, " have you suddenly become deaf since last Thursday ? "

He made no reply, and affected an air of disdain, as if he would not compromise himself by as much as one word with a baggage like that.

She burst out into angry laughter.

"You're dumb, are you? Has Madame there bitten out your tongue?"

With a furious gesture and in an exasperated voice he broke out.

"Who gave you permission to speak to me? Get out of this or I'll have you arrested."

Then with flaming eyes and heaving bosom she screamed :

"So that's it, is it? You silly mug! If you carry on with a woman, the least you can do is to say 'How do you do' to her. Because you happen to be with someone else to-day isn't a reason for cutting me. If you had only made a sign when I passed you just now, I'd have left you alone. But you meant to give yourself airs. You wait. I'll pay you out. What, you can't even say good evening to me when I meet you——"

She would have kept it up, but Madame de Marelle had opened the door of the box, and was escaping through the crowd, frantically looking for the exit.

Duroy had darted after her and was endeavouring to rejoin her.

Rachel, seeing them in flight, shouted after them triumphantly :

"Stop her! stop her! She has stolen my man."

The spectators began to laugh. Two men, for the joke of the thing, seized Clotilde by the shoulders, and endeavoured to bring her back, at the same time attempting to kiss her. But Duroy who had caught her up, pulled her roughly away, and dragged her out into the street.

She threw herself into an empty cab which was standing outside. He jumped in after her, and when the driver asked, "Where to, mister?" he replied, "Oh, anywhere you like."

The cab rolled away slowly, rattling over the paving-stones. Clotilde, seized by an attack of nerves, was gasping for breath, and Duroy did not know what to do or what to say.

At last he heard her burst into tears, and he stammered out :

" Listen Clo, my little Clo, let me explain things to you. It's not my fault. I used to know that woman a long time ago—in the early days——"

She uncovered her face, and seized with the rage of a woman in love who finds herself betrayed, a furious rage which restored her power of speech, she panted in rapid, broken phrases :

" Oh, you wretch, you wretch ! What a cad you are ! Is it possible ! What a disgrace ! Oh, heavens, what a disgrace ! "

Then growing more and more beside herself as her ideas gained in lucidity and new arguments occurred to her.

" And it was my money you paid her with ! I actually gave him money—for that woman. Oh, what a wretch ! "

For some moments she seemed to be vainly searching her brain for a still stronger word. Suddenly she spat at him.

" Oh, you beast, you beast, you beast ! You paid her with my money, you beast, you beast ! "

She could think of nothing else and went on repeating :

" You beast, you beast."

Suddenly she leaned out and clutched the driver by the sleeve ordered him to stop. Opening the door, she jumped out into the road.

George was about to follow her, but she exclaimed :

" I forbid you to get out," in so loud a voice that the passers-by began to collect round her, and Duroy did not stir for fear of a scandal. She drew her purse from her pocket and extracted some coins by the light of the street lamp. She placed two francs fifty in the driver's hand and said to him in a resonant voice :

" Here you are, here's your fare for an hour. From me, not from him. And drive that sweep to the Rue Boursault near the Batignolles."

The group of people surrounding her were much amused. One gentleman said :

" Bravo, little woman," and a young rascal who was standing between the wheels of the cab, thrust his head in through the open door, and called out in a squeaky voice :

" Good night, pet."

Then the cab moved off, pursued by peals of laughter.

VI

THE next morning George Duroy awoke to a sad world.

He dressed slowly, and then seated himself at the window and began to reflect. He felt stiff all over, as if he had had a sound thrashing the night before. At last, goaded by the necessity for raising money he went to Forestier's house. His friend received him in his study with his feet at the fire.

" What got you out of bed so early ? "

" Oh, a very serious matter. I have a debt of honour."

" A gambling debt ? "

Duroy hesitated. Then he assented.

" Yes, a gambling debt."

" A large one ? "

" Five hundred francs."

He owed only two hundred and eighty.

Forestier asked, sceptically :

" To whom do you owe it ? "

Duroy had no answer ready.

" Why, to—to—to—to a gentleman from Carleville."

" Indeed. What is his address ? "

" His address is—his address is——"

Forestier burst out laughing.

" Mr. Nobody of Nowhere. I know that gentleman, my dear fellow. If you'd like a louis it's at your disposal, but no more."

Duroy accepted the coin.

Then he went from door to door, to all his acquaintances, and by five o'clock he had scraped together eighty francs

As he still had to raise another two hundred, he resolved to hold on to what he had collected.

" Hang it," he muttered, " I'm not going to put myself out for a minx like that. I'll pay her when I can."

For a fortnight he lived a well-regulated life of strict economy, his mind full of energetic resolutions. Suddenly he was seized by an access of amorousness. It seemed to him several years since he had clasped a woman in his arms, and like the sailor, beside himself at the mere sight of land, every petticoat he met made him tremble.

One evening he returned to the Folies-Bergère in the hope of seeing Rachel. He caught sight of her, as soon as he entered, for she never deserted the place.

He went towards her smiling, with outstretched hand. But she looked him up and down.

" What do you want with me ? "

He tried to laugh it off.

" Look here, don't put on frills with me."

She turned on her heel remarking :

" I don't associate with scum like you."

At this insulting expression, carefully selected by her, Duroy felt himself growing purple in the face, and he went home alone.

Forestier, ailing, losing strength and troubled with a perpetual cough, led Duroy a dog's life at the office. He seemed to make a point of providing him with unpleasant tasks. One day in a moment of nervous irritation, following upon a long paroxysm of choking, when Duroy had failed to bring him some required information, he growled :

" Good heavens, you are a bigger fool than I took you for."

Duroy nearly boxed his ears, but he restrained himself and went away muttering :

" I'll pay you out for this."

A thought flashed swiftly across his mind and he added :

" I'll do it through your wife, my boy."

And he went away rubbing his hands together and delighted with his idea. He intended to set to work the very next day. So he paid Madame Forestier a visit of reconnaissance. She was lying at full length on the sofa reading a book.

Without changing her position, and merely turning her head, she said :

" How do you do, Bel-Ami ? "

He felt as if he had had his ears boxed.

" Why do you call me that ? "

" I saw Madame de Marelle the other day," she said with a smile, "and I heard how you had been christened at her house."

His hostess's pleasant manner set him at ease. After all, why should he be afraid of her ?

" You spoil her," she continued. " As for me, people come to see me when it occurs to them, generally on the 30th of February."

He had seated himself near her and was regarding her with a new interest, the interest of a collector of rarities. She was charming with the warmth and delicacy of her fair colouring, and she seemed made for caresses.

" She's certainly superior to Clotilde," he reflected.

He had no doubts of his success ; it seemed to him that he had only to stretch out his hand and to take her as one plucks a fruit. He said resolutely :

" The reason why I did not come to see you, was because it was better that I shouldn't."

" Really ? " she asked, not undertsanding him, " Why ? "

" Why ? Can't you guess ? "

" No, I haven't an idea."

" Because I'm in love with you—oh, only a little, a very little—but I don't want it to become serious."

She appeared neither surprised, nor shocked, nor flattered. With her usual placid smile she answered calmly :

" Oh, you can come just the same. No one is ever in love with me for long."

He was even more surprised by the tone of her voice than by her words.

" Why ? "

" Because it's useless, and I make that clear from the beginning. If you had confided your fears to me earlier, I should have reassured you. In fact, I should have insisted on your coming as often as possible."

He exclaimed with pathos in his voice :

" As if one could control one's emotions."

She turned towards him.

" My dear friend, as far as I'm concerned a man in love with me simply doesn't count. I regard him as mad, and not only mad, but dangerous. I break off all intimate relations with people who are, or profess to be in love with me, in the first place because they bore me, secondly because I regard them with distrust, like mad dogs liable to sudden paroxysms. And so I keep them in a moral quarantine until they have recovered. Don't forget this. I am quite aware that with you love is merely a kind of appetite ; with me, on the other hand, it would be a communion of souls, and that forms no part of a man's religion. You understand its letter and I its spirit. Now look me straight in the face."

Her smile had vanished. Her face was calm and cold, and she said, laying stress on each word :

" Understand that I shall never, never be in love with you. It is therefore utterly useless, and it would in fact be bad for you, to persist. And now that—the operation has been performed—let us be friends, good friends, real, true friends without any mental reservation."

Realising that every attempt would be futile in the face of this sentence, and that there was no appeal, he made up his mind at once. Overjoyed at securing such an ally he held out both hands.

" I am yours, Madame Forestier, on whatever terms you please."

She caught the inflection of sincerity in his voice and gave him her hands.

He kissed them, one after the other. Then looking up at her he said ingenuously :

" Good heavens, if I had only met a woman like you, with what joy I should have married her."

This time she was touched and flattered by his remark, like all women by a compliment that goes straight to their heart, and she threw him one of those swift looks of gratitude which enslave us. Then as he could find no appropriate words with which to resume conversation, she laid her hand on his arm, and said in a gentle voice :

" I am going to start at once on my office of friend. You don't play your cards well, dear Monsieur Duroy."

She hesitated.

" May I speak freely ? "

" Certainly."

" Absolutely ? "

" Absolutely."

" Well then, go and see Madame Walter. and make yourself pleasant. She has a high opinion of you. You will find your compliments well received in that quarter, although she is a good woman, I would have you understand, a thoroughly good woman. Oh, there's no hope for a free lance there either. But you might find something better than that if you show up frequently. I know that you are still in a subordinate position on the paper. But don't be afraid. The Walters receive all their reporters with the same friendliness. Take my advice and go and call."

" Thank you. You're an angel," he said, with a smile, " a guardian angel."

Then they spoke of one thing and another. He remained a long time, anxious to prove to her that it was a pleasure to him to be near her. When he left her, he asked once more :

" It's agreed that we're to be friends ? "

" Yes, it's agreed."

As he had noticed the effect of his recent compliment, he emphasised it by adding :

" And in case you're ever a widow, you may regard me as a candidate."

Then he hastened off, so as to give her no time to take offence.

Duroy was a little perplexed about his visit to Madame Walter. He had never been invited to call and he did not wish to commit a solecism. But Monsieur Walter had shown good-will towards him, thought highly of his services, and employed him by preference when there was difficult work to be done. Why should he not take advantage of the favour shown him to gain a footing in his house ?

Rising early one morning he went to the market, and for about ten francs secured a score or so of fine pears. Carefully packing them in a hamper to give them the appearance of having come from a distance, he left them with the porter at Madame Walter's house, with a card on which was written:

"George Duroy, hoping that Madame Walter will deign to accept a little fruit, which arrived from Normandy this morning."

The next day in his pigeon-hole at the office he found a card from Madame Walter, "With many thanks to Monsieur George Duroy. Madame Walter is at home every Saturday."

The next Saturday he went to call.

Monsieur Walter owned and occupied a double house on the Boulevard Malesherbes ; one part of it was let, according to the economical custom of practical people. A porter who had his lodge between the two courtyard gates, acted as door-keeper for both landlord and tenant. Dignified as a verger, with his large white-stockinged calves and his full dress with gold buttons and scarlet facings, he lent to each entrance the impressive air of a luxurious, well-ordered house.

The reception-rooms were on the first floor. Leading into them was a tapestried anteroom shut off by curtains. Two footmen sat dozing on chairs. One of them took Duroy's overcoat, the other seized his walking stick and threw open a door. Walking a few steps in front of Duroy, he then stood to one side and announced his name to an empty room, and allowed Duroy to pass.

Duroy glanced all round him in embarrassment. In a mirror, he caught sight of some people who seemed very far away. At first confused by the mirror he mistook the direction, but eventually he made his way through two other empty drawing-rooms until he reached a small boudoir hung with blue silk with gold spots, where four ladies were chatting round a tea-table.

Notwithstanding the self-confidence he owed to his residence in Paris and more especially to his profession of reporter, which brought him into daily contact with notable people, Duroy felt a little abashed by the formality of his reception and his journey through the empty drawing-rooms.

Endeavouring to catch the eye of his hostess, he said haltingly :

" Madame Walter, I have ventured——"

She held out her hand and he bowed over it.

" It is very nice of you to come and see me, Monsieur Duroy," she said.

She offered him a chair, on which, misjudging its height, he sat down with a bump.

The conversation which had ceased was resumed. The subject was that of the cold snap which, though severe, was not sufficiently so to check the epidemic of typhoid or to make skating possible. Each of the guests gave her opinion about the frost ; then they expressed their personal preferences for the different seasons, repeating all the commonplace reasons that litter a mind like dust in a room.

A slight noise at the door made Duroy turn his head, and through two glass screens he saw a stout lady approaching. As soon as she entered the boudoir, one of the other visitors rose, shook hands and went away. As she disappeared through the drawing-rooms, Duroy's eyes followed her black mantle with its trimming of glittering jet beads.

When the disturbance caused by this change of guests had subsided, the conversation turned abruptly to the question of Morocco, the war in the East, and England's difficulties in South Africa. The ladies gave their opinions like parrots or as if they were repeating frequently rehearsed parts in a comedy of social life.

A new visitor entered, a small, fair woman with curly hair. Her arrival was the signal for the departure of a tall, spare woman, of uncertain age.

The discussion now turned on Monsieur Linet's chances of admission to the Academy. The new-comer was firmly convinced that he would be beaten by Monsieur Cabanon-Lebas, who had written in French verse a fine adaptation of Don Quixote for the stage.

" You know it's to be produced at the Odéon next winter."

" Oh, really. I shall certainly go to see it. It's an experiment of real literary value ! "

Madame Walter made her replies urbanely, with calm

indifference, never hesitating as to what she should say, all her opinions being cut and dried. It was growing dark and she rang for the lamps and while she listened to the conversation which flowed on languidly, she was thinking that she had forgotten to call at the engraver's about the invitation cards for her next dinner party.

Madame Walter was inclined to be stout. She was a fine looking woman still, but at the critical age when one begins to go to pieces. She took a great deal of trouble to preserve herself, using hygienic precautions and face-creams.

She appeared a model of discretion, one of those women whose minds are as orderly as a French garden, in which one strolls about with no sense of surprise, yet is conscious of a certain charm. Her judgment was acute and sound, and took the place of imagination. She had kindness too, and devotion, and a calm, comprehensive, all-embracing benevolence.

She noticed that Duroy had said nothing; that no one had spoken to him and that he seemed a little embarrassed. As the ladies had not yet dropped the subject of the Academy, a favourite topic, which always occupied them for a long time, she asked :

" But you, Monsieur Duroy, you must know more about this matter than any of us. Whom do you prefer ? "

He replied without hesitation.

" On this question, Madame Walter, I should never consider the vexed subject of the candidates' merits, but their age and health. I should not inquire into their claims, but into their diseases. I should not ask whether they had produced a rhymed version of Lopez da Vega, but I should carefully inquire into the condition of their liver, heart, kidneys and spinal cord. In my opinion a good hypertrophy or albuminuria, and especially a promising locomotor ataxy, would be a recommendation a hundred times higher than forty volumes of digressions on the idea of patriotism in barbaric poetry."

This utterance was received in amazed silence.

" But why ? " asked Madame Walter with a smile.

" Because," he replied, " I care only for what may give

pleasure to the ladies   Now, Madame Walter, the Academy has really no interest for you, except when an Academician dies.   The oftener they die, the happier you must be.   But if you want them to die quickly, you must nominate the old and the sick."

Seeing that his audience still manifested some surprise, he added :

" Besides I'm just like you ; I'm always delighted to see the news of the death of an Academician in Paris society notes.   Immediately I ask myself who will succeed him. And I make out a list.   It's a game, a very amusing little game, played in all the drawing-rooms of Paris on the decease of an Immortal, the game of Death and the Forty Greybeards."

Though still somewhat disconcerted, the ladies, were nevertheless moved to smile at the truth of his remarks.

As he rose to go he concluded :

" It is you ladies who nominate them, and you only nominate them for the pleasure of seeing them die.   So choose them old, very old, as old as possible, and don't trouble about anything else."

Then he gracefully withdrew.

As soon as he had left the room, one of the women exclaimed :

" What an amusing young fellow !   Who is he ? "

" One of our reporters," replied Madame Walter, " he still does only unimportant work for the paper, but I feel sure he will get on."

Duroy walked gaily down the Boulevard Malesherbes with long, swinging strides, pleased with his parting remarks, and murmuring to himself : " A good send off."

That evening he made friends again with Rachel.

The following week was remarkable for two events. He was made editor-in-chief of the Echoes and was invited to dinner by Madame Walter.   He did not fail to see a connection between the two occurrences.

The *Vie Française* was essentially a business paper, the director being a business man to whom the press and the Chamber of Deputies had served as levers.   He conducted his campaigns under a smiling mask of amiability and good-fellowship. But for carrying out his various schemes, he employed only persons whom he had sounded, tested, and instinctively approved, whom he considered shrewd, audacious and adroit. Duroy, whom he was appointing editor-in-chief of the Echoes, seemed to him a fellow worth having. Hitherto that post had been filled by the secretary of the editorial department, Monsieur Boisrenard, an experienced journalist, accurate, painstaking and a good subordinate. During thirty years he had been secretary of the editorial departments of eleven different newspapers, without modifying in a single respect his methods of work and observation. He had passed from one editorial office to another, as one changes one's restaurant, hardly noticing the change in one's diet. Political and religious opinions were sealed books to him. He was devoted to his paper, whichever it happened to be, well versed in his craft and valuable for the sake of his experience. He did his work like a blind man who sees nothing, like a deaf man who hears nothing, and like a dumb man who never utters a word. At the same time he had a strong sense of professional loyalty, and he would not have lent himself to any scheme which he did not consider honourable, straightforward and right from the special point of view of his calling.

Monsieur Walter, much as he appreciated him, had nevertheless often wished for another man to whom he could entrust the Echoes, which he said, were the backbone of the paper. By means of these paragraphs news are promulgated, rumours spread abroad, influence exercised upon the public and the funds. One must know how to slip in, casually, between two accounts of fashionable evening parties, some item of importance which is implied rather than definitely stated. It is essential to ensure by means of hints that as much as is convenient shall be guessed ; to make a denial have the effect of a confirmation and *vice-versâ*. Further, in order that the Echoes shall be universally read, it is of vital importance that every reader, each day, shall find there at least one line that interests him. All things and all men have to be considered, all strata of society, all the professions, Paris, the provinces, the army, the artists, the clergy, the university, the magistrates, the *demi-monde*.

The man in charge of the Echoes, must, with his battalion of reporters, be continually on the watch, continually on guard, distrustful, far-seeing, subtle, alert, pliant, armed with every artifice and endowed with an infallible instinct for detecting at a glance an item of false news, for deciding what it is expedient to say and what to conceal, and for divining what will make an impression upon the public. He must also know how to present his information in such a way as to enhance its effect.

Monsieur Boisrenard, who had experience in his favour, lacked authority and style ; above all he had not the acuteness necessary for anticipating day by day the director's private thoughts. But Duroy seemed made for the part. He put the finishing touches to this portion of the paper, which was, in the words of Norbert de Varenne, " floated by state banks over political sandbanks."

The moving force of the *Vie Française* came from half a dozen Deputies with an interest in all the speculations started or supported by the director. In the Chamber they were known as " Walter's gang," and were objects of envy because they were bound to make money through him.

Forestier, the political editor, was merely a man of straw to these business men, carrying out suggestions made by them. They inspired the leading articles which, as he said, he always took home to write in peace.

A flavour of literature and a Parisian atmosphere were provided by two celebrated writers, differing from each other in style. They were Jacques Rival, who based his articles on facts, and the poet, Norbert de Varenne, author of imaginative articles, or rather, stories in the modern style. Among the great mercenary band of hack writers, critics of the arts of music, painting and drama, an editor for police news, and another for racing intelligence, had been engaged at low salaries. Two society women, " Pink Domino " and " Pale Hands," contributed miscellaneous notes on social matters. They dealt with questions of dress, fashionable life, etiquette, and good breeding, and indulged in indiscretions on the subject of ladies in high position. And the *Vie Française* steered by all these different hands floated over its banks and its sandbanks.

While Duroy was at the height of his joy over his new appointment, he received a small printed card which said :
" Monsieur and Madame Walter request the pleasure of Monsieur George Duroy's company at dinner on Thursday, January 20th."

This new mark of favour, following close upon the other, filled him with such rapture that he kissed the invitation as he would have kissed a love letter. Then he went to see the cashier to negotiate with him on the sordid question of funds.

An editor of Echoes has, as a rule, his own allotment, out of which he pays his reporters for the items of news, good or indifferent, brought to him by one or other of them, as gardeners bring their early fruit to a dealer. Duroy was to start with an allowance of twelve hundred francs a month, and he proposed to keep a large proportion of it for himself. On his urgent representations, the cashier eventually advanced him four hundred francs. At first he had the intention of returning to Madame de Marelle the two hundred and eighty francs he owed her, but almost at once he realised that this would leave him only one hundred and twenty francs, a sum utterly inadequate for carrying out in a proper manner his new duties. So he postponed the repayment until a later date.

For two days he was busy settling in. He succeeded to a private table and a set of pigeon-holes for letters. in the large editorial common-room. He occupied one end of the apartment, while the other was occupied by Boisrenard, whose hair, ebony black despite his age, was for ever drooping over a sheet of paper.

The long table in the centre was reserved for the occasional staff. As a rule they used it as a bench and sat on it either with their feet dangling over the edge, or squatting, Turkish fashion, in the middle. There were sometimes five or six of them on the table, perseveringly playing cup-and-ball, in attitudes like grotesque Chinese images. Duroy had acquired a taste for this diversion and was becoming an expert, under the instruction and guidance of Saint-Potin.

Forestier, more and more of an invalid, had made over to him his beautiful cup-and-ball of Antilles wood, his latest acquisition, which he found a little heavy for him. With a vigorous arm Duroy swung the big black ball at the end of its string, counting softly, " One, two, three, four, five, six." He had just succeeded for the first time in scoring twenty, the very day on which he was to dine with Madame Walter.

" This is my lucky day," he said, " everything goes well."

Skill at cup-and-ball really conferred a kind of superiority in the office of the *Vie Française*.

He went home early so as to have time to dress, and as he was walking up the Rue de Londres he saw tripping ahead of him, a small woman of the same build as Madame de Marelle. He felt a wave of heat rising to his face, and his heart began to throb. He crossed the street to obtain a view of her profile. She, too, stopped short with the intention of crossing. He found that he was mistaken, and he breathed again. He had often asked himself how he should behave if he met Clotilde face to face. Should he raise his hat to her, or should he pretend not to see her ?

" I shouldn't look at her," he thought to himself.

It was cold, and the frozen gutters had a film of ice. The pavements were dry and showed grey in the gas light.

When he reached home, he thought to himself :

" I must change my lodgings. These won't do for me now."

He felt excited and in high spirits, ready to dance a break-down, and as he went from his bed to his window he exclaimed out loud :

" Has my luck turned ? I believe it has. I must write to Papa."

From time to time he wrote to his father and the letter always brought joy to the little Norman wineshop by the road side, on the top of the high hill overlooking Rouen and the wide valley of the Seine. From time to time, too, a blue envelope reached him, its address traced in a large trembling hand. The opening lines of his father's letters were always the same.

My dear Son,
    This is to inform you that we are quite well, your mother and I. Nothing much new in this part of the world. But I must tell you——"

Duroy continued to take an interest in the affairs of the village, in the news of the neighbours, and the conditions of the ground and the crops.   He said to himself again, as he tied his white tie before his little looking-glass :

" I must write to Papa to-morrow.   If the old man could see me this evening, in the house I'm going to, wouldn't he be struck all of a heap ?   By Jove, I shall presently have such a dinner as he never ate in all his life."

Suddenly he saw again the dark kitchen of his father's house, behind the deserted coffee-room, with the copper saucepans throwing yellow gleams upon the walls, the cat in the chimney corner its nose in the fire and in the attitude of a crouching chimera, the wooden table with the year-old grease of spilt liquids upon it, a smoking soup tureen in the middle and a lighted candle with a plate on either side. And he saw, too, his father and mother, slow-moving peasants, taking their soup with deliberation.   He knew every wrinkle on their old faces, every little gesture of the arm or head.   He even knew what they said to each other every evening, as they took their supper, face to face.

He thought to himself.

" I really must go and pay them a visit some day."

He finished dressing, put out his light and went downstairs.   All along the outer Boulevard he was accosted by young women.   Shaking his arm free, he exclaimed with angry disdain :

" Can't you leave me in peace ? "   As if they had insulted him and mistaken their man.   For what did they take him ?   These creatures did not know one sort of man from another.

The evening dress in which he had arrayed himself to dine with these very rich, very well-known and very important people, created in him the sense of a new personality.   He felt a new man, a man of the world. the world of fashion.

Confidently he entered the antechamber, which was

lighted with lofty bronze candelabra, and with easy unconcern he handed his stick and overcoat to the two footmen.

All the drawing-rooms were brightly lighted. Madame Walter received her guests in the second room, which was the largest. She welcomed Duroy with a charming smile and he shook hands with the two men who had arrived before him, Monsieur Firmin and Monsieur Laroche-Mathieu, Deputies and anonymous editors of the *Vie Française*. Monsieur Laroche-Mathieu exercised special authority over the paper ; this was due to his great influence in the Chamber. No one doubted that he would be in the Government some day.

Then the Forestiers arrived, Madame Forestier looking ravishing in pink. Duroy was amazed at seeing her on familiar terms with the two Deputies. For more than five minutes she exchanged whispers with Laroche-Mathieu in a corner by the fire. Forestier appeared to be exhausted. He had grown very thin during the last month and he coughed incessantly, and kept repeating :

" I shall have to make up my mind to go south for the rest of the winter."

Norbert de Varenne and Jacques Rival arrived together. A door opened at the end of the room and Monsieur Walter entered with two grown-up girls of sixteen and eighteen, one of them plain, the other pretty. Although Duroy had been aware that the director was the father of a family, he was taken by surprise. He had never thought about his daughters, any more than one thinks about the distant countries one never expects to see. Besides, he had imagined them quite small, and he found that they were grown women. He felt the slight mental confusion consequent upon a changed point of view.

After he had been introduced they both shook hands with him and seated themselves at a small table, evidently reserved for them, where they began to toy with some reels of silk in a little basket.

Another guest was expected and the company waited in silence, experiencing that sense of constraint which is felt in the moments preceding dinner, when the guests are not in touch with each other owing to their different occupations of the day.

Duroy was idly scanning the walls and Monsieur Walter called out to him with the obvious desire of showing off his possessions :

" Are you looking at my pictures ? " He emphasised the word " my." " Let me show them to you." And he held up a lamp so that the details could be clearly discerned.

" Here are the landscapes," he said.

In the centre of the panel hung a large canvas by Guillement representing a Norman seashore under a stormy sky. Beneath it hung a wood by Harpignies ; then a plain in Algeria by Guillaumet, with a camel standing up on its long legs, like a curious piece of sculpture.

Monsieur Walter passed on to the next wall and announced, in the grave tones of a master of ceremonies :

" These are very fine."

There were four canvases, " A Visit to a Hospital," by Gervex ; " A Reaper," by Bastien-Lepage ; " A Widow," by Bougereau ; and " An Execution," by Jean-Paul Laurens. The last work represented a Vendean priest up against the wall of his church and facing a firing party of Blues.

A smile flitted over the director's solemn face as he pointed out the next panel.

" Here is something more fanciful."

The first picture that caught the eye was a small canvas by Jean Beraud, entitled, " Above and Below." It represented a pretty Parisian girl mounting the staircase of a tram in motion. Her head appeared at the level of the roof, and the men seated on the benches took note with eager delight, of the youthful face approaching them, while the men standing on the platform below were contemplating the young woman's legs with a somewhat different expression of countenance.

Monsieur Walter held the lamp out at arm's length and laughed coarsely :

" Funny, isn't it ? Very funny."

Then turned the light on to " A Rescue," by Lambert. In the middle of a half-cleared table a kitten was sitting up

on its hindquarters, watching with surprise and perplexity
a fly drowning in a glass of water. It had raised its paw for
a sudden grab at the insect. But it could not make up its
mind. It was hesitating. What would it do?

Then he pointed out a Detaille, "The Lesson," representing a soldier in a barrack-room teaching a poodle to play the
drum.

"I call that very humorous."

Duroy laughed his appreciation and went into raptures:

"It's charming, charming, perfectly charm——"

He broke off suddenly, hearing behind him the voice of
Madame de Marelle, who had just entered the room.
Monsieur Walter continued to hold the light up to his pictures
and to explain them. Next he showed Duroy a watercolour
by Maurice Leloir, "The Obstruction." It represented
a sedan-chair brought to a standstill in a street which was
blocked by a fight between two roughs, two great fellows
who wrestled like Hercules. At the window of the sedan-
chair appeared the charming face of a woman, who kept her
eyes steadily fixed, without impatience or apprehension, and
with a certain admiration, on the conflict between these
two brutes.

Monsieur Walter continued:

"I have other pictures in the adjoining rooms, but they
are by less known and less distinguished artists. This is
my Salon Carré. At present I am buying the works of
young men, quite young men, and I shall hold them up in
the private rooms until the artists have become famous."
Then he said, in a low voice:

"Now's the time to buy pictures. The artists are starving.
They haven't a sou, not a sou."

But Duroy saw nothing, and listened without understanding. Madame de Marelle was there, behind him.
What was he to do? If he greeted her, would she not
turn her back on him or insult him? On the other hand,
if he did not speak to her, what would the others think?

He said to himself:

"At all events I'm gaining time."

He was so much perturbed that for a moment he thought

of feigning a sudden indisposition and going away. The inspection of the walls was over. The director set down the lamp, and shook hands with Madame de Marelle, while Duroy began to examine the pictures again by himself, as if he could never weary of admiring them. He was greatly agitated. What was he to do ? He heard voices ; words penetrated to his ears. Madame Forestier was calling him. He hastened towards her. She wanted to say a good word on behalf of a friend of hers who was going to give a party and was anxious to have it noticed in the Echoes of the *Vie Française.*

" Certainly, Madame Forestier, with pleasure," he stammered.

Madame de Marelle was now quite close to him. He dared not turn round to go away. Suddenly he thought he must be mad ; for she had said in a clear voice :

" Good evening, Bel-Ami. Have you forgotten me ? "

Hastily he swung round. She was standing before him smiling, her eyes full of merriment and affection, and she held out her hand to him. He took it in trepidation, still dreading some trick or some act of treachery.

" What has become of you ? " she asked calmly. " I never see you now."

Without recovering his self-possession, he faltered :

" I have been very busy, Madame de Marelle, very busy indeed. Monsieur Walter has entrusted me with new duties, which give me an immense amount to do."

She looked him in the face, and he could discover nothing but friendliness in her eyes.

" Yes, I know. But that's not a reason for forgetting your friends."

They were interrupted by the arrival of a stout lady with red arms and red cheeks. She was ostentatiously arrayed in a low-necked gown, with her hair elaborately dressed. She walked with so heavy a tread that from watching her gait one gained some notion of the weight and solidity of her limbs.

She appeared to be treated with a great deal of deference, and Duroy asked Madame Forestier :

" Who is that lady ? "

" The Viscountess de Percemur, who signs herself ' Pale Hands.' "

He was amazed and could hardly restrain his laughter. " Pale Hands ! Pale Hands ! Why, I had pictured to myself a young woman like yourself. So that's Pale Hands ? O ! she's splendid, simply splendid."

A servant appeared at the door and announced that dinner was ready. The dinner was commonplace and cheerful, one of those dinners at which one speaks about everything and says nothing. Duroy was placed between Walter's elder daughter, the plain one, Rose, and Madame de Marelle. Madame de Marelle's proximity embarrassed him a little, although she seemed very much at her ease and talked away with her usual vivacity. At first he was confused and awkward, and hesitated like a musician who has lost the right key. By degrees, however, his confidence returned to him, and their eyes, continually meeting, mutually questioning, mingled their glances in the intimate, almost sensuous fashion of former days. Suddenly he thought he felt a light touch on his foot under the table. He gently moved his leg forward and met that of Madame de Marelle. She did not shrink from the contact. At the moment they were not talking to each other, but to their other neighbours. With beating heart, Duroy advanced his knee a little further. A slight pressure responded. He realised that their relations were to be resumed.

After that, what did they say ? Nothing particular. But whenever they looked at each other, their lips quivered.

From time to time, however, Duroy, who wished to make himself agreeable to his chief's daughter, addressed a remark to her. She answered him just as her mother would have done, never hesitating as to the correct reply.

The Viscountess de Percemur on Monsieur Walter's right was giving herself the airs of a princess. Duroy, who found amusement in watching her, asked Madame de Marelle in an undertone :

" Do you know the other, the one who signs her articles ' Pink Domino ' ? "

" Yes, quite well.   You mean Baroness de Livar."

" Is she like this one ? "

" No, but just as odd.   She is a tall, lean creature, sixty years old, with false curls and prominent teeth like an Englishwoman's.   Her wit dates from the Restoration, and so do her gowns."

" Where did they dig out these literary phenomena ? "

" The waifs and strays of the aristocracy are always sure of a welcome from middle-class upstarts."

" No other reason ? "

" None whatever."

The director entered into a political discussion with the two Deputies, Norbert de Varenne and Jacques Rival, which lasted till dessert.

When the party returned to the drawing-room, Duroy again approached Madame de Marelle.   Looking into her eyes, he asked :

" May I take you home to-night ? "

" No."

" Why ? "

" Because Monsieur Laroche-Mathieu, who is my neighbour, always drops me at my door when I dine here."

" When shall I see you ? "

" Come and lunch with me to-morrow."

And they parted without another word.

Duroy did not stay late, finding the evening dull.   On his way downstairs he caught up Norbert de Varenne, who had also just left.   The old poet took his arm.   As he no longer feared him as a rival on the newspaper, their work being essentially different, he now treated the young man with grandfatherly benevolence.

"Well, are you coming part of the way with me ?" he asked.

" With pleasure, my dear sir," replied Duroy.

And they began strolling slowly down the Boulevard Malesherbes.   The streets were almost deserted.   It was a cold night, one of those nights that seem more spacious than other nights, when the constellations are higher in the heavens, and the air seems to bring in its icy breath something from beyond the stars

For the first few moments neither man spoke. Then, to break the silence, Duroy said :

" That fellow Laroche-Mathieu seems very intelligent and well-informed."

" You think so ? " replied the old poet.

Duroy hesitated in surprise.

" Why, certainly. Besides, he is considered one of the most capable men in the Chamber."

" Possibly. In the kingdom of the blind the one-eyed is king. All these people, you see, are mediocrities. Their minds are hemmed between two barriers, money and politics. They are pedants, my dear fellow, with whom it's impossible to discuss anything, anything we care about. Their intelligence is mud through and through, or rather sewage like the Seine at Asnières. Ah ! How rare are the men of spacious thought, whose presence is like a deep fresh breath of air from the wide ocean. I have known a few such men, but they are dead."

Norbert de Varenne spoke in a clear but restrained voice, which would have echoed in the stillness of the night if he had given it full utterance.

He seemed over-excited and sad with a melancholy which sometimes comes upon the soul and makes it vibrant like the frost-bound earth.

" After all," he continued, " what does it matter, a little more or a little less talent ? It must all come to an end."

He fell silent. Duroy, who was feeling lighthearted, said with a smile :

" You are in the blues to-night, my dear sir."

" I always am, my lad," replied the poet, " and so will you be when you are as old as I am. Life is a hill. While you are climbing it you look at the summit and feel happy ; but when you reach the top, you suddenly catch sight of the descent, and of the end, which is death. The ascent is slow, but the descent is rapid. At your age, you are full of joy, and of many hopes, which after all are never fulfilled. At my age, you expect nothing, except death."

Duroy laughed.

" You give me cold shudders down my spine."

" No," replied Norbert de Varenne. " you won't understand me now, but later on you will remember what I have
been saying to you. One day, and with many it happens
early in life, the laughter stops, and behind everything you
look at you see death lurking. Death ! Why you don't
even understand the word. At your age it has no significance. At mine it is terrible. Suddenly without rhyme
or reason you grasp it and the whole aspect of life is changed.
For fifteen years, now, I have felt it working within me, like
a beast gnawing my vitals. I have felt it demolishing me
little by little, month by month, hour by hour, like a house
that is crumbling away. It has disfigured me so completely
that I no longer recognise myself. There is nothing of
me left, nothing of the man, brilliant, youthful, strong, I
was at thirty. I have watched it bleach my dark hair, by
a process skilful, malicious, deliberate. It has stolen from
me my smooth skin, my muscles, my teeth, all my youthful
body, leaving me nothing but a despairing soul which it will
likewise soon carry off. Yes, I am crumbling away under
its base attacks. Moment by moment, with a horrifying
gentleness, it accomplishes its long task, the destruction of
my being. And now, whatever I do, I feel myself dying.
Every step brings me nearer to death, every movement,
every breath, hastens its hideous work. Breathing, sleeping,
eating, drinking, working, dreaming, everything we do is a
process of dying. Life itself is death. Oh, you will come
to realise it. Fifteen minutes thought will bring it home
to you. What do you look for ? Love ? A few more
kisses and there will be an end. What else ? Money ?
What for ? To buy women ? I wish you joy of them.
To eat too much, to grow fat, and to groan all night with
the pangs of gout ? And what besides ? Fame ? Of
what use is fame when one no longer can pluck it in the
form of love ? And finally ? It is always death in the end.
I now see death so close to me that I often feel that I must
stretch out my arms to push it away. Death broods over
the earth and pervades space. I see signs of it everywhere.
Insects lying crushed in the road, falling leaves, a white
hair seen in a friend's beard, all these devastate my heart

and cry to me, Death is here. It casts a blight on all that I do, all that I see, all that I eat and drink, all that I love, moonlight, sunrise, the wide ocean, splendid rivers, the air of summer nights, so sweet to breathe."

He moved along quietly, a little breathless, uttering his thoughts aloud, almost forgetting that he had a listener.

" And not one returns," he continued, " not one. The moulds of statues are preserved, the matrices that will always reproduce the same forms, but my body, my face, my thoughts, my desires will never reappear. And yet millions and millions of beings will be born, who within the limits of a few square inches will possess, like me, nose, eyes, forehead, cheeks, mouth, and also like me a soul, but without my personality, without anything even recognisably mine reappearing in these countless individuals differing infinitely, and yet infinitesimally. To whom should we cling ? Whom assail with our cries of distress ? In what can we believe ? All religions are monstrously stupid, with their puerile morality, their egoistical promises. Death is the one sure thing."

He stood still, seized Duroy by the lapels of his overcoat, and in a slow voice added :

" Think of all this, young man, think of all this for days and months and years, and you will look at life from a different point of view. Endeavour to break away from all that hems you in, make the superhuman effort necessary for detaching yourself while still alive, from your body, your interests, your thoughts, and humanity in general, to turn your eyes elsewhere, and you will understand of how little importance are the disputes between the romanticists and the realists, and the discussions on the Budget."

He walked on at a rapid pace.

" But you will also experience the terrible agony of those who despair. You will struggle, bewildered, overwhelmed by doubt. You will cry for help in all directions and no one will answer. You will stretch out your arms, you will clamour for succour, love, comfort, salvation, and no one will come to you. Why do we suffer thus ? It is doubtless because we were born to live according to things material rather than things spiritual. But, as the result of thought, the balance between our state of increased intelligence and the unfavourable conditions of our life has been upset. Look at people of moderate intelligence. Unless some great disaster overwhelms them, they are content, and do not suffer from the universal woe. Nor do animals feel it."

He halted again, reflected for a moment, then continued with an air of weary resignation :

" As for me, I am one of the lost. I have neither father, mother, brother, sister, wife, children, nor God." He added after a silence, " I have nothing left to me but poetry."

Raising his head towards the sky, where the pale disc of the full moon was shining, he recited :

" *To this dark mystery I seek reply,*
Where floats a pale star in the empty sky."

They reached the Pont de la Concorde and crossed it in silence ; then they strolled along by the Palais-Bourbon. Norbert de Varenne began again :

" Get married, my friend. You can't conceive what it is to live alone at my age. Nowadays solitude fills me with horrible anguish, the solitude of home, by the fire, of an evening. It seems to me then as if I were alone on earth, terribly alone, but surrounded by vague dangers, things unknown and frightful. The partition, which separates me from my unknown neighbour, removes me as far from him as from the stars which I see through my window. A fever possesses me, a fever of pain and fear, and the silence of the walls appals me. It is so profound, and so sad, the silence of a room in which one lives alone. It is not merely a silence around one's body, but silence around the soul. When a chair creaks, you are shaken to the heart, for all sounds are unexpected in that mournful dwelling."

Again he was silent. Then he added :

" After all, when one is old, how good it must be to have children."

They were half-way down the Rue de Bourgogne. The poet stopped in front of a tall house, shook Duroy's hand and said :

" Forget all this old man's talk, young fellow, and live as befits your age. Good night."

And he disappeared down the dark passage.

Duroy went on his way, with heavy heart. He felt as if someone had shown him a pit full of bones, a pit that he could not avoid, into which he must fall some day.

He muttered :

" Upon my word, his home can't be very cheerful. I shouldn't care for a front seat to watch his ideas go past."

He stood still to allow a scented woman to pass him. She had just stepped out of her carriage and was entering her house. He eagerly drew in a deep breath of air perfumed with verbena and orris root. Suddenly his lungs and his heart palpitated with hope and joy, and the thought of Madame de Marelle, whom he would see on the morrow, thrilled him from head to foot. All things smiled upon him ; life welcomed him affectionately. How sweet was the realisation of one's hopes !

In this state of exaltation he went to bed. He rose early to take a walk in the Avenue of the Bois-de-Boulogne before keeping his appointment. During the night the wind had changed and the weather had turned milder, and had the warmth and sunshine of an April day. All the frequenters of the Bois were out that morning, attracted by the smiling blue sky.

Duroy walked along slowly, drinking in the soft air, delicious as a spring dainty. He passed the Arc de Triomphe, and entered the great avenue, opposite the riding track. He watched the riders, trotting and galloping past, wealthy society people, and at that moment he scarcely envied them. He knew most of them by name, was acquainted with the extent of their fortunes and the secret histories of their lives, his professional duties having made him a sort of record of the celebrities and scandals of Paris. Women rode past him, slim in their tight-fitting dark habits, and with that disdainful air of aloofness, which many women have on horseback. Duroy amused himself by repeating in an undertone, as one repeats litanies in church, the names, titles, and qualities of the lovers they had had, or that had been ascribed to them. And sometimes instead of saying :

"Baron de Tanquelet, Prince de la Tour—Enguerrand," he would murmur, Lesbos-fashion : "Louise Michot of the Vaudeville—Rose Marquetin of the Opera."

He derived much amusement from this pastime, as if he had verified, beneath austere appearances, the eternal and profound corruption of men, and as if it had delighted, excited and solaced him.

He exclaimed aloud :

"What a crew of hypocrites ! "

And his eyes sought out among the horsemen those about whom the grossest scandals were current.

He saw many who were suspected of cheating at cards, to whom the clubs were their chief, indeed their only, resource, and one that was unquestionably tainted. Others, celebrated men, lived entirely, as every one knew, on their wives' incomes, others, it was said, on those of their mistresses. Many had paid their debts (an honourable act) without its having ever been discovered where they procured the necessary money (a shady mystery). He saw financiers whose immense wealth had grown out of a theft, and who were received everywhere in the most aristocratic houses ; others who were held in such respect that plain middle-class men raised their hats to them when they passed them, but whose shameless robberies, in great national enterprises, were no secret to anyone behind the scenes. And they all had a haughty air, a scornful expression and insolent eyes ; some sported moustaches, some whiskers.

Still laughing, Duroy exclaimed again :

"A nice crew they are, a lot of rips and blackguards."

A well-turned out, low-hung, open carriage drove past, drawn at a fast trot by two small white horses with floating manes and tails. Two grooms sat in the back seat and the reins were held by a slim young woman with fair hair, a famous courtesan. Duroy stood still. He had an impulse to take his hat off to her, to express his admiration of this upstart, who flaunted audaciously, in this avenue and at this hour sacred to those aristocratic hypocrites, the ostentatious luxury she had earned in her profession. Perhaps he felt vaguely that he and she had something in common, some natural bond, that they were of the same breed and nature, and that he would owe his success to audacities like hers.

He returned at a more leisurely pace, his heart aglow with satisfaction, and a little before his time, he reached Madame de Marelle's door. When they met she kissed him as if there had been no quarrel between them, and for a few moments she even forgot the wise discretion with which in her own house she opposed their caresses. Kissing the curled ends of his moustache, she said :

" Such a tiresome thing has happened, my dear. I was looking forward to a lovely honeymoon, and here am I, saddled with my husband for six weeks. He has taken leave. But I don't propose to be six weeks without seeing you, especially after our little quarrel, and this is how I have arranged matters. You must invite yourself to dinner on Monday. I have already spoken of you to him. I shall introduce you."

Duroy hesitated, a little disconcerted. He had never yet been face to face with a man in such circumstances. He feared lest he should betray himself in some way, by a slight sign of embarrassment, by a look, by some slip or other. He stammered out :

" No, I should prefer not to make your husband's acquaintance."

Greatly surprised, she stood before him, her eyes wide open and ingenuous.

" But why not ? " she persisted. " What a funny idea. These things happen every day. I really shouldn't have thought you so simple-minded."

He was hurt.

" Very well, I'll come to dinner on Monday."

" To make it seem quite natural," she added, " I shall ask the Forestiers. All the same it doesn't amuse me a bit to have people to the house."

Duroy thought no more of the meeting until Monday came, but as he was mounting Madame de Marelle's stairs, he experienced a curious sensation of discomfort, not because he felt any reluctance to take the husband's hand, to drink his wine and eat his bread. What disquieted him was some sensation which he could not define.

He was shown into the drawing-room and was kept waiting as usual. Then the door opened and he saw a tall white-bearded man of composed and correct demeanour, wearing the ribbon of an order. He came towards him with punctilious politeness.

"My wife has often spoken of you, Monsieur Duroy, and I am delighted to meet you."

Duroy stepped forward, endeavouring to assume an expression of cordiality, and he wrung his host's outstretched hand with unnecessary energy. Then, seating himself, he could think of nothing to say.

Monsieur de Marelle put a piece of wood on the fire, and said :

"Have you been long engaged in journalism ? "

"Only some months," replied Duroy.

"Indeed. You have got on rapidly."

"Yes, fairly rapidly," and he began to talk at random, scarcely thinking of what he was saying and uttering all the commonplaces usual among people who do not know each other. His confidence had returned and he was beginning to be much amused at the situation. As he looked at Monsieur de Marelle's dignified face, laughter trembled on his lips.

"I have made a fool of you, old man," he thought to himself.

And a secret and depraved feeling of satisfaction possessed him, the joy of a successful thief whom no one suspects, a sneaking but delicious emotion. All at once he longed to become the man's friend, to win his confidence, to make him relate to him the secret things of his life.

Suddenly Madame de Marelle entered, and surveying them with a smiling, impenetrable glance, she went towards Duroy, who did not, in her husband's presence, venture to kiss her hand, as was his custom.

She was serene and cheerful, like a person equal to any

situation. Thanks to the innate and undisguised artfulness of her character, she considered this meeting a perfectly natural and simple affair. Laurine came in. Awed by the presence of her father, she went up to George more sedately then usual and offered him her forehead.

" Aren't you going to call him Bel-Ami to-day ? " asked her mother.

The child flushed as at some gross indiscretion, as if something that ought not to have been told had been revealed, some deep, and not quite innocent secret of her heart.

When the Forestiers arrived, every one was shocked at Charles's condition. In a single week he had grown terribly thin and pale, and he coughed unceasingly. He said that he and his wife were going to Cannes the following Thursday by the express orders of the doctor.

They left early and Duroy said, shaking his head :

" I'm afraid he's in a bad way. He won't make old bones."

Madame de Marelle said calmly :

" O ! there's no hope for him. What luck he had to find a wife like that ! "

" Does she help him much ? " asked Duroy.

"Why she does it all. She is up to everything ; she knows everyone, without appearing to see anybody. She gets what she wants, in her own way and at her own moment. O ! there's no one like her for subtlety, cleverness and intrigue. There's a treasure for a man who has ambition."

" No doubt she will very soon marry again ? " suggested George.

" Yes," replied Madame de Marelle, " I shouldn't be surprised if she had somebody in view already—a Deputy—provided that he doesn't object—there might perhaps be serious obstacles—moral I mean. Well, there it is. I know nothing about it."

Monsieur de Marelle remonstrated with mild impatience :

" You are always making insinuations that I dislike. We should never meddle with the affairs of others. A man's own conscience keeps him well employed. That should be the rule for everybody."

Duroy took his leave, his mind perturbed and full of vague schemes.

The following day he paid a visit to the Forestiers and found them finishing their packing. Charles, lying on a sofa, exaggerated the difficulty he had in breathing, and said repeatedly :

"I ought to have gone a month ago." He gave Duroy a number of injunctions concerning the newspaper, although everything had been arranged and settled with the director.

When George went away he shook his friend's hand with energy.

"Well, my dear fellow, we shall meet again soon."

But when Madame Forestier accompanied him to the door, he said to her eagerly :

"You haven't forgotten our compact ? We are friends and allies, are we not ? And so, if you have need of me, on any account whatever, do not hesitate. A telegram, or a letter, and I shall obey."

"Thank you, I shall not forget," she said softly. And her eyes likewise said "Thank you," in a way that was even deeper and sweeter.

As Duroy descended the stairs he met Monsieur de Vaudrec slowly ascending, whom he had seen once before at Madame Forestier's. The Count seemed to be sad, perhaps because of the Forestiers' departure.

Anxious to show himself a man of the world, Duroy bowed to him effusively. The Count acknowledged his greeting with civility, but with a touch of haughtiness.

The Forestiers left Paris on Thursday evening.

VII

In Charles's absence Duroy became of more importance on the editorial staff of the *Vie Française*. He put his name to several leaders, and also signed his Echoes, the director liking each writer to assume the responsibility for his own copy. Duroy engaged in several controversies in which he acquitted himself with credit, and his constant relations with public men gradually prepared him to become in time an adroit, clear-sighted, political editor.

There was one cloud only on his horizon. This was a censorious little paper which was continually attacking him, or rather attacking the editor of the Echoes in the *Vie Française*, " Monsieur Walter's shockers," as the anonymous writer in *La Plume* called them. Every day it contained malicious comments, biting sarcasms, insinuations of every description.

One day Jacques Rival said to Duroy :

" You're very long suffering."

" What am I to do ? " said Duroy, disconcerted. " He hasn't made a direct attack on me."

One afternoon as he entered the editor's room, Boisrenard held out to him that day's issue of *La Plume*.

" Look, there's another unpleasant paragraph for you."

" What about ? "

" Nothing at all. The arrest of a lady of the name of Aubert by the guardians of public morals."

George took the paper that Boisrenard offered him, and under the title, " The Diversions of Duroy," he read as follows :

The distinguished reporter of the Vie Française *informs us to-day that the lady of the name of Aubert whose arrest we announced at the hands of the odious guardians of public morals, exists only in our imagination. Now the lady in question lives at No. 18, Rue de L'Ecureuil, at Montmartre. We understand only too well what interest, or interests, the agents of Walter's bank may have in supporting those of the prefect of police, who shuts his eyes to their proceedings. As for the reporter, he would be better advised to give us one of those excellent items of sensational news of which he has the secret ; reports of deaths contradicted the next day ; of battles that have never taken place ; important statements by Royal personages who have never uttered a word, in short all the information that goes to make up " Walter's profits " ; or perhaps one of those indiscreet little paragraphs about evening parties given by women in the swim, or about the excellence of certain products which are a source of profit to some of our colleagues.*

Duroy remained speechless ; he was more than annoyed ; he understood that there was something in all this with a very unpleasant significance for him.

" Who brought you that Echo ? " asked Boisrenard.

Duroy thought for a moment. Suddenly it flashed upon him.

" It was Saint-Potin, of course."

He read the paragraph in *La Plume,* and blushed suddenly, outraged by the accusation of venality.

" What ! " he exclaimed, " he means to insinuate that I'm paid to——"

Boisrenard interrupted him.

" Yes, of course he does. It's very annoying for you. The director has strong views on that subject. There are so many openings for that in the Echoes."

At that moment Saint-Potin entered the room. Duroy darted towards him.

" Have you read the paragraph in *La Plume ?* "

" Yes, and I have just been to see Madame Aubert.

She really does exist, but she has not been arrested. That report has no foundation."

Duroy rushed to see the director, who treated him coldly and had a suspicious look in his eyes. After hearing the facts he said :

" Go and see the lady yourself, and make your contradiction in such a way that people won't write any more things like that about you. I am referring to the last part. It is very annoying for the paper, for me and for you. A journalist, like Cæsar's wife, must be above suspicion."

With Saint-Potin for guide, Duroy took a cab and drove to 18, Rue de L'Ecureuil, Montmartre.

It was a big house and he had to climb to the top of its six stories. An old woman in a woollen jacket opened the door to them.

" What do you want now ? " she asked when she saw Saint-Potin.

" I have brought this gentleman to see you," he replied, " he is an inspector of police and wants to know about your affair."

She showed them in and began her tale.

" Since you were here, two more people came from some paper or other, I don't know which."

She turned to Duroy :

" So you're the gentleman who wants to know about it ? "

" Yes. Were you arrested by a guardian of public morals ? "

She threw up her hands.

" Never in my life, my good sir, never in my life. This is what happened. I have a butcher who sells good meat, but gives bad weight. I had often noticed it, without saying anything. But when I asked him for two pounds of cutlets, because my daughter and my son-in-law were coming, I noticed that he was weighing me waste bits, cutlet bones, to be sure, but not mine. I could have made them into a stew, it's true, but when I ask for cutlets I don't want bones other people have left. So I refused to have them. Then he called me an old cat, and I called him an old cheat ; and we had such a row that there were more than a hundred people outside the shop roaring and laughing. At last a policeman came along and we were asked to go to the police station and explain things, so we went and the case was dismissed. Since then I buy my meat elsewhere, and I don't even pass his door, to avoid a scandal."

" Is that all ? " asked Duroy.

" The whole truth, my dear sir."

After she had offered him a glass of ratafia, which he declined, the old woman urged him to mention the butcher's false weights in his report.

When he returned to the office, Duroy drafted his reply.

" An anonymous scribbler in *La Plume*, with a plume plucked from the editorial goose, is picking a quarrel with me about an old woman whom he declares to have been arrested by a guardian of the peace, a statement which I deny. I have seen Madame Aubert myself. She is sixty years old at least, and she told me in detail about her quarrel with a butcher on the subject of the weighing of certain cutlets, which involved an explanation at the police station.

" That is the whole truth.

" As for the editor's other insinuations, I despise them. I may add that one does not reply to such accusations when they are delivered from behind a mask."

George Duroy, Monsieur Walter and Jacques Rival who had just come in, considered the reply adequate, and it was decided that it should go in that same day, at the end of the Echoes.

Duroy went home early somewhat agitated and perturbed. What would the other man say in his answer ? Who was he ? Why this brutal attack ? With the reckless ways of journalists this silly business might go far, very far. He slept badly. When he read his reply in the paper the next day, he thought it more aggressive in print than in manuscript. He might, he felt, have toned it down. He was in a fever all that day and the next night he again slept badly. He rose at dawn to procure a copy of the issue of *La Plume* which would contain the answer to his paragraph. The weather had turned cold again ; it was freezing hard.

The running water in the gutters was frozen and lay alongside the pavement like ribbons of ice.

The papers had not arrived yet at the kiosks, and this reminded Duroy of the day when his first article appeared. His hands and feet grew numb and began to hurt him, especially at the extremities, and he started running round the glass-sided kiosk. Nothing could be seen of the woman crouching inside over her brazier, except a nose and two red cheeks emerging from a woollen hood. At last the packet of newspapers was passed in through the square window and the woman handed Duroy an unfolded copy of *La Plume*.

He glanced down it looking for his name and at first did not see it. He was already breathing a sigh of relief, when he caught sight of the expected paragraph between two dashes.

> *His Lordship Duroy, in the* Vie Française, *gives us the lie, and in doing so, is himself a liar. He admits the existence of the woman Aubert; he admits that a guardian of the peace conducted her to the police station. It is only necessary to add the three words " and of morals " and the inference is obvious.*
>
> *But the conscience of certain journalists is on a level with their talent.*
>
> *I have the honour to sign myself,*
> Louis Langremont.

George's heart began to beat violently, and hardly knowing what he was doing, he went home to finish dressing. Apparently he had been insulted and in such a way that there was only one course open to him. And what was the reason? There was none. It was merely because an old woman had quarrelled with her butcher. He dressed very quickly and went to see Monsieur Walter, although it was barely eight o'clock in the morning. Monsieur Walter was already up and was reading *La Plume*.

"Well," he said with a grave face, as soon as he saw Duroy, "you cannot draw back now."

Duroy made no reply. The director continued:

" Go and see Rival at once ; he will act for you."

Duroy stammered some vague words and went away to see Rival who was still asleep. When the bell rang, Rival jumped out of bed, and as soon as he had read the paragraph, he exclaimed :

" By Jove, you're in for it now ! Whom do you think of having as your other second ? "

" I haven't the slightest idea."

" What about Boisrenard ? "

" Yes, Boisrenard."

" Are you a good swordsman ? "

" Far from it."

" The deuce ! What about pistols ? "

" I can shoot a bit."

" Good. You can go and practise, while I arrange things. Wait a moment."

He went into his dressing-room and soon reappeared, washed, shaved and well turned out.

" Come along," he said.

He occupied the ground floor of a small house, and he took Duroy down to a huge cellar, which he had converted into a salle d'armes and shooting gallery, closing up all the openings to the street. He lighted a row of gas jets which stretched away to the far end of a second cellar where an iron figure painted red and blue was set up. He laid upon the table two pairs of breechloading pistols of a new pattern, and then started giving the words of command in abrupt tones, as if they were already on the duelling ground.

" Ready ? Fire ! one—two—three."

Too much overcome to resist, Duroy raised his arm, took aim and fired. He hit the dummy repeatedly full in the stomach, having in his boyhood often used an old horse pistol of his father's for killing birds in the yard. Jacques Rival exclaimed with satisfaction :

" Good—very good—you'll do, you'll do. Go on practising till twelve. Here is ammunition. Don't be afraid of wasting it. I'll call for you at luncheon and bring you the news "

Then he went away.

Left alone, Duroy fired a few more rounds and then sat down and began to reflect.

After all what a silly business it was. What did it prove? Was a scoundrel any less of a scoundrel after fighting a duel? What did a decent man, who had been insulted, gain by risking his life against a blackguard? Brooding thus dismally, he remembered Norbert de Varenne's remarks on man's limited intelligence, uninspired ideas and futile morality, and he exclaimed aloud:

" By Jove, he's right!"

He felt thirsty, and hearing the drip of water behind him he discovered a showerbath apparatus and had a drink from the nozzle. Then he resumed his meditations. The cellar was gloomy, as gloomy as a tomb. The remote, muffled sound of carriage wheels sounded like the rumbling of a distant storm. He wondered what time it was. The hours passed in that place as in the depths of a prison, where there is nothing to mark their passage except the visits of the jailer bringing food. He waited a long time, a long, long time. Suddenly he heard steps and voices, and Jacques Rival reappeared accompanied by Boisrenard. As soon as he saw Duroy, Rival called out:

" Everything is arranged."

Duroy imagined that the matter had been settled by a letter of apology. With a thrill of joy he thanked Rival, who replied:

" Langremont is a very decent fellow; he has accepted all our conditions. Twenty-five paces, and raise your pistol at the word of command. This makes your arm much steadier than if you have to bring it down. Look, Boisrenard, this is what I was telling you."

Picking up a pistol, he fired some shots to show how much more accurate one's aim was with a rising arm.

Then he said:

" Come and have luncheon. It's past twelve."

They went to a restaurant close at hand. Duroy did not say a word. But he took some food, so that he should not appear frightened. In the afternoon he went with Boisrenard to the office and did his work in an absent-minded mechanical way. His colleagues were impressed by his coolness.

Later in the afternoon Jacques Rival came to see him. It was agreed that his seconds should call for him in a landau the next morning at seven o'clock and that they should proceed to the Vesinet Wood, where the encounter was to take place. All this had been arranged without Duroy's knowledge or participation, without his having said a word, or expressed an opinion, without his approval or disapproval, and with such suddenness that he remained bewildered and aghast, hardly realising what had happened. He returned home about nine in the evening after dining with Boisrenard. who had stayed by his side devotedly all day. As soon as he was alone, he paced his room rapidly for several minutes. He was too much agitated to think. His mind had room for only one idea, to-morrow's duel, and the thought of it aroused in him a confused though strong emotion. He had been a soldier ; he had had shots at Arabs, but with no great danger to himself, rather as one fires at a wild boar when out hunting. However he had done what he was bound to do. He had come up to the mark. His conduct would be discussed ; he would be commended and congratulated. Speaking aloud, as one does in moments of great agitation, he exclaimed :

" What a brute the man is ! "

He sat down and began to think. On his little table lay his adversary's card, which Rival had given him for the sake of the address. He read it again for the twentieth time that day, " Louis Langremont, 176 Rue Montmartre." That was all.

He considered this group of letters, which seemed to him full of mystery and sinister import. " Louis Langremont." Who was this man ? What was his age, his build, his appearance ? Was it not revolting that a perfect stranger should wantonly force this trouble upon one, for no reason whatsoever, except that an old woman had quarrelled with her butcher ?

Again he said aloud :

" What a brute ! "

He sat motionless, pondering, his eyes fixed on the card. This scrap of paper roused in him fierce anger, mingled with a strange sensation of discomfort. How idiotic the whole business was ! He snatched up a pair of nail scissors and thrust them through the printed name as if he were stabbing someone.

So he was going to fight a duel, a duel with pistols. Why had he not chosen swords ? He might have got off with a scratch on the arm or the hand, whereas with pistols no one knew what might happen.

" Come, come," he said, " I must put a bold front on it."

He started at the sound of his own voice, and looked all round him. He began to feel very nervous. He drank a glass of water, and went to bed. As soon as he was in bed he blew out the candle and closed his eyes. Although it was cold in his room he felt hot under the blankets, and could not get to sleep. He tossed about, lay for five minutes on his back, then threw himself on his left side, then on his right. He was still thirsty. He got up for a drink. Then seized with anxiety, he wondered if he could be feeling frightened. Why did his heart beat so wildly at every familiar sound in the room ? When his cuckoo clock was about to strike, the little creak of the spring made him jump, and for some seconds he had such a sense of oppression that he had to open his mouth to breathe. He began to argue out the matter. Was he afraid ? No, assuredly he could not be afraid. He had made up his mind to see the thing through, to fight the duel, and not to show the white feather. But he felt so much agitated that he asked himself :

" Is it possible to be afraid, in spite of oneself ? "

And he was seized by this feeling of doubt, anxiety and dismay. If a force stronger than his own will, a dominating, irresistible force, mastered him, what would happen ? What might not happen ? He would certainly appear on the duelling ground, because he was determined to do so. But supposing he showed signs of fear ? Supposing he fainted ? He thought of his position, his reputation, his future. He was moved with a curious desire to go and look at himself in the mirror. He lighted his candle again. When he saw his face reflected, he hardly recognised it. He felt as if he had never seen himself before. His eyes looked to him enormous, and he was pale ; he was certainly pale, very pale indeed. Suddenly a thought struck him with the force of a bullet :

"This time to-morrow I may be dead." And his heart began to race furiously.

He turned towards his bed, and had a distinct vision of himself lying on his back on the sheets he had just left. His face was the cavernous face of the dead, and his hands had the whiteness of hands that would never move again. The sight of his bed frightened him and to avoid looking at it he threw open the window and put his head out. The biting air chilled him from head to foot, and he shrank back, gasping. It occurred to him to light the fire. He kindled it deliberately, without looking behind him. His hands shook with slight nervous tremors whenever they came in contact with anything. His head was swimming, he was tormented with incoherent and elusive thoughts ; his mind felt confused, as if he had been drinking. And unceasingly he asked himself :

"What is this thing I am doing ! What will be the end of it all ? "

He began to pace the room, repeating mechanically and monotonously :

"I must be firm, very firm."

Presently he said to himself :

"I had better write to my parents in case of accidents."

He sat down again, took some notepaper and wrote :

"My dear Papa and Mamma——"

Then it seemed to him that this beginning was too familiar for such tragic circumstances. He tore up the first sheet and started again.

My dear Father and Mother,
I am going to fight a duel at daybreak, and as I may possibly——

He dared not finish the sentence and he started up from his chair. He now began to be tormented by the following reflection. He was going to fight a duel. That he could no longer avoid. Then what was the matter with him ? He had every intention of fighting ; he was firmly resolved to do so. Yet he felt that in spite of every effort of his will he would never retain the strength to reach the duelling ground.

Occasionally his teeth chattered a little.

" I wonder if Langremont has ever been out before," he said to himself. " Does he go to shooting galleries ? Is he known as a shot ? "

He had never heard Langremont's name mentioned. And yet if he were not remarkably handy with a pistol, he would surely not have accepted, without demur, that deadly weapon. Duroy pictured to himself their encounter, his own behaviour and that of his adversary. He wore himself out imagining the minutest details of the duel. Suddenly he seemed to see pointing at him the pistol's small, black, hollow bore whence the bullet would issue, and a terrible paroxysm of despair overwhelmed him. His whole body was shaken by spasmodic shudders. He clenched his teeth to repress his screams and he had a mad desire to roll upon the ground, tearing and biting things. But at that moment he caught sight of a tumbler on the mantelpiece and he remembered that his cupboard contained nearly a whole quart of brandy, for he still retained the military habit of a morning nip. He seized the bottle, and drank from it greedily, in great gulps. And he did not put it down until he was out of breath. It was emptier by a third.

Soon he felt a burning heat in his stomach ; it diffused itself through his limbs, and fortified his mind by blunting its sensibilities.

He said to himself :

" I know the remedy now." And as his skin was burning he opened the window again.

Day dawned, calm and very cold. The stars died away in the brightening sky, and in the deep railway cutting, the green, red and white signal lights grew pale. The first locomotives were emerging from the engine house uttering a succession of shrieks, their waking cries, like cocks in the country crowing.

" Perhaps I shall never see all this again," thought Duroy. He was once more on the verge of self-pity, but he resisted the impulse resolutely.

" Come, I mustn't think of anything at all until the meeting. That's the only way to keep up one's courage."

He began to dress. As he was shaving he had another moment of weakness at the thought that this was perhaps the last time that he would see his own face. He took another nip of brandy and finished dressing   The next hour went slowly. He walked up and down, endeavouring to stifle his thoughts. But when he heard a knock at the door it gave him such a shock that he nearly fell flat on his back. His seconds had arrived. Already !

They were wrapped in fur coats. After shaking hands with his principal, Rival said :

" It's as cold as Siberia." Then he added, " Everything all right ? "

" Yes, perfectly, thank you."

" Not feeling excited ? "

" Not a bit."

" That's all right. You'll do. Have you had something to eat and drink ? "

" Yes, everything I want."

In honour of the occasion, Boisrenard was wearing the green and yellow ribbon of a foreign order, which Duroy had never seen on his coat before. They went downstairs. Another gentleman was waiting for them in the landau.

" Dr. Le Brument," said Rival, introducing him.

Duroy shook hands with him, and muttered :

" I'm much obliged to you."

As he was taking his place on the front seat he came upon something hard, which made him shoot up again as if he had touched a spring. It was the case of pistols.

" Not there," said Rival, " Duroy and the doctor are to sit on the back seat." At last Duroy understood what he was to do, and sank down beside the doctor. The seconds entered the carriage and the coachman drove away. He had been told where he was to go.

But the case of pistols bothered everyone, especially

Duroy, who would have preferred not to see it at all. When they placed it behind their backs, it bruised them. When they stood it up between Rival and Boisrenard, it kept tumbling down. At last they put it under their feet on the floor.

Conversation languished. The doctor related anecdotes, but Rival alone took any notice of them. Duroy would have liked to give some proof of calmness but he was afraid of losing the thread of his ideas, and thus betraying the disturbed state of his mind, and he was tormented by the fear of a sudden fit of trembling. Presently the carriage reached the open country. It was about nine o'clock on one of those sharp winter mornings, when everything in nature seems as radiant, as brittle and as hard as crystal. The rime-covered trees seem to have exuded frost ; the earth rings out under the feet ; the dry air carries the least sounds to a great distance ; the blue sky has the glitter of a mirror, and the sun, brilliant and cold, moves through space, casting heatless rays upon a frost-bound world.

" I got the pistols at Gastine-Renette's," said Rival, " he loaded them himself. The box is sealed. We shall decide by lot whether these or your opponent's are to be used."

" Thank you," replied Duroy mechanically.

Rival then gave him minute instructions, for it was a point of honour with him that his principal should make no mistake. He dwelt repeatedly on each detail.

" When they ask you, ' Are you ready, gentlemen ? ' you reply in a loud voice, ' Yes.' When the order to fire is given you raise your arm quickly and you pull the trigger before the word ' three ' is uttered."

Duroy kept saying over and over to himself :

" When I'm ordered to fire, I raise my arm. When I'm I'm ordered to fire I raise my arm. When I'm ordered to fire I raise my arm."

He learned it off as children learn their lessons, murmuring it over and over to impress it thoroughly on his mind.

" When I'm ordered to fire, I raise my arm."

The landau entered a wood, turned to the right down an avenue, and then again to the right. Suddenly Rival opened the door and called out to the coachman, " There, down that narrow road." And the carriage proceeded along a rough lane between thickets in which dead leaves quivered in the frost.

Duroy continued to mutter :

" When I'm ordered to fire I raise my arm."

And he reflected that a carriage accident would simplify everything. O, if only the carriage would upset, and if he could but have the luck to break a leg !

But at the far side of a clearing he saw another carriage and four gentlemen who were stamping to warm their feet. He was obliged to open his mouth, so difficult did he find it to breathe.

The seconds stepped out first, followed by the doctor and Duroy. Rival had taken the case of pistols, and he and Boisrenard went forward to meet the other seconds who were coming towards them. Duroy saw them exchange ceremonious greetings. Then they walked about the clearing together, looking first at the ground, and then at the trees, as if they were seeking for something that had either dropped down or flown away. They measured out paces, and with great difficulty drove two walking-sticks into the frozen ground. Then they stood in a group and went through the action of tossing up, like children at play.

" You're feeling quite well ? " Dr. La Brument asked Duroy, " there's nothing you require ? "

" No, thank you, nothing."

He felt that he must be either mad, or asleep and dreaming, that he was actuated by some power outside himself. Was he afraid ? Perhaps he was. He hardly knew. Everything around him seemed changed. Jacques Rival came back and whispered to him in tones of satisfaction :

" It's all ready. Fortune favoured us about the pistols."

This was a matter of profound indifference to Duroy. He allowed his seconds to remove his overcoat. They felt the pockets of his frock-coat, to satisfy themselves that he had no papers or pocket-book which would stop a bullet.

Meanwhile he kept saying to himself, as if it were a prayer :

" When I'm ordered to fire I raise my arm."

Then he was conducted to a spot marked by one of the walking-sticks, and his pistol was placed in his hand. He caught sight of another man standing opposite him, a very short distance away, a corpulent little man, with a bald head and eyeglasses. It was his opponent.

He saw him perfectly, but he thought of one thing only :
" When I'm ordered to fire, I raise my arm."

A voice broke the deep stillness of the air, a voice which seemed to come from very far away. It said :
" Are you ready, gentlemen ? "
" Yes," cried George.

And the same voice commanded :
" Fire."

He heard nothing more ; he had no clear idea of what was happening. He was merely conscious that he raised his arm and pressed the trigger with all his might. No sound reached his ears. But immediately he perceived a small puff of smoke round the muzzle of his pistol. The man facing him remained standing, in the same attitude as before, and he noticed another little puff of smoke vanishing into the air above his head. Both of them had fired. It was all over. His seconds and the doctor touched him and felt him, unbuttoned his clothes, asking anxiously :
" You're not wounded ? "

He replied at random :
" No, I don't think so."

Langremont had remained unhurt, like his adversary, and Jacques Rival muttered in disgust :
" With these wretched pistols that's what always happens ; you either miss altogether, or you kill. What a beastly weapon ! "

Duroy stood there paralysed with surprise and joy. It was all over. His weapon, which he still grasped in his hand, had to be taken from him. It seemed to him now that he could have fought the whole world. It was all over. What bliss ! He felt brave enough now to challenge anyone.

The four seconds conversed for a few minutes and

arranged to meet during the day to draw up their report. Then they entered the carriage, and the coachman, who was laughing on the box, drove away, cracking his whip.

Duroy and his friends lunched together in a restaurant on the Boulevard, and discussed the incident. Duroy spoke of his sensations.

" It didn't upset me at all, not in the very least. But you must have noticed that."

" Yes," replied Rival, " you behaved very well."

When the report had been drafted it was handed over to Duroy, who was to insert it in the Echoes. He was surprised to read that he had exchanged two balls with Monsieur Louis Langremont, and in some concern he said to Rival :

" But we only fired once."

Rival smiled. " Yes, once—once each—that makes twice."

Satisfied with this explanation, Duroy did not press the point. Old Monsieur Walter embraced him :

" Bravo, bravo, you have stood up for the colours of the *Vie Française*, bravo ! "

That evening George showed himself at the offices of the leading newspapers and at all the most important cafés on the Boulevards. Twice he ran across his opponent, who was also showing himself. They did not bow to each other. If either of them had been wounded they would have shaken hands. Each of them, by the way, swore with conviction that he had heard his opponent's ball whistle past him.

The next morning about eleven o'clock, Duroy received a telegram :

" Heavens, how frightened I was. Come at once to the Rue de Constantinople. I want to kiss you, darling. How brave you are. I love you.—CLO."

He went to the rendezvous and Clotilde threw herself into his arms, and smothered him with kisses.

" Oh my darling, if you only knew my feelings when I read the papers this morning. Oh, do tell me about it. Tell me everything. I want to know all."

He had to describe the affair to her in great detail.

"What a terrible night you must have had just before the duel," she exclaimed.

"Not at all. I slept very well."

"I shouldn't have closed an eye. Now tell me exactly what happened on the ground."

He gave her a dramatic account.

"We were opposite each other, at a distance of twenty paces, only four times the length of this room. After asking us if we were ready, Jacques gave the order to fire. I raised my arm immediately to the proper level, but I made the mistake of trying to aim at his head. My weapon was very stiff, and I am used to pistols that go off easily so the resistance of the trigger sent the shot too high. All the same it can't have missed him by much. He shoots well, too, the beggar ; his ball whizzed past my temple. I felt the wind it made."

She was sitting on his knee, clasping him in her arms, as if to share his danger.

"Oh my poor darling," she exclaimed in a broken voice, "my poor darling."

When he had finished his tale she said to him :

"You know, I can't get on without you now. I simply must see you, and with my husband in Paris, it's not at all easy. But I have often a spare hour in the morning, before you are up, when I could come and pay you a visit. Only I don't want to enter your horrible house again. What are we to do ? "

He had a sudden inspiration.

"What do you pay for this flat ? " he asked.

" A hundred francs a month."

"Very well. I shall take it on and live here altogether. Mine is no longer suited to my new position."

She thought for a moment ; then she replied :

"No, I don't want you to."

"Why not ? " he asked in surprise.

"Just because."

"That's not a reason. These rooms suit me. Here I am. Here I stay."

He began to laugh.

" Besides, it's taken in my name."

But she still refused.

" No, no, I don't want you to."

" Well then, tell me why not ! "

At last she whispered softly and tenderly :

" Because you would bring other women here, and I don't want you to."

He protested indignantly.

" What an idea. I wouldn't for the world. I promise you."

" Yes, you would all the same."

" I swear to you."

" Really and truly ? "

" Really and truly. On my word of honour. This is our own home, yours and mine, and nobody else's."

She threw her arms around him in a passion of love.

" Very well, then, darling, I consent. But you know, if you deceive me once, once only, all will be over between us, for ever and ever."

He assured her with further protestations, and it was agreed that he should move in that very day, so that she could see him when she passed the door.

" In any case," she said, " come to dinner on Sunday. My husband thinks you charming."

He felt flattered.

" Really ? "

" Yes, you have made a conquest of him. And listen, you told me that you were brought up on an estate in the country, didn't you ? "

" Yes. Why ? "

" Then you must know something about agriculture."

" Certainly."

" Well, talk to him about gardening and crops. He likes that sort of thing."

" Good. I shan't forget."

She left him after a lingering embrace, the duel having stimulated her affection for him.

On his way to his office, Duroy thought to himself :

" What a queer, flighty little creature she is ! You

never know what she will take into her head. And what
an odd household. What humorist arranged the match
between old Marelle and that scatter-brain? What can
have induced the inspector to marry such a tomboy? It's a
mystery. Who knows? Perhaps it was love. After
all," he concluded, " she is very charming, and I should be a
perfect fool to let her go."

VIII

THANKS to his duel Duroy had attained a leading position on the staff of the *Vie Française*. But as he had great difficulty in hitting upon new ideas, he made a speciality of invectives on the decadence of manners, the degeneration of character, the collapse of patriotism, and the anæmia of French honour. (He had discovered the word "anæmia" and was very proud of it.) When Madame de Marelle, with the mocking, sceptical, cynical wit which is characteristic of Paris, laughed at his tirades and crushed them with an epigram, he would reply with a smile :

"Pooh ! I am building up a reputation for later on."

He was now living in the Rue de Constantinople, whither he had transferred his trunk, his hair-brushes, his razor and his soap, which completed the business of his installation. Two or three times a week, Clotilde visited him before he was up. She would undress quickly, and slip into bed, shivering with the cold air of the streets.

Duroy dined every Thursday at her house, and ingratiated himself with the husband by talking agriculture. As he himself was interested in cultivation, they sometimes became so much absorbed in their conversation that they quite forgot Clotilde, their common property, who sat dozing on the sofa. Laurine, too, would drop off to sleep, sometimes on her father's knee, sometimes on Bel-Ami's.

When Duroy had gone away, Monsieur de Marelle never failed to declare in the pedantic tone in which he uttered the most trivial remarks :

"Really he's a very agreeable young fellow and very well informed."

February drew to a close. As one passed the barrows of the flower-girls one perceived a scent of violets in the air.

There was not a cloud on Duroy's sky. One night, however, when he returned home he found a letter under the door. He looked at the postmark and saw that it was Cannes. Opening the letter he read :

Cannes, Villa Jolie.

My dear Friend,

You told me, you remember, to count on you in any emergency. So I am going to ask a painful service of you. It is that you will come to my assistance and not leave me to face Charles's last moments all by myself. He is dying. He may not last out the week, although he still gets up. The doctor has told me to be prepared. I have neither the strength nor the courage to witness his continual sufferings and I think with terror of his last moments, which are now so near. There is no one but you to whom I can turn, for my husband has no relations. You were his comrade ; he opened to you the door of the Vie Française.

Come, I implore you. There is no one else I can ask.

Believe me your devoted friend,

Madeleine Forestier.

George was conscious of a curious sensation like a breath of fresh air, a feeling of relief, as if a wide space were opening out before him. He murmured :

" Of course I'll go. Poor old Charles ! But after all, it's what we all come to."

The director, to whom he showed Madame Forestier's letter, gave his consent grudgingly.

" Come back soon," he said repeatedly, " we can't spare you."

After telegraphing to the Marelles, George Duroy left for Cannes the next morning by the seven o'clock express. He arrived the following afternoon. A porter showed him the way to the Villa Jolie. It stood half-way up the pine-clad hill which, with its sprinkling of white houses, extends from Le Cannet to Golfe Juan. It was a low house, in the Italian style, built by the side of the road which winds upwards, in and out among the trees, and presents at each turning point an exquisite view.

The servant opened the door and exclaimed, "Oh, sir, the mistress will be so glad to see you."

"How is your master?" asked Duroy.

"Not at all well, sir; he can't last much longer."

Duroy entered the drawing-room. It had hangings of pink and blue chintz and the wide, high window looked out over the town and the sea.

Duroy murmured: "By Jove, this is a delightful country house! Where the deuce do they get all the money from?"

Hearing the rustle of a skirt he turned round. Madame Forestier held out both her hands.

"How kind you are! How good of you to come!"

And suddenly she kissed him, and they gazed at each other.

She had grown a little pale and thin, but still looked young and fresh and perhaps all the prettier for her somewhat fragile air.

"He is terrible," she said, "you see, he knows there's no hope for him, and he has become a dreadful tyrant. I have told him that you have arrived. But where is your luggage?"

"I left it at the station," replied Duroy. "I did not know what hotel you would advise me to go to, so as to be near you."

She hesitated; then said:

"You must stay here, in the Villa. Your room is quite ready. He might die at any moment, and if it happened during the night I should be all alone. I will send for your luggage."

He bowed.

"I am at your disposal."

"Let us go upstairs now," she said.

He followed her. She opened a door on the first floor. In an arm-chair by the window sat Forestier, wrapped in rugs, and little more than a corpse, livid in the sunset light. He looked at Duroy, who scarcely recognised him, and could hardly believe that this was his friend Forestier. The place smelt of fever, potions, ether and tar, and had the indescribable and heavy odour of a room in which a consumptive labours for breath.

Forestier held out his hand with a slow, painful effort.

"Here you are," he said. "You have come to see me die. I am very grateful to you."

Duroy affected to laugh it off.

"To see you die ? That wouldn't be at all an amusing experience, and I shouldn't choose an occasion like that for a visit to Cannes. I have merely come to see you, and to take a little holiday."

"Sit down," murmured Forestier, and his head drooped as if he were plunged in despairing thoughts. His breathing was quick and laboured, and now and then he uttered a kind of groan, as if to remind the others how ill he was. Seeing that he was not disposed to talk, his wife came and leaned against the window. Nodding towards the distant view, she exclaimed :

"Look at it ! Isn't it beautiful ? "

In front of them lay the hill with its sprinkling of villas, sloping down to the town, which formed a semicircle along the line of the beach. Its right extremity touched the jetty, which was dominated by the old city with its ancient belfry towering above it ; its left the point of La Croisette, opposite the Lérin Islands These two islands looked like two green patches on the blue water. Viewed from above, they had the appearance of huge flat leaves. On the opposite side of the bay, beyond the jetty and the belfry, the far horizon was bounded by a long chain of mountains. The irregular and picturesque outline of the rounded, jagged or pointed summits was etched against the dazzling sky, and culminated in a great pyramidal peak with its base planted in the sea.

"The Esterels," said Madame Forestier.

The sky behind the dark mountain tops was red, a fierce glowing red, insupportably bright, and in spite of himself, Duroy was affected by the majesty of the dying day. Finding no other term vivid enough to express his admiration, he murmured :

"Yes, it's amazing."

Forestier turned his head towards his wife.

" Let me have some air."

" Be careful," she said, " it's late. The sun is setting ; you will catch another cold, and you know it wouldn't be good for you in your present state of health."

With his hand he made a feeble, feverish gesture, intended for a thump of his fist. His face was distorted with rage, and the approach of death had emphasised the thinness of his lips, the hollowness of his cheeks, and the prominence of every bone. " I tell you I'm suffocating," he muttered. " What does it matter to you if I die a day sooner or later ? I'm done for anyhow."

She threw the window wide open.

The air stole in upon the three like a caress. It was a soft, mild, gentle breeze, a spring breeze already laden with the heady fragrance of the shrubs and flowers of that coast. A strong scent of resin and the aromatic essence of eucalyptus were perceptible. Forestier drank in the air with quick feverish gasps. Then he dug his finger nails into the arms of his chair, and hissed in a low, angry voice :

" Shut the window, it's hurting me. I'd rather snuff out in a cellar."

His wife slowly closed the window. Then she gazed into the distance, leaning her forehead against the panes. Ill at ease, Duroy would have liked to talk to the sick man. But he could think of nothing comforting to say.

" Then you're no better since you came here ? "

Exhausted and impatient, Forestier shrugged his shoulders.

" You can see for yourself." And again his head drooped.

" By Jove, this is a very jolly place compared with Paris ! " exclaimed Duroy. " There it's midwinter ; it's snowing, hailing and raining, and it's so dark that you have to light the lamps by three o'clock."

" Anything new at the office ? " asked Forestier.

" No. Young Lacrin, who has left the *Voltaire*, has been put on to your work. But he hasn't sufficient experience. It's time you came back."

" I ? " muttered the invalid. " All my articles will be written six feet underground."

This fixed idea recurred, like the clang of a bell, in each

topic of conversation ; it presented itself in every thought, in every phrase. There was a long silence, a deep and painful silence. The brilliance of the sunset was slowly fading ; and the mountains were turning black against the red sky, now darkening. A sombreness, suffused with colour, the sombreness of incipient night, which still like dying cinders retained its glow, pervaded the room and tinged the furniture, walls, hangings and corners with mingled tones of purple and inky black. The mirror above the mantelpiece, which reflected the sky, was like a pool of blood. Madame Forestier remained motionless, with her back to the room and her face against the window pane.

Forestier began to speak in a jerky, breathless voice, which it was torture to hear.

" How many more sunsets shall I see, eight, ten, fifteen, twenty ? Thirty, perhaps, but not more. There's time before you yet, you two. But it's all over for me. And all this will go on—after me, just as if I were still here."

After a brief silence, he continued :

" Whenever I look at a thing, I remember that in a few days I shall see it no more——. It's horrible—I shall see nothing—nothing of all that exists—not the least of all the little things one uses—the tumblers—the plates—the beds where one rests so comfortably—the carriages. It's pleasant to go for a drive in a carriage of an evening. How I used to enjoy it all ! "

He made little nervous movements with the fingers of both hands, as if he were playing the piano on the arms of his chair. And each pause of his was more poignant even than his words, so keenly did one feel that he was thinking of things that horrified him. Suddenly Duroy remembered what Norbert de Varenne had said to him a few weeks back.

" I now see death so close to me that I feel I must stretch out my arms to repel it. I see signs of it everywhere. Insects lying crushed in the road, falling leaves, a white hair seen in a friend's beard, all these devastate my heart and cry to me, Death is here."

He had not understood then, but now when he looked at Forestier he understood all. And a strange and terrible pang shot through him. It was as if he had perceived, quite close to him, there on that arm-chair, where the sick man was panting for breath, the hideous form of death, within reach of his hand. He wanted to rise from his chair and run away, to escape, to return to Paris at once. If he had only known, he would never have come.

Night had now fallen upon the room, like a pall, flung hastily over the dying man. Only the window was visible, and framed in its square of light, Madeleine's motionless silhouette.

Forestier exclaimed irritably :

" Well, aren't they ever going to bring the lamp to-day ? That's what they call looking after an invalid."

The silhouette vanished from the window and the sound of an electric bell rang through the echoing house. Presently a servant entered and placed a lamp on the mantelpiece.

" Will you go to bed or will you come down to dinner ? " Madame Forestier asked her husband.

" I'll come down," he replied.

They were kept waiting another hour for dinner. They hardly moved. Now and then one of them would utter a word, a casual commonplace word, without significance, as if there were danger, some mysterious danger, in allowing the silence to remain too long unbroken, and the air to stagnate in that room where death was lurking.

At last dinner was announced. It seemed to Duroy interminably long. They did not talk, they ate in silence, crumbling their bread with their fingers. And the servant waited and moved about the room with inaudible footsteps. Charles had been irritated by the noise of his leather soles and the man was now wearing soft felt slippers. The sharp regular ticking of a clock was the only sound that broke the stillness of the room.

Directly after dinner, Duroy pleaded weariness and withdrew to his room. Leaning on his elbows at the window, he gazed at the full moon high in the sky, like the globe of a vast lamp, shedding upon the white walls of the villas its cold, subdued light, and diffusing over the sea ripples of soft, pearly radiance. He tried to invent an excuse for going away immediately ; he thought out schemes, telegrams or an urgent recall from Monsieur Walter. But when he woke up the next morning, his plans for flight seemed more difficult to put into execution. Madame Forestier would certainly not be deceived by his pretext and his cowardice would cost him all that he had gained by his devotion. He said to himself :

" Of course it's a nuisance. But it can't be helped. There are disagreeable predicaments in life. After all it can't last long."

The skies were blue, with that blue of the south which rejoices the heart. Duroy went down to the sea, thinking to himself that it would be time enough to see Forestier later in the day. When he returned for luncheon, the servant said to him :

" The master has been asking for you two or three times, sir. Would you mind going up to his room ? "

Duroy went upstairs. Forestier appeared to be asleep in his arm-chair and his wife was lying on the sofa, reading.

The invalid raised his head.

" Well," said Duroy, " How are you ? You look to me quite cheerful this morning."

" Yes, I'm better," Forestier replied, " I'm feeling stronger. Be quick and have luncheon with Madeleine ; we're going for a drive."

As soon as she was alone with Duroy, Madame Forestier said :

" You see, to-day he thinks he's going to get well. He has been making plans all the morning. We are going to Golfe-Juan this afternoon to buy faience for our flat in Paris. He is determined to go out, but I'm terribly afraid that something will happen. He is not strong enough to stand the jolting on the road."

When the landau had come, Forestier descended the stairs step by step, on his servant's arm. As soon as he saw the carriage, he ordered it to be opened. His wife remonstrated :

" You will catch cold. It's madness."

He insisted.

" No, I'm much better. I feel sure I am."

They drove through the shady roads with gardens on either side, which give Cannes the appearance of an English park ; then they entered the Antibes road which runs along the coast. Forestier acted as guide. He pointed out, among others, the villa of the Count de Paris. He was gay with the self-conscious, forced and feeble gaiety of a condemned man. He raised his finger, lacking the strength to stretch out his arm.

" Look, there's the island of St. Marguerite and the castle from which Bazaine escaped. What a lot of sentry-go they gave us, after that affair ! "

Memories of the regiment came back to him. He mentioned the officers by name, and this recalled various incidents to their minds. Suddenly, at a bend of the road, the whole bay came into view, with the white village of Golfe-Juan in the background and the Cape of Antibes beyond.

Forestier cried in childish glee :

" Ah, there's the fleet ! You'll see the fleet ! "

In the middle of the wide bay lay half a dozen big ships, like rocks with branches sprouting from them. They were bizarre, misshapen, enormous, with excrescences and towers, and cut-waters that plunged into the waves as if to take root beneath the sea. One could scarcely believe that they were capable of any change of position, or of motion, so heavy they seemed, so firmly anchored. There was a floating battery, round and high, shaped like an observatory, or a lighthouse on a reef. A great three-master passed them on its way to the open sea, with all its gay white sails set. It was a gracious and beautiful sight by the side of those hideous, iron monsters of war crouching on the water. Forestier endeavoured to identify them. He named them : the *Colbert*, the *Suffren*, the *Admiral Duperre*, the *Redoubtable*, the *Devastation*. Then he corrected himself.

" No, I'm wrong, that one over there is the *Devastation*."

They came to a large pavilion on which was inscribed : " Art faience of Golfe-Juan," and the carriage skirted a lawn and drew up at the door.

Forestier wished to buy two vases for his library. As he

could not get out of the carriage, he had specimans brought to him. He took a long time to make his choice, and consulted his wife and Duroy.

" You know it's for the bookshelves at the end of my study. When I'm in my chair they catch my eye all the time. I've set my heart on an antique form, a Greek form."

He examined the samples, sent for others and then returned to those he had looked at first. At last he made his selection, and after paying, he ordered his purchase to be dispatched at once.

" I shall be returning to Paris in a few days," he said.

They turned home, but as they drove along by the side of the bay a gust of cold air from one of the valleys suddenly caught them, and the invalid began to cough. At first it was only a slight attack, but it grew worse, until it became an interminable paroxysm, then a kind of hiccough, accompanied by a rattling in the throat. Forestier was choking, and every time he tried to breathe, his deep-seated cough tore his throat. Nothing would check it or relieve it. He had to be carried from the landau to his room, and Duroy, who was holding his legs, felt his feet shake at every convulsion of his lungs. The warmth of bed did not check the attack, which lasted till midnight ; then the deadly paroxysm of coughing yielded to the influence of narcotics. The sick man remained till daybreak, sitting up in bed with his eyes wide open.

His first words were a request for the barber, for he insisted on being shaved every morning. He rose for this operation, but had to be put to bed again immediately. His breathing became so quick and laboured that Madame Forestier was frightened and called Duroy, who had gone to bed, and begged him to fetch the doctor. He returned immediately with Dr. Gavaut who prescribed a potion and gave some advice, but when Duroy accompanied him to the door, in order to ask his opinion, he said :

" It's the end. He will be dead by to-morrow morning. Prepare his poor young wife and send for a priest. There is nothing that I can do, but I place myself entirely at your disposal."

Duroy summoned Madame Forestier.

" He is dying. The doctor suggests sending for a priest. What are your wishes ? "

She hesitated for a long time. Then after thinking it over, she said in deliberate tones:

" Yes, that will be best, in many ways. I will prepare him and tell him that the priest would like to pay him a visit——Oh I don't really know what I shall say——It would be very kind if you would go and fetch one, preferably a parish priest, and if you would choose him carefully. Bring one who won't make too much fuss. Try to induce him to content himself with the confession and to let us off the rest."

Duroy returned wth an obliging old ecclesiastic, willing to adapt himself to the situation. When he entered the dying man's room, Madame Forestier came out and sat with Duroy next door.

" It has upset him," she said. " When I mentioned a priest a terrible expression appeared on his face, as if he had felt—had felt—a breath of—you know. He realised that it was the end at last and that his hours were numbered."

She was very pale. She continued :

" I shall never forget the expression on his face. Surely he saw death in that moment. He saw death——"

They could hear the priest, who was a little deaf and spoke in a somewhat loud voice.

" No, no," he was saying, " you are not as bad as all that. You are ill, but in no danger. And the proof of that is that I've come to see you as a friend, as a neighbour."

They could not catch Forestier's reply. The old man answered :

" No, I am not going to administer the Sacrament to you. We will talk of that when you are better. But if you care to take advantage of my visit to make your confession, I shall be very glad. You see I am a pastor, and I seize every chance of bringing back my sheep to the fold."

There was a prolonged silence. Doubtless Forestier was speaking in his choking voice, which had no resonance

All of a sudden, in a new tone, the tone of an officiating priest at the altar, the confessor spoke again.

"The mercy of God is infinite. Repeat the Confiteor, my son. You may have forgotten it ; I will help you. Say after me, ' Confiteor Deo omnipotenti—Beatæ Mariæ semper virgini——"

From time to time he waited for the dying man to repeat the words. Then he said :

"Now make your confession."

Madeleine and Duroy remained motionless in the grip of some painful emotion, troubled by anxious expectation. The sick man had murmured some reply. The priest resumed :

"You have culpably indulged yourself. In what way, my son ? "

Madeleine rose and said with simplicity :

"Let us go into the garden. We must not listen to his secrets."

They seated themselves on a bench outside the door, beneath a flowering rose tree and behind a clump of carnations which shed their strong, sweet perfume upon the clear air.

"Will it be long before you return to Paris ? " asked Duroy after a few minutes' silence.

"Oh no," she replied, "when it's all over, I shall come back."

"In about ten days ? "

"Yes, at the most."

"He has no relations at all ? " he resumed.

"Only cousins. His father and mother died when he was quite young."

Together they watched a butterfly drawing its sustenance from the carnations, flitting from one to another with fluttering wings, which continued to beat slowly after it had alighted on a flower. They sat in silence for a long time till the servant came to tell them that the priest had finished. They they returned to the house together.

Forestier looked even more wasted than on the previous evening. The priest was holding his hand.

"Au revoir, my son. I will come and see you again to-morrow."

And he went away.

As soon as he had left the room, the dying man, who was panting for breath, tried to raise his hands towards his wife, and gasped :

"Save me, save me, my darling. I don't want to die ; I don't want to die—oh, save me. Tell me what to do. Send for the doctor. I will take anything you like. I don't want to die—I don't want to die."

His hands, which had dropped back on to the bed, began a continuous movement, slow and regular, as if trying to pick up something from the sheets.

Bursting into tears, his wife said in a broken voice :

"No, no, it's nothing. It's only an attack ; you will be better to-morrow. The drive yesterday was too much for you."

Forestier's breath came faster than that of a panting dog ; it was so quick that it was impossible to count it, and so feeble that it was barely audible.

He kept repeating :

"I don't want to die. O God, O God, O God, what will happen to me ? I shall never see anything again, never again, never again. O my God ! "

His gaze was fixed on something in front of him, invisible to the others, something frightful of which his staring eyes reflected the terror. His hands continued their dreadful and exhausting movement. All at once a sudden shudder passed over his whole body, and he gasped out :

"The cemetery ! I ! O my God ! "

He did not speak again. He remained motionless, haggard, panting for breath.

Time went on. The clock in the neighbouring convent struck twelve. Duroy left the room to take some food, but Madame Forestier refused to eat. He returned an hour later. The sick man had not changed his position and his thin fingers still strayed over the sheet as if to draw it towards his face. His wife was seated in an arm-chair at the foot of the bed. Duroy took another chair at her side, and they waited in silence.

The doctor had sent a nurse, who was dozing by the window. Duroy himself began to feel drowsy, when he suddenly had a sensation as if something had happened. He opened his eyes just in time to see Forestier close his own, like two expiring lights. A small hiccough shook the dying man's throat, and two trickles of blood appeared at the corners of his mouth, and flowed down on to his nightshirt. His hands ceased their terrible restlessness. He had breathed his last.

His wife realised the truth, and uttering a cry, flung herself on her knees, sobbing into the bedclothes. Startled and dismayed, George mechanically made the sign of the cross. The nurse, who had woken up, approached the bed.

" It is all over," she said.

Duroy had regained his composure, and murmured with a sigh of relief :

" It wasn't as long as I had expected."

After the first shock was over, and the first tears had been shed, they busied themselves with all the cares and offices that are entailed by a death. Duroy was running errands till nightfall. He came home very hungry ; Madame Forestier ate a little food. Then both of them took up their position in the chamber of death to watch by the body. On the small table by the bedside two candles were burning, near a spray of mimosa in water. They had not been able to procure the customary branch of boxwood. They were alone, in the presence of him who was no more. They remained speechless, deep in thought, gazing at him.

Oppressed by the surrounding gloom, George looked fixedly at the body. His eyes and his thoughts were attracted and fascinated by that wasted countenance, which seemed more wan than ever in the flickering light. There lay his friend, Charles Forestier, who had been speaking to him only yesterday. What a strange and terrible thing was this utter annihilation of a living person. How well he remembered now those words of Norbert de Varenne, who was haunted by the fear of death.

"Not one ever returns." Millions, tens of millions would be born, almost exactly alike, with eyes, nose, mouth, skull, and brains within the skull, but never would that man lying there on the bed reappear. For some years he had lived, eaten and drunk, laughed, loved, hoped, like every one else. And now it was over for him, over for ever. One life! a few days and then nothing. One is born, grows up, is happy, waits a while, and then one dies. Farewell, man or woman, you will never return to earth again. And yet each one bears within him the feverish, impossible yearning for immortality; each is a kind of world within the world and is soon utterly annihilated and cast upon the dung heap where new life germinates. Plants, animals, men, stars, worlds, all quicken and then die that they may be transformed. And not one returns, insect, man or planet.

Duroy's spirit was oppressed by a vague overwhelming terror, the terror inspired by that infinite, irresistible nothingness, which destroys ruthlessly our fleeting and paltry lives. Already his head was bowed before its menace. He thought of flies that live a few hours, insects that live a few days, men that live a few years, worlds that live a few centuries. What difference is there between one and the other? Only a few dawns more or less. He turned away his eyes from the corpse.

Madame Forestier, who sat with bent head, seemed also to be plunged in painful thoughts. But her fair hair made so charming a frame to her sorrowful face that an agreeable sensation, like a gleam of hope, stole into Duroy's heart. Why distress himself when he had still so many years before him? He began to study her. Buried in her thoughts, she was unaware of his scrutiny.

"After all," he said to himself, "the only thing in life worth having is love. To clasp in one's arms the woman one loves! That is the height of human bliss."

How fortunate the dead man had been, to secure so intelligent and charming a companion. How had they become acquainted? Why had a woman like that consented to marry a man without distinction or wealth? By what means had she succeeded in making something of him?

Then he thought of all the hidden mysteries in people's lives. He remembered whispers about Count de Vaudrec, who, it was said, had given her a dowry and married her off.

What would she do now ? Whom would she marry ? Perhaps a Deputy, as Madame de Marelle had suggested, or some dashing adventurer, a superior sort of Forestier ? Had she any projects, plans, fixed ideas ? He would have given anything to know. But why this anxiety about her plans, he asked himself, and he realised that his uneasiness originated in one of those vague, secret, deep-seated thoughts which one does not avow, even to oneself, and discovers only when one probes one's inmost heart.

Yes, why should not he himself attempt her conquest ? With her help, how strong he would be, how formidable ! How swiftly, how surely he would make his way. And why should he not succeed ? He was aware that he had an attraction for her ; that she felt more than mere sympathy for him. It was rather the affinity that links two kindred natures, and which springs as much from mutual attraction as from a kind of unavowed complicity. She knew him to be intelligent, resolute, determined, she could rely upon him.

Had she not sent for him at this serious emergency ? Why had she summoned him ? Did not her act imply choice, confession, purpose ? If she had thought of him, at the very moment when she was about to become a widow, it was perhaps because she was turning to one who was to become her new companion and ally.

He felt an impatient desire to make sure, to question her and learn her intentions. But he was to leave on the second day, as he could not remain alone in the house with his hostess. So he had no time to lose. Before he went back to Paris, he must skilfully, and delicately, elicit from her her plans, and forestall the possibility of her yielding on her return to the solicitations of another man and entangling herself inextricably.

There was a deep silence in the room ; nothing was audible but the regular, metallic ticking of the pendulum clock on the mantelpiece.

" You must be very tired," he said softly.

" Yes," she replied, " but morally rather than physically."

They were startled by the sound of their own voices, which echoed strangely in that sinister place. They threw a quick glance at the dead man's face, as if they expected him to move and speak, as he had done a few hours ago.

" It's a great blow for you," replied Duroy, " a complete change in your life, a real catastrophe in your affections and existence."

She sighed deeply, but made no reply.

" It is terribly sad for a young woman to find herself as lonely as you will be."

He was silent. But as she said nothing, he continued, hesitatingly :

" Whatever happens you must remember our compact. I am entirely at your disposal. I am wholly yours."

She gave him her hand, and threw him one of those glances of gentle melancholy, which thrill us to the marrow of our bones.

" Thank you ; you are kind, more than kind. If I might venture, and if there were anything I could do for you, I, too, should say, count on me."

He had taken her outstretched hand, and clasped it firmly, longing to kiss it. At last he decided to venture. He raised it and pressed the smooth fingers, hot and feverish, but very fragrant, lingeringly to his lips. When he felt that this friendly caress had lasted long enough, he discreetly released the little hand. It sank back gently on to Madame Forestier's knee. She said gravely :

" Yes, I shall be very lonely, but I shall try to be brave."

He did not know how to convey to her how happy, how very happy, he would be to make her his wife. He could not tell her this in so many words at such a time and in such a place, in the actual presence of her dead husband. Yet he might, he thought, hit upon one of those ambiguous, decently involved phrases, with a hidden meaning in their words, and expressing by their calculated reticence exactly what one desires to say.

But he was restrained by the presence of the corpse, the

rigid corpse that lay stretched out before their eyes, and which he felt as a barrier between them. Moreover, for some time he had been conscious of a suspicious odour in the close atmosphere of the room, an exhalation of corruption issuing from Forestier's breast, that first breath of the charnel house, which the poor dead body lying on its bed, casts upon the relatives watching by its side, that terrible breath with which it soon will fill the empty coffin.

" Couldn't we open the window a little ? " asked Duroy. " It seems to me that the air is tainted."

" Yes, do," she replied, " I had noticed it too."

He went to the window and opened it. The cool, fragrant night air rushed in, making the two lighted candles by the bedside flicker. Again the moon shed its ample, peaceful light upon the white walls of the villas and the great shining expanse of sea. As Duroy drew deep breaths of air into his lungs, hopes suddenly thronged upon him, and he exulted in the quivering approach of joy.

He turned round.

" Come and get a breath of fresh air," he said, " it is a lovely night."

Quietly she moved to the window and leaned her elbows on the sill, close beside him.

Then in a low voice he whispered :

" Listen to me, and try to understand what I want to say. And above all do not be angry with me for speaking to you on such a subject at a time like this. But I'm leaving you the day after to-morrow, and when you return to Paris it may be too late. Well—as you know I am only a poor devil with no fortune, who has still to make a position for himself. But I have determination and am, I think, not without intelligence, and I have made a good start. With a man who has arrived, you know where you are ; with a man at the beginning of his career, you never can tell to what he may attain. So much the better, or so much the worse. This is the point. I told you one day at your house that it would have been my cherished dream to marry a woman like you. To-day I repeat that aspiration. Do not answer me. Hear me out. I am not making you a proposal. In such a place, and at such a time, it would be atrocious. All that I want is that you should be aware that you can take me for a brotherly friend, or, if you please, a husband. I am yours, soul and body. I do not want you to answer me now, and we will not discuss it here. When we meet again in Paris, you will convey to me your decision. Until then, not another word."

He spoke without looking at her, as if he were scattering the words abroad upon the night air. And she seemed not to have heard, she remained so still, gazing with staring, unconscious eyes, straight at the wide landscape, that lay white in the moonlight. For a long time they stood there side by side, silent and deep in thought. Then she said softly :

"It's rather cold." And turning round, she moved again towards the bed. Duroy followed her example.

As he approached, he perceived that the body was really showing signs of decomposition, and he drew his chair away.

"We must place him in the coffin to-morrow morning," he said.

"Yes, that has been arranged," she replied, "the under-taker is coming about eight o'clock."

"Poor fellow," sighed Duroy. And she in her turn heaved a deep sigh of heart-broken resignation.

They glanced less frequently at the body. They were already becoming accustomed to the idea of his death, and reconciled to his disappearance, which a moment ago had filled with revolt and indignation these two, who were likewise mortal. They did not speak, but continued to keep watch decorously, without going to sleep. But towards midnight Duroy fell into a doze. When he woke he saw that Madame Forestier, too, had dropped off to sleep, and moving into a more comfortable posture, he closed his eyes again, muttering :

"By Jove, a man is more comfortable between the sheets."

A sudden noise made him jump. It was the nurse coming in and it was broad daylight. Madame Forestier, in the arm-chair facing him, seemed as much surprised as himself. She looked somewhat pale, but none the less attractive, fresh and charming, in spite of having sat up all night. Glancing at the body, Duroy shuddered and exclaimed :

" Oh, look at his beard."

On the decomposing flesh the beard had grown in a few hours as much as it would have grown in several days on a living face. And they were appalled at the life which lingered on in the dead, as at some horrible prodigy, a supernatural portent of resurrection, one of those abnormal and terrible signs that unhinge and confound the intelligence.

Both of them went away and rested till eleven o'clock. At that hour Charles was laid in the coffin, and immediately they were conscious of a sense of relief.

They sat opposite each other at luncheon eager to talk of comforting and cheerful things and to get back to life again, since they had done all they could for the dead. Through the wide open window came the mild warmth of spring, wafting to them the perfume of the carnations flowering by the door. Madame Forestier suggested a stroll in the garden, and they began to walk slowly round the little lawn, enjoying the soft air, fragrant with pine and eucalyptus. Suddenly, without turning her head towards him, just as he had done during the night in that room upstairs, she spoke. She uttered her words deliberately in a low, grave voice :

" Listen, dear friend, I have thought over carefully— already—what you proposed to me, and I will not let you go without one word in reply. I shall say neither yes nor no. We will wait and see and get to know each other better. You for your part should think it over seriously. Do not yield to a sudden impulse. If I talk to you of this, even before poor Charles is laid in his grave, it is because, what you have said to me makes it essential that you should have a clear idea of me. If your character is not such that you can understand and help me, you must not entertain further the wish that you have expressed to me. I want to make this clear to you. I look upon marriage, not as a bond, but as a partnership. I claim freedom, perfect freedom always in all my acts, in all my proceedings, in my goings and comings. I could not endure control or jealousy or any discussion of my conduct. I should, of course, pledge myself never to compromise the name of the man I married, and never to bring upon him odium or ridicule. But on his part he must pledge himself to look upon me as an equal, an ally, and not as an inferior being, or an obedient, submissive wife. I know that my ideas are not universally accepted. but I do not propose to change them. There it is. One thing more. Do not answer me now ; it would be useless and unseemly. We shall see each other again and perhaps talk about all this later on. Now go for a stroll. I must return to him. We will meet again this evening."

He printed a lingering kiss upon her hand and left her without a word.

That evening they only saw each other at dinner time. Afterwards they went up to their rooms, both of them prostrate with weariness.

Charles Forestier was buried quietly the next day in the Cannes cemetery.

George Duroy proposed to catch the Paris express which left at half-past one. Madame Forestier took him to the station. They walked quietly up and down the platform, awaiting the time of departure, and talking of indifferent matters. The train arrived ; a very short train, a real express with only five carriages. Duroy selected his seat, then got out of the train to chat to her for a few moments more. Suddenly he was seized with sadness, grief and violent regret at leaving her, as if he were about to lose her for ever.

A guard shouted.

" Marseilles, Lyons, Paris. Take your seats."

Duroy entered the train, and leaned out of the window to say a few last words to her. The engine whistled, and the train began slowly moving out of the station. Leaning out of the carriage window, Duroy gazed at Madeleine standing motionless on the platform and following him with her eyes. Just as he was losing sight of her he threw her a kiss with both hands. Discreetly, hesitatingly, with a mere shadow of his own gesture, she returned his salute.

PART II

I

GEORGE DUROY had resumed all his old ways.

Now that he was installed in the little ground-floor flat in the Rue de Constantinople, he was leading the well-regulated existence of a man who is laying the lines for a reform in his mode of life. His relations with Madame de Marelle were even invested with a conjugal staidness, as though he were practising for a coming event, and that lady, astonished at the well-ordered tranquillity of their union, used to say with a laugh :

" You are even more of a home bird than my husband. It was hardly worth while making the change."

Madame Forestier had not returned, but was prolonging her stay at Cannes. Duroy received from her a letter announcing her return in the middle of April, but there was not a word of allusion to their farewells. He waited. He was now fully determined to use every means to persuade her to become his wife, if she should appear to hesitate. Moreover he retained his faith in his own good luck and his confidence in that power of seduction which he was conscious of possessing, a power undefined but irresistible, a power to which all women yielded.

He received a briefly worded missive which intimated the approach of the fateful hour :

I am in Paris. Come and see me.
Madeleine Forestier.

That was all. The letter had reached him by the nine o'clock delivery, and he went to call on her at three o'clock on the same day. She held out both hands to him and smiled her pleasing and attractive smile ; and for a few minutes they gazed deep into each other's eyes.

Then she murmured :

" How sweet it was of you to come all that way in those terrible circumstances ! "

" I would have done anything you ordered me," he replied.

They seated themselves, and she listened to his news about the Walters and the newspaper and the staff. The newspaper was often in her thoughts.

" It's a dreadful loss to me," she said, " dreadful. At heart I had become a journalist. I can't help it. I just love journalism."

Then she fell silent, but he thought he understood ; he believed he had discerned in her smile, in the tone of her voice, and in her very words, a sort of invitation, and although he had cautioned himself against being too precipitate, he found himself saying brokenly :

" Well then—why, why not take it up again—journalism —under the name of Duroy ? "

Of a sudden she again became serious. She put her hand on his arm and said gently :

" Don't let us talk of that just yet."

But he divined her acceptance. He fell on his knees and began to kiss her hands passionately. In faltering accents he repeated :

" I love you, I love you. How can I ever thank you ? "

She rose from her chair and he from his knees. He noticed that she was very pale, and knew that he had found favour with her, possibly had long done so. They were standing face to face ; he clasped her in his arms and imprinted on her forehead a long, tender, reverent kiss.

Slipping out of his embrace she freed herself, and resumed gravely :

" Listen, my friend. I have not yet made up my mind. Still, it is possible that I may say yes. But in any case you must promise me absolute secrecy until you have my leave."

He gave her his promise, and then took his departure, with a heart overflowing with joy.

From that day he was highly discreet in his conversation with her ; he never pressed for a more definite consent, for she had a way of talking of the future, of asking him to " wait a little," of making plans assuming a common existence which never failed to meet the situation in a manner that was more convincing, and at the same time less crude, than a formal acceptance.

Duroy continued to work hard and to spend little, in an endeavour to save something, so that he should not be absolutely penniless on his wedding day. He was becoming as parsimonious as he had once been prodigal.

Summer and autumn passed without any suspicions being aroused, for they saw little of each other and that only in circumstances that seemed normal.

One evening Madeleine looked him straight in the face and said to him :

" You have said nothing of our plans to Madame de Marelle ? "

" No, my dear. I promised you it should remain a secret and I haven't told a living soul."

" Well then, she might be told now. I shall let the Walters know. This week do you think ? "

" Certainly. To-morrow."

He had blushed. She turned away her eyes gently, as if to avoid noticing his confusion, and resumed :

" If you like, we could be married at the beginning of May. That would be quite correct."

" I shall joyfully obey your wishes in everything."

" The tenth of May is a Saturday and I should like that date because it is my birthday."

" Very well then, the tenth of May."

" Your parents live near Rouen, don't they ? At least you told me so."

" Yes, near Rouen. At Canteleu."

" What are they ? "

" They are—they have a small income of their own."

" Ah, I should very much like to know them."

He hesitated in great perplexity.

" Well, as a matter of fact—they——"

He took the bull by the horns.

" My dear, they are just peasant folk. They keep a little drinking shop and they sweated to give me an education. Of course I'm not ashamed of them. Still they are so simple—and—countrified, that you might find them embarrassing."

Her smile at this was exquisite ; her face lighted up with goodness and sweetness.

" Not at all. I shall be very fond of them. We will go and see them. I really want to. We will talk about this again. My own people were nobody in particular. Unlike you, I have lost sight of mine. I have nobody left to me in the world."

She stretched out a hand to him :

" Except you," she added.

He felt touched and moved, vanquished by her, as never before by any other woman.

" I have had an idea," she went on. " But it is rather difficult to explain."

" What is it ? " he asked.

" Well, my dear, to tell you the truth, I have my little weaknesses like all women. I love sound and glitter. I should adore a name that showed rank and family. Couldn't you manage, when we get married, to assume just a touch of the—aristocratic ? "

It was her turn to blush now ; one would have supposed that she had proposed something not quite proper.

He replied frankly :

" What you suggest has often occurred to me, but it does not seem easy."

" How so ? "

" Because," he laughed, " I am afraid of making myself ridiculous."

She shrugged her shoulders.

" Oh, not at all, not at all. Everybody does it and nobody laughs at it. Divide your name into two, so, Du-Roy. That would do very nicely."

His reply came promptly. He had been evidently considering the problem.

" No, that won't quite do ; it's too simple, too common, too obvious. I had been thinking myself of first adopting the name of my birthplace as a literary pseudonym. Then I would gradually link it up with my real name, and eventually I would divide up my name as you suggested."

" You come from Canteleu ? " she asked.

" Yes."

She still seemed to hesitate.

" No. The termination does not please me. Could we not modify the word Canteleu a little ? "

She had picked up a pen and was scribbling names and studying the impression they made on her. Suddenly she exclaimed :

" Look here, I have it ! "

On the paper she gave him, he read :

" Madame Duroy de Cantel."

He thought it over for a few moments and then said gravely :

" Yes, it's very good."

She was in raptures and kept repeating :

" Duroy de Cantel. It's splendid, splendid ! " With an air of conviction she continued :

" And you will see how easily it will go down with everybody. But we must lose no time about it. It would be too late after our marriage. Beginning from to-morrow you must sign your articles D. de Cantel, and your Echoes simply Duroy. This sort of thing is done every day in the press and nobody will be surprised at seeing you take a pseudonym. At our marriage we can carry it a step further by telling our friends that you have given up the *du* through modesty, and in view of your position, or, if you like, we needn't say anything at all. What is your father's Christian name ? "

" Alexander."

She repeated Alexander several times, listening to the sonorousness of the syllables. Then she took a blank sheet of paper and wrote on it :

" Monsieur and Madame Alexander du Roy de Cantel have the honour to inform you of the marriage of their son, Monsieur George du Roy de Cantel with Madame Madeleine Forestier."

He held the writing at a little distance and was enraptured with the effect.

She exclaimed :

" With a little management you get everything you want."

Once in the street again, Duroy felt that his determination to call himself henceforth Du Roy had conferred on him new importance. He was walking with an increased swagger, with his head held higher ; his moustaches had a prouder curl and he had the gait of a man of assured position. He was conscious of a joyous impulse to impart to the passers-by the news that his name was now Du Roy de Cantel.

Hardly had he reached home, however, when he was disquieted by the thought of Madame de Marelle, and he wrote at once to her to fix an appointment for the following day.

" It will be no joke," he reflected. " I am in for the very devil of a row."

However, he made up his mind to this with the natural callousness which made him disregard the disagreeable things of life. Then he set himself to concoct a mock-serious article on the new imposts, which were to be introduced to ensure an equilibrium in the Budget. In his list of taxes he suggested one of a hundred francs a year for having a preposition in one's name, and that all titles, from baron to prince, should pay from five hundred to a thousand francs. And he signed himself D. de Cantel.

Next day he received from Madame de Marelle a telegram to say that she would be with him at one o'clock. It was with a slight sense of discomfort that he awaited her. He had made up his mind not to mince matters ; to be quite frank from the beginning and then, when the first emotions had subsided, to argue it all out reasonably with her and prove to her that he could not refrain indefinitely from marriage and that, in view of her husband's perverse refusal to die, it was only due to himself to think of some other woman whose companionship could be sanctioned by law.

Nevertheless he had his emotions, and when the bell rang, he felt his heart beating.

She threw herself into his arms.

" How are you, Bel-Ami ? "

Discerning a coldness in his embrace, she looked at him and asked :

" What is the matter ? "

" Sit down," he said. " I want to have a serious talk with you."

She seated herself. She did not take off her hat, but merely raised her veil and waited for him to speak. He had lowered his eyes ; he was preparing his opening. His words came slowly.

" My dear, you see me much troubled and grieved and embarrassed by what I have to confess to you. I love you intensely and from the depths of my heart, and the fear of causing you pain afflicts me even more than the actual news I have to tell you."

She felt herself trembling ; she turned pale and faltered :

" What is the matter ? Oh, tell me at once."

In a sad but resolute tone, and with the factitious grief with which are announced calamities that have a silver lining, he said :

" The matter is that I am going to get married."

She gave a sigh, as if she were going to faint, a dolorous sigh from the depths of her being ; she caught her breath, unable to speak, and seemed on the point of suffocating.

Seeing her speechless, he resumed :

" You cannot conceive how greatly I have suffered before coming to this decision. You are aware that I have neither fixed employment nor money. I am alone, lost in Paris. I need someone near me to advise and console and fortify me. What I have sought is a partner, an ally, and I have found her."

He fell silent, hoping that she would make some reply. He was prepared for abuse. She rested one hand upon her heart as though to repress it ; her bosom heaved and her head was shaken by the painful spasms in which her breath came and went. He took the hand which was resting on the arm of the chair, but she snatched it away, and she repeated dully, as though in a sort of stupor :

" Oh, my God,"

He kneeled before her, not however daring to touch her. More deeply moved by her silence than he would have been by transports of anger, he said brokenly :

" Clo, my little Clo, try to understand my position, try to realise what I am. Oh, if I had been able to make you my wife, what happiness it would have been ! But you are already married. What could I do ? Only consider, my dear. I have to make my place in the world, and that is impossible until I have a home. If you only knew—— There have been days when I have wanted to kill your husband . . ."

His words were uttered in a soft, veiled, seductive voice, a voice that fell upon the ear like music. In Clotilde's staring eyes he saw two tears slowly forming ; they grew larger, and even as they trickled down her cheeks, two fresh tears were already forming on her eyelids.

" Don't cry, Clo," he murmured. " Oh, don't cry, I implore you. It cuts me to the heart."

At that she made an effort, a great effort, to retain her dignity and pride, and she asked him, in the quivering voice of a woman on the verge of sobs :

" Who is it ? "

He hesitated a moment, but realised that there was no escape for him :

" Madeleine Forestier."

She started violently, but she remained dumb, concentrating her thoughts so intently that she seemed to have forgotten that he was still at her feet. And the crystal teardrops never ceased to form in her eyes and brim over, and ever new tears took their place. She rose from her chair, and Duroy saw that she was going to leave him without a word either of reproach or forgiveness, and this wounded and humiliated him to the bottom of his soul. He did not want to let her go ; he threw his arms about her and through her dress he felt her rounded limbs stiffening to resist him.

" I entreat you not to leave me like that," he replied,

Then she looked down on him with those eyes brimming with tears and despair, so charming and so sad, and revealing all the grief of a woman's heart. In broken accents she said :

"I have—I have nothing to say—or do—— You are right : you—you have done what was best for yourself."

She freed herself with a backward step and left him, and he made no further effort to detain her. When he was alone, he rose to his feet. He felt stunned as by a blow on the head, but he presently collected himself and said :

"For better or worse, there it is. There was no scene. It's just as well."

With a great weight off his mind he realised that he was a free man, unfettered, with nothing to hinder him in his new life, and he began to attack the wall with great blows of his fists, in a sort of intoxication of success and energy, as though he were fighting against destiny.

When Madame Forestier asked whether he had told Madame de Marelle, he calmly replied :

"Why, certainly."

Clear-eyed, she scrutinised him.

"Was she put out about it ? "

"Not at all. Quite the contrary. She seemed to approve highly."

The news soon spread abroad. Some admitted their astonishment, others declared that they had foreseen it, others again smilingly gave one to understand that a thing like that could hardly have escaped them.

He was now signing his news items D. de Cantel, his Echoes Duroy and his occasional political articles Du Roy. He passed half his days at the house of his betrothed, who treated him with sisterly familiarity, in which however there was sincere but disguised tenderness, real desire, but veiled as a weakness. She had decided that the marriage should take place very quietly, in the presence of the witnesses only, and that she and her husband would leave the same evening for Rouen. Next day they would go and pay their respects to his old parents and they would stay in the neighbourhood for a few days.

Duroy had done his best to induce her to give up this plan, but in the end he had had to yield. Accordingly on the tenth of May the newly married couple, who had agreed that as there were no guests, there was no object in having a religious ceremony, went back home to pack up their things, after the brief proceedings at the town hall. At the Saint-Lazare station they took the six o'clock train which carried them off towards Normandy.

Until they found themselves alone together in the carriage they had barely exchanged twenty words, but as soon as they felt they had fairly started, they looked at each other and burst out laughing, to conceal a certain awkwardness which they did not wish to admit. The train glided smoothly through the long station at Batignolles and then crossed the squalid flats that reach from the fortifications to the Seine. Every now and then Duroy and his wife would exchange some futile remark and would then turn again towards the carriage window. When they passed the Asnières bridge, their spirits rose at the sight of the river crowded with boats, fishermen, and people rowing about. The powerful May sun shed its slanting rays on the little boats and on the calm river, which seemed stationary, without current or eddy, motionless in the clear warmth of closing day. A sailing boat in midstream had on either side, to catch the lightest puffs of air, a huge triangle of white sail cloth, and had the appearance of a great bird ready to take to its wings.

" I love the environs of Paris," said Duroy, " and my memories of its fried fish are the happiest of my existence."

" And the dear little boats," she replied. " How sweet it is to glide at sunset on the surface of the water."

They then stopped talking, as though they were rather afraid to let themselves go on the subject of their past life, and in silence they were perhaps already savouring the poetry of regrets.

Duroy, seated opposite his wife, took her hand and imprinted a lingering kiss on it.

" When we get home again," he said, " we will go and dine sometimes at Chatou."

" There will be so much to do," she murmured, in a

tone which seemed to imply, "We must sacrifice the agreeable to the expedient."

He retained his hold of her hand, but he kept asking himself uneasily how he was to make the transition to caresses. This would not have worried him in the same way had he been confronted with the ignorance of a young girl, but his position was rendered embarrassing by his consciousness of Madeleine's alert and subtle intelligence. He was afraid of seeming silly in her eyes, either over-timid or over-bold, too slow or too forward. He gave little squeezes to her hand but she did not respond to his appeal. He said :

" It seems very odd to me that you should be my wife."

She appeared surprised. " Why so ? "

" I don't know. Somehow it seems odd. I should like to kiss you and yet I am surprised to think that I have a right to do so."

She presented her cheek to him calmly and he kissed it as if it were his sister's.

He resumed :

"The first time I saw you, at that dinner to which Forestier invited me I thought, ' if only I could find a wife like that ! ' And I have. Here she is."

She murmured :

" How nice of you," and from smiling eyes she threw him a glance at once direct and subtle.

" I am too cold," he thought, " I am stupid. I ought to get on faster than that." And he said, " Tell me how you made the acquaintance of Forestier."

With provoking archness she replied :

" Are we going to Rouen to talk about him ? "

He blushed.

"What a fool I am. But you do frighten me so."

She was enraptured.

" I ? Impossible ! How can that be ? "

He had seated himself quite close to her. She exclaimed :

" Oh, a stag ! "

The train was traversing the forest of St. Germain, and she had seen a startled stag bounding across a drive. While she was looking out of the open window, Duroy leaned over and long and lovingly kissed the curls on the nape of her neck. She remained a few moments without moving ; then she raised her head :

" You are tickling me.   Stop it."

But he would not desist and he moved his moustache gently over her white skin in an enervating and prolonged caress.   She gave herself a shake, " Do stop."

He slipped his right hand behind her head and turned her face towards him, and swooped down on her lips like a hawk on its prey.   She struggled, pushed him away, tried to free herself, and at last succeeded.   Again she said :

" Oh, do stop."

But he would listen no longer ; he clasped her in his arms and devoured her with greedy and trembling kisses.   She freed herself with a great effort and jumped to her feet.

" Really, George, you must stop this.   We are not children.   Surely we can wait until we get to Rouen."

He remained seated.   He was very red in the face and felt abashed by her reasonable words, but he presently regained his self-possession.

" So be it.   I shall wait," he said gaily, " but the deuce take me if I say twenty words more before we arrive.   And remember that we have only got as far as Poissy."

" You can trust me to do the talking," she said, gently resuming her place beside him.   And she did in fact speak, and with precision, of what they would do on their return. They would keep on the flat which she had occupied with her former husband and Duroy would also step into the duties and emoluments of Forestier on the *Vie Française*. As regarded the financial details of housekeeping, she had, before their marriage, arranged everything with as sure a touch as any business man.

Their legal status was that of separate estates, and every possible contingency had been provided for, such as death, divorce, and the birth of one or more children.   The husband had brought with him four thousand francs according to his own statement, but fifteen hundred of this had been borrowed.   The rest had accrued from savings effected during the year, against his marriage.   The wife had forty thousand francs which she said Forestier had left her, and she recurred to him, quoting his example :

" He was very thrifty and steady and devoted to his work. He would have been rich in quite a short time."

But Duroy was not listening, his mind was otherwise engaged. Occasionally she fell silent in order to pursue some private train of thought, and then, resuming :

" From now on, for the next three or four years, you should have no difficulty in making an income of thirty or forty thousand francs. It's what Charles would have had if he had lived."

George was beginning to find the discourse somewhat boring.

" I thought," he said, " that we weren't going to Rouen to talk about him."

She gave him a playful tap on the cheek.

" Quite true," she laughed, " My mistake ! "

He assumed the air of a very well-behaved little boy and placed a hand on each of his knees.

" You look silly doing that," she remarked.

" It is the part you want me to play," he retorted. " You have just reminded me of it. I shall stay like this."

" Why ? " she asked.

" Because you have taken charge of the house, and of me as well, as far as I can see. And quite right, too, since you are a widow."

" What exactly do you mean by that ? " she said in surprise.

" What I mean to say is that you will be able to enlighten my ignorance with your experience. You know all about marriage. It is for you to arouse me from my virgin innocence."

" Really," she exclaimed, " you are going too far."

" That is how it stands," he retorted. " I can't be expected to know anything about women, whereas you, being a widow, know all about men, eh ? You must take me in hand to-night, and you can begin right away if you like, eh ? "

" Oh, come now, you can hardly count on me for that."

" Yes. I do." He assumed the voice of a schoolboy who stammers through his repetition. " I count on your putting me through a proper course—twenty lessons—ten in the rudiments—reading and grammar—ten in the higher branches, including rhetoric. I am an absolute ignoramous."

" You silly ! " she ejaculated, greatly amused.

" Now you are becoming familiar," he retorted, " and I shall follow your example. I assure you, my love, that I adore you more and more every second, and to my mind Rouen is an unconscionable way off."

He was now using the intonations of an actor, with a pleasing play of facial expression which entertained Madeleine who was accustomed to the manners and gaiety of the upper circles of literary Bohemia. She cast a sidelong glance at him and he struck her as really charming. She felt the desire one has to pluck and nibble a fruit from the tree, despite the restraint of one's reason, which counsels one to wait till dinner to eat it at the right time. Blushing a little at the thoughts that assailed her, she said :

" My little pupil, believe me. I have great experience. Kisses in a railway carriage are not worth it. They don't agree with you." And she blushed still more as she added :

" You must never cut your corn until it is in the ear."

Excited by the subtle significance of the utterances of her pretty mouth, he chuckled. Then he crossed himself and moving his lips like a rabbit as if he were murmuring a prayer, he announced :

" I have just put myself under the protection of St. Anthony, the patron saint of the tempted. I am proof now."

Night came gently on, enveloping with its transparent shadow, like filmy crêpe, the wide expanse of country on their right. The train ran along the banks of the Seine, and the young couple began to admire in the river which lay alongside the track like a broad ribbon of polished metal, rosy reflections, patches fallen from the sky, which the departing sun had burnished with purple and fire. Little by little these patches of light were extinguished ; they grew darker and faded sadly away into the night. The landscape was plunged in obscurity, and over it passed a slight shudder, that shudder of death which the earth feels each day at twilight. This nocturnal sadness stole in by the open window and penetrated the hearts that had lately been so gay, and the two were stricken with silence. They had come nearer to each other to watch the dying moments of this lovely and cloudless evening of May. The little oil-lamp which had been lighted at Mantes shed over the grey cloth of the cushions its flickering yellow rays. Duroy clasped his wife in his arms and strained her to him. His fierce desire softened to tenderness, a languorous tenderness, a soft yearning for those comforting little endearments with which infants are lulled to sleep.

He murmured in a low voice :

" I shall be your true lover, my little Madeleine."

The young wife was stirred by the gentleness of these words, and a quick tremor passed through her.

He had pillowed his cheek on her warm bosom, and she leaned over him and offered him her lips to kiss. The kiss was lingering and silent and passionate, and was succeeded by a violent embrace. After it they rested in each other's arms, both somewhat disillusioned, but still languid and loving, until the whistle of the locomotive announced an approaching station. With the tip of her fingers she touched lightly the disordered hair on his temples and said :

" That was very silly. What a way to behave ! "

But he kissed her hands, first one and then the other, with feverish rapidity, and said :

" I adore you, my darling Madeleine."

As far as Rouen they remained almost motionless, cheek to cheek, their eyes fixed on the outside darkness and on the house lights that flashed past from time to time. They were dreaming idly, content in their proximity to each other and in the growing anticipation of a more unrestrained intimacy.

They put up at a hotel with the windows facing upon the quay and after a light supper they went to bed. The chambermaid called them the next morning just after eight o'clock. When they had drunk the cups of tea which had been placed on the tables beside their beds, Duroy looked at his wife and with the elation of a lucky man who has just come upon a treasure, he seized her in his arms and faltered :

" My little Madeleine, I love you, I love you, I love you."

She smiled a confident and satisfied smile and giving him back his kisses, whispered :

" And I you—perhaps."

He was still uneasy about the visit to his parents. He had often warned his wife, what to expect, but he thought fit to begin again.

" You know, they are peasants, real country peasants, not the comic-opera kind."

" I know that already," she laughed. " You have told me so often enough. Do get up now and let me get up too."

He jumped out of bed and put on his socks.

" We shan't be at all comfortable there, not at all. There is only an old bed with a straw palliasse in my room. They've never heard of mattresses at Canteleu."

To all appearances she was enchanted.

" So much the better. It will be charming to lie awake beside—beside you—and to be roused in the morning by the crowing of cocks."

She had slipped on her morning gown, an ample garment of white flannel, which Duroy recognised at once with a displeasure he could not explain. He knew that his wife had a complete dozen of these morning gowns. And she could hardly be expected, could she, to destroy her whole wardrobe and replace it with a new one ? No matter. Still he would have preferred her honeymoon outfit to contain nothing that recalled her former husband. It seemed to him as if the soft warm material could not but retain some trace of contact with Forestier. He lighted a cigarette and went to the window.

The view of the port, with its wide river full of slender-masted sailing vessels and sturdy steamships, of which the cargoes were being noisily discharged upon the quays by revolving cranes, aroused in him a lively emotion, familiar as the sight had been to him for many years.

" By Jove, how fine that is ! " he exclaimed.

Madeleine ran to him and placing both hands on her

husband's shoulder, leaned towards him with an unrestrained gesture and remained at the window enraptured and thrilled.

" Oh, how pretty it is ; how pretty. I never knew that there were so many ships as that."

An hour later they set forth, for they were to have their luncheon with the old people, who had had several days' notice. An open cab with rusty ironwork carried them off with a clatter like a tinsmith's wares rattling up and down. They drove along an unprepossessing boulevard, across meadows intersected by a stream, and then began to climb a slope. Madeleine, who was tired, had fallen into a doze under the potent caresses of the sun which warmed her deliciously as she lay back in the old vehicle, in a warm bath of sunlight and country air.

Her husband awoke her.

" Look," he said.

Two thirds of the way up the slope they had halted at a celebrated view-point which all strangers visited. Below them lay the immense valley, stretching far and wide with the unpolluted river flowing through it, in great sweeping curves. Its course could be traced a long distance, with its many islands, and the bend it described before it passed Rouen. On the right bank lay the city, swimming in the morning haze ; there were flashes of sunshine on the roofs ; there were a thousand airy belfries, pointed or square, fragile structures, carved like gigantic jewels ; there were towers, square or circular, capped by heraldic crowns, there were steeples and bell-turrets, the multitudinous variety of Gothic architecture displayed in church tops, and all were dominated by the pointed spire of the Cathedral, that astonishing spike of bronze, unlovely, weird, portentous, the loftiest in the world.

On the opposite bank of the river, slender, round, bulging at the top, the factory chimneys of the wide-spreading Saint-Sever quarter shot up into the sky. More numerous than the church spires, they could be seen rearing their lofty brick columns far out into the country and sending their black exhalations of coal-smoke into the azure sky. Loftiest of all these, high as the Pyramid of Cheops—the second highest altitude attained by human labour, and almost the equal of its proud gossip, the spire of the Cathedral—the great water tower of the Foudre had an air of being queen of the working and smoking factory throng just as its neighbour was queen of the pointed and carved array of sacred monuments.

Farther out, beyond the factory town, stretched a forest of fir trees; and the Seine, after passing between the two cities, hugged a great undulating slope, wooded on top and showing here and there its bones of white rock. After describing a second sweeping curve it was lost to view on the horizon. Ascending and descending were sailing ships, in tow of steam tugs which looked no larger than flies and belched forth dense clouds of smoke. The water was dotted with islands linked end to end, or set at wide intervals, like beads irregularly strung in a green rosary.

The driver of the cab waited for the travellers to get their raptures over. He knew by experience the duration of the enthusiasm of every variety of sight-seer. Hardly had he set his horse going again when Duroy suddenly caught sight at a little distance of an old couple approaching. He jumped from the carriage, calling out:

"There they are, I recognise them."

They were two peasants, man and woman, who walked with swaying, irregular steps, sometimes bumping each other with their shoulders. The man was slight, stunted, of a ruddy complexion and somewhat pot-bellied, but vigorous for his age; the woman was tall, withered, round-shouldered, set of countenance; a typical agricultural labouring woman who had worked since she was a child and had not laughed once in her life, while her husband had been drinking and cracking jokes with the customers. Madeleine had also got out of the carriage, and as she watched these two poor creatures coming nearer, she felt a constriction of the heart, a quite unexpected sadness. They did not recognise their son in the dandified gentleman and would never have suspected a daughter-in-law in this fine lady in the light-coloured frock. In silence and at a good pace, they were walking to meet their son, and did not cast a glance at these two townspeople, with their carriage. They were passing by, when George laughed and called out :

" Good day to you, father Duroy."

They stopped short, both of them, at first stunned with the shock and then dazed with astonishment. The old woman was the first to collect her senses, and without moving from where she stood, she stammered :

" Is it you ? Our son ? "

" Why, mother Duroy," George replied, " to be sure it's me." And he went up to her and kissed her on both cheeks with a hearty filial kiss. Then he embraced his father who had taken off his cap, which was in the Rouen fashion, made of black silk, like those worn by cattle dealers.

" This is my wife," announced George. The two country folk looked at Madeleine ; looked at her as one looks at a prodigy, with uneasy timidity, accompanied on the father's part with something approaching contented approval, and on the mother's with jealous hostility.

The old man, who was naturally cheerful and was moreover saturated with the gaiety that comes from alcohol and soft cider, plucked up courage and said with a roguish twinkle in his eye :

" Perhaps I might have a kiss ? "

" To be sure," the son announced, and Madeleine, with a feeling of awkwardness, proffered her cheeks to the resounding kisses of the old peasant, who thereafter wiped his mouth with the back of his hand.

The old woman, when her turn came, kissed her daughter-in-law with hostile reserve. No, this was not at all the daughter-in-law of her dreams ; this was no big unspoiled country lass as rosy as a pippin and as round as a brood-mare. She had the air of a street-walker, had this lady, with her furbelows and her musk ; for all perfumes were musk to the old woman.

All four turned to follow in the train of the cab in which was the trunk of the newly wedded pair. The old man took his son by the arm and drawing him back behind the others, asked with interest :

" Well, how goes business ? "

" Very well."

" So much the better. And what about your wife, has she got anything ? "

" Forty thousand francs," replied Duroy.

A gentle whistle betrayed his father's admiration. " The deuce ! " was all he could say, so greatly was he thrilled by the amount.

" My soul and body ! " he next exclaimed with profound conviction : " she's a beauty."

For he found her to his taste, he did, and he had been thought a good judge in his time.

Madeleine and her mother-in-law were walking side by side without exchanging a word, and the two men rejoined them. They arrived at the village, which consisted of a row of ten buildings on each side of the road. Some of them were the usual country-town houses, built of brick and with slate roofs ; the others were farm hovels of clay and thatch. Old Duroy's café, " The Belle Vue," was a tiny place, consisting of a ground floor and a loft. It was at the near end of the village, on the left. A fir branch suspended on the door indicated, after the ancient fashion, that thirsty folk might enter.

Places were laid in the common room of the tavern, on two tables which had been brought together and covered by two napkins. A woman who had come in to help in serving the meal dropped a deep curtsy at the appearance of such a fine lady. Then she recognised George and exclaimed :

" Lord, is that you, child ? "

" Yes, it's me, Mother Brulin," he replied gaily, and he kissed her at once, just as he had kissed his father and mother.

He turned to his wife : " Come to our room," he said, " and take your hat off."

By a door on the right he brought her into a cold room, paved with stone, and with white limewashed walls and a bed with white cotton curtains. A crucifix above the holy water, and two coloured pictures representing Paul and Virginia under a blue palm tree, and Napoleon the First on a yellow horse, were the sole ornaments of this clean but depressing chamber.

As soon as they were alone Du Roy kissed his wife.

"Well, Madeleine, how are you feeling? I am quite pleased to see the old people. At Paris they never cross one's thoughts but all the same it is pleasant when one does meet again."

The old man rapped the partition with his fist and called out :

"Come along ; the soup is ready."

They seated themselves at table. It was a prolonged meal, a peasants' meal, with a succession of dishes all in the wrong order, chitterlings after a leg of mutton, and an omelette to follow the chitterlings. The old man, cheered by the cider and some glasses of wine, turned on the tap of the choice pleasantries which he reserved for great occasions, indecent anecdotes of things which he declared had happened to his friends. George knew all these stories, but laughed at them nevertheless. His native air had gone to his head. He had been recaptured by his innate love of his homeland and the places he had known so well in his childhood, by all the sensations and recollections that thronged back to him, all the old-time trifles that he was recognising—a knife mark in a door, a rickety chair which recalled some petty incident, the earthy odours, the great breath of resin and foliage that came in from the neighbouring wood, the smells of house and brook and dunghill.

The old woman did not say one word, but remained gloomy and sour, spying upon her daughter-in-law with hatred in her heart, the hatred which an old working woman, an old field-hand with worn fingers and joints twisted by hard tasks, naturally felt for this town-bred woman who provoked in her the repulsion of an accursed reprobate thing, an unchaste creature made for slothfulness and vice. She got up from her chair continually to fetch new dishes, to pour into the glasses the acid yellow fluid from the decanter or the darker cider, foaming and sweet, from bottles from which the corks leaped as from aerated lemonade.

Madeleine ate hardly anything, spoke hardly at all, and remained depressed. She had her customary smile on her lips but it was a smile of sadness and resignation. She was disillusioned and distressed. Why? She had wanted to come. She had been perfectly well aware that she was going to the house of peasants, humble peasants. She who so seldom dreamed, what had her dreams about them been? She hardly knew. But have not women a habit of hoping that things will always be other than they are? Viewing them from afar had she seen them in a more poetic light? Hardly, but perhaps she had expected them to be better educated, more distinguished, warmer hearted, more ornamental. At the same time, she had no desire that they should be out of the common, like peasants in a novel. Whence came it then that they shocked her in a thousand little intangible things, by a thousand uncouthnesses that one could not seize upon, by the ineradicable boorishness of their gestures and their mirth. She recalled the memory of her own mother, of whom she never spoke to anyone. She was a governess who had been seduced. She was educated at Saint Denis, and had died of want and grief when Madeleine was twelve years old. An unknown man had seen to the little girl's education. Her father, doubtless. But who was he? She had never known precisely, although she had vague suspicions.

The meal seemed interminable. Some customers presently came in, shook hands with old Duroy, exclaimed on seeing his son, and looking sideways at the young wife, winked waggishly, as much as to say :

" My word, there are no flies on her, not on George Duroy's wife."

Others, less intimate, seated themselves at the wooden tables and called for a glass of beer, a litre of wine, a mug of beer, two brandies, a glass of camphor-cordial, and so forth.

Then they began to play dominoes, slapping down the little black-and-white oblongs of bone and making a great noise.

The old lady never ceased coming and going, waiting upon the customers with her desolate air, taking the money, wiping the tables with the corner of her blue apron. The smoke of clay pipes and halfpenny cigars filled the room. Madeleine began to cough and said :

"Suppose we go out? I can't stand this any longer."
As the meal was not yet finished, old Duroy was annoyed.
She left the table and seated herself on a chair before the
door, on the road, and waited until her father-in-law and her
husband had finished their coffee and liqueurs. Presently
her husband joined her.

"Would you like to stroll down to the Seine?"

She joyfully agreed. They descended the hill-side and
hired a boat at Croisset, and passed the rest of the afternoon
beside an island, under the willows. Both felt drowsy in
the soft warmth of springtime, and were lulled by the movement of the little waves of the river. When night came
on they ascended the hill again.

The evening repast, taken by the light of a single candle,
Madeleine found even more distressing than the morning
meal. Old Duroy was half tipsy and did not speak, and the
old lady remained intractable.

The wretched light threw on the grey walls shadows of
heads with enormous noses and exaggerated movements.
Whenever anyone turned his profile slightly towards the
yellow and flickering flame a gigantic hand would raise a
fork the size of a pitchfork towards a mouth which opened
like the jaws of a monster.

After dinner Madeleine drew her husband outside so as
to escape from the ill-lighted room and its pungent odour
of old tobacco pipes and spilled drinks. When they were
alone, he said :

"You are bored already."

She seemed about to protest but he stopped her.

"No. I see it quite clearly. We will go back to-morrow
if you like."

She agreed and they strolled on together. It was a mild
night and its profound and soothing darkness seemed filled
with faint noises, rustlings and sighings. They had entered
a narrow avenue, with tall trees meeting overhead and on
either side coppices of impenetrable obscurity.

"Where are we?" she asked.

"In the forest," he replied.

"Is it a big forest?"

" Very. One of the biggest in France."

The smell of earth and trees and moss, that perfume, old yet fresh, that comes from bushy thickets and is compounded of the sap of buds and the dead and mouldy grass of the undergrowth, hung about the path. Raising her eyes, Madeleine could see the stars shining through the treetops, and though the branches were stirred by no breeze, she yet felt around her the vague throbbing of that ocean of leaves. A strange shudder swept over her body and soul ; and a vague anguish constricted her heart, why, she could not say. She had a sense of being lost, submerged, surrounded by dangers, abandoned by everybody ; she felt alone, alone in the world, under the living vault that trembled overhead.

" I am rather frightened," she said. " I should like to go back."

" Very well. Let us go home."

" And—we leave for Paris to-morrow ? "

" Certainly."

" To-morrow morning."

" To-morrow morning, if you like."

When they entered the house the old people were already in bed. Madeleine slept badly. She was continually awakened by all those country noises which were new to her, such as the screeching of owls, the grunting of a pig in a sty next to the house wall, the crowing of a cock that began at midnight. The first light of dawn found her up and ready to go.

When George informed his father and mother that they were going, they were taken aback, but they were not long in realising with whom this wish had originated.

" I shall see you again ? " the father asked simply.

" Yes, in the course of the summer."

" That's good."

The old lady muttered ungraciously :

" I hope you won't regret what you've done."

He appeased their displeasure with a gift of two hundred francs. A boy was sent to fetch a cab which arrived about ten o'clock, and the newly wedded pair kissed the old peasants and set out for home. As they descended the slope into Rouen Duroy began to laugh.

"There you are," he said, "I told you so. It would have been better if I hadn't introduced you to Monsieur and Madame du Roy de Cantel senior."

She joined in his laughter and said:

"I assure you I am delighted. They are excellent old people and I am beginning to be quite fond of them. I shall send them little presents from Paris." And she continued in a lower tone: "Du Roy de Cantel . . . You will see. No one will be in the least surprised when we tell them. We shall say that we have been spending a week at your parents' place."

She came closer to him and brushed the tip of his moustache with a kiss.

"How goes it, George?"

"All right, Madeleine," he replied, sliding his arm round her waist.

Far away in the bottom of the valley they saw the great river, like a silver ribbon, unrolled beneath the morning sun; on one side all the factory chimneys were belching out their clouds of smoke into the sky, and on the other all the pointed spires of Rouen were towering above the ancient city.

II

The Duroys had been back in Paris two days. Duroy
had for the nonce resumed his former work, but would
presently take over Forestier's duties, and devote himself
entirely to politics.

He was gay at heart that evening as he mounted the stairs
to dine in the house which was once his predecessor's home,
but now his own. He had an eager desire to embrace his
wife, to whose physical charm and insensible domination he
had yielded with keen delight. As he was passing a florist's
at the end of the Rue Notre-Dame-de-Lorette, it had occurred
to him to buy a bouquet for Madeleine and he purchased a
great bunch of half-open roses, a posy of sweetly perfumed
buds. At every story of the staircase, now his own, he
regarded himself complacently in the mirror which invariably
reminded him of the first visit to the house.

Having forgotten his key, he rang the bell and the door
was opened by the same servant, whom he had retained on
his wife's advice.

" Has Madame Du Roy come in ? " George asked.

" Yes, sir."

But as he passed through the dining-room he was greatly
surprised to see that the table was laid for three. Through
the looped-up curtain of the drawing-room he caught sight
of Madeleine arranging in a vase on the mantelpiece a
bouquet of roses precisely similar to his own. He was
annoyed and disappointed, as if someone had robbed him
of his idea, his little attention, and all the pleasure he expected
from it.

Entering the drawing-room he asked :

" Have you invited someone to dinner ? "

She continued to arrange the flowers and without turning her head, replied :

" Yes and no. It is my old friend the Comte de Vaudrec who always dines here on Mondays. He is coming as usual."

" Ah, quite so," said George.

He stood behind her with his bouquet in his hand. He had a mind to hide it or throw it away. Resisting this impulse he said :

" Look, I've brought you some roses."

Alert and smiling she turned and exclaimed :

" Ah, how nice of you to think of it."

She held out her arms to him and offered him her lips with a thrill of pleasure which was so sincere that his chagrin vanished. She took the flowers, inhaled their perfume and with the vivacity of an enraptured child put them in the vase that stood empty opposite the first one. Admiring the effect, she said :

" How lovely they are. My mantelpiece is just perfect now." Almost immediately she went on with an air of conviction :

" Vaudrec is charming, you know. You will be great friends with him at once."

The bell rang. The Count had arrived. He came in, calm, as much at his ease as if he were in his own house. After kissing his hostess's fingers with an air of gallantry, he turned to her husband, held out his hand to him cordially and said :

" How are you, my dear Du Roy ? "

He had nothing of his former stiffness and affected composure ; the geniality of his manner showed clearly that the situation was changed. Du Roy was surprised, and in response to these advances made himself as pleasant as possible. You would have thought, after five minutes, that they had known and liked each other for ten years.

Madeleine's face was radiant.

" I will leave you two together," she said. " I want to take a look at my kitchen."

She disappeared, both men following her with their eyes. When she came back she found them talking about the stage, discussing a new play, and they were so entirely of the same opinion that a sort of sudden friendship kindled between them at the discovery of their complete similarity of ideas. It was a delightful dinner full of intimate cordiality ; and the Count stayed very late, so happy did he feel in this house, with its new and agreeable domesticity.

When he had left, Madeleine said to her husband :

" Isn't he perfect ? And the more you know him, the better you like him. He is a real friend, true, devoted, loyal. Ah, without him——"

She did not finish her reflection, and George replied :

" Yes, he is most agreeable. I think we shall get on very well together."

She resumed without delay :

" You don't know yet, but we have some work to do to-night before we go to bed. I hadn't time to speak to you about it before dinner, because Vaudrec arrived immediately. But I heard some important news just now, news from Morocco. I got it from Laroche-Mathieu the Deputy, the future minister. We must make a great article out of this, one that will create a stir. I have the facts and figures. We had better set to work at once. Fetch the lamp."

He brought it and they passed into the study.

The shelves held the same rows of books as before, and in the cornices stood the three vases which had been purchased by Forestier at Golfe-Juan the day before he died. Under the table lay the foot-muff of the deceased ready for the feet of Du Roy, who, after seating himself, picked up an ivory penholder bearing the tooth marks of his predecessor.

Leaning against the mantelpiece, Madeleine lighted a cigarette, imparted her news, and then expounded her ideas, and the plan of the article she had in her head. He listened attentively, scribbling notes the while, and when she had finished, he criticised, went through the question again, enlarged its scope, and finally developed it until it was no longer the sketch of an article, but a plan of campaign against the ministry in power. This article would sound the attack. Madeleine had stopped smoking, so deeply was her interest roused, so wide and distant a prospect was revealed to her when she pursued her husband's speculations. Every now and then she expressed her approval :

" Yes, yes, very good. Excellent. It is very strong . . ."

When he had had his say, she exclaimed :

" Now let us get it down in writing."

But he was always bad at starting and words did not come easily to him. So she came to him gently and leaning on his shoulder began whispering phrases into his ear. Now and then she asked hesitatingly :

" Does that express your meaning ? "

" Perfectly," he replied.

She was an adept at strokes of a certain kind, pointed, feminine, venomous, calculated to wound the President of the Council, and she made fun simultaneously of his face and his politics in a quaint fashion which not only provoked laughter but at the same time carried a conviction of truth.

Du Roy sometimes added a few lines which lent depth and strength to the attack. His work on the Echoes had given him complete command of the art of underhand insinuation, and whenever any fact stated by Madeleine as certain seemed to him doubtful or compromising, he made use of his knack of imposing it on the mind by indirect suggestion, which was more convincing than if he had actually affirmed it.

When the article was finished George read it aloud from beginning to end like a speech. They agreed that it was admirable, and exchanged smiles of delighted surprise as if they had just revealed themselves to each other. They looked deep into each other's eyes, thrilled with admiration and tenderness, and embraced with a transport, a warmth of love, communicated by their minds to their bodies.

Du Roy picked up the lamp.

" And now, darling," he said, his face alight.

" Pass on, my master," she replied, " since it is you who light the way."

He went first and she followed him into their bedroom. She tickled his neck between his collar and his hair, knowing that he disliked this habit of hers and that it would make him go more quickly.

The article appeared over the signature of George Du Roy de Cantel and created a great sensation, even in the Chamber of Deputies. Old Walter congratulated the author and made him political editor of the *Vie Française*. The Echoes reverted to Boisrenard.

This was the signal for the commencement of an able and violent campaign against the ministry concerned. The attack was always adroit and well supported by facts. It was sometimes ironical, sometimes serious, sometimes jocular, sometimes virulent ; but it was delivered with a certainty and a persistence which astonished every one. The other newspapers were continually quoting from the *Vie Française*, and extracting entire passages, while the men in power asked whether this unknown and implacable enemy could not be gagged with a prefecture.

Du Roy was becoming a celebrity in political circles. By the way people shook hands with him and took off their hats to him, he realised how much his influence was increasing. He was filled with astonishment and admiration at his wife's subtlety of mind, her skill in making inquiries, and the extent of her knowledge. At any moment when he came home, he might find in his drawing-room a senator, a deputy, a magistrate, a general, all of whom treated her intimately, like an old friend, and took her seriously. Where had she made the acquaintance of all these people ? In society, she said. But he could not understand how she had managed to enlist their trust and their affection.

" She's a born diplomatist," he reflected.

She would often arrive home late for meals, out of breath, flushed, and trembling, and even before taking off her veil she would say :

" I got a real tit-bit to-day. Would you believe it, the minister of justice has just appointed two magistrates who were members of the mixed commissions ? We are going to smite him hip and thigh, and he won't forget it."

So they smote him once, and the next day they smote him again and on the third day yet again. Laroche-Mathieu, the Deputy who dined every Tuesday at the Rue Fontaine, Monday being Count de Vaudrec's day, would shake their hands with excessive demonstrations of joy. He was continually exclaiming :

"Heavens, what a campaign ! We are bound to succeed after this."

What he was really hoping to succeed in was his effort to unhook the portfolio of the Ministry of Foreign Affairs. He had had his eye on it for a long time.

He was one of those double-faced politicians, without convictions or great means, without audacity or serious knowledge, a country lawyer, a buck from the provinces, walking the tight-rope between political extremes, a sort of republican Jesuit, a mushroom liberal of doubtful wholesomeness, such as sprout by hundreds on the popular dunghill of universal suffrage.

His rustic Machiavellism enabled him to pass for a strong man among his colleagues, the outcasts and the misbegotten, from whom deputies are recruited. He was sufficiently presentable, correct, affable and agreeable for purposes of success, and succeed he did, in the mixed and not very refined society of the high officials of the moment. It was commonly said of him that he would be in the Government some day, a prophecy in which he had a more implicit belief than anyone. He was one of the principal shareholders in Walter's journal and was his colleague and associate in many financial affairs.

Du Roy gave him his confident support, nourishing vague hopes of the future. He was merely carrying on the work initiated by Forestier, to whom Laroche-Mathieu had promised the cross of the Legion of Honour, when his day of triumph arrived. Now the decoration would be worn on the breast of Madeleine's new husband, that was all. In reality nothing was changed. So clearly was this felt that the men at the office started a game which annoyed Du Roy. They never called him anything but Forestier. The moment he arrived at the office someone would call out :

"I say, Forestier."

He would pretend not to hear and would go on looking for letters in his pigeon-hole. A second time, but louder, would come the call for " Forestier," and repressed laughter ran round. As Du Roy reached the door of the director's private room, the man who had called him, stopped him.

" I beg your pardon. It is you I wanted to speak to. It is stupid of me, but I am always mixing you up with poor Charles. Your articles are so confoundedly like his, you know. Everybody gets taken in by them."

Du Roy raged silently and a dull resentment against the deceased began to grow in him.

Old Walter had himself declared, when people were commenting on the startling identity of style and inspiration between Forestier and Du Roy :

" Certainly, this is Forestier, but it's Forestier with more substance, more energy, more virility."

On another occasion Du Roy happened to open the cup-and-ball press and found his predecessor's toy with a crape band round the handle, whereas his own, with which he practised under the guidance of Saint-Potin, was adorned with a pink favour. All the cups and ball had been laid out on the same shelf in order of size, and there was a ticket, such as one sees in museums, with the inscription :

" Ancient collection, made by Forestier and Co. Successor, Forestier Du Roy. Patented without government guarantee, indestructible, can be used in all circumstances, even while travelling."

He closed the press calmly but he said loud enough to be heard :

" There are idiots and jealous people everywhere."

Nevertheless he felt the wound to his pride and vanity, the pride and vanity peculiar to authors who, be they pressmen or poets, are ever ready to take offence, ever a prey to nervous, watchful susceptibility.

The word Forestier grated on his ear ; he dreaded to hear it, and when he did hear it, he felt himself blushing. To him this name was biting mockery, or, worse than mockery, it was almost an insult. It cried at him :

" It is your wife who is doing your job for you, just as she did the other man's. You would be nothing without her."

He was quite prepared to admit that Forestier would have

been nothing without Madeleine, but as for himself, that was another matter.

Even at home the obsession continued. It came to this : the whole house, the furniture, the knick-knacks, everything he touched, brought back Forestier. In the early stages he hardly ever thought of it ; but his colleagues' raillery had fretted in his spirit a wound on which trifles hitherto unnoticed acted like poison. He could not touch an object without at once imagining that he saw Charles's hand laid on it. He could only bear to look at and handle things he had himself bought, cared for and possessed. He actually began to feel irritated by the thought of the former relations of his friend and Madeleine.

He could not understand this revulsion of feeling and sometimes said to himself in astonishment :

" How the devil does this come about ? I am not jealous of Madeleine's friends. I never worry about what she does. She comes in and goes out at her pleasure, and yet the recollection of that beast Charles puts me in a rage."

He reasoned with himself :

" At bottom Forestier was no better than an idiot, and it is that idea that hurts my feelings. It vexes me to think that Madeleine could ever have married such a fool."

And incessantly he kept saying to himself :

" How on earth could a woman like that put up with such a nonentity ? "

His rancour was augmented daily by a thousand insignificant details which pierced him like pin-pricks, Forestier being incessantly recalled to his mind by a chance word from Madeleine or the man-servant or the housemaid.

One evening Du Roy, who was fond of sweets asked :

" Why don't we have sweets for dinner ? You never order them."

His wife replied lightly :

" It is quite true. It didn't occur to me. That is because Charles hated them."

He interrupted her with an uncontrollable gesture of impatience.

" You know, Charles is beginning to get on my nerves.

It is always Charles here and Charles there, Charles liked this and Charles liked that. Now that Charles has snuffed out, suppose we let him be."

Madeleine looked at her husband with stupefaction, understanding nothing of his sudden anger. But with her fine sensibility she divined more or less this slow working of posthumous jealousy which was momentarily augmented by all that recalled Forestier. She thought it puerile, perhaps, but it flattered her. She made no reply.

Du Roy himself felt mortified at the irritation which he had been unable to conceal. Then, that evening after dinner, as they were writing an article for the following day, he fell foul of the foot-muff. He could not manage to turn it over, so he kicked it away with his foot and asked with a laugh :

" Charles always had cold paws, had he ? "

Laughing in her turn Madeleine replied :

" Oh, he lived in terror of catching cold. His chest wasn't strong."

Du Roy retorted savagely :

" He has proved that, anyhow." Then he added with gallantry, " Happily for me." And he kissed his wife's hand.

But when they went to bed, he was still haunted by the same thought.

" Did Charles," he asked, " wear cotton nightcaps to keep the draughts out of his ears ? "

She lent herself to his frivolous humour and replied :

" No. He wore an Indian handkerchief with the knot tied on his forehead."

George shrugged his shoulders and said with the air of a man who was above that sort of thing.

" What a muff ! "

From that time onward Charles was the constant subject of his discourse. He never lost a chance of dragging him in, and he never alluded to him except as " poor Charles," with an air of infinity pity. When he came home from the office where he had heard himself addressed two or three times as Forestier, he took his revenge by pursuing the deceased into his tomb with odious mockery. He recalled his defects, his absurdities, his smallnesses, went over them one by one complacently, making the most of them and exaggerating them as though to combat in his wife's heart the influence of a redoubtable rival.

" I say, Madeleine," he would ask, " do you remember the day when that green-horn Forestier wanted to prove to us that fat men were more energetic than thin ones ? "

Next he wanted to know a number of intimate and secret details about the deceased, but Madeleine did not like this and refused to tell him. But he insisted obstinately :

" Come along now, tell me all about it. He must have looked jolly funny when he was doing that."

She replied pettishly :

" Can't you leave him alone now ? "

" No, do tell me," he urged. " He must have been a clumsy animal to go to bed with."

And always he ended up with the same remark :

" What a silly ass he was ! "

One evening towards the end of June as he was smoking a cigarette at the window, the fine weather suggested a drive and he said :

" Madeleine, my dear, would you like to come as far as the Bois ? "

" Yes, very much."

They took an open carriage and drove to the Champs-Elysées and the avenue of the Bois de Boulogne. It was a windless night, one of those nights when Paris is like a sweating-room and the overheated air enters one's lungs like hot blasts from a kiln. A fleet of hackney-carriages was conveying a whole host of lovers to the wood. The carriages moved on in an endless file one behind the other.

George and Madeleine were diverted by the sight of all these couples with their arms round each other, the women in light coloured dresses and the men in dark suits. It was an immense stream of lovers pouring towards the Bois under the hot and starry sky. No sound could be heard except the dull rolling of wheels on the ground On and on they passed, one couple to each carriage, lying back on the cushions, not saying one word, pressed against each other, lost in the hallucination of desire, trembling in the expectation of the coming embrace. The warm darkness seemed full of kisses. A flood of tender sensation, a universal sexual yearning, permeated the air, rendered it heavy, stifling. All these linked couples, intoxicated with the same emotion, with the same ardour, created a surrounding atmosphere that pulsated with febrile warmth. This swarm of vehicles, all laden with love, pullulating with caresses, gave out, as it passed along, a sort of sensual emanation, subtle and disturbing.

George and Madeleine felt themselves yielding to this contagion of tenderness. They clasped hands gently and in silence, somewhat subdued by the heaviness of the atmosphere and by the emotion that was penetrating them. As they arrived at the turning which leads along by the fortifications, they kissed each other and Madeleine murmured somewhat shamefacedly :

" Really this is hardly decent. It's as bad as our journey to Rouen."

The great stream of vehicles divided up when it came to the coppices. In the Chemin des Lacs which the Du Roys took, the carriages fell farther apart. The dense shade of the trees, the freshening of the air by the foliage and by the humidity of the brooks heard trickling beneath the branches, the coolness of a large open space at night, all decked with stars, lent a more penetrating sweetness, a more mysterious darkness, to the embraces of those who drove past, two by two.

" Oh, my little Madeleine," murmured George, pressing her closer to him.

" You remember," she said, " the forest near your home, how sinister it was ? It seemed to me to be thronged with terrifying beasts. It seemed to go on and on for ever. But here it is charming. The wind is caressing and it is a comfort to know that Sèvres is just beyond the trees."

" In the forest near my home," he replied, " there is nothing but red deer and foxes and roe and wild-boar and here and there the house of a *forestier*."

This word, the name of her dead husband, gave him a

shock, as if someone had shouted it at him from the depths of a thicket. He fell abruptly silent. Again he felt himself under the sway of that strange and obstinate discomfort, that jealous, gnawing, insuperable irritation which had been spoiling his life for some time.

A minute later he asked :

" Did you ever come here at night like this, with Charles ? "

" Yes, often," she replied.

On this he was seized by a sudden desire to go home ; a nervous desire which gave him a feeling of constriction to his heart. But the image of Forestier had come back to his mind and taken firm possession of it. He could think and speak of nothing but Forestier.

" I say, Madeleine," he said in a spiteful tone.

" Yes, dear ? "

" Did you ever deceive that poor beggar ? "

" How silly you are, always harping on him."

But he stuck to his idea.

" Look here, darling. Be quite frank, own up. You made a fool of him, didn't you ? Confess that you made a fool of him."

Shocked as all women are by the suggestion, she was silent, and he resumed obstinately :

" By Jove, if any man had a head for that decoration, he had. Of course. Yes, yes. If there's one thing that would amuse me it would be to know that Forestier had been made a fool of. Eh ? The silly mug ! "

He was conscious that she was smiling, possibly at some recollection, and he insisted :

" Come now, speak up. What does it matter ? On the contrary, I should think it an excellent joke if you confessed that you had deceived him ; confessed it to me, I mean, to me."

He was simply quivering with the hope and desire that Charles, that odious Charles, the detested and execrated deceased, should prove to have incurred this ridiculous and shameful fate. And yet—and yet, there was a second and vaguer emotion spurring him on in his desire to know.

" Madeleine, my sweet Madeleine," he urged, " tell me,

I beg you. He was just the man for it. It would be simply a sin if you hadn't given him that to wear. Come, darling, tell me."

It seemed clear that she did not find this insistence disagreeable for she was laughing short staccato laughs. He put his lips close to his wife's ear :

" Come now, tell me."

She drew away from him with a sharp movement, and exclaimed abruptly :

" How silly you are. Who would think of replying to questions like that ? "

She said it in a tone so peculiar that a cold shudder ran through his veins and he remained confounded, alarmed, a little breathless, as if he had received a moral concussion.

The carriage was now proceeding along the edge of the lake, into which the sky seemed to have shed its stars. Two spectral swans, hardly visible in the obscurity, were swimming about slowly.

" Home ! " cried George to the driver, and the carriage turned, meeting other carriages that were moving at a walk, their great lamps shining like eyes in the darkness of the Bois.

" How curious her manner had been when she made that remark ! Was it a confession ? " he asked himself.

It was almost a certainty that she had been untrue to her first husband, and the thought was now putting him in a frenzy of rage. He wanted to beat her, strangle her, tear her hair out. If she had only replied : " My dearest one, if I had ever thought of deceiving him it would have been with you," how he would have kissed and clasped and adored her !

He sat motionless with his arms crossed, looking at the sky, his mind too much agitated for reflection. All that he felt was the fermenting in him of that rancour and anger, which smoulder in the hearts of all males at the caprices of feminine desire. For the first time in his life he was experiencing the distraught anguish of the suspicious husband. He was neither more nor less than jealous, and his jealousy was for the sake of a dead man, it was on behalf of Forestier ! It was a strange and poignant emotion and into it entered a sudden hatred of Madeleine. She had been untrue to the other man ; how could he himself have any confidence in her ?

After that, little by little, a sort of calm came over his spirit. Bracing himself against his suffering, he reflected :

" All women are rotters ; the right thing to do is to make use of them and give them nothing of oneself."

The bitterness of his heart rose to his lips in words of contempt and disgust, but for the present he managed to keep them to himself. He said inwardly :

" The world is to the strong. The one thing necessary is to be strong and have everything under one's feet."

The carriage was moving more rapidly ; it passed the fortifications again. Looking straight in front of him, Du Roy saw in the sky a ruddy glow like the reflection of a gigantic blast-furnace, and he heard a confused uproar, vast, continuous, made up of innumerable different noises, clamorous yet dull, near yet distant, a vague and prodigious pulsation of life, Paris breathing and panting in the summer night, like a Colossus exhausted with fatigue. He reflected :

" I should be a fool to get angry about it. Every man for himself. Victory is to the bold. Everything is simply egoism. And the egoism that pursues fame and fortune is of more account than the egoism that pursues women and love."

The Arc de Triomphe came in sight as they approached the town. Erect on its two monstrous legs it seemed a sort of misshapen Titan, about to set out on a march down the long avenue that lay open before it. Again George and Madeleine took their place in the procession of carriages, each with its silent amorous couple, driving homewards to bed. The whole human race, intoxicated with joy, pleasure and happiness, seemed to be gliding along with them.

Madeleine, who had divined something of her husband's thoughts, asked him gently :

" What are you thinking of, my dear ? You haven't said a word for half an hour."

With a sneering laugh he replied :

" I was thinking of all these cuddling fools and I was

saying to myself that really there are other things to do in life."

"Yes," she murmured, "but sometimes this is good."

"Good? Yes, good, when there is nothing better."

His thoughts pursued their course, in a sort of perverse rage, stripping life of its garment of poetry:

"I should simply be a fool to go on worrying and doing without things and fretting and bothering and eating my soul out the way I have been doing for some time."

The image of Forestier flashed on his mind, but it no longer caused him any irritation. He and Forestier seemed somehow to have affected a reconciliation; they were friends again. He felt like calling out a greeting to him.

Madeleine was annoyed by his silence.

"Suppose," she suggested, "before returning home we go and have an ice at Tortoni's."

He cast a side-glance at her. Her clear-cut profile was lighted up by the brilliant glare of a wreath of gas jets which advertised a café-chantant. "She is pretty," he reflected. "And so much the better. Set a thief to catch a thief. But if anybody finds me tormenting myself on your account, you can look for heat at the North Pole."

"Certainly, my darling," he replied.

And he kissed her, to keep her from guessing anything. It seemed to Madeleine that her husband's lips were cold as ice. But when he gave her his hand to help her out of the carriage at the café, his lips wore their customary smile.

III

WHEN Du Roy arrived at the office on the following day, he went to Boisrenard and said to him :

" My dear fellow, I want you to do something for me. For some time past people have been thinking it amusing to call me Forestier. I am beginning to find it a bore. Will you be so kind as to let our friends know quietly, that I propose to box the ears of the first man who indulges himself again in that pleasantry ? It will be for them to consider whether it's worth crossing swords for. I am addressing myself to you because you don't get excited, and will be able to prevent things going too far, and also because you have already acted as my second."

Boisrenard accepted the charge. Du Roy went out to do his rounds, and on his return an hour later no one ventured to call him Forestier.

On reaching home, he heard women's voices in the drawing-room and asked who was there. The servant replied :

" Madame Walter and Madame de Marelle." His heart beat a little more rapidly. Then he said to himself, " Come, we'll see," and opened the door.

Clotilde was in the corner by the fire-place. A bright light from the window shone on her. It seemed to George that she turned a little pale when she saw him come in. After shaking hands with Madame Walter and her two daughters who were seated like sentinels one on each side of their mother, he turned towards Clotilde. She stretched out her hand to him and he took it and pressed it significantly as though to say, " I love you always." She returned the pressure.

" You have been quite well since we last met ?   It is a century ago."

She replied without embarrassment :

" Yes, very well, thank you.   And you, Bel-Ami ? "
Then she turned to Madeleine and said :

" You don't mind my still calling him Bel-Ami ? "

" Not at all, my dear.   You can call him what you please."   There seemed a shade of irony lurking in her remark.   Madame Walter spoke of an entertainment which Jacques Rival was going to give in his bachelor quarters. It was to be a great assault-at-arms and society ladies were to be present.

" It will be very interesting," she said.   " But I am in despair because we have no one to take us, as my husband will be away."

Du Roy immediately offered his services, which were accepted.

" My daughters and I will be very grateful to you," she said.

He looked at the younger of the two girls.

" That little Suzanne," he thought, " really isn't at all bad."

She had the air of a fragile fair-haired doll, somewhat too small, but finely made ; her figure was slight, slender in the hips and bust ; she had a face like a miniature, with eyes of blue-grey enamel finished off with a subtle, fanciful brush.   Her skin was excessively white, smooth and polished, without a flaw or hint of colour, and her hair was fluffy, curly, a sophisticated mop, an airy fascinating cirrhus, exactly similar in effect to the heads of hair that one sees on expensive dolls carried by little girls who are not nearly as big as their playthings.

The elder sister, Rose, was plain, dull and insignificant ; she was one of those girls whom no one notices, speaks to, or talks about.

Madame Walter rose and turned to George :

" Well then, I shall expect you next Thursday at two o'clock."

" You can depend on me," he replied.

As soon as Madame Walter had left, Madame de Marelle, too, rose to go.

" Au revoir, Bel-Ami."

It was now her turn to bestow upon him a long firm pressure of her hand, and he felt himself thrilled by this silent avowal. He was seized again by a sudden passion for this little middle-class Bohemian, who was such a good sort and who, it was possible, had a true affection for him.

" I shall go and see her to-morrow," he resolved.

As soon as he was alone with Madeleine, she began to laugh lightly and gaily. Looking him full in the face she said :

" Do you know that you have inspired a passion in Madame Walter."

" Nonsense," he replied incredulously.

" It is a fact, I assure you. She spoke about you to me with extravagant enthusiasm. It is singular of her. She said she would like to find two husbands like you for her daughters. Fortunately in her case things like that are of no importance."

He did not take her meaning.

" Of no importance ? How so ? "

She replied with the conviction of a woman sure of her judgment :

" Oh, Madame Walter is one of those women who have never been gossiped about. Never, never, you understand. She is impregnable in every respect. As for her husband, you know him as well as I do. But she is quite a different sort. She has gone through a good deal too for marrying a Jew, but she has remained true to him. She is absolutely straight."

Duroy expressed his surprise :

" I thought she was Jewish too."

" She ? Not at all. She is patroness to all the good works at the Madeleine. She even insisted on a religious marriage ceremony. I can't tell you whether her husband went through any form of baptism or whether the Church winked at it."

" Ah, indeed "—said George, " and she—she has taken a fancy to me ? "

" Absolutely and completely. If you weren't already married I should advise you to ask for the hand of—of Suzanne, I should say, rather than Rose."

Twisting his moustaches, he replied :

" Well, the mother isn't a backnumber yet."

But Madeleine said impatiently :

" As for the mother, my dear, get her if you can. I'm not afraid. It is not at her age that one goes wrong for the first time. You have to take to it earlier than that."

" All the same," George reflected, " suppose it's true that I could have married Suzanne." He shrugged his shoulders. " Pooh, what nonsense. Her father would not have looked at me."

Nevertheless he resolved henceforth to observe carefully Madame Walter's manner towards him. He had not as yet, however, asked himself of what advantage her affection would be.

All that evening he was haunted by recollections of his affair with Clotilde, and by memories at once tender and sensual. He recalled how droll and charming she was, and what fun they had had.

" She is really very sweet," he said to himself. " Yes, I shall go and see her to-morrow."

On the following day, immediately after luncheon, he carried out his intention of going to the Rue Verneuil. The same maid opened the door to him, and with the familiarity common in the servants of lower middle-class housemaids, she asked him how he was.

" Very well, my dear," he replied.

He entered the drawing-room where someone was playing scales on the piano with unpractised hands. It was Laurine. He had expected her to throw her arms round his neck. But she rose solemnly, made a ceremonious bow like a grown-up person, and quitted the room with dignity. She had so much of the air of a woman who has been affronted that he was struck with surprise. Her mother came in and he caught and kissed her hands.

" How much I have been thinking of you," he said.

" And I of you," she replied.

They seated themselves. They looked into each other's eyes, smiling, and with a desire to kiss each other.

" My dear little Clo, I love you."

" And I you."

" Then—then, you haven't been bearing me any ill will ? "

" Yes and no. It did hurt me, what you did, but I understood your reasons and I said to myself that some day or other you would come back to me."

" I was afraid to come back. I couldn't say what sort of reception I would get. I was afraid, but I wanted to terribly. By the way, tell me what is wrong with Laurine. She would hardly say how d'you do to me, and she took herself off like a fury."

" I can't say, but since your marriage she won't hear you spoken of. I really think she is jealous."

" Oh, come now ! "

" Yes, really, my dear. She doesn't call you Bel-Ami any longer. She calls you Monsieur Forestier."

Du Roy reddened. He came closer to Clotilde :

" Your mouth, please."

She gave it to him.

" Where can we see each other again ? "

" Why—the Rue Constantinople."

" Ah, the flat hasn't been let yet ? "

" No, I kept it on."

" You kept it on ? "

" Yes. I thought you would come back."

He heaved a breath of joy and pride. Here indeed was a woman who loved him with a deep, true, constant love.

" I adore you," he murmured. Then he asked : " Is your husband all right ? "

" Yes, thank you. He has just spent a month with me. He left the day before yesterday."

Du Roy could not help laughing.

" That chimes in splendidly."

" Yes, indeed it does," she replied artlessly. " But all the same you understand, don't you, that he doesn't interfere with me when he is here ? "

" I'm positive of that.   He's a delightful fellow."

" And you," she asked, " how are you taking to your new life ? "

" Neither well nor ill.   My wife is a comrade, a partner."

" Nothing more ? "

" Nothing more.   As for her heart . . . "

" I understand perfectly.   She is very sweet, none the less."

" Yes, but I don't find her exciting."

He came closer to Clotilde and asked in a low voice :

" When are we going to meet again ? "

" To-morrow, if you like."

" Yes, to-morrow.   At two o'clock ? "

" Two o'clock."

As he rose to go, he said hesitatingly, with a shade of annoyance :

" You know, I propose to take that flat in the Rue de Constantinople in my own name.   I insist upon it.   It would be the last straw if you were to pay for that."

It was her turn now to kiss his hands with a movement of adoration.

" You shall do as you please," she said.   " It is enough for me to have kept it for us to meet in again."

Du Roy went away well content.

As he was passing in front of a photographer's show-case, he was reminded of Madame Walter by the portrait of a big woman with large eyes.

" After all," he mused, " she ought to be passable still. How did it happen that I never noticed her ?   I am anxious to see what sort of reception she will give me on Thursday."

He rubbed his hands together and marched along with an inward joy, the joy of success in all its forms, the egotistic joy of the adroit man who succeeds, and the subtle joy, composed of flattered vanity and gratified sensuality which is conferred by the affection of women.

When Thursday came he said to Madeleine :

" You are not coming to this assault-at-arms at Rival's ? "

" Oh, no.   That sort of thing doesn't amuse me at all. I shall go to the Chamber of Deputies."

It was beautiful weather and he went to call for Madame Walter in an open landau. When he saw her he was surprised at the beauty and youthfulness of her appearance. She was wearing a light-coloured dress, with the corsage a little open, and the voluptuous contours of her bosom were just visible under filmy white lace. She had never seemed to him so young and fresh, and to his thinking she was eminently desirable. She had a quiet and correct air of her own, and a calm matronly way with her which had the effect of causing her to pass almost unnoticed by ladies' men. She had moreover the habit of conversing only on topics that were common property, conventional, and in restrained taste, her ideas being circumspect, methodical, well-ordered, and carefully moderated.

Her daughter Suzanne was dressed in pink and resembled a freshly varnished Watteau. The elder daughter was like the governess-companion to this pretty little doll.

There was a file of carriages drawn up in front of Rival's door. Du Roy offered his arm to Madame Walter and they went in.

The assault-at-arms was given for the benefit of the orphans of the sixth arrondissement of Paris, and was under the patronage of the wives of the senators and deputies who were connected with the *Vie Française.*

Madame Walter had promised to bring her daughters, but had refused the title of lady patroness, because she only lent her name to works undertaken by the clergy. This was not because she was exceptionally pious, but she believed that her marriage with a Jew forced her to adopt a certain religious attitude, and the entertainment organised by Rival had a sort of republican significance which might be deemed anti-clerical.

For the past three weeks the following notice had appeared in newspapers of all shades of opinion :

"Our eminent colleague Jacques Rival has just thought of a scheme as ingenious as it is generous. He proposes to organise, on behalf of the orphans of the sixth arrondissement of Paris, a grand assault-at-arms in the charming *salle d'armes* attached to his bachelor flat. Invitations are issued by

Mesdames Laloigne, Remontel, Rissolin, the wives of the senators bearing these names, and by Mesdames Laroche-Mathieu, Percerol, Firmin, the wives of the well-known deputies. There will be one collection only, which will take place during the interval of the assault-at-arms, and the amount collected will be immediately placed in the hands of the Mayor of the arrondissement or his representative."

The whole thing was a vast advertisement which the adroit pressman had conceived for his own advantage.

Jacques Rival received the guests in the hall of his flat where he had installed a buffet of which the expenses were to be met from the collection. Then with a hospitable gesture he pointed out the small staircase leading down to the cellar where he had installed the *salle d'armes* and the shooting gallery, and he said :

" Downstairs, please, ladies, downstairs. The assault-at-arms will take place in the subterranean apartments."

He darted forward to receive Madame Walter and then shook hands with Du Roy :

" How do you do, Bel-Ami ? "

Du Roy in surprise asked :

" Who told you that——"

Rival interrupted him :

" It was Madame Walter here. She thinks it's a very nice nickname."

Madame Walter blushed.

" I confess, if I knew you better, I should do like little Laurine and call you Bel-Ami. It suits you very well."

" Then pray do so, Madame Walter," said Du Roy, laughing.

She cast down her eyes.

" No, we are not intimate enough."

" May I hope," he said, " that we may become more so ? "

" Perhaps," she replied, " we shall see later on."

As they descended the narrow, gas-lighted staircase, he kept himself in the background. The abrupt transition from daylight to this yellow illumination had in it a touch of the lugubrious. An underground odour came up the spiral staircase, a warm, damp smell of mould-covered walls that had been brushed clean for the occasion. There were also whiffs of gum benjamin which recalled church services, and there were feminine emanations of eau de Lubin, verbena, orris-root and violet. From this den arose a great clamour of voices and the agitation of an excited crowd.

The whole cellar was illuminated with gas crescents and Venetian lanterns concealed in the foliage with which the nitre-encrusted walls were screened. Nothing was visible but this greenery. The ceiling was adorned with ferns and the ground was covered with leaves and flowers. Everyone was charmed and thought it revealed an exquisite imagination. In the small cellar at the farther end a stage had been erected for the competitors, with two rows of chairs for the judges. The total seating accommodation of the cave was about two hundred and consisted of benches in rows of ten, equally divided on either side of the cellar. Four hundred people had been invited.

In front of the stage the young competitors, slim, long-limbed, with chests thrown out, and moustaches with turned-up ends, were already posing, in their fencing costumes, before the spectators, who picked them out by name and pointed out the professionals and the amateurs, all the notabilities of the fencing world. Around them frock-coated gentlemen of all ages, who had a family likeness to the men in fighting costume, were engaged in conversation. These also were not averse to being seen and recognised and mentioned by name ; they were the masters of the foils in plain dress, the experts in fencing.

Almost all the benches were filled with ladies, from whom arose a great rustling of dresses and a loud murmur of voices. They fanned themselves as at a theatre, for this leafy grotto had already the heat of a vapour bath. A wag in the audience called out from time to time :

" Orgeat, lemonade, beer ! "

Madame Walter and her daughters reached their reserved seats in the front row. Du Roy, having seen them safely there, prepared to depart.

" I have to leave you," he said ; " men are not allowed to take up room on the benches."

Madame Walter replied hesitatingly :

" I should like very much to keep you here all the same. You could tell me who the fencers are. Look, if you were to stand at the corner of this bench, you wouldn't be in anybody's way."

She looked at him with her large soft eyes, and insisted :

" Do stay with us, Monsieur—Monsieur Bel-Ami. We need you."

" I shall obey with pleasure, Madame Walter," he replied.

On all sides could be heard the words :

" It is very quaint, this cellar, quite a good idea."

This vaulted hall was perfectly familiar to George. He recalled the morning he had spent there the day before his duel, all by himself, facing the little white disc that like an enormous and terrifying eye stared at him from the far end of the smaller cellar.

Jacques Rival's voice rang out from the staircase :

" Ladies, the assault-at-arms is about to begin."

Six gentlemen, in clothes that fitted them so tightly as to make their chests more prominent, mounted the stage and took their places on the chairs assigned to the jury. Their names ran as follows : General de Reynaldi, a little man with a heavy moustache ; the painter Joseph Roudet, a tall bald man with a long beard ; Matthéo de Ujar, Simon Ramoncel, Pierre de Carvin, three young men of fashion ; and Gaspard Merleron, a master of fencing.

Two labels were suspended on either side of the recess. That on the right bore the name Monsieur Crèvecœur and that on the left, Monsieur Plumeau.

These two men were masters, good men of the second rank, of lean build, with a military air and gestures inclining to stiffness. Having made the salute with movements like automata they began to attack, looking, in their costume of cloth and white leather, very like a couple of pierrot soldiers fighting for fun.

Every now and then was heard the word *Touché*. And the six gentlemen of the jury leaned their heads forward with the air of connoisseurs. All that the public could see was two living marionettes dancing about, each with an arm out-stretched. The spectators understood nothing, but were perfectly satisfied. None the less, these two worthy men, far from being particularly graceful, were in a vague way absurd. They made one think of the wooden wrestlers sold on the Boulevards on New Year's Day.

The first pair were succeeded by Monsieur Planton and Monsieur Carapin, fencing masters, the former civil, the latter military. Monsieur Planton was quite small and Monsieur Carapin very big. One would have thought that the first touch with the foil would have deflated this balloon of a man like an elephant made of goldbeater's skin. There was a general laugh. Monsieur Planton skipped here and there like a monkey. Monsieur Carapin made no movement except with his arm. The rest of his body was immobilised through his corpulence. During the five minutes' bout he lunged with such weightiness and with so strenuous a forward effort that he seemed to be taking the most energetic resolution of his life. He had great difficulty in recovering after a lunge. But the connoisseurs declared his sword-play to have been very firm and close, and the public accepted their verdict and accorded their appreciation.

These two were followed by Monsieur Porion and Monsieur Lapalme, a professional and an amateur, who threw themselves without restraint into an exhibition of acrobatics. They ran at each other with fury and forced the judges to retreat for safety, taking their chairs with them. They went the whole length of the stage, backwards and forwards, one advancing and the other retreating by vigorous and comical bounds. They indulged in little backward leaps which made the ladies laugh, but they also frightened them a little with great forward rushes. This acrobatic display provoked some unknown wag to call out, " Don't break your backs. You're working by the hour." The spectators were offended by this lack of taste and said " Hush." The judgment of the experts was passed round among the audience. It was that the fencers had shown great vigour, but that it was not always quite effective.

The first part of the programme closed with a very fine

passage at arms between Jacques Rival and the famous Belgian professor, Lebègue. Rival was much appreciated by the ladies. He was really a fine young man, well built, supple, agile, and more graceful than those who had preceded him. In his manner of standing on guard and lungeing he displayed a certain pleasing elegance of style which was a contrast to the energetic but less polished bearing of his adversary. The remark went round, " You can see he is a gentleman." He won the best of three, and there was general applause.

For some minutes an extraordinary clamour coming from the floor above had been causing uneasiness among the spectators. People were stamping loudly to the accompaniment of bursts of noisy laughter. Doubtless the two hundred invited ones who had been excluded from the cellar were amusing themselves in their own fashion. There were about fifty men packed into the little spiral staircase. The heat below became terrible. There were cries of " More air," " Something to drink," and the same wag kept yelping in a shrill tone that was heard above all the conversation : " Orgeat, lemonade, beer ! "

Rival looked very red in the face ; he had kept on his fencing costume.

" I am going to have some refreshments brought," he said, and he ran to the staircase. But all communication with the ground floor was blocked. It would have been as easy to make a way through the ceiling as through the human wall piled up on the stairs.

" Pass down some ices for the ladies," Rival shouted, and fifty voices echoed, " Ices, ices," and a tray at last made its appearance, but there was nothing but empty glasses on it, the refreshments having vanished on the way down.

Somebody bellowed in a loud voice : " They are all being suffocated in there. Let us stop the show and get away."

Another person shouted : " The collection." And all present, gasping yet gay, caught up the cry, " The collection, the collection."

Six ladies began to walk round among the benches and the tinkle of silver dropping into collection bags was heard.

Meanwhile Du Roy was telling Madame Walter the names of the celebrities. There were people of fashion ; and newspaper men, on the staff of important, old-established journals. They looked down on the *Vie Française*, with a certain reserve which was the fruit of long experience. They had witnessed the extinction of so many of these politico-financial sheets of ambiguous origin, collapsing with the fall of a ministry. There were also painters present, and sculptors, who are in general addicted to sport ; a poet, who was a member of the Academy, and two musicians, and a number of distinguished foreigners, to whose names Du Roy added the syllable Rast, to indicate the foreign adventurers known as Rastaquouères, and in imitation, as he said, of the English who put Esq. on their cards.

He heard someone greeting him :

" My dear fellow, how are you ? "

It was Count de Vaudrec. Du Roy made his excuses to the ladies and went to shake hands with the Count. When he came back he declared :

" Vaudrec is a charming fellow. He has such an air of breeding."

Madame Walter made no reply. She was a little tired, and her bosom rose with the effort of breathing. This attracted Du Roy's attention. From time to time he met her glance, a glance full of agitation and doubt, a glance that rested upon him only to take flight at once.

" I wonder, I wonder," he reflected. " Can it be that I have flushed this bird too ? "

The collectors passed by, their bags full of silver and gold. A new ticket was hung up on the platform announcing, " A Great Surprise." The members of the jury returned to their places. There was a pause. Two women appeared with foils in their hands. They were dressed in gymnasium costume, black tights, very short skirts reaching half-way down the thighs, and on their chests a fencing-pad which was so thick that it forced up their chins. They were young and pretty, and they smiled as they saluted the audience. They were received with prolonged applause.

They threw themselves on guard, to the accompaniment

of a buzz of compliments and whispered pleasantries. An amiable smile settled on the faces of the judges, who applauded successful thrusts with little bravos.

The audience, delighted with this bout, conveyed their appreciation to the two combatants, who appealed to the passions of the men and gratified in the women the natural taste of the Parisian public for diversions that are not quite nice, for refinements that are a trifle vulgar, for the mock-pretty and the sham-graceful, café-concert music and operetta poetry. Every time one of these performers lunged, a tremor of joy coursed through the spectators. The one who turned her back—and a lusty back it was—to the hall provoked a gaping of mouths and a rounding of eyes ; and it was not the play of her wrist that attracted most attention. They were applauded madly.

A bout with sabres succeeded, but no one looked at it, for the attention of all was distracted by what was going on upstairs. For some minutes they had been listening to a great noise of furniture being shifted and dragged over the floor, as if a removal was going on. Then suddenly the sound of piano-playing was heard through the ceiling, and the rhythmic fall of feet dancing in time became distinctly audible. The people upstairs were getting up a dance for themselves as a compensation for having seen nothing. At first there was a great burst of laughter in the *salle d'armes*, but presently the women wanted to go and dance and they no longer paid any attention to what was happening on the stage, but began to talk at the top of their voices. That the late arrivals should get up a dance struck them as a droll idea. They had evidently no intention of being bored. It must be rather fun to be up there.

But two new combatants had saluted each other and taken up their positions so authoritatively that all eyes followed their movements. They lunged and recovered with elastic grace, with controlled energy, with such sure use of their strength, such sobriety of gesture, such correctness of demeanour, such measured mastery in their play, that even the ignorant throng were astonished and delighted. Their calm readiness, their cautious adroitness, their rapid movements, so under control as to seem leisurely, attracted and captivated the eye by their mere perfection. The spectators realised that they were witnessing a rare and beautiful thing. Two men, great artists in their profession, were showing them the finest of all sights, all that it lay in the power of two masters to display of skill, cunning, reasoned knowledge and physical dexterity. So closely were they watched that conversation ceased. Then, after the last thrust of the foils, when the combatants had shaken hands, there was an outburst of shouts and hurrahs. People stamped and roared. The names of the combatants were known to all ; they were Sergent and Ravignac.

Excitement made men quarrelsome, and they looked at their neighbours with a desire to fall out with them. A smile would have roused them. Men who had never held a fencing-foil in their hands were demonstrating thrusts and parries with their walking-sticks.

Little by little however, the crowd made its way up the small staircase. There was general indignation when it was found that the dancing people, after stripping the buffet, had gone away declaring that it was uncivil to put two hundred people to so much trouble and then show them nothing. Not a cake was left, not a drop of champagne, liqueur, or beer, not a sweetmeat or a fruit, nothing, not the ghost of anything. Everything had been plundered, ravaged, swept clean. They had the details from servants who kept serious faces which concealed their wish to laugh.

" The ladies were even more furious than the men," they declared. " They ate and drank in a way to make themselves ill."

It was like listening to tales of survivors after the sack and pillage of a town in 1870. However, it was time to be off. Some regretted the louis they had contributed to the collection and were indignant because those upstairs had junketed without paying.

The lady patronesses had collected over three thousand francs. When all costs had been defrayed the orphans of the sixth arrondissement benefited to the extent of two hundred and twenty francs.

Du Roy, in attendance upon the Walter family, was awaiting his landau. As he drove away with Madame Walter he was seated facing her and again he met her caressing but timid and confused glance.

" By Jove," he reflected, " I believe she is nibbling."

He smiled as he realised how fortunate he was with women. Madame de Marelle, too, since the renewal of their tender relations, seemed to be madly in love with him. It was with a joyful step that he entered his house.

Madeleine was awaiting him in the drawing-room.

" I have news for you," she announced. " The Morocco business is getting complicated. It is quite on the cards that France will send an expedition there in a few months' time. In any case it will give us a good handle for upsetting the ministry, and Laroche will seize the opportunity to become Foreign Minister."

To tease his wife, Du Roy pretended not to believe a word of it. No one would be such a madman as to begin that Tunis folly over again. But she shrugged her shoulders impatiently.

" I tell you it is so, it is so. You don't seem to understand that it is simply a question of money with them. Nowadays, my dear, when political complications arise you don't say ' *Cherchez la femme*,' you try to ferret out the business interests."

" Pooh ! " he ejaculated, assuming an air of contempt in order to annoy her.

" Really," she exclaimed with irritation, " You are as green as Forestier."

Her desire was to wound him and she expected an outburst of anger, but he only smiled.

" As green as the man you made a fool of ? "

She was shocked.

" Oh, George ! "

With an insolent, jeering air he went on :

" Well what about it ? Didn't you own up to me the other evening that you had ? "

And he added : " Poor devil ! " in a tone of profound compassion.

Disdaining to reply, Madeleine turned her back on him, but after a momentary silence she resumed :

" We are having some people here on Tuesday. Madame Laroche-Matthieu and the Viscountess de Percemur are coming to dinner. Will you invite Rival and Norbert de Varenne ? To-morrow I will go and invite Madame Walter and Madame de Marelle. Perhaps we could have Madame Rissolin too."

She had for some time been cultivating relations with people of note and making use of her husband's political influence to attract to the house, either by inclination or expediency, the wives of senators and deputies who needed the support of the *Vie Française*.

" Very well," replied Du Roy, " I'll see about Rival and Norbert."

He rubbed his hands with satisfaction at the thought of having discovered a goad with which to torment his wife and to gratify the obscure rancour, the vague gnawing jealousy he had conceived since that drive in the Bois. Henceforward he would never mention Forestier without this gibe at him, and he was convinced that in the long run it would drive Madeleine to fury. No less than ten times that evening he managed to use, with ironical bonhomie, the expression " that poor fool Forestier."

No longer did he entertain any grudge against the deceased ; on the contrary, he was avenging him. His wife pretended not to understand and faced him with smiling unconcern.

On the following day, as his wife was about to address her invitation to Madame Walter, it occurred to him to anticipate her in the hope that he might find Madame Walter alone and discover if she really had a predilection for him. The idea amused and flattered him. And after that . . . why not ? . . . if the thing was possible . . .

By two o'clock he was at the Boulevard Malesherbes ; he was shown into the drawing-room, and there he waited. Madame Walter appeared and shook hands with him with pleased cordiality.

" What good wind blows you here ? "

" No good wind, but my wish to see you. I felt that I had to come to you ; I don't know why. I have nothing to say to you. But I have come, and here I am. Will you pardon me for coming so early, and for the frankness of my explanation ? "

He spoke in a tone of playful gallantry ; with smiling lips but serious voice.

She was astonished, blushed a little, and faltered :

" But . . . really . . . I don't understand . . . you surprise me . . . "

" It is a declaration," he continued, " but I'm talking lightly, so as not to frighten you."

They had seated themselves close to each other. She treated the matter playfully.

" Indeed ! It is a declaration ? . . . Serious ? "

" Yes, certainly. I have been wanting to make it for a long time, oh, ever so long. But I hadn't the courage. People say you are so severe, so strict."

She had recovered her self-possession and replied :

" Why did you choose to-day ? "

" I don't know." Then he lowered his voice, " Or rather, it is because I can think of nothing but you, since yesterday."

She suddenly grew pale and she stammered :

" Now please, enough of this childishness. Let us talk of something else."

But he had thrown himself so suddenly on his knees that she was startled. She wanted to get up, but he held her in her chair by main force, clasping her in his arms.

" Yes," he urged in passionate tones, " It is true that I have long loved you to distraction. Don't answer me. I am mad. I love you. Oh, if you only knew how I loved you."

She was choking for breath ; she tried to speak, but could not say a word. She repulsed him with her hands, seized him by the hair to prevent the approach of his mouth, which she knew was coming closer and closer to her own. She turned her head from side to side rapidly, and closed her eyes so as to shut out further sight of him. He touched her through her dress, passed his hands over her, pressed her with his fingers, and she grew faint under his strong and brutal caresses. He rose hastily to his feet and would have embraced her but, freed for one second, she leaped backwards and escaped, fleeing from chair to chair. He thought it ridiculous to pursue her and he threw himself into a chair, buried his face in his hands, and feigned convulsive sobs. Then he rose to his feet, called out " Adieu, adieu," and fled. In the vestibule he picked up his walking-stick and he reached the street, he said :

" Good Lord, I believe I've done it this time."

Then he went along to the telegraph office to send a message to Clotilde, fixing an appointment for the next day.

When he arrived home at his usual hour he said to his wife :

" Have you got all your guests for your dinner ? "

" Yes," she replied, " Only Madame Walter isn't quite sure that she will be free. She is doubtful. She mentioned something, a previous engagement, some difficulty or other. To tell you the truth, her manner seemed to me rather odd. But never mind, I expect she'll come all the same."

" Of course she'll come," he said, shrugging his shoulders. But he was not sure of it, and until the day of the dinner party his mind was not at ease. But in the morning, Madeleine received a short note from Madame Walter :

I have managed to disengage myself though with great difficulty, and shall join your party. But my husband will not be able to come with me.

Du Roy thought to himself, " It was very wise of me not to go back there. She seems to have quieted down. Now go slow ! "

Nevertheless he awaited her arrival with a certain disquiet. Her demeanour was very calm, somewhat frigid and a little disdainful. He grew very humble and discreet and submissive.

Madame Laroche-Mathieu and Madame Rissolin were there with their husbands. Viscountess de Percemur talked about the aristocratic world. Madame de Marelle was ravishing in a fanciful and original gown of yellow and black, in Spanish style, which was closely moulded to her pretty figure, her bust and her dimpled arms, and which lent an air of pertness to her small bird-like head.

Du Roy had Madame Walter on his right and during dinner spoke to her of nothing but serious things and with exaggerated respect. Every now and then he cast a glance at Clotilde.

"Really," he thought, "she is prettier and fresher than ever."

Then his eyes would turn again to his wife whom also he could not but admire, although he still nursed against her a suppressed anger, tenacious and vindictive. But he was provoked by the difficulty he anticipated in Madame Walter's conquest and by that element of novelty which is ever an attraction to men. She wished to return home early and he offered to escort her, but she refused. He insisted :

"Why won't you let me ? You will hurt me very much. Do not let me think that you have not forgiven me. You see how calm I am."

"You cannot desert your guests," she replied.

He smiled :

"Pooh, I shall only be away twenty minutes. My absence won't even be noticed. If you refuse you will wound me to the heart."

"Very well," she said, "you can come."

But as soon as they were in the carriage, he seized her hand and kissed it passionately.

"I love you. I love you. Do not forbid me to tell you so. I won't touch you. I simply want to tell you again that I love you."

"Oh," she faltered, "after your promise . . . it is wrong, it is wrong."

Simulating a great effort, he resumed in a tone of restraint :

"Look ! you can see how I control myself. And yet . . . let me tell you this one thing, I love you . . . Suffer me to come every day and kneel at your feet for five minutes so that I may repeat those three words while I gaze on your adored face."

She had surrendered her hand to him and she replied with a catch in her breath :

"No. I cannot. I will not. Think what people would say. My servants, my daughters. No, no, it is impossible."

"I cannot live without seeing you. Either at your house or elsewhere I must see you, were it only for a minute a day. I must touch you hand, I must breathe the air your dress has stirred, I must gaze upon your form and your beautiful great eyes that drive me distracted."

She listened, trembling, to these commonplace outpourings of love and she replied in a broken voice :

"No, no. It is impossible. You mustn't talk like that."

He continued to whisper softly in her ear, realising that a woman of her simple nature must be captured by degrees, that he must persuade her first to accord him rendezvous where she wished, but afterwards, as it pleased him.

"Listen. It must be. I must see you. I shall wait outside your door, like a beggar. If you don't come down to me, I shall go in. But see you I must, to-morrow."

But she said again :

"No, no. You must not come. I cannot receive you. Think of my daughters."

"Then tell me some place where I can meet you, in the street or anywhere, at any hour you please, as long as I see you. I shall greet you, I shall tell you I love you, and then I shall go away."

Bewildered, she hesitated, and as the carriage was passing through the gateway of her house, she said in a quick whisper :

"Very well, I shall be at the Trinity Church to-morrow at half-past three."

When she had stepped out of the carriage she ordered the coachman to take Monsieur Du Roy home. On his return his wife asked him where he had been.

He replied in a low voice :

"I went to the telegraph office to send an urgent message."

Madame de Marelle came up to him.

"You must take me back, Bel-Ami. You know it is only on that condition that I dine out so far from home."

Then she turned to Madeleine.

"You are not jealous?"

Madame Du Roy replied deliberately:

"No. Not very."

The guests took their leave. Madame Laroche-Mathieu looked like a little maidservant from the provinces. She was a notary's daughter whom Laroche had married while he was yet an obscure advocate. Madame Rissolin, full of years and affectation, gave the impression of an ex-midwife who had picked up her education in public reading rooms. Viscountess de Percemur looked down her nose at them. Her "pale hands" shrank from the touch of their plebeian fingers.

Clotilde, swathed in lace, said to Madeleine, as she was passing through the door opening on to the staircase:

"Your dinner was perfect. You will presently be having the first political *salon* in Paris."

As soon as she was alone with George, she clasped him in her arms.

"Oh, my dear Bel-Ami, I love you more and more every day."

"This isn't as good as our room," she said.

"Oh no," he replied.

But he was thinking of Madame Walter

IV

THE Place de la Trinité was almost deserted under the blazing July sun. Paris lay crushed under overwhelming heat as if the upper air, grown heavy and parched, had sunk down on the city, a sluggish and baking atmosphere making it difficult to breathe.

The water of the fountain in front of the church fell in languid trickles that seemed too tired to flow, they were so slow and feeble, and the liquid in the basin of the fountain, in which leaves and scraps of paper were floating, looked thick and of a bluish grey.

A dog had jumped on to the stone ledge of the fountain and was bathing in the doubtful fluid, and was watched with envy by people seated on the benches of the little circular garden, which curves round the west door.

Du Roy looked at his watch ; it was only three o'clock ; he was half an hour too soon.

As he thought of this rendezvous he laughed.

"In her eyes," he said, "churches are useful for all purposes. They soothe her conscience for marrying a Jew, they give her an attitude of protest in the political world, an air of correctness amongst people of distinction, and they serve as a screen for her assignations. She uses her religion as one uses an *en-tout-cas*. If it is a fine day, it is a walking stick ; if it is sunny it is a parasol ; if it rains it is an umbrella, and if you don't go out, you leave it in the hall. There are hundreds of women like that ; they have no more respect for God than they have for a cherry, but they won't let you speak ill of Him and they use Him as a go-between whenever it is convenient. If you suggested that they should come with you into a furnished house, they would think it an infamous proposal, but in their eyes it is quite natural to carry on at the foot of a church altar."

He strolled slowly up and down by the side of the fountain. He looked again at the church clock, which was two minutes in advance of his watch. It pointed to five minutes past three. He decided that it would be pleasanter inside the church and he entered accordingly. The air was as cool as in a cellar, and he breathed it gratefully. He walked up and down the nave to familiarise himself with the place. From the farther end of the great church, the sound of a measured tread, sometimes stopping and then beginning again, came as in response to the noise of his own footsteps, which echoed in the lofty vaulted roof. He looked to see who it was, and caught sight of a fat, bald man who walked with his head in the air and his hat held behind his back. Here and there was an old woman kneeling in prayer with her face in her hands. He was struck by a sense of solitude, loneliness, rest ; the light, tinted by the painted windows, was pleasant to the eyes. Du Roy decided that it was " dashed fine " in there.

He came back to the door and consulted his watch again. It was only a quarter-past three. He took a seat by the entrance to the central aisle, regretting that he could not smoke a cigarette. From the other end of the church, near the choir, came the sound of the stout gentleman's slow promenade.

Someone came in and George turned quickly. It was a woman of the people, in a woollen petticoat, a poor woman, who fell on her knees beside the nearest chair and remained motionless, with her hands clasped, her eyes fixed on heaven, her soul soaring upwards in prayer.

Du Roy looked at her with interest, wondering what mortification, what grief, what despair could be bruising this humblest of hearts. It was evident that she was crushed under the weight of sorrow. She had perhaps a husband who beat her cruelly, or, it might be, her child was dying.

" Poor things," he reflected. " There are always those who suffer."

A gust of rage against the pitilessness of nature swept

over him. His next thought was that these wretches at least had the belief that they were an object of concern to someone up above, and that their record was kept in heaven, with a debit and credit balance. Up above? Where?

And Du Roy, who was impelled to these far-reaching speculations by the silence of the church, summed up all creation in a single reflection, and pronounced his contemptuous verdict :

"What a silly business it all is ! "

He started on hearing the rustle of a dress. It was Madame Walter. He rose and went quickly towards her. She did not offer to shake hands with him, but said in low tones :

"I have only a few moments. I have to get back home. Kneel down near me so that we shan't attract attention."

She walked up the great nave, seeking a safe and suitable place, as one who knew the building well. A heavy veil concealed her face and her steps were hardly audible. On arriving near the choir she turned and muttered in that repressed tone which is always used in church :

"The side aisles will be better. This place is too conspicuous." She bowed low and curtsied to the High Altar, then turned to the right, went a short distance back towards the entrance, and coming to a decision, took a *prie-Dieu* and fell on her knees. George took possession of the adjoining *prie-Dieu* and soon they were both motionless in the attitude of prayer.

"I am very grateful to you," he said. "I adore you. I should like to keep repeating it again and again, telling you how my love for you began, how I lost my heart to you the first time I saw you . . . Will you suffer me some day to pour out my heart to you, to tell you all ? "

She listened in an attitude of profound meditation, as though she had heard nothing. Then she replied through her fingers :

"It is madness to let you speak to me like this, madness for me to have come here, to be doing what I am doing, to let you believe that this . . . , this passion of yours can have any sequel. Forget it. You must forget it, and never again speak to me of it."

She paused. He sought for a reply; for convincing, passionate words, but he had difficulty in combining gesture and speech and found that his power of action was paralysed. He began again.

"I expect nothing. I hope for nothing. I love you. Whatever you do, I shall continue to tell you that so often, with such strength and ardour that you cannot but end by realising it. I wish my affection for you to penetrate you. I want to pour it into your soul, word by word, hour by hour, day by day, so that at last impregnating you like a fluid falling drop by drop, it may sweeten and soften you and at some later time may force you to reply to me, 'I also, I love you.'"

He felt her shoulder tremble in contact with him; her throat was throbbing; and she said, very quickly, in a broken voice:

"I also, I love you."

He started violently as if he had had a severe blow on the head, and he gasped:

"O my God!"

Her breathing was still agitated when she spoke again:

"Ought I to tell you that? It makes me feel guilty and contemptible, me, the mother of two girls . . . but I cannot—I cannot . . . I couldn't have believed . . . thought . . . I cannot help it . . . I cannot help it . . . Listen, listen, I have never loved anyone . . . but you. I swear it. And I have loved you this year past, in secret, the secret of my heart. Oh, believe me, I have suffered and wrestled, but I can do no more. I love you . . ."

Her hands were before her face and her tears rained down on them and all her body trembled and shook under the violence of her emotion.

"Give me your hand," said George, "that I may touch it and press it."

Slowly she took one hand from her face. He saw her cheek all wet with tears, and on her lashes a teardrop hovered, ready to fall.

He took the hand and pressed it.

" Oh, how I should love to drink your tears."

In a low broken voice she moaned :

" You mustn't take advantage of me. I am a lost woman."

He suppressed a smile. How could he take advantage of her in a place like that ? He pressed to his heart the hand that lay in his.

" Do you feel it beating ? " he asked. His stock of impassioned phrases was exhausted.

The measured tread of the man who was walking about the church came nearer. He had visited all the altars and now, for the second time at least, was coming down the small aisle on the right. When Madame Walter heard him near the pillar which concealed her, she snatched her fingers from George's clasp and covered her face again. The two remained motionless and kneeling as if they had both together been offering ardent supplications to heaven. The stout gentleman passed close to them, cast a glance of indifference at them and withdrew towards the lower end of the church, still holding his hat behind his back.

Du Roy, however, was meditating a rendezvous elsewhere than at Trinity Church.

" When can I see you to-morrow ? " he whispered.

She made no reply ; seemed lifeless, as if changed into a statue of Prayer.

" To-morrow," he urged. " Would you like me to meet you at the Parc Monceau ? "

She turned towards him her face, now uncovered ; it was livid, contracted by hideous sufferings. In broken phrases she pleaded :

" Leave me . . . leave me now . . . go away . . . go away . . . for five minutes only . . . I am suffering too much, near you . . . I want to pray . . . I cannot . . . go away . . . let me pray . . . alone . . . five minutes . . . I cannot . . . let me implore God to forgive me, to save me . . . leave me . . . five minutes . . ."

Her face manifested such utter distress and grief that he rose without saying a word, but after a little hesitation he asked :

" Shall I come back soon ? "

She made an affirmative sign with her head and he moved away towards the choir.

Then she tried to pray. She made a superhuman affort of invocation, of appeal to God, and with trembling body and bewildered soul, she cried to Heaven for pity. She closed her eyes angrily to shut out the sight of the man who had just left her. She drove him from her thoughts, she strove against him, but instead of the celestial apparition which she yearned for in the anguish of her heart, she could see only her lover's curled moustache. For a whole year she had wrestled daily, nightly, against this growing obsession, against the image that haunted her dreams, her whole frame, and harassed her nights. She felt that she had been snared like an animal, bound, and thrown into the arms of this male who had made of her his victim and his prey by virtue merely of the hair on his lip and the colour of his eyes.

And now, in this church, with God so near, she felt more feeble, more deserted, more lost than even in her own home. No longer could she pray ; no longer could she bend her thought to any but him. Already she was suffering because of his absence. None the less she struggled desperately, defending herself and calling out for succour with all the strength of her soul. She would have died rather than succumb thus, she who had never transgressed. While from her lips came bewildered words of supplication, she was listening to the echo of his footsteps as it grew fainter in the lofty arches.

She knew now that it was all over, her struggle had been in vain. But she was not yet ready to yield ; and she was seized by one of those hysterical crises in which women cast themselves palpitating, screaming and contorted, on the ground. She trembled in all her limbs, feeling that she was about to fall and roll amongst the chairs with piercing shrieks.

She heard someone approaching with rapid steps. Turning, she saw a priest. She rose to her feet, ran to him holding out her clasped hands, and cried :

" Save me, oh, save me ! "

He halted in surprise.

" What is it that you wish, madam ? "

" I want you to save me. Have pity on me. If you don't help me, I am lost."

Wondering whether she was not mad he looked at her and asked :

" What can I do for you ? "

He was young, tall, and inclined to stoutness ; his cheeks were chubby and pendulous, and darkened by a closely shaven growth of beard. He was one of those good-looking town curates living in a rich parish and accustomed to well-to-do penitents.

" Receive my confession," she implored him, " and give me your counsel. Support me and tell me what to do."

" My hours for confession," he rejoined, " are on Saturdays from three to six."

She seized his arm and held it tight and insisted :

" No, no, no . . . Immediately. Immediately. You must. He is there. He is in this church. He is waiting for me."

" Who is waiting for you ? " asked the priest.

" A man . . . who is going to ruin me . . . he will get me if you don't save me . . . I have no more strength to flee from him . . . I am too weak . . . too weak . . . so weak . . . so weak."

She threw herself down on her knees and sobbed :

" Oh have pity on me, father. In the name of God, save me, save me."

She held him by his black gown to prevent him escaping, and he looked around him uneasily to see whether some malevolent or pious eye were not observing him and the woman at his feet. Realising at last that escape was impossible, he said :

" Get up from your knees. It so happens that I have the key of the confessional on me."

He rummaged in his pocket and drew out a key-ring with a number of keys on it. Having selected one, he went quickly towards one of the little wooden cabinets, receptacles for the impurities of the soul, the places into which believers void their sins. He entered by the middle door which closed on him. Madame Walter threw herself into the narrow compartment at the side and poured out her confession with fervour and in an impassioned transport of hopefulness.

"Bless me, father, for I have sinned."

* * * * *

Du Roy walked round the choir and came down the left aisle. Half-way along he met the stout bald man who was still walking at an equable pace.

"What can that individual be up to here?" Du Roy wondered.

The stout man had also slackened his pace and looked at George with an obvious desire to address him. When he had come quite near him, he bowed and said very politely:

"I'm sorry to trouble you, sir, but can you tell me at what epoch this church was built?"

"Upon my word," Du Roy replied, "I really know nothing about it. I think it must have been twenty or twenty-five years ago. To tell you the truth, it is the first time I have been here."

"I too, I have never seen it before."

Yielding to his growing curiosity Du Roy continued:

"You seem to be doing it very thoroughly. You are studying it in detail."

"I am not here to examine the church," the other replied in a resigned tone. "I am waiting for my wife, who arranged to meet me here. She is very late."

After a short silence.

"It's beastly hot outside."

Du Roy, who was taking his measure, rather liked the look of him, and was struck by the idea that he had a resemblance to Forestier.

"You are from the Provinces?" he asked.

"Yes. I am from Rennes. May I ask if you have come to this church to see it?"

"No. I am waiting for a lady."

Du Roy bowed and withdrew, with a smile on his lips.

As he came near the main doorway, he caught sight of the poor woman, who was still on her knees and praying incessantly.

" Good Lord," he thought, " she does stick to her praying."

He no longer felt any emotion, or any pity for her. Passing by, he made his way softly up the right aisle in search of Madame Walter. He looked from a distance for the place where he had left her, but to his surprise she was no longer there. He thought he must have mistaken the pillar, so he went right to the end and then came back. It was true. She had gone away. He was angry and astonished. It then occurred to him that perhaps she was looking for him, and he walked right round the interior. Having failed to find her, he came back to the chair which she had occupied, in the hope that she would return to him there. And he waited.

His attention was presently attracted by a low murmuring. He had seen no one in this corner of the church. Whence then could this whispering be coming ? He rose in order to make a search and observed the doors of the confessional in the adjoining chapel. From one of the doors the end of a dress was visible, trailing on the paved floor. He came nearer for a closer view of the wearer, and recognised Madame Walter. She was confessing . . . He felt a violent desire to seize her by the shoulders and drag her away from the box. But a second thought came to him :

" Pooh, it's the priest's turn to-day, it will be mine to-morrow."

He sat down with an easy mind in front of the confessional. His time was coming. The adventure in its present aspect made him laugh.

He waited a long time, but at last Madame Walter rose to her feet, and turned, and seeing him, came up to him. Her expression was cold and severe.

" Monsieur Du Roy," she addressed him, " I must beg of you not to wait for me, and not to follow me, and never again to come to my house alone. If you did come, you would not be received. Good-bye."

And she withdrew with dignity. Du Roy allowed her to go ; it was a principle of his never to force events. But when the priest, somewhat troubled, came out in his turn from his recess, Du Roy marched right up to him and looking him straight in the eyes, and thrusting his face into his, growled :

" See here, you. If it wasn't for your petticoat, you would get a couple of fine smacks on your ugly snout."

Then he turned on his heel, and as he left the church he was whistling softly. The stout man, weary of waiting, was standing under the portico, with his hat on his head and his hands clasped behind his back, and his eyes were searching all over the vast square and the streets leading into it. As Du Roy passed near him, the two bowed to each other.

Being disengaged, Du Roy went down to the offices of the *Vie Française*. The moment he entered, he guessed from the busy demeanour of the office-boys that there was something unusual in hand, and he went briskly into the director's private room. Old Walter was on his feet, nervously dictating an article in inconsequent phrases, issuing instructions, between one paragraph and another, to the reporters round him, making references to Boisrenard and opening letters. When Du Roy come in, Walter gave utterance to a cry of joy :

" Ah, what luck ! Here comes Bel-Ami."

Somewhat confused, he stopped short and apologised :

" I beg your pardon for calling you that, but I am much upset by the state of affairs. And, you know, I hear my wife and daughters calling you Bel-Ami from morning to night, so I've picked up the habit myself. You don't mind ?"

" Not at all," George laughed, " there is nothing in that nickname to displease me."

" That's all right," Monsieur Walter replied. " Then I baptize you Bel-Ami as everyone else does. Well now, look here, we are in the middle of great happenings. The ministry has been turned out by three hundred and ten votes to a hundred and two. Our holidays have all been postponed to the Greek kalends, and here we are at the twenty-eighth of July. Spain has taken umbrage over Morocco and that is what has upset Durand de l'Aine and his acolytes. We are in the trough, up to the neck. Marrot has been told to form a new Cabinet. He is taking General Boutin d'Acre for War Minister and our friend Laroche-Mathieu for Foreign Affairs. He is keeping Home Affairs for himself, with the presidency of the Council. We are to be the official organ. I am now doing a leader, a declaration of our principles and an indication of ministerial policy."

He smiled genially and resumed :

" The policy they propose to follow, you understand. But I must have some interesting stuff about Morocco ; what I want is something realistic, some actual experience that will produce an effect, a sensation. You must get that for me, Du Roy."

Du Roy reflected an instant and replied :

" I have the very thing for you. I shall do you a study on the political situation of all our African colonies with Tunis on the left, Algeria in the middle, and Morocco on the right. I shall give a description of the races that inhabit this immense territory and an account of an expedition on the Morocco frontier up to the great oasis of Figuig to which no European has yet penetrated and which is the actual cause of the present trouble. Will that suit you ? "

" Admirably," exclaimed Monsieur Walter. " And the title ? "

" From Tunis to Tangier."

" Superb."

Du Roy went forthwith to look up in the back numbers of the *Vie Française* his first article, " The Recollections of an African Light Horseman," which when touched up, adapted, and issued under a new name, would suit the purpose admirably, inasmuch as the question at issue was one of colonial policy, and concerned the population of Algeria and an expedition into the Province of Oran.

In three-quarters of an hour the thing was re-written, patched and polished ; it had the savour of actuality and contained praise of the new Cabinet. The director read the article.

" It is perfect," he declared. " You are a valuable man. All my compliments ! "

When Du Roy went home to dinner, he was enchanted with the success of his day, in spite of the rebuff at the Trinité, for he was quite sure that he had won his game. His wife, in a fever of expectation, awaited him. When she saw him she called out :

" You know that Laroche is Minister of Foreign Affairs?"

" Yes. I've just been writing an article on Algeria, in relation to that."

" What ? "

" You know it. It's the first one we did together, ' Recollections of an African Light Horseman,' revised and corrected to suit the occasion."

" Ah ! " she smiled. " The very thing."

After a moment's reflection.

" I was thinking," she said, " of that series which you were to do then and which you . . . lost sight of. We could set ourselves to that now. It would make a splendid series and very much to the point."

As he sat down to his soup he replied :

" Certainly. There is nothing in the way now that that poor fool Forestier is dead."

Offended, she replied sharply :

" That joke is quite out of place. I beg of you to let us have no more of it. It has lasted too long already."

He was on the point of making a sarcastic retort, when an unsigned telegram was brought him containing the following words :

I lost my head. Forgive me, and come to-morrow, four o'clock, Parc Monceau.

The situation was clear to him and his heart was suddenly filled with joy. He slipped the blue paper into his pocket.

" I won't do it again, my love. It is silly, I admit."

He began his dinner. All the time he was eating he was repeating the words :

" I lost my head, Forgive me and come to-morrow, four o'clock, Parc Monceau."

She had yielded. The meaning of the message was :
" I surrender. I am yours, whenever and wherever
you want me."

He began to laugh and Madeleine asked :

" What is the matter with you ? "

" Nothing much. I am thinking of a priest I met lately.
He was a real funny-face."

On the following day Du Roy arrived punctually at the
rendezvous. On all the benches in the park were seated
middle-class people, overcome by the heat, and careless
nurses who seemed to be dreaming while the children rolled
about in the sand of the pathways.

He discovered Madame Walter in the little antique ruin
which had a spring of running water. She was walking
round the narrow circle of dwarf columns and wore a restless,
unhappy expression. As soon as he greeted her, she said :

" What a number of people there are in this garden."

He seized the opportunity.

" Yes. That is true. Would you like to come somewhere else ? "

" Yes, but where ? "

" No matter where. What about a carriage ? You could
let down the blinds on your side, and you would be quite
well screened."

" Yes. I should prefer that. I am frightened to death
here."

" Well then, meet me in five minutes at the gate opening
on the outer Boulevard. I shall be there with a cab."

He left her at a run, and as soon as she had rejoined him
and had carefully drawn the blind over the window on her
side of the carriage, she asked :

" Where did you tell the driver to take us ? "

" Leave everything to me. The driver knows what he
is about."

He had given the man the address of his flat in the Rue
Constantinople.

" You can't imagine," she went on, " what I suffer
because of you, what torments and tortures I endure.
Yesterday in church I was unkind, but I wanted to escape

from you at any cost. I have such a dread of finding myself alone with you. Have you forgiven me ? "

He pressed her hand.

" Yes, yes. How could I fail to forgive you, loving you as I do ? "

" Listen," she supplicated. " You must promise to respect me ; not to . . . not to . . . Otherwise I could never meet you again."

For a moment he made no reply, under his moustache lurked that subtle smile which troubled women's peace of mind. At last :

" I am your slave," he said.

Next she began to tell him how she had first realised that she loved him when she learnt of his engagement to Madame Forestier. She gave details, trifling details of dates and things that had touched her closely.

Of a sudden she fell silent. The carriage had stopped, and Du Roy opened the door.

" But where are we ? "

" At my house. It is my bachelor's quarters. I took them on again . . . for a few days . . . so as to have a corner where we could meet."

Terrified at the idea of this *tête-à-tête*, she clung to the upholstery of the carriage and exclaimed in agitation :

" No, no. I won't. I won't."

Earnestly he assured her :

" I swear to respect you. Come. You can see there are people looking at us. There will be a crowd round us presently. Quick, quick. Come out."

And again he said :

" I swear to respect you."

A man standing at the door of his wine-shop was looking at them inquisitively. She made a terror-stricken rush for the house. She started going upstairs, but he caught her arm.

" It is down here, on the ground floor."

He pushed her into his flat. As soon as the door was closed, he fell on her like a bird of prey. She resisted, struggled, stammered :

" Oh my God . . . oh my God."

He kissed her frenziedly on the neck, the eyes, the mouth. She could not avoid the fury of his caresses, and even while she repelled him and avoided his lips she was giving him back his kisses, in spite of herself. Suddenly she ceased struggling. She was defeated.

V

Autumn had come. The Du Roys had spent the whole
summer in Paris, conducting an energetic campaign in the
Vie Française on behalf of the new Cabinet during the brief
holidays of the Deputies. Although it was only the beginning of October, the Chambers were about to resume their
session on account of the threatening aspect of Moroccan
affairs.

No one at heart believed that there would be an expedition
to Tangier, although on the day that Parliament rose a
Deputy of the Right, Count Lambert-Sarrazin, in a witty
speech which was applauded even by the Centre, had offered,
following the example of a celebrated Viceroy of India, to
bet his moustaches against the President of the Council's
whiskers, that the new Cabinet could not restrain itself from
imitating the old one and would send an army to Tangier
to balance the one to Tunis, for the love of symmetry,
just as one puts two vases on a chimney-piece.

" If you come to think of it, gentlemen," he said, " Africa
is just a fire-place for France, a fire-place that consumes our
best wood, a fire-place with a strong draught, and we light
our fire with bank-notes. Indulging your artistic fancy,
you have embellished the left hand corner with a Tunisian
ornament, a very expensive one, and you will find that
Monsieur Marrot will want to follow the example of his
predecessor and embellish the right hand corner with a
knick-knack from Morocco."

This speech became celebrated and served Du Roy as a
text for ten articles on the Algerian colony, for the entire
series which had been interrupted at the time when he was

doing his earliest work for the paper. He had vigorously supported the idea of a military expedition, although convinced that no such thing would take place. He had twanged the patriotic chord, and had bombarded Spain with the whole arsenal of contemptuous argument which is directed against nations whose interests do not coincide with one's own.

The *Vie Française* had acquired considerable importance from its known relations with those in power. In advance of the old established newspapers it would give political intelligence, hinting at the intentions of its friends, the ministers of State, and the entire press of Paris and the provinces went for its information to the *Vie Française*. It was quoted, it was feared, it even began to be respected. It was no longer the suspected organ of a group of political intriguers ; it was the avowed mouthpiece of the Cabinet. Laroche-Mathieu was its soul and Du Roy its megaphone. Old Walter, a dumb Deputy but a crafty administrator, had the art of effacing himself, and was rumoured to be busy in the background with a big Morocco copper-mine concern.

Madeleine's drawing-room had become an influential centre, at which there was a weekly gathering of several Cabinet Ministers. Even the President of the Council had twice dined there, and the wives of men in office, who had formerly hesitated to cross her threshold, now boasted of their friendship with her and paid more visits to her than they received in return. The Minister of Foreign Affairs ruled the household almost as if he had been its master. He came there at all hours with dispatches, intelligence, information, which he dictated either to husband or wife as though they were his secretaries.

When the Minister was out of the house and Du Roy was left alone with Madeleine, he would inveigh, in a threatening tone and with malicious innuendo in his words, against the ways of this mediocre upstart. She shrugged her shoulders contemptuously.

" Do as much as he has done. Become a Minister yourself. Then you can talk. Until you've done that you can hold your tongue."

He twisted his moustache and looked askance at her.

" People don't know yet what I can do," he said. " Perhaps they will find it out some day."

" We shall believe that when we see it," she replied coolly.

On the morning of the day on which the Chamber was to meet, Madeleine, who was still in bed, had innumerable directions to give her husband. He was dressing for a luncheon with Monsieur Laroche-Mathieu, where he was to receive his instructions for next day's political article. This article was to be a sort of official declaration of the Cabinet's real policy.

" And above everything," she enjoined him, " do not forget to ask him whether General Belloncle is to go to Oran. There was a talk of that. It would be most significant."

George retorted testily :

" I know just as well as you what to do. Can't you let me alone with your eternal repetitions ? "

" My dear," she replied calmly, " you always forget half the messages I give you for the Foreign Minister."

" You and your minister," he growled. " He is becoming a nuisance. He is a noodle."

" He is no more my minister than yours," she retorted calmly. " He is more useful to you than to me."

He turned slightly in her direction and said with a snigger :

" Pardon me. It isn't me he is paying attentions to."

" Or to me either, for that matter," she said in a deliberate tone. " But he is making our fortune."

This silenced him, but after a little he resumed :

" If I had to make my choice among your admirers, I should prefer that old booby de Vaudrec. What has come over him ? I haven't seen him for a week."

Without betraying emotion, she replied :

" He is not well. He has written to say that he is actually confined to bed with an attack of gout. You might go along there and find out how he is. He is very fond of you, you know, and he would be delighted to see you."

" All right," George agreed, " I'll go there soon."

He had finished dressing and with his hat on his head he was looking to see whether he had forgotten anything.

Satisfied that everything was in order, he went to the bed and kissed his wife's forehead.

" See you later, my love. I shan't be home before seven at the earliest."

Then he went out. Monsieur Laroche-Mathieu was awaiting him. Their luncheon was at ten o'clock, as there was a council meeting at noon, before the re-opening of Parliament.

Madame Laroche-Mathieu had declined to change her luncheon hour, so they lunched alone with the private secretary. As soon as they were seated Du Roy spoke of his article, indicated its tenor, consulting notes scribbled on visiting cards. When he had finished,

" My dear sir, do you see anything in that requiring modification ? "

" Very little, my dear fellow. You are perhaps rather over-positive about the Morocco business. Talk of the expedition as if it ought to take place, but let it be well understood that it won't and that you haven't the remotest degree of faith in it. Put it so that the public will read between the lines that we have no intention of poking our noses into such an adventure."

" Precisely. I understand, and I shall make it clear. By the way, my wife told me to ask you whether General Belloncle was to be sent to Oran. I conclude not, after what you have told me."

" No," was the reply.

Then they conversed about the coming Session.

Laroche-Mathieu began to hold forth ; he was trying on Du Roy the phrases which he proposed to shower on his colleagues a few hours later. He kept moving his right hand, sometimes brandishing his fork in the air, sometimes his knife, sometimes a piece of bread. Looking at nobody, and addressing the invisible assembly, he emitted the luscious eloquence one would expect from a good-looking young fellow who was particular about his hair. A very small, twisted moustache adorned his upper lip with two points like scorpions' tails, and his hair, which glistened with brilliantine and was parted in the middle, was plastered down over his temples and gave him an air of provincial foppishness. He was a little too fat and though still young, somewhat bloated ; his waistcoat was slightly distended. The private secretary went on calmly eating and drinking ; he was evidently used to these floods of eloquence ; but Du Roy, consumed with envy at his success, was thinking :

" Oh, shut up, you booby ! What idiots these politicians are ! "

And comparing his own worth with the babbling self-importance of this Minister of State, he said to himself :

" Good Lord, if I only had a clear hundred thousand francs, I would stand for the Deputyship of my own pretty Rouen, and take my honest Normans, my crafty thick-headed Normans, and bake them in the pie of their own coarse malice. What a real statesman I would make beside these blackguards who can't see an inch in front of them."

Monsieur Laroche-Mathieu did not cease speaking until the coffee arrived. Then seeing that he was late, he rang for his brougham, and extending his hand to Du Roy, said :

" Now you know where we are, my dear fellow."

" Perfectly, my dear sir. You can depend on me."

Du Roy went his way in complete peace of mind to the office in order to begin his article, having no other engagement until four o'clock. At four he was to go to the Rue de Constantinople to meet Madame de Marelle, whom he saw regularly twice a week, Mondays and Fridays. But when he entered the editorial department he was handed a sealed telegram. It was from Madame Walter, and ran as follows :

It is absolutely necessary for me to speak to you to-day. It is important, most important. Expect me at two o'clock, Rue de Constantinople. I can render you a great service. Your friend until death.—Virginie.

" Good God," he swore. " What a leech the woman is," and in a burst of ill-temper he dashed out of the office, too exasperated to do any work.

For six weeks he had been trying to shake her off but he

had failed to wear out her frantic affection. After her fall
she had suffered an access of terrifying remorse and at three
successive rendezvous had overwhelmed her lover with
reproaches and maledictions.

Bored by these scenes and already surfeited with this
mature and melodramatic female, he had simply kept out
of the way, in the hope that the adventure would thus come
to an end. But the next development was that she grappled
on to him desperately, hurling herself into this love-affair
as one would hurl oneself into a river after tying a stone
round one's neck. His weakness, complaisance and deference had led to his recapture ; she had confined him in the
prison of her unbridled and exhausting passion, and had
persecuted him with her devotion. She wanted to see him
every day, and summoned him with perpetual telegrams to
hasty interviews at street corners, in shops, in public gardens.
Over and over again in the same phrases she told him that
she adored him, idolised him, and when she left him she
would swear that the sight of him had made her so happy.

She turned out quite different from what he had expected.
She tried to charm him with girlish graces and infantine
endearments that were laughable at her age. Up to that
time she had always been rigidly virtuous, of virgin heart,
closed to all sentiment, entirely destitute of sensuality, and
love had come like a thunderbolt upon this prudent woman
whose calm forty years seemed like a wan autumn after a
chill summer. She was experiencing a sort of faded springtime, full of little flowers that had missed their blossoming,
buds that had failed to open, a young girl's strange bursting
into love, a love delayed, ardent, and ingenuous, made up of
unlooked for impulses, of the little ejaculations of a girl
of sixteen, of embarrassing endearments and graces that had
attained old age without ever having been young. She would
write him ten letters a day, letters betraying an imbecile
obsession, in a grotesque style combining the poetical and
the absurd, full of Oriental imagery and the names of animals
and birds.

The moment they were alone together she would caress
him with the clumsy endearments of a coarse street-girl,

absurd poutings, skips and jumps that made her too bountiful bosom shake under her bodice. What disgusted him more than anything was to hear her calling him, "My rat, my cat, my jewel, my blue bird, my treasure," and to see her persist in offering herself to him with a small comedy of infantine modesty, of little gestures of timidity which she thought attractive, and all the little wantonnesses of a depraved schoolgirl. She would ask : "Whose mouth is this ?" and when he was slow of replying, "It is mine," she insisted until he grew pale with weariness.

He considered that she ought to have felt that the qualities necessary in love are tact, adroitness, prudence and rigid propriety ; that, having given herself to him, mature and matronly woman of the world as she was, she ought to have surrendered with seriousness, with a sort of restrained transport, without levity, with tears perhaps, but with the tears of a Dido and not of a Juliet.

Incessantly, over and over again, came the words, "How I love you, my little one. Do you love me as much ? Tell me, baby mine."

He could not hear the words "my little one," "my baby" without wanting to call her "old girl."

"How mad I was to give in to you," she said. "But I don't regret it. It is so good to love."

All of which on her lips George found irritating. She murmured, "It is so good to love" just as an actress would have done, playing the *ingénue* at a theatre.

She exasperated him, too, by the awkwardness of her caresses. Kindling in the embraces of this good-looking young fellow, she brought to her love an unskilful ardour and a resolute earnestness which roused Du Roy's mockery and made him think of old men trying to learn to read. And when she ought to have crushed him in her arms, looking at him ardently with that profound and terrible expression, characteristic of women who have passed their youth but are superb in their expiring flame ; when her lips should have been dumb and trembling, as wearied but insatiable she enfolded him, she frisked about like a street-girl and used baby-talk to make herself attractive.

It was on such occasions that he felt a furious desire to swear, to take up his hat, and go away after slamming the door.

At first they met frequently at the Rue de Constantinople, but Du Roy was afraid of her coming across Madame de Marelle and he found a thousand pretexts for declining these rendezvous.

The next thing was, that he was obliged to come almost daily to her house, to luncheon or dinner. She would squeeze his hand under the table, and would try to kiss him behind the door. His chief amusement, however, was playing with Suzanne, whose quaint ways cheered him up. In spite of her doll-like appearance, she exercised a wit that was agile and roguish, unexpected and sly, and she was for ever showing off like a marionette at a fair. She treated everything and everybody with ridicule, mordant and to the point. George excited this spirit in her, incited her to sarcasm, and they were on excellent terms. Every moment she called to him :

"Listen, Bel-Ami. Come here, Bel-Ami."

And he would leave the mother at once and run to the daughter who would whisper some piece of mischief in his ear, and they would laugh heartily.

As time went on his dislike of the mother grew to an insurmountable repugnance. He could not see or hear her, or even think of her, without falling into a rage. No longer would he go to her house, answer her letters or give way to her entreaties. She came at last to understand that he no longer loved her, and her sufferings were terrible. But she was inexorable. She spied on him, followed him about, and waited for him in cabs with the blinds down, at the door of his office or his house, or in the streets along which she expected him to come.

He wanted to be harsh to her, to abuse her, to slap her, to say to her straight out :

"Hang it, I've had enough of you. You're boring me to death."

But he always preserved a certain circumspection, with his eye on the *Vie Française*. It was by means of coldness and harshness under a mask of deference ; occasionally, even by deliberate rudeness of speech, that he endeavoured to bring it home to her that it was high time the affair was ended. She was particularly bent on devising plans for drawing him to the Rue de Constantinople, and he was in perpetual trepidation lest the two women should confront each other one day on the doorstep.

His fondness for Madame de Marelle had, on the other hand, increased during the summer. He called her his "street-arab," and there was no doubt of the pleasure she gave him. Their own natures had a similar bent ; both of them undeniably belonged to that adventurous breed, the vagabonds of life, the vagabonds of society, who have, without suspecting it, a strong likeness to the gipsies of the high roads.

They had had a delightful summer of love-making, like a pair of students on the spree. They would slip away and lunch or dine at Argenteuil, Bougival, Maisons, or Poissy and would pass hours in a boat, plucking the flowers that grew along the banks. She adored fried fish from the Seine, rabbit stews, fish stews, the trellised arbours of tavern gardens, and the cries of the boating people. On a fine day he loved to traverse with her, on the roof of a train, the outskirts of the town, and, engaged in gay and foolish talk, to cross the ugly country round Paris, with its crop of hideous middle-class villas. And when he had to return for dinner at Madame Walter's, his mind was full of Clotilde whom he had just left, who had reaped the harvest of his ardour in the grass by the river side. And he hated the old woman who loved him with such frenzy.

He believed that he had at last almost freed himself from Madame Walter, to whom he had expressed in clear and almost brutal fashion his resolution to break with her, when he received the telegram summoning him to meet her at two o'clock at the Rue de Constantinople. As he walked along he read it again.

It is absolutely necessary for me to speak to you to-day. It is important, most important. Expect me at two o'clock, Rue de Constantinople. I can render you a great service. Your friend until death.—Virginie.

" What does the old owl want with me now ? " he wondered. " I bet she has nothing to say. She wants to tell me again that she adores me. I shall have to go and see all the same. She speaks of something very important and a great service. Perhaps it is true. But there is Clotilde due at four. I shall have to get rid of the first one by three o'clock at the latest. I hope to goodness they don't meet. What hussies women are."

His own wife, he reflected, was the only woman who never plagued him. She lived her own life, yet she showed every sign of great affection at the proper time, for she never tolerated any derangement in the fixed order of life's customary occupations.

As he proceeded with reluctant steps towards his rendez-vous, he worked himself up against Madame Walter.

" Ah, I'll give her a pretty reception if she has nothing to say to me. The language of Cambronne will be academic compared with mine. I shall tell her plainly that I'll never come near her house again."

He went in and waited for her and she arrived almost immediately. As soon as she saw him :

" Ah," she exclaimed, " you got my message ? What luck ! "

He had a vicious expression on his face.

" Of course I found it at the office just as I was setting out for the Chamber of Deputies. What do you want with me now ? "

She had raised her veil to kiss him. She came up to him with the timid and submissive air of a dog that is often beaten.

" How cruel you are to me ! How harshly you talk. What have I done ? You can't conceive what suffering you cause me."

" You aren't going to begin again ? " he growled.

She was standing quite close to him, ready at a smile or a sign to throw herself into his arms.

" If you meant to treat me like this," she protested, " why did you have anything to do with me ? You might have left me quiet and happy, as I was. Do you remember what you said to me in the church and how you compelled me to come into this house ? And see how you speak to me now, and the sort of a reception you give me. Oh Heavens, how badly you treat me."

He stamped on the floor and exclaimed violently :

" Oh hang it all ! I've had enough of it. I can't be with you for one minute without your harping on that. People would imagine you were twelve years old when I got you, and that you were as innocent as a cherub. No, my dear. Let us get back to the facts. There wasn't any seduction of a girl under age. When you gave yourself to me you were of full age and understanding. I thank you for it, I am as grateful as possible for it, but I am not obliged to tie myself to your apron strings for the rest of my life. You have a husband and I have a wife. We are neither of us free. We indulged ourselves in a frolic ; no one saw it, no one knows about it ; it is over."

" Oh how brutal you are," she protested. " What a coarse wretch you are. No, I was no longer a young girl, but I had never loved, never gone wrong . . ."

" You have told me that twenty times already. I know it," he interrupted. " But after all, you had had two children . . ."

She shrank back.

" Oh, George, how unworthy . . ."

She carried her hands to her bosom and began to choke with sobs which strangled her utterance.

When he saw tears coming, he took his hat from the corner of the chimney-piece.

" Ah, now you are going to cry ! Very well then. Good evening. Is that the exhibition you wanted me for ? "

She took one step and barred his way. Drawing a handkerchief from her pocket she wiped away her tears briskly. She steadied her voice by an effort of will, and in spite of a quiver of grief, she said :

" No . . . I came to . . . to give you a piece of news . . . political news . . . to give you the means of getting fifty thousand francs . . . or even more . . . if you wish."

His violence suddenly assuaged, he asked :

" How so ?   What do you mean ? "

" Yesterday evening I chanced to overhear some words spoken by my husband and Laroche.   In any case they were pretty frank in my presence.   My husband advised Laroche not to let you into the secret, otherwise you would give everything away."

Du Roy had replaced his hat on a chair and was listening attentively.

" Well, what is it ? "

" They are going to take Morocco."

" Oh come now.   I've just been having luncheon with Laroche and he as good as dictated the intentions of the Cabinet to me."

" No, my love, they were playing with you.   They are afraid of their schemes being discovered."

" Sit down," said George.

He seated himself in an arm-chair, and she drew a little footstool along the floor and sat down on it, between Du Roy's knees.   She resumed in a coaxing tone :

" As I am always thinking of you, I pay attention now to all the whisperings that go on round me."

Then she began quietly to explain to him how she had divined for some time past that a plan was being prepared without his knowledge and that he was to be made use of although his co-operation was feared.

" You know," she said, " when one is in love, one grows cunning."

At last, on the preceding evening she had understood the scheme.

It was a business transaction, on a very large scale, and the plans for it were being kept dark.

She was now smiling with pleasure at her own cleverness. She put on airs, and spoke as a financier's wife, accustomed to witness the contriving of Stock Exchange manœuvres, the making of prices, of which the raising and depressing may ruin in a couple of hours thousands of petty tradesmen and annuitants who have put their savings into funds that are guaranteed by the names of men, honoured and respected in politics and finance.

" It is a wonderful scheme, this of theirs," she said.
" Really wonderful.   It is my husband who has arranged it
all, and he knows what he is up to.   I assure you, it is a
great scheme."

This beating about the bush made him impatient.

" Look here, tell me quickly."

" Very well.   Here it is.   The expedition to Tangier
was decided between them on the very day Laroche became
Foreign Minister.   Little by little they have bought up
the whole Morocco Loan, which had fallen to sixty-four
or sixty-five francs.   They bought it up very skilfully,
through brokers of little account who aroused no distrust.
Even the Rothschilds were taken in.   They were surprised
at the steady absorption of Morocco stock, but it was pointed
out to them that the dealers were all low-class outsiders.
That kept the Rothschilds quiet.   Well, the next thing now
is that the expedition is going to come off after all and as
soon as we get to Tangier the Government will guarantee
the debt.   Our friends will have made fifty or sixty millions.
You see the idea ?   You will realise that they distrust
everyone, and fear the slightest indiscretion."

She was resting her head against Du Roy's waistcoat and
had her arms in his lap, she pressed very close to him, aware
that for the moment she had aroused his interest, and ready
to do anything on earth for a caress or a smile.

" Are you quite sure ? " he asked.

" Absolutely," she replied with confidence.

" You are right," he declared,   " It's a great scheme.
As for that scum Laroche, that's a fellow I'll get between my
finger and thumb.   The scoundrel ?   Let him look out
for himself . . . let him look out for himself.   I shall have
his ministerial carcass between my fingers."

He began to reflect.

" All the same," he said, " there ought to be some profit
to be got out of it."

" You can still buy stock," she said.   " It has only gone
to seventy-two."

" Quite so," he rejoined, " but I have no money available."

She raised her eyes full of supplication, towards him.

" I thought of that, my pet, and if you were very kind and loved me a little, you would let me lend you some."

He replied abruptly, almost harshly :

" No, no, none of that, none of that."

" Listen," she implored. " There is a way you can do it without borrowing the money. I intended to buy ten thousand francs of the loan myself, so as to have a little nest-egg. Well, I'll buy twenty thousand, and you can go halves. You understand, of course, that I shan't pay my husband anything. For the present there will be nothing to pay. If it succeeds, you get seventy-two thousand francs. If it fails, you will owe me ten thousand which you can pay when it suits you."

Again he refused.

" No. I have no fancy for an arrangement like that."

Then she argued with him persuasively, and made it clear to him that he was really pledging ten thousand francs on his word, and taking all the risk and that she was advancing him nothing, inasmuch as all the disbursements were made by her husband's bank. Further she pointed out to him that it was he who had conducted, in the *Vie Française*, all the political campaign which had rendered this affair possible, and that he would be very silly if he did not get something out of it.

He was still hesitating and she went on :

" If you will only consider that it is my husband who is advancing the ten thousand francs to you and that you have rendered him services which are worth far more than that."

" Very well," he said. " Be it so. I will go shares with you. If we lose, I shall pay you back ten thousand francs."

She was so delighted that she rose and took his head between her hands and began to kiss him eagerly. At first he made no attempt to defend himself, but as she grew bolder, straining him in her arms and devouring him with caresses, it occurred to him that the other lady was due to arrive quite soon and that if he showed weakness he would be wasting his time and would lose in the arms of the elder woman the ardour which would be better kept for the younger. So he repulsed her gently.

"Come now," he said, "you must behave yourself."
She looked at him disconsolately.

"Oh, George, I'm not allowed even to kiss you."

"No," he replied. "Not to-day. I have a nervous headache, and it hurts me."

Docilely she resumed her seat between his knees, and asked:

"Will you come and dine with us to-morrow? It would be such a joy to me."

He hesitated but feared to refuse.

"Yes, certainly."

"Thank you, my darling."

With a fondling motion, she rubbed her cheek up and down against Du Roy's chest, and one of her long black hairs caught in his waistcoat. She observed it, and a wild idea crossed her mind, one of those superstitious notions which often constitute a woman's only logic. She started very gently winding this hair round a button. Then she wound another round the next button below, a third round the next one above; until she had attached a hair to every button. When he rose he would presently tear them all out. He would hurt her. What happiness! And without knowing it he would carry away something of hers, a small tress of her hair, a thing he had never asked her for. It was a bond by which she attached herself to him, a bond, secret and invisible, a charm left on him by her. Whether he would or not, he would think of her, dream of her, and on the morrow love her a little more.

"I must leave you," he announced suddenly. "I am expected at the Chamber of Deputies for the end of the sitting. I mustn't fail them to-day."

"Oh, already!" she sighed. Then in a resigned tone:

"Go, my love, but come to dinner to-morrow."

Briskly she moved away from him and felt on her head a quick keen pang as though her skin had been pricked with needles. Her heart beat; she was happy, because she had endured a little pain through him. She bade him adieu. He took her in his arms with a compassionate smile and kissed her eyes coldly. Again at the contact she lost her self-control and she whispered, "Already?" and her suppliant glance wandered to the open door of the room. He broke away from her, saying as if in haste :

" I must get away or I shall be late."

She offered him her lips which he hardly brushed with his, and after giving her her umbrella which she was forgetting, he urged her :

" Come, come, we must hurry up. It is past three."

She preceded him ; again she said :

" To-morrow at seven."

" To-morrow at seven," he replied.

They separated, she turned to the left and he to the right. Du Roy walked as far as the outer Boulevard ; then he turned slowly back along the Boulevard Malesherbes. As he passed a confectioner's he noticed some *marrons glacés* in a crystal bowl and he thought :

" I will take Clotilde a pound of them."

He bought a bag of these sugar-plums, for which she had a passion. By four o'clock he was at the flat again, awaiting Clotilde. She was a little late in arriving, because her husband had just come home for a week.

" Can you dine with us to-morrow ? " she asked. " He would be delighted to see you."

" No. I'm dining with Walter. We are busy with a lot of political and financial schemes."

She had taken off her hat, and was now removing her bodice, which was too tight for her. He pointed to the bag on the mantelpiece :

" I bought you some *marrons glacés*."

She clapped her hands.

" How jolly ! What a darling you are."

She took one, tasted it, and declared :

" They are lovely. I have a feeling that I shan't leave one of them."

And casting at George a look both sprightly and voluptuous she added :

" You encourage me in all my weaknesses."

She continued slowly eating the *marrons glacés*, continually glancing at the bottom of the bag to see whether there were any left.

" Look here," she said. " You take the arm-chair and I'll sit between your knees and nibble my sweets. I shall enjoy that."

He smiled and sat down, and took her between his knees, just as he had a moment before held Madame Walter.

She raised her face to speak to him and said, with her mouth full :

" Do you know, my love, I've been dreaming about you. I dreamt we were both of us making a great journey on a camel. The camel had two humps and we were each of us astride one of them and we were crossing the desert. We had sandwiches in a paper parcel and a bottle of wine and we were having our dinner on our humps. But I was annoyed because we couldn't do anything else. We were too far away from each other, so I wanted to get down."

" So do I want to get down," he replied.

Amused by her story he laughed, and incited her to say foolish things and chatter and utter all the childish absurdities of lovers. The prattle which charmed him on the lips of Madame de Marelle would have exasperated him on Madame Walter's. Clotilde, too, called him " my darling, my little one, my pet," and these words seemed to him soft and caressing, although it was only a moment since the same endearments from the other woman had aroused his irritation and disgust. Terms of affection are always the same, but they derive their flavour from the lips that utter them.

But even while he was diverted by this trifling his thoughts were occupied with the seventy thousand francs which he hoped to make, and, tapping her head with his fingertips he put an abrupt stop to her chattering.

" Listen, puss. I am going to give you a message for your husband. Tell him from me to buy to-morrow ten thousand francs of Morocco stock, now standing at seventy-two. I guarantee that he will make sixty to eighty thousand francs within three months. You must enjoin absolute silence. Tell him from me that the expedition to Tangier has been settled and France will guarantee the Morocco debt. But keep it to yourself. It is a State secret that I am trusting you with."

She listened gravely and replied :

" Thank you. I shall let my husband know this very evening. You can depend on him. He won't chatter. He is thoroughly trustworthy. There is no danger."

She had finished the *marrons glacés*, and she crumpled up the bag in her hands and threw it in the fire-place.

Without rising from her footstool, she began to unbutton George's waistcoat. All of a sudden she stopped. She had found a long hair in a button-hole, and she drew it out between finger and thumb.

" Look ! " she laughed. " You have one of Madeleine's hairs on you. There's a faithful husband ! "

Then she became serious and laid the hair on her hand and examined it closely.

" It is not Madeleine's," she said. " It is a brown one."

He smiled.

" It is probably the housemaid's."

But she inspected the waistcoat as minutely as a detective and she picked out a second hair which was coiled round another button ; then she saw a third. She trembled a little and turned pale, and exclaimed :

" Oh, you've been with a woman who has wound hairs round all your buttons."

Taken by surprise he faltered :

" Oh no . . . you are crazy . . . "

Suddenly he remembered and understood. At first he was taken aback, but presently he denied it with a suppressed laugh, not wholly displeased that she should suspect him of other intimacies. She continued seeking and finding other hairs which she unwound quickly and threw on the carpet. With her subtle feminine instinct she had divined their significance, and in a fury of rage and on the verge of tears she clamoured :

" She loves you, this woman. She wants you to carry something of her about with you . . . oh, what a traitor you are . . . "

Then she shrieked ; a strident shriek of glee :

"Oh, oh . . . it's an old woman! Here is a white hair . . . ah, you are taking old women now. Do they pay you anything? Tell me, do they pay you? Ah, you've come down to old women . . . Then you don't want me any longer. You can keep the other one."

She rose to her feet, snatched her bodice off the chair and put it on rapidly. Ashamed and stammering he tried to detain her.

"Come now . . . Clo . . . this is silly of you . . . I don't know what it's all about. Listen . . . do stay . . . Oh! come now, do stay . . ."

"Keep your old woman," she said. "Keep her. Have a ring made of her hair, her white hair . . . you have enough of it for that . . ."

With impetuous and hasty movements she had put on her bodice, her hat and her veil, and when he tried to catch her, her arm swung round through the air and caught him a slap on the face. While he was still stunned with the blow, she opened the door and took to flight. As soon as he was alone he broke out into a furious rage against Madame Walter. Ah, he would send that old jade about her business, and sharply too. He bathed his scarlet cheek and, meditating vengeance, left the house in his turn. This time he would not forgive her. No, he would not. He went along as far as the Boulevard, and loitered before a jeweller's window to look at a chronometer which he had long coveted and which was priced at eighteen hundred francs. He thought suddenly, with his heart leaping with joy:

"If I get my seventy thousand, I shall be able to pay for that watch."

And he began to dream of all the things he would do with the seventy thousand francs.

First he would be elected Deputy, then he would buy his chronometer, then he would gamble on the Stock Exchange, and then . . . and then . . . He had no wish to go back to the office. He wanted to have a talk with Madeleine before seeing Walter again and writing his article, and he turned in the direction of home.

He reached the Rue Drouot when he stopped short. He

had forgotten to enquire for Count de Vaudrec, who lived in the Chaussée d'Antin. He turned accordingly, still with loitering step and his mind in a happy dreamland, thinking of a thousand pleasant things, and of the wealth within his grasp, but also of that blackguard Laroche and that scurvy old Madame Walter. He was however not in the least put out by Clotilde's anger, well aware that she would soon forgive him.

He asked the hall-porter at de Vaudrec's house :

" How is Count de Vaudrec ? I hear that he hasn't been well these last few days."

" The Count is not at all well, sir," the man replied, " he is not expected to last the night. The gout has gone to his heart."

Du Roy was so much shocked that he did not know what to do. Vaudrec dying ! His head was thronged with confused and disquieting thoughts which he dared not avow. He stammered :

" Thanks . . . I shall come back . . ."

But he did not know what he was saying.

He jumped into a cab and drove home. His wife was there. Out of breath, he thrust his way into her room and announced abruptly :

" Haven't you heard ? Vaudrec is dying."

She was sitting reading a letter. She raised her eyes.

" What ? You say . . . you say . . . you say . . ." she repeated three times.

" I tell you that Vaudrec is dying of an attack of gout which has gone to his heart. What are you going to do ? " he added.

She stood up, livid, her cheeks shaken with nervous tremors ; then she gave way to a passion of tears and buried her face in her hands. She remained standing, convulsed by sobs and torn with anguish. But suddenly she controlled her grief. Wiping her eyes, she said :

" I am . . . I am going to him . . . don't worry about me . . . I don't know what time I shall be back . . . don't wait for me."

" Very well. Go," he said.

They pressed each other's hands, and she left in such a hurry that she forgot her gloves. After a solitary dinner, George set himself to write his article. He did it exactly according to Laroche's instructions, letting the reader understand that there would be no expedition to Tangier. Then he took it to the office, chatted a few moments with Monsieur Walter, and went away smoking. His heart was light, he did not know why. His wife had not come home yet. He went to bed and fell asleep. She returned about midnight. Suddenly awakened, George sat up in bed.

" Well ? " he asked. He had never seen her so pale or so strongly moved.

" He is dead," she murmured.

" Ah . . . and . . . he said nothing to you ? "

" Nothing. By the time I arrived he had lost consciousness."

George was thinking. Questions, which he dared not put, occurred to him.

" You had better go to bed," he said.

She undressed quickly and slipped in beside him.

" Had he any relations by his death-bed ? "

" Only one nephew."

" Ah ! did he often meet this nephew ? "

" Never. They hadn't met for ten years."

" Had he any other relations ? "

" No—I believe not."

" Well, then it is this nephew who is the heir ? "

" I don't know."

" Vaudrec was very rich ? "

" Yes. Very."

" Have you any idea how much he had ? "

" No. Not exactly. One or two million francs, perhaps."

He said no more, and she blew out the candle. They lay side by side in the darkness, silent, wakeful, thinking. Du Roy had no further disposition to sleep. The seventy thousand francs promised him by Madame Walter seemed to him now a paltry sum. He suddenly had the impression that Madeleine was crying. To make sure of it he said :

" Are you asleep ? "

" No."

Tears trembled in her voice.   He went on :

" I forgot to tell you that your Laroche has let us in."

" How is that ? "

He narrated to her at length and with all the details, the
scheme that Laroche and Walter had concocted between
them.   When he had finished, she asked him :

" Where did you learn that ? "

" With your permission," he said, " I shall not tell you.
You have sources of information to which I have no access.
I have mine and I intend to keep them.   All the same I
can vouch for the accuracy of my information."

She said thoughtfully :

" Yes.   It is possible.   I had my doubts as to whether
they were not doing something and leaving us out."

George, who was no nearer to sleep, came closer to his
wife and kissed her ear softly, but she repulsed him sharply.

" Leave me alone, please, will you.   I'm not in a playful
mood."

Resignedly he turned his face to the wall, closed his eyes
and at last fell asleep.

VI

THE church was draped in black and on the west door was a great hatchment surmounted by a coronet which apprised the passers-by that a person of noble birth was being interred.

The ceremony was over and those who had been present were departing, filing slowly out in front of the coffin, after shaking hands with Count de Vaudrec's nephew. When George and Madeleine Du Roy had left the church they walked homeward sides by side. They were preoccupied and silent. At last George, as if speaking to himself, ejaculated:

" Really it is most astonishing ! "

" What is astonishing, my dear ? "

" That Vaudrec has left us nothing."

She reddened violently as if a rosy veil, rising up from her neck to her forehead, had suddenly covered her white skin.

" Why should he have left us anything ? " she asked. " There was no reason why he should."

But after a short silence she continued :

" Perhaps there is a will at some notary's. We could not know yet."

" Yes," he said thoughtfully, " that is possible. After all he was our best friend, mine as well as yours. He dined with us twice a week and was always dropping in. He was at home with us, absolutely at home. He loved you like a father, and he had no family, no children or brothers or sisters, nothing but a nephew of sorts. Certainly there must be a will. I don't expect anything much ; just a keepsake to show that he thought of us and was fond of us and acknowledged our affection. He certainly owes us a mark of friendship."

Pensive and indifferent, she said, " I dare say there is a will."

On their return to their house, the servant handed Madeleine a letter. She opened it and held it out to her husband.

Chambers of Maître Lamaneur,
Notary.
17, *Rue des Vosges.*

Madam,
I have the honour to request that you will have the goodness to attend at my chambers, between the hours of two and four, on Tuesday, Wednesday or Thursday, in relation to a matter of business which concerns you.

Believe me, etc.,
Lamaneur.

It was George's turn to blush.

" That must be it. It is odd that he should send for you and not me, seeing that I am legally the head of the family."

At first she made no reply, but after a brief reflection :

" Would you like us to go at once ? " she asked.

" Yes, certainly."

They set out immediately after luncheon. As they entered Maître Lamaneur's chambers, the chief clerk rose with marked alacrity and showed them in to his master.

The notary was a small man and very round, round all over ; his head looked like a ball fixed on top of another ball, to which were attached two legs so small and short as almost to resemble balls too. He shook hands with them, offered them chairs, and turning to Madeleine, said :

" Madam, I have sent for you to acquaint you with the terms of the testament of Count de Vaudrec which concerns you."

George could not refrain from interjecting a remark.

" I thought as much."

The notary proceeded :

" I am going to inform you of the contents of this document which is, I may say, extremely brief."

He took a paper from a case which lay before him, and read as follows :

273

I, the undersigned, Paul Emil Cyprien Gontran Count de Vaudrec, being in good health and full possession of my faculties, hereby express my last wishes.

As we are all liable to death at any moment, I desire in prevision to take the precaution of writing my testament, which will be deposited with Maître Lamaneur.

Having no direct heirs, I bequeath my entire fortune, consisting of securities valued at six hundred thousand francs and real estate valued at about five hundred thousand francs, to Madame Claire Madeleine Du Roy, free from all charge or obligation. I beg her to accept this gift from a departed friend, as a testimony of devoted, profound and respectful affection.

" That is all," remarked the notary. " This document bears date last August, and supersedes a document of similar intention made two years ago, in favour of Madame Claire Madeleine Forestier. I have the prior document which will serve to prove, in case of any dispute on the part of the family, that Count de Vaudrec's intentions remained unaltered."

Madeleine had turned pale and was looking at her feet. George was twisting the ends of his moustache nervously between his fingers. After a moment's silence the notary resumed :

" It is understood, of course, Monsieur Du Roy, that your wife cannot accept this legacy without your consent."

Du Roy rose to his feet and said dryly :

" I must have time to think it over."

The notary smiled, bowed, and said in an amiable voice :

" I understand the scruple which makes you hesitate, Monsieur Du Roy. I may add that Monsieur de Vaudrec's nephew, who was acquainted this very morning with the last intentions of his uncle, expressed his readiness to respect them on condition that a sum of a hundred thousand francs is made over to him. In my opinion the will is unassailable, but legal proceedings would attract an amount of public attention which you might prefer to avoid. The world is apt to be uncharitable in its verdicts. In any case, will you be able to communicate to me your decision on all these points before Saturday ? "

George bowed his assent and took leave ceremoniously. He opened the door for his wife, who had remained silent, and he went away with so inflexible an air that the notary smiled no longer.

As soon as they were at home again, Du Roy shut the door sharply and threw his hat on the bed.

" You were de Vaudrec's mistress ? "

Madeleine, who was taking off her veil, turned round with a start.

" I ? Oh ! "

" Yes, you.   A woman doesn't have a fortune left her unless——"

She had begun to tremble, and was unable to take out the pins with which her veil was fastened.   After a moment's thought, she stammered, in an agitated voice :

" Look here.   Come now.   You are mad—You are —you are.   Didn't you yourself—only a moment ago —Weren't you hoping that he would leave you something ? "

George remained standing near her, keeping a close eye on all her emotions, like a police magistrate trying to take advantage of the slightest weakness of an accused.   Emphasising each word, he made his pronouncement :

" Yes, he could have left something to me—to me, your husband—to me, his friend, you understand—but not to you—a woman and my wife.   The distinction is of the utmost importance ; it is essential, from the point of view of propriety ; of public opinion."

Madeleine, in her turn, looked him fixedly and straight in the eyes, with a certain depth and singularity of scrutiny, as though to read in them and discover that unknown element of character, which is never wholly revealed, and of which one can barely catch a fleeting glimpse at unguarded or reckless moments that are like doors ajar disclosing the mysterious recesses of the mind.   With slow articulation, she said :

" Nevertheless, it seems to me as if—that people would

have thought a legacy of such importance at least as strange from him—to you."

" Why so ? " he asked sharply.

" Because——" She hesitated, but resumed presently :

" Because you are my husband. You have really known him only a short time and I have been his friend for ages, since his first will, which was made during Charles's lifetime, was already in my favour."

George had begun to stride up and down.

" You can't accept the legacy," he declared.

She replied with indifference :

" Very well. Then we needn't wait until Saturday. We had better let Monsieur Lamaneur know at once."

He stopped in front of her, and again they remained some instants, eye to eye, each straining to reach the impenetrable secret of the other's heart, to pierce down to the quick of thought. Each tried in one fierce dumb interrogation to see the other's conscience naked ; it was a hand-to-hand struggle between two beings who, though living side by side, remained ignorant of each other, suspected, watched and lay in wait without ever reaching the slimy profundities of the other's soul.

Abruptly, and looking into her face, he said in a low voice :

" Come now, confess that you were Vaudrec's mistress."

She shrugged her shoulders.

" How stupid you are ! Vaudrec had a very great affection for me, but nothing more—ever."

He stamped his foot.

" You lie. It is impossible."

" It is as I have told you nevertheless," she replied calmly.

He began again to walk up and down. Presently he stopped.

" Then will you explain to me why he is leaving all his fortune to you—, to you—"

She did so with quiet unconcern.

" It is quite simple. As you were just saying, he had no friends but us, or me rather, for he knew me as a child. My mother was companion to some relatives of his. He was continually coming here and as he had no natural heirs he thought of me. It is possible that he loved me a little. But where is the woman who has never inspired that sort of love? Why should not this secret affection have influenced him to write my name when he was thinking of making his last dispositions? He used to bring me flowers every Monday. You were not surprised at that, but he didn't bring any flowers for you, did he? Now he has given me his fortune for the same reason, and because he has no one else to give it to. It would, however, be extremely surprising if he had left it to you. Why should he? What were you to him?"

She spoke so calmly and naturally that George hesitated. Then he resumed:

"All the same, we can't accept the legacy under these conditions. It would have a deplorable effect. Everyone would believe it was true; everybody would talk and make fun of me. As it is, the other men on the staff are jealous and far too ready to attack me. More than anyone, I am bound to have a care of my honour and reputation. It is out of the question for me to make the admission involved in allowing my wife to accept a legacy of that sort from a man, whom public rumour already credits with being her lover. Perhaps Forestier could have stood it. He might, but not I."

"Very well, my dear," she replied gently, "Don't let us accept it. It will be a million francs less in our pockets, that's all."

He continued pacing up and down and began to speak his thoughts aloud, talking at his wife without directly addressing her.

"Well then—yes—a million—so much the worse. When he was making his will he didn't realise what an error in tact, what a breach of propriety he was committing. He never noticed what a false and ridiculous position he was going to place me in. These niceties are everything in life. He ought to have left me half. Then there would have been no fuss."

He sat down and crossed his legs and began to twist the

tips of his moustaches as was his habit when bored or uneasy or puzzled. Madeleine took up a piece of embroidery which she occasionally worked at, and while selecting her wools, said :

" As for me, I have only to hold my tongue. It is for you to do the thinking."

He did not reply for a long time. Finally he said, with hesitation :

" People will never understand how Vaudrec came to make you his sole heir and I to allow it. To accept this fortune on these terms would be to admit on your part a guilty liaison and on mine an infamous complaisance. Do you realise what interpretation would be placed on our acceptance ? We should have to invent some subterfuge, some adroit way of toning the thing down, for instance, we should have to let it be understood that he divided his fortune between us, giving half to the husband and half to the wife."

" I don't see," she replied, " how that can be done, seeing that the terms of the will are explicit."

" Oh, that is quite simple," he rejoined. " You could make over half the inheritance to me by a deed of gift. We have no children, so it can be done. In that way we should close the mouth of public slander."

With a certain loss of patience, she retorted :

" Even then I don't see how the mouth of public slander would be closed, considering that the document is there with Vaudrec's signature."

He replied angrily :

" Do we have to show it and placard it on the walls ? It is you who are stupid, if it comes to that. We can say that Count de Vaudrec has left half his fortune to each of us. There you are ! . . . Now, you can't accept this legacy without my authorisation. I give it to you on the sole condition of a division which will prevent me from becoming a general laughing-stock."

Again she flashed a piercing glance at him.

" Very well. I agree."

He rose to his feet and began to walk about again. He

seemed to hesitate anew and he was now avoiding the penetrating eyes of his wife.

" No," he said, " Decidedly no. Perhaps it would be better to renounce it altogether, more dignified, more correct, more honourable . . . Still, in this way, there could be no ground for suppositions, none whatever. The most scrupulous could not but accept it."

He halted in front of Madeleine.

" Very well, then, if you so desire, my love, I shall go back alone, to Maître Lamaneur to consult him and explain matters. I shall make it clear to him that it is a point of honour and that we arrived at the notion of a division for the sake of propriety and to prevent people from chattering. From the moment that I accept half this inheritance it is quite obvious that no one will have any right to smile. It is equivalent to saying in a dignified manner, ' My wife accepts because I accept—I, her husband, who am the judge of what she can do without compromising herself.' Otherwise it would have caused a scandal."

Madeleine contented herself with saying, " As you will."

He began to talk fluently.

" Yes, it is clear as daylight, with this plan of dividing it in halves. We inherit from a friend who has been reluctant to create any difference between us, who would make no distinction, and did not want to seem to say, ' I continue after my death the preference I had while I was alive.' He was fonder of the wife, to be sure, but by leaving his fortune equally between the two he wanted to express clearly that his preference was entirely platonic. And you may be sure that that is precisely what he would have done, if he had thought of it. But he did not think. He did not foresee the consequences. As you put it so well just now, it is to you that he offered flowers every week, it is to you that he wanted to leave his last keepsake, but he forgot that——"

With a shade of annoyance, she interrupted him :

" It is all settled. I understand the position. There is no need for so many explanations. You can go to the notary immediately."

He reddened and stammered.

" You are right.   I'll go."

He took his hat, and as he was going out, he said :

" I might try to arrange the difficulty with the nephew for fifty thousand francs, don't you think ? "

" No," she replied disdainfully, " Give him the hundred thousand that he is asking for.   And take it out of my share, if you prefer."

" Why, no," he replied, suddenly ashamed of himself : " We will each pay half.   If we each give up fifty thousand there is a clear million left for us."

Adding, " I shall be back soon, my dear," he went away to explain to the notary the scheme which he pretended had originated with his wife.

On the following day they signed a deed of gift of half a million francs which Madeleine Du Roy had made over to her husband.

When they left the notary's chambers George proposed, as it was a fine day, to walk as far as the Boulevards.   His demeanour was gentle, attentive, respectful, and tender. Everything pleased him and made him laugh.   She on the other hand remained meditative and serious.

It was an autumn day and rather cold.   People had a hurried air and were walking fast.   Du Roy brought his wife in front of the shop where he had so often gazed upon the longed-for chronometer.

" Would you like me to give you a piece of jewellery ? "

" If you would care to," she replied with indifference.

They entered the shop and he asked her :

" What would you prefer ?   A necklace, a bracelet, or ear-rings ? "

The sight of the pretty things in gold and precious stones broke down her assumed coldness, and, her eyes sparkling with interest, she looked over the show-cases full of jewels. Suddenly something caught her fancy, and she said :

" That is a pretty bracelet."

It was a chain of bizarre design, every link being set with a different stone.

" How much is this bracelet ? " asked George.

" Three thousand francs, sir," replied the jeweller.

" If you will let me have it for two thousand five hundred, we will call it a bargain."

The man hesitated before replying.

" No, sir, it is impossible."

" Look here," said Du Roy, " throw in this chronometer for fifteen hundred, that makes four thousand, and I pay cash. How will that do? If you don't agree, I shall go elsewhere."

The jeweller was at first perplexed, but ended by accepting.

" Very well, sir. It's a bargain."

Du Roy gave his address and continued :

" On the chronometer I want the initials G.R.C. engraved in a monogram, under a baron's coronet."

Madeleine was surprised and smiled, but when they left the shop she took his arm affectionately. There was real address and strength in him, and now that he had an independent income he must, to be sure, have a title. The jeweller bowed them out.

" You can depend on me, Baron. It will be ready on Thursday."

They passed in front of the Vaudeville, where there was a new play on the programme.

" We might go to the theatre to-night, if you would like to," he suggested. " Let us see if we can get a box."

They secured their box, then he said :

" Suppose we dine at a restaurant."

" I should love it."

He was as happy as a king and kept thinking of things to do.

" We might go and see Madame de Marelle and ask her to spend the evening with us. I hear that her husband is at home. I should very much like to see him."

They went to the Marelles, and George, who was a little timid at the prospect of meeting his mistress again, was not displeased at his wife being present and thus making explanations impossible. But Clotilde seemed to remember nothing, and persuaded her husband to accept the invitation.

They had a festive dinner and a delightful evening. It was late when George and Madeleine got home. The gas was out. To light them up the staircase Du Roy kept striking wax-matches. On the first floor landing, they saw their faces flash out at them from the mirror, in the sudden flaring of a match in the surrounding darkness of the staircase. They had the air of phantoms that come forth out of the night and are ready to vanish into it again.

Du Roy raised the match to illuminate their reflections more closely, and with a triumphant laugh he exclaimed:

" Look at the millionaires."

VII

IT was now two months since the conquest of Morocco had been accomplished. France, now mistress of Tangier, was in occupation of the entire African coast line as far as the regency of Tripoli, and had guaranteed the debt of the newly annexed country. It was rumoured that two ministers of State had made a profit of twenty million francs, and Laroche-Mathieu's name was mentioned without much pretence of secrecy. As for Walter, everybody in Paris knew that he had made a double *coup* and had netted between thirty and forty millions on the loan and eight to ten millions on the copper and iron mines, not to mention the profits on immense tracts of land which he had bought for a song before the conquest and had sold to colonisation companies the day after the occupation. In a few days he had become a world power, one of those omnipotent financiers, stronger than kings, who can force heads to bow and lips to tremble, and can evoke from the depths of man's heart the whole compass of the base, the ignoble and the envious.

He was no longer Walter the Jew, owner of a doubtful bank, director of a shady newspaper, a Deputy suspected of disreputable intrigues. He was Monsieur Walter, the wealthy Israelite. And he intended to let people see it.

Aware of the pecuniary embarrassment of the Prince of Carlsbourg, who owned one of the finest mansions in the Rue du Faubourg Saint Honoré, with a garden overlooking the Champs Elysées, he made a proposal to buy the property from him, furniture and all, without moving as much as a single arm-chair, at twenty-four hours' notice. He offered three million francs for it. Tempted by this sum, the Prince accepted, and on the following day Walter installed himself in his new domicile.

Soon afterwards he had another idea, the idea of a conqueror, eager to take Paris by storm, a Napoleonic idea. At that moment the whole town was flocking to see a great picture by the painter Karl Marcowitch, which was exhibited by Jacques Lenoble the expert. It represented Christ walking on the waves. The art critics declared enthusiastically that this painting was the masterpiece of the century.

Walter bought it for half a million francs, and carried it off, thus holding up the tide of public curiosity, from one day to another, and forcing all Paris to talk about him, in envy, blame or approval.

His next move was to issue an announcement in the papers that he would invite all Parisian Society to his house one evening to see the masterpiece of the foreign painter, so that it should not be said that he had hidden away a work of art. His house would be thrown open. Anyone who pleased could come. It would be sufficient to show at the door the letter of invitation.

The invitation was couched in these terms :

" Monsieur and Madame Walter request the honour of your company on the thirtieth of December, from nine to twelve, at their house, to see Karl Marcowitch's picture, ' Christ Walking on the Waves,' by electric light."

Then followed a postscript in quite small letters.

" After twelve o'clock there will be dancing."

Those who wished to stay on for the dance would do so, and from among them the Walters would recruit their future circle of acquaintance. The others insolent or indifferent would look at the picture, the house and its owners with worldly curiosity. Then they would go as they had come. Old Walter was perfectly aware that they would return some day, just as they had done to the houses of his brother Israelites who had grown rich like himself.

The first thing was to attract to his house all the impecunious people of title whose names figure in society papers. They would be curious to see the face of a man who had made fifty million francs in six weeks ; they would come, too, in order to observe who else was there; also because he had had the good taste and tact to invite them to admire a Christian picture in the house of a son of Israel.

It was as if he said to them:

"Look here, I gave half a million for Marcowitch's sacred masterpiece, 'Christ Walking on the Waves.' And this masterpiece will always remain here, under my eyes, in the house of Walter the Jew."

In society, the society of duchesses and the Jockey Club, this invitation, which after all did not bind one to anything, was much discussed. People would go, just as they went to see the water-colours at Monsieur Petit's. It came to this. The Walters owned a masterpiece and were throwing open their doors for one evening to give everyone a chance of admiring it. That was all.

For a fortnight the *Vie Française* had had a paragraph every morning about the evening party, fixed for the 30th of December, and was doing its utmost to kindle public curiosity.

Du Roy was enraged at his director's triumph. He had considered himself rich with the five hundred thousand francs he had extorted from his wife, but now he thought himself poor, miserably poor, as he compared his paltry fortune with the rain of millions that had fallen around him, none of which he had been able to pick up for himself.

His jealous rage increased daily. He was furious with everybody, with the Walters whom he refused to visit, with his wife, who, misled by Laroche, had dissuaded him from buying Morocco Loan. Above all he nursed a grudge against the minister who had tricked him, made use of him and dined at his table twice a week. George acted as Laroche's secretary, agent, amanuensis. When he wrote to his dictation, he had a mad desire to strangle the triumphant coxcomb. As minister, Laroche had been moderately successful, and in order to retain his portfolio, he carefully concealed the fact that it was bulging with gold. But Du Roy divined the presence of this money in the haughtier tone assumed by this upstart lawyer, his more insolent demeanour, his bolder assertions and his complete confidence in himself.

Laroche was supreme now, in Du Roy's house. Vaudrec's place and Vaudrec's dinners were now Laroche's, and he talked to the servants as if he were a second master.

George trembled but endured, like a dog that wants to bite but dares not. He was however often harsh and brutal to Madeleine, who would shrug her shoulders and treat him like a tiresome child. She was astonished at his constant ill-temper and would say :

" I simply don't understand you. You are always complaining. And yet you're in a splendid position."

He turned his back on her without a word. At first he had declared that he would not go to the director's party nor set foot in the house of that dirty Jew. For the last two months he had had daily letters from Madame Walter imploring him to come and see her, or to arrange a meeting wherever he pleased, so that she might hand over to him the seventy thousand francs which she had gained for him. He did not answer these desperate appeals, but threw them in the fire, not because he had decided to refuse his share of their common profits, but because he wished to madden her, to treat her with contempt, to trample her underfoot. She was too rich, and he wanted to show his scorn.

On the day of the reception Madeleine pointed out to him that he was making a great mistake in refusing to go. He retorted :

" Can't you leave me alone ? I shall stay at home."

After dinner he suddenly declared :

" After all it might be better to endure the infliction. Hurry up and get ready."

She was expecting this, and replied :

" I shall be ready in quarter of an hour."

He grumbled as he dressed, and even in the cab he continued to show his bad temper.

The great courtyard of the Carlsbourg House was illuminated at each corner by electric globes, which looked like four small bluish moons. A magnificent carpet was laid all down the high flight of stairs, and on each step stood a man in livery, as rigid as a statue.

" What ostentation ! " said Du Roy.

He shrugged his shoulders and his heart contracted with envy.

" Be quiet," said his wife, " and see if you can't do as much yourself."

They entered and left their heavy wraps with the footman who came forward. Several women were there with their husbands, and were taking off their furs. They were heard to murmur, " It's very fine ! very fine ! "

The enormous entrance hall was hung with tapestries representing the story of Mars and Venus. To right and left branched the two wings of a monumental staircase, which united on the first floor. The balustrade was a marvel of wrought iron, and its ancient and faded gilding cast a subdued gleam upon the red marble steps. At the entrance to the drawing-rooms two small girls, one in pink, the other in blue fancy dress, presented bouquets to the ladies. This was thought a charming idea. The *salons* were already crowded. Most of the ladies were in afternoon dress so as to make it quite clear that they had come there as they would to any other private view. Those who intended to remain for the ball had bare arms and necks.

Madame Walter, surrounded by friends, was receiving her guests in the second drawing-room. Many of them did not know her by sight, and wandered about as if they were in a museum, without troubling their heads about their hosts.

As soon as she caught sight of Du Roy she turned livid and made as if she would go to him. She remained, however, rooted to the spot, waiting for him. He greeted her ceremoniously, while Madeleine lavished upon her affectionate words and compliments. George left his wife with Madame Walter, and mingled with the throng in order to hear the spiteful things which would certainly be said.

Five drawing-rooms opened out of one another ; they were hung with valuable materials, Italian embroideries and Oriental tapestries of varied colour and workmanship, and on the walls were exhibited pictures by ancient masters. A small Louis XVI room was the chief centre of attraction, a boudoir upholstered in pale blue silk with pink bouquets.

The low gilt chairs, covered with the same material as the walls, were of exquisite workmanship.

George recognised the celebrities, the Duchess of Terracine, Count and Countess de Ravenel, General the Prince d' Andremont, the perfectly lovely Marchioness des Dunes, and besides them all the ladies and gentlemen who attend first nights.

Someone seized him by the arm, and a gay youthful voice exclaimed in his ear :

" Oh here you are at last, you naughty Bel-Ami. Why do you never come near us now."

It was Suzanne Walter, who was looking at him with her eyes of enamel blue, beneath the wavy cloud of her fair hair. He was delighted to see her again, and shook her hand heartily.

" I wasn't able to come," he apologised. " I have had so much to do these two months that I have not been out at all."

She resumed gravely :

" It was wrong, very, very wrong of you. You hurt our feelings very much. Mamma and I both adore you. I simply can't get on without you. When you are not there I am bored to death. I tell you this quite frankly so that you will have no excuse for disappearing like that again. Give me your arm. I want to be the one to show you 'Christ Walking on the Waves.' It's right at the back, behind the conservatory. Papa put it at the far end, so that people would be obliged to pass through all the rooms. It's surprising how Papa peacocks with this house."

They made their way slowly through the crowd. People turned their heads to look at the handsome young man by the side of that ravishing doll. A well-known painter declared :

" What a handsome couple ! They're a pleasure to see."

" A really strong man," George was thinking, " would have married this girl. It was quite within my power. How was it I didn't think of it ? Why did I allow myself to go after Madeleine ? What madness ! One always acts without sufficient reflection."

And envy, bitter envy, filtered into his soul drop by drop, like gall, poisoning all his joys, and making his existence hateful.

" Oh, do come often, Bel-Ami," exclaimed Suzanne, " we shall have such fun now that Papa is rich. We shall enjoy ourselves like mad."

Still following up his thought, he replied :

" Oh, you will be getting a husband soon. You will marry some fine prince, rather hard up, and we shall never see each other."

She exclaimed ingenuously :

" Oh no, not yet. I shall marry somebody I like, some- body I like very much, somebody I like more than anyone else. I am rich enough for two."

He smiled a cynical, disdainful smile and began to name to her some of the guests, men of noble birth, who had sold their tarnished titles to financiers' daughters, like her, and who now lived with or without their wives, but in any case independent and insolent, well known and treated with deference.

" I don't give you more than six months," he concluded, " before you are caught by the same bait. You will be a Marchioness, a Duchess, or a Princess, and then you will look down on me, young woman."

She was indignant, and tapping him on the arm with her fan, vowed that she would never marry except to please her heart.

He laughed mockingly :

" We shall soon see ; you're too rich."

" But you, too," she replied. " You have had a legacy."

" Oh that ! " he ejaculated contemptuously. " It is hardly worth mentioning. A bare twenty thousand francs a year. It doesn't go far nowadays."

" But your wife got the same amount."

" Yes, a million between us. Forty thousand francs a year. We can't even keep a carriage on that."

They came to the last *salon*, and reached the open door of the conservatory. It was a large winter garden, full of tall trees from the tropics ; and under them masses of rare flowers. Beneath this dark green canopy, where the light filtered through like a silver stream, one breathed the warm earthy scent of the damp soil and the perfume-laden atmosphere. It was a curious sensation, unwholesome yet delicious, artificial, enervating and relaxing. Underfoot were spread carpets like moss and on either side were dense rows of shrubs. On his left Du Roy caught sight of a large white marble basin under a lofty dome of palm trees. It was big enough to bathe in, and on its rim were four great swans in Delft faience, with jets of water pouring from their open bills.

The bottom of the basin was sanded with gold dust and swimming about in it could be seen several enormous gold fish, grotesque monsters from China, with goggle eyes and blue-edged scales, mandarins of the water. Floating about over the golden bottom of the fountain they recalled the strange embroideries of that land.

Du Roy stood still with throbbing heart.

"This is luxury, real luxury. This is the sort of house to live in. Others have attained it. Why shouldn't I ?"

He thought of possible means of doing so, but as no idea immediately occurred to him he was exasperated by a sense of powerlessness. His companion likewise remained silent and thoughtful. He cast a sidelong glance at her and reflected :

"And all I had to do was to marry this human doll."

Suddenly Suzanne seemed to wake up.

"Come along," she said.

She urged George through a group of people who were blocking the way, and made him turn sharply to the right.

Embowered in strange plants which spread their quivering leaves wide open, like hands with slender fingers, was the motionless figure of a man standing upon the waves. The effect was startling. The sides of the picture were concealed in the living verdure and it had the appearance of a dark recess, with a fantastic and striking background. To take it in, a close scrutiny was necessary. The frame cut through the middle of the ship, on which were the apostles, dimly illuminated by the slanting rays of a lantern, whose light one of them, seated on the bulwarks, threw full on the advancing figure of Christ. Christ was about to step upon a wave which appeared to subside, allayed and soothed, ready to caress the divine foot. Everything surrounding the Saviour was in shadow, but the stars were shining in the sky. Seen in the faint light of the lantern, the faces of the apostles expressed amazement.

Undoubtedly it was a masterpiece, powerful and arresting, one of those works that make a profound impression upon the mind and for years afterwards give it food for reflection. Those who gazed at the picture did so in silence and went away thoughtful. It was not until later that they spoke of its worth as a painting.

After contemplating it for some time, Du Roy exclaimed :
" It's a feather in one's cap to be able to afford toys like that."

People were jostling and pushing him to obtain a view, so he turned away with Suzanne's little hand still on his arm. He pressed it gently.

" Won't you have some champagne ? " she asked. " Come to the buffet ; we shall find Papa there."

They returned slowly through the reception-rooms, where the increasing crowd, the fashionable crowd that frequents public entertainments, was making itself at home.

Suddenly George thought he heard someone say :
" There are Laroche and Madame Du Roy."

The words fell upon his ear like distant sounds wafted by the wind. Who had uttered them ? He looked all round him, and at that moment he happened to catch sight of his wife on Laroche's arm. They were talking in low confidential voices, smiling into each other's eyes. He thought he noticed people whispering and looking at them and he felt a brutal and foolish impulse to hurl himself upon the pair and batter them with his fists. Madeleine was making him ridiculous. He thought of Forestier. Perhaps people were saying :
" That poor fool Du Roy."

Who was she ? Nothing but a little upstart, clever enough, but without great resources. People came to his house, because they feared him and felt that he was formidable, but doubtless they talked freely about their modest way of living. He would never go very far with a woman like Madeleine, who would always be compromising herself and giving the house a doubtful reputation, and whose demeanour betrayed the adventuress. Henceforth she would always be a drag on his feet. Ah! if only he had guessed! If only he had known! He would have played a deeper, more daring game. With little Suzanne for the stake, how splendid his winnings would have been. How could he have been so blind as not to realise it?

They reached the great dining-room with its marble pillars and its walls hung with Gobelin tapestry. Walter caught sight of Du Roy and darted forward to shake hands with him. He was delirious with joy.

" Have you seen everything? Suzanne, have you shown him everything? Isn't there a crowd, Bel-Ami? Did you see Prince de Guerche? He has just been here drinking a glass of punch."

Then he rushed at Senator Rissolin, who was dragging along his bewildered wife, bedizened with all the frippery of a pedlar's pack.

A man bowed to Suzanne, a tall thin man, slightly bald, with fair whiskers, and an unmistakable air of fashion. George heard his name, the Marquis de Cazolles, and immediately became jealous of him. How long had he known her? Doubtless since she had possessed a fortune. He suspected him of being a suitor.

Someone took his arm. It was Norbert de Varenne, indifferent and languid, with his greasy hair and shabby coat.

" This is what is called enjoying oneself," he said. " Presently there will be dancing and then bed, and all the little girls will have had a good time. Have some champagne; it's excellent."

He filled his glass and bowing to Du Roy, who had taken another, said:

" To the triumph of mind over millions."

Then he added mildly, " not that I resent other people having them. I protest on principle."

George was not listening to him. He was looking for Suzanne who had just disappeared with the Marquis de Cazolles. Abruptly breaking away from Norbert de Varenne, he went in pursuit.

A dense throng, anxious for something to drink, delayed him. When he had at last made his way through it, he found himself face to face with the Marelles. He and Madame de Marelle still met, but it was a long time since he had seen her husband. Monsieur de Marelle seized both his hands.

"How can I thank you, my dear fellow, for the advice you gave me through Clotilde. I made nearly a hundred thousand francs out of the Morocco Loan. I owe it all to you. You are really a friend worth having."

Several men turned to look at the pretty dark woman in her elegant gown.

"As a reward, my dear fellow," said Du Roy, "I shall take away your wife. Or rather I offer her my arm. Husband and wife ought always to be separated."

Monsieur de Marelle bowed.

"Quite right. If I lose sight of you, we will meet here in an hour's time."

"Very good."

Du Roy and Clotilde disappeared in the crowd, followed by Monsieur de Marelle.

"What luck these Walters have!" exclaimed Clotilde. "That's what comes of being in the know."

"Pooh," replied George, "a strong man will always make his way, somehow or other."

"Those two girls will have twenty or thirty million francs each. And Suzanne is pretty into the bargain."

He made no reply. His own thoughts, issuing from another person's mouth, irritated him. She had not yet seen "Christ Walking on the Waves." He offered to take her there. They amused themselves with ill-natured remarks about people, and by making fun of all the unknown faces. Saint Potin passed close to them, with many ribbons on his coat, and this amused them very much. There was a former ambassador just behind them, whose row of decorations was less conspicuous.

"What a hotchpotch of society," said Du Roy.

Boisrenard shook hands with them. He, too, had adorned his buttonhole with the green and yellow ribbon which he had worn on the day of the duel. The Viscountess de Percemur, enormous and bedizened, was chatting with a duke in the little Louis XVI boudoir.

George murmured :

"A flirtation in high life."

As they went through the conservatory, he caught another glimpse of his wife and Laroche-Mathieu, almost hidden behind a group of plants. It was as if they had said :

"We have arranged a rendezvous here, a public rendezvous. We snap our fingers at public opinion."

Madame Marelle admitted that Karl Marcowitch's Christ was very striking and they went away. They had shaken off the husband.

"How is Laurine?" he asked. "Is she still angry with me?"

"Yes, just the same. She refuses to see you, and goes away when we talk about you."

He made no reply. The little girl's sudden hostility piqued and troubled him.

Suzanne caught them as they entered a door.

"Oh, there you are. Well, Bel-Ami, you're going to be left all alone. I want to carry the fair Clotilde off, to show her my room."

The two women went away together, gliding swiftly through the throng with the sinuous snake-like movement which women can adopt in a crowd.

Almost immediately a voice murmured his name. It was Madame Walter who addressed him, speaking very low.

"Oh, how ruthless and cruel you are. What unnecessary sufferings you cause me. I told Suzanne to take Madame de Marelle away so that I could have a word or two with you. Listen. I must, I must speak to you this evening . . . or . . . or . . . you don't know what I shall do. Go into the conservatory. You will find a door on the left.

Make your way into the garden, and follow the path in front of you. Right at the end you will see an arbour. Meet me there in ten minutes' time. If you don't agree to this I swear that I'll make a scene now on the spot."

He replied disdainfully :

" Very well, I shall be there in about ten minutes."

They separated. But Jacques Rival nearly made him late. He had taken him by the arm, and was chatting away with an elated air. Doubtless he had been visiting the buffet. At last Du Roy, transferring him to the hands of Monsieur de Marelle, whom he found in a doorway, made his escape. He had to take precautions to avoid being seen by his wife and Laroche and in this, thanks to their absorption in their conversation, he was successful. He made his way into the garden.

The night air chilled him like an iced bath.

" Hang it," he thought, " I shall catch cold," and he put his handkerchief round his neck like a muffler.

On either side, he distinguished leafless shrubs whose slender branches quivered. He walked slowly along the path hardly able to see after the brightness of the drawing-rooms. Silvery gleams of light from the windows of the house filtered through the twigs. Midway on the path in front of him he noticed something white. It was Madame Walter, with bare arms and neck. She exclaimed in a trembling voice :

" Ah, there you are. Do you want to kill me ? "

He replied calmly :

" No scenes if you please, or I shall make tracks at once."

She had clasped her arms round his neck, and with her lips close to his own, she murmured :

" What have I done to you ? You're treating me shamefully. What have I done to you ? "

He tried to shake her off.

" Last time I saw you you twisted some of your hairs round all my buttons, and it very nearly led to a rupture between my wife and me."

At first she was taken by surprise, then she shook her head.

" Oh, your wife doesn't care. It must have been one of your mistresses who made a scene."

" I have no mistresses."

" Don't talk nonsense. Why don't you ever come to see me ? Why do you even refuse to dine with us once a week ? My sufferings are appalling. I love you so much that I have no thought except for you ; I can look at nothing without seeing you before my eyes. I cannot utter a word without dreading that your name will slip out. Of course you can't understand this. It's as if I were caught in a trap, bound hand and foot. I can't describe it. The memory of you is always present ; it compresses my throat, tears something within my bosom, paralyses my limbs, so that I haven't the strength to walk. And I sit in a chair all day long, like a senseless animal, thinking of you."

He looked at her in amazement. This was no longer the awkward frolicsome hoyden whom he had known, but a distracted, desperate woman, capable of anything.

A vague idea, however, began to shape itself in his mind.

" My dear," he replied, " love isn't eternal. We come together and then we part. But when it drags on, as it did with us, it becomes a horrible burden. I have had enough of it. That's the plain truth. But if you can behave reasonably, receive me and treat me simply as a friend, I will come again as I used to. Do you think you're capable of that ? "

She laid her bare arms on George's black coat and whispered :

" I'm capable of anything for the sake of seeing you."

" Then it's agreed," he replied. " We're friends, nothing more."

She replied in a broken voice :

" It's agreed."

Then offering him her lips,

" One kiss, one last kiss."

Gently he refused.

" No, we must keep our compact."

She turned her head and wiped away two tears. Then she

drew from her bodice a bundle of papers, tied up with pink ribbon, and offered it to Du Roy.

" This is your share of the profits out of that Morocco business. It gave me such pleasure to make the money for you. Take it."

He wanted to refuse.

" No, I can't take it."

She was indignant.

" Oh, you mustn't behave like that now. This is yours, all yours. If you don't take it, I shall throw it down a drain. You mustn't treat me like that, George."

He took the small packet and slipped it into his pocket.

" We must go in," he said. " You'll catch pneumonia."

" All the better," she replied. " If only I could die."

She seized his hand, kissed it in a passion of love, rage and desperation, and fled into the house.

He followed her slowly and thoughtfully. He returned through the conservatory with his head held high and a smile on his lips.

Laroche and Madeleine had disappeared. The crowd was dispersing. Evidently people were not staying for the ball. He saw Suzanne holding her sister by the arm. They both came up to him to ask him to make up the first quadrille with Count de Latour-Yvelin.

" Who on earth is that ? " he asked in surprise.

Suzanne replied, teasingly :

" He's a new friend of my sister's."

Rose flushed and retorted :

" How silly you are, Suzanne. He's no more my friend than yours."

" We know all about that," said Suzanne, smiling.

Indignantly Rose turned her back on them and went away.

Du Roy took Suzanne familiarly by the elbow, and said in a caressing voice :

" Listen, my dear girl. You do believe that I'm your friend."

" Oh yes, Bel-Ami."

" You trust me ? "

" Absolutely."

" Do you remember what I said to you just now ? "

" About what ? "

" About your marriage, or rather about the man you'll marry."

" Yes."

" Well, will you promise me something ? "

" Yes. What ? "

" To consult me whenever you receive a proposal, and not to accept anyone without asking my advice."

" Yes, certainly I will."

" And it's to be a secret between you and me. Not a word either to your father or your mother."

" Not a word."

" Promise ? "

" I promise."

Rival came up to them with an air of importance.

" Mademoiselle Suzanne, your father wants you for the ball."

" Let's go, Bel-Ami."

But he refused. He decided to go home at once, anxious to be alone with his thoughts. Too many new ideas had entered his head. He went to look for his wife. After a while he found her at the buffet, drinking chocolate, with two men he did not know. She introduced her husband to them but without mentioning their names.

Presently he said :

" Shall we go ? "

" Whenever you like."

She took his arm, and they went back through the drawing-rooms, where only a few guests now remained.

" Where is Madame Walter ? " Madeleine asked. " I want to say good-bye to her."

" Better not. She would try to keep us for the ball and I've had enough."

" That's true."

They were silent all the way home. But when they entered their room, Madeleine, without waiting to take off her veil, said with a smile :

" You don't know what a surprise I've got for you."

" What is it ? " he growled ill-temperedly
" Guess."
" I can't be bothered."
" The day after to-morrow is New Year's Day."
" Yes."
" It's the time for presents."
" Yes."
" Here's yours. Laroche gave it to me just now."

She handed him a small black box like a jewel case. He opened it carelessly and found that it contained the cross of the Legion of Honour. He turned a little pale. Then he exclaimed with a smile :

" I should have preferred ten million francs. This doesn't cost him much."

She had been expecting an outburst of joy and his coldness exasperated her.

" You really are an incredible person. Nothing is good enough for you now."

" The man is only paying his debt," he replied quietly. " He owes me a great deal."

She was surprised at the tone of his voice, and rejoined :

" All the same, it's a great thing at your age."

" All values are relative," he answered, " I could do better than that now."

He had taken the case, and laying it open on the mantelpiece, he gazed fixedly at the sparkling star. Then he closed it again, shrugged his shoulders, and went to bed.

The Gazette of the first of January announced the appointment of Monsieur Prosper George Du Roy, journalist, to be Chevalier of the Legion of Honour for his distinguished services. The name was written in two syllables, and this pleased him even more than the decoration itself.

An hour after he had read the public announcement of the news, he received a note from Madame Walter inviting him and his wife to dine with her that evening to celebrate the distinction that had been conferred on him. He hesitated a few minutes. Then he threw the note, which was written in somewhat compromising terms, into the fire.

"We are dining with the Walters this evening," he announced to Madeleine.

She was surprised.

"Why, I thought you weren't going to set foot in their house again."

"I've changed my mind," was all he said.

When they arrived, Madame Walter was alone in the little Louis XVI boudoir, which she used for informal gatherings. She was dressed in black, and had powdered her hair and this added a charm to her appearance. Viewed from a distance she seemed an old woman, but close at hand she looked young and there was a fascination about her which captivated an attentive eye.

"Are you in mourning?" asked Madeleine.

She replied sadly:

"Yes and no. I have not lost anyone belonging to me. But I have reached the age when one mourns for one's youth. I am wearing black to-day to inaugurate it. After this I shall wear it in my heart."

"Will this resolution last?" Du Roy wondered.

Dinner was rather a gloomy affair. Only Suzanne chattered incessantly. Rose seemed preoccupied. Du Roy received many congratulations.

After dinner the party went strolling and chatting through the drawing-rooms and the conservatory. Du Roy walked behind with Madame Walter. She held him back by the arm.

"Listen," she said in a low voice, "I am not going to talk about things, ever again. But do come and see me, George. You see I'm not using terms of love. It's impossible, utterly impossible, for me to live without you. It's unimaginable torture. I am conscious of you, day and night you are in my eyes, my heart, my body. It is as if you had made me drink a poison that consumed me. I can't stand it. I can't. I am ready to be nothing more to you than an old woman. I powdered my hair to-day to show you, but do come here sometimes, just as a friend."

She had seized his hand and was pressing it, crushing it and digging her nails into the flesh.

" It's agreed," he replied calmly. " It's unnecessary to discuss it again. You see, I came to-day at once, in response to your letter."

Walter who was on ahead with his two daughters and Madeleine, waited for Du Roy before the picture of " Christ Walking on the Waves."

" Just imagine," he laughed, " Yesterday I found my wife on her knees before this picture, as if she was in a chapel. She was saying her prayers. How I laughed ! "

Madame Walter replied in a firm voice, a voice that vibrated with secret exaltation :

" That picture of Christ will save my soul. Whenever I look at it, it gives me courage and strength."

And standing before the picture of the Saviour, she exclaimed :

" How beautiful He is. How those men fear Him and love Him ! Look at His head and His eyes. He is so simple, and the same time so divine."

Suzanne exclaimed :

" Why He is like you, Bel-Ami, I'm sure He is. If you had a beard, or if He were shaven you would be exactly alike. Oh, it's a striking resemblance."

She made him stand beside the picture and it was admitted that the two faces were really alike.

Everyone was surprised. Walter considered it a strange coincidence. Madeleine said with a smile that she thought Christ had the more manly air.

Madame Walter remained motionless, gazing fixedly at the face of her lover beside that of Christ. She had turned as white as her white hair.

VIII

DURING the rest of the winter, the Du Roys went often to the Walters. George dined there frequently without Madeleine, his wife professing to be tired and preferring not to go out. He had chosen Friday as his day for the Walters and Madame Walter on these evenings had no one else to dinner. They were Bel-Ami's nights and his only. After dinner they played cards, or fed the Chinese fish, and they were like members of one family in their behaviour and diversions. Several times, behind a door, or screened by a clump of foliage, or in some dark corner, Madame Walter had flung her arms round Du Roy and straining him to her bosom with all her strength, had whispered fiercely : " I love you, I love you, I am dying of love for you." But he always repulsed her coldly.

" If you begin that again," he would say dryly, " I shan't come here any more."

Suddenly, towards the end of March, the marriage of both sisters was talked of. Rose, it was said, was to marry Count de Latour-Yvelin, and Suzanne the Marquis de Cazolles. These two men were now quite at home in the house, and obviously occupied a position of special favour and privilege. George and Suzanne treated each other with the intimate freedom of brother and sister, chatting together for hours on end, making fun of everybody and seemingly well content in each other's society. They had never spoken again of the possibility of Suzanne getting married, nor of the suitors who were now coming forward.

One morning when Walter had brought Du Roy home to luncheon, Madame Walter was called away after the meal to speak to a tradesman, and George said to Suzanne :

" Let's go and feed the gold fish."

Each took a large piece of crumb from the table and they went off to the greenhouse. On the floor alongside the marble basin of the fountain, cushions had been placed so that people might kneel down and examine the fish from close quarters. The young people each took a cushion, and leaning over the water side by side, began to roll bread-pellets in their fingers and throw them into the water. As soon as the fish caught sight of them, they approached with tails and fins in motion. Their goggle eyes rolling, they twisted and dived after the sinking morsels, and rose again to ask for more, with grotesque movements of their mouths, with quick abrupt dashes here and there, like tiny parodies of strange monsters. Their warm red colouring stood out vividly against the golden sand. They darted like flames through the translucent water, and when they came to rest, the narrow edging of their scales gleamed blue.

Looking into the water George and Suzanne saw their faces in it, and they smiled at their reflections. Suddenly George said in a low voice :

"Suzanne, you ought not to practise these concealments with me."

"What concealments do you mean, Bel-Ami ? "

"Don't you remember the promise you made me on this very spot, the night of the fete."

"No. What was it ? "

"You said you would always consult me when anyone wanted to marry you."

"Well, what then ? "

"Well, some one does want to marry you ? "

"Who, pray ? "

"You know quite well."

"I swear I don't."

"Oh, yes, you do. It is that great coxcomb the Marquis de Cazolles."

"To begin with, he isn't a coxcomb."

"Perhaps not. He's a bit of an ass all the same. He has gambled away all his money and he is worn out with dissipation. He's a nice sort of a match for a fresh, pretty, clever girl like you."

" What have you got against him ? " she asked with a smile.

" I ? Nothing."

" Yes, you have. He isn't as bad as you make out."

" Oh ! come now ! He is a fool, and an intriguer too."

She stopped looking into the water and turned towards him:

" Tell me now, what is the matter with you ? "

As if a secret were being torn from the bottom of his heart, he declared :

" The matter is . . . that I am jealous of him."

" You ? " she said, without excessive surprise.

" Yes. I."

" How can that be ? "

" Because I am in love with you, and you know it quite well, you naughty girl."

Severely :

" You are mad, Bel-Ami."

" I know that very well," he rejoined. " Is it right that I, a married man, should make a declaration like that to you, a young girl ? I am more than mad. I am guilty. I am a scoundrel. There is no possible hope for me, and when I realise that, I am distracted. When I hear it said that you are to be married, I could go and kill someone, I have such paroxysms of rage. But you must forgive me for that, Suzanne."

He fell silent. The fishes, not getting any more bread, remained motionless in line like English soldiers, and looked at the faces of these two human beings who were still leaning over but thought no more of them.

Half sorrowful, half gay, Suzanne said :

" It is a pity you are married, but what can we do about it ? Nothing. It's all over."

He turned abruptly to her and with his face close to hers :

" Would you marry me," he asked, " if I were free ? "

" Yes, Bel-Ami," she replied frankly, " I would marry you. I love you much better than any of the others."

He rose to his feet.

" Thank you. Thank you a thousand times. I implore you not to accept anyone. Wait just a little longer, I implore you. Will you promise me that ? "

" I promise," she replied, confused and not realising what he had in his mind.

Hurling into the water the lump of bread which he was still holding in his hands, Du Roy took to flight, like one beside himself. The fishes made greedily for this piece of bread which, not having been kneaded, floated on the surface ; and they tore it to pieces voraciously. They dragged it to the other end of the fountain, wriggled about under it, packed together like a cluster of grapes or an animated flower caught in an eddy, a living flower thrown head downwards into the water.

Surprised and uneasy, Suzanne rose and went softly away. Du Roy had gone.

When he reached home he showed no signs of agitation. He found Madeleine writing letters and he asked her :

"Are you dining with the Walters on Friday ? I am going."

" No," she said. " I am not feeling well. I should prefer to stay at home."

" As you please," he said. " No one's forcing you."

He took up his hat and went out again immediately. For a long time he had been spying on her, watching her and following her about. He was familiar with all her movements. The hour for which he was waiting had at last arrived. He knew well what underlay the tone in which she had replied, " I should prefer to stay at home." During the intervening days he behaved amiably to her. His manner was unusually cheerful, and she said :

" You are becoming quite agreeable again."

When Friday came, he dressed early in order, as he declared, to call at one or two places before going to the Walters'. He kissed his wife and went out at about six o'clock. Having secured a cab on the Place Notre-Dame-de Lorette, he said to the driver :

"Stop in front of 17, Rue Fontaine ; and stay there till I tell you to go on. After that you can take me to the Cock Pheasant restaurant in the Rue Lafayette."

The horse set off at a slow trot, and Du Roy pulled down the blinds of the cab.

Once before his **own door**, he kept his eyes fixed on it.

He waited ten minutes. Then he saw Madeleine come out and turn towards the outer Boulevards. When she had gone a short distance he put his head out of the window and told the cabman to drive on. The cab put him down in front of the Cock Pheasant, a middle-class restaurant well known in the quarter. George entered the public room and ate his dinner without haste. Every now and then he consulted his watch. At half-past seven, having drunk his coffee and two glasses of liqueur brandy and slowly smoked a good cigar, he went out, hailed an empty cab and drove to a house in the Rue La Rochefoucauld. Without putting any questions to the hall-porter, he ascended to the third story and said to the maid who opened the door to him :

" Monsieur Guibert de Lorme is at home, I think ? "

" Yes, sir."

He was shewn into the drawing-room where he waited a few moments. Then a tall man entered ; he wore a decoration and was of soldier-like bearing. His hair was grey, though he was still young.

Du Roy bowed to him and said :

" As I foresaw, sir, my wife is dining to-night with her lover in the furnished apartments which they have rented, in the Rue des Martyrs."

The Commissary bowed.

" Sir, I am at your service."

" You have up to nine o'clock, haven't you ? " George resumed. " After that you have no power to break into a private dwelling in order to establish an adultery."

" That is so. Seven o'clock in the winter and nine o'clock after the 31st March. As this is the 5th April, we have up to nine o'clock."

" Very well, I have a carriage and there will be room for your men. We can wait a little while outside the door. The later we arrive the more chance we have of catching them in the act."

" As you please."

The commissary left the room and returned wearing an overcoat which concealed his tricolour sash. He stood to one side to allow Du Roy to precede him. But Du Roy's

mind was taken up with other matters and he refused to go
out first.

"After you, after you," he said.

But the commissary insisted.

"Go first, please. This is my house."

Du Roy bowed and passed out.

First they went to the police station, where they found
three policemen in plain clothes awaiting them, George
having in the course of the day given notice that the surprise
visit was to take place that evening. One of the policemen
mounted the box beside the driver. The other two entered
the cab which then drove away to the Rue des Martyrs.

"I have the plan of the flat," Du Roy remarked. "It is
on the second floor. First we come to a little vestibule, and
then comes the bedroom. The three rooms lead into one
another. There is no way of escape. There is a locksmith
a few doors off, who is in readiness in case you should want
him."

It was only a quarter-past eight when they arrived in
front of the house, and they waited more than twenty minutes
in silence. When he saw the third quarter about to strike,
George said :

"Now we can go up."

They ascended the staircase without troubling the hall-
porter, who in any case had not noticed them. One of the
men stayed below to watch the door. The other four
stopped at the second story. The first thing Du Roy did
was to put his ear to the door, and then his eye to the keyhole.
But he heard and saw nothing. He rang the bell. The
commissary addressed his men :

"Stay here in case you are wanted."

They waited, and after two or three minutes, George
rang the bell several times in succession. A noise was heard
at the farther end of the flat ; then a light footstep approached.
Someone was coming to spy. Thereupon Du Roy rapped
briskly on the door-panels with his knuckles. A woman's
voice, evidently disguised, asked :

"Who is that ?"

The police officer replied :

" Open, in the name of the law."

" Who are you ? " said the voice.

" I am the commissary of police.   Open the door or I
shall have it forced."

" What do you want ? "

" It is I," Du Roy replied.   " It is useless to attempt to
escape."

The pattering of bare feet was heard as the woman withdrew.
After a few seconds it was heard again and George exclaimed :

" If you won't open the door, we'll break it in."

He seized the copper doorhandle and pushed lightly against
the door with one shoulder.   There was no word from
within, and he suddenly gave so vigorous a push that the
ancient lock yielded.   The screws drew out of the wood-
work, and Du Roy nearly fell over Madeleine, who was
standing in the vestibule.   She was clad in chemise and
petticoat ;   her hair was loose, her legs were stockingless,
and in her hand she carried a candle.

" It's she," he cried.   " We've got them."

He flung himself into the flat.   The commissary took
off his hat and followed.   Madeleine, terror-stricken,
followed with the candle.   They went through the dining-
room.   The table had not been cleared, and still had on it
the remains of a meal.   There were empty champagne
bottles, an open dish of *foie-gras*, a chicken, and some half
consumed pieces of bread.   Two plates on the sideboard
were piled with oyster shells.   The room was in the utmost
disorder.   On one of the chairs was a dress ;   over the arm
of another some underclothing.   At the foot of the bed two
pairs of shoes, one large and one small, lay on their sides.

It was a typical sample of furnished lodgings.   The
furniture was mean.   Every corner was pervaded by that
hateful sickly odour of hired rooms, the odour that emanates
from curtains, mattresses, walls, chairs, the odour of all the
people who have slept or lived there for one day or six months.
Each person adds a whiff of his personality to this odour,
until it accumulates and forms the vague, fetid, intolerable
stench characteristic of all these places.   A plate of cakes,
a bottle of Chartreuse, and two half-empty liqueur glasses

were on the chimney piece. The group of figures on the ornamental bronze clock was hidden under a man's tall hat.

Turning sharply the commissary looked straight at Madeleine.

" Is it a fact that you are Madame Claire Madeleine Du Roy, legitimate wife of Monsieur Prosper George Du Roy, editor, here present ? "

In a strangled voice she replied :

" Yes."

" What are you doing here ? "

She made no reply, and the commissary repeated :

" What are you doing here ? I find you, away from your own house, almost unclothed, in a furnished flat. What was your intention in coming here ? "

He waited a few moments, and then continued :

" As soon as you show yourself unwilling to admit it, I must take steps to establish it by evidence."

On the bed concealed under the sheet, a human form could be discerned. The commissary went up to the bed and called out :

" Sir."

The man in the bed did not move. He seemed to have his back turned and his head was buried under a pillow. The police officer touched what appeared to be his shoulder, and addressed him again.

" Sir, I beg of you not to compel me to use force."

But the body under the sheet remained as still as if it had been dead. Du Roy came briskly forward, caught hold of the sheet, whipped it off, and snatching away the pillow uncovered the livid face of Monsieur Laroche-Mathieu. He leaned towards him, trembling with a desire to seize him by the throat and strangle him and he said to him through his clenched teeth :

" At any rate have the courage of your infamous conduct."

The commissary repeated his question, " Who are you ? "

The bewildered lover making no reply, he continued :

" I am commissary of police and I charge you to tell me your name."

Quivering with brutal anger George exclaimed :

" Answer, you coward, or I will give your name myself."

The man in the bed protested feebly :

" Commissary, you shouldn't let this person insult me. Is it with you or him that I have to do ? Is it to you or him I have to answer ? "

He spoke as if his mouth were quite dry.

" It is with me, sir, and me only," replied the officer. " I ask you to tell me who you are."

The other was silent. He held the sheet tight round his neck and rolled his terror-stricken eyes. His little upturned moustaches seemed dead black on his pallid face.

" You will not answer ? " said the commissary. " Then I shall be compelled to arrest you. In any case you must get up. I shall interrogate you when you are dressed."

With a nervous movement he replied :

" But I can't, in front of you."

" Why not ? " asked the commissary.

The other answered hesitatingly :

" The fact is . . . the fact is . . . I am . . . I am ; . . I have no clothes on."

Du Roy laughed jeeringly, and picking up a shirt from the floor flung it on the bed.

" Come on, get up," he cried, " If you can undress in front of my wife, surely you can dress in front of me."

He swung round on his heel and returned to the fireplace.

Madeleine had regained her self-possession, and recognising that all was lost, she was ready to go to all lengths. Her eyes sparkled defiantly. She made a spill, and as if for a reception she lighted the ten candles in the ugly candelabra on the corner of the mantelpiece. Then she leaned back against the marble, stretching out one of her bare feet to the expiring fire, in an attitude in which her petticoat, which had almost slipped from her hips was hitched up at the back. She took a cigarette from a pink paper case, lighted it, and began to smoke.

The commissary had returned to her, while he waited for her companion to get up.

She asked him insolently :

" Do you often do this kind of work ? "

" As seldom as possible, madam," he replied gravely.

" I congratulate you," she said with a sneer, " it is not work for a gentleman."

She affected neither to look at, nor even to seem aware of her husband.

Meanwhile the gentleman from the bed was dressing. He had put on his trousers and shoes, and as he approached the commissary, was slipping on his waistcoat. The police officer turned to him :

" Now, sir," he said, " Will you tell me who you are ? "

Again the other made no reply.

" I see I shall have to arrest you," declared the commissary.

At that the man cried out sharply :

" Don't lay a hand on me. I am immune from arrest."

Du Roy hurled himself at him as though to fell him to the ground and snarled into his face :

" It is *flagrant délit . . . flagrant délit.* I can have you arrested if I wish. Yes, I can."

Then in a resonant voice :

" This man's name is Laroche-Mathieu. He is Minister of Foreign Affairs."

The commissary shrank back in amazement.

" I beg of you, sir, to tell me truthfully who you are."

At last Laroche-Mathieu made up his mind and said resolutely :

" For once in his life, that scoundrel has told the truth. I admit that I am Laroche-Mathieu, Minister of State."

Then pointing with his hand towards George's chest on which gleamed a little spot of red he exclaimed :

" And that rascal there wears on his coat the cross of honour which I gave him."

Du Roy had become livid. With a swift gesture he tore from his button-hole the little flame-coloured ribbon and flinging it into the fireplace, exclaimed :

" That's what I think of a decoration that comes from a dirty dog like you."

They snarled into each other's faces, clenching their fists in a fury, the one man lean and with bristling moustaches, the other fat and with moustaches twisted upwards.

The commissary thrust himself hastily between the two men and pushing them apart with his hands :

" Gentlemen," he said, " you are forgetting yourselves. Remember who you are."

In silence they turned their backs on each other. Madeleine, never moved but continued to smoke with a smile on her face.

The police officer resumed :

" Monsieur Laroche-Mathieu, I surprised you alone with Madame Du Roy, here present. You were in bed and she was almost undressed. Your clothes had been thrown in confusion about the room. These facts constitute *flagrant délit* in a case of adultery. You cannot deny the evidence. Have you any thing to say ? "

Laroche-Mathieu replied in a low voice :

" I have nothing to say. Do your duty."

The commissary turned to Madeleine :

" Do you admit, madam, that this gentleman is your lover ? "

She replied brazenly :

" I do not deny it. He is my lover."

" That is sufficient."

The commissary proceeded to take some notes concerning the condition and arrangement of the flat. As he was completing his report, Monsieur Laroche-Mathieu, who had finished dressing and was waiting with his overcoat on his arm, and his hat in his hand, asked him :

" Have you any further need of me, sir ? What am I to do ? May I retire ? "

Du Roy turned to him with an insolent smile.

" Why should you retire ? We have finished. You can go back to bed again. We shall leave you two alone."

And laying his hand on the police officer's arm :

" Let us withdraw, sir," he said, " we have nothing further to do here."

Somewhat surprised the commissary followed him, but on the threshold of the room, George waited for him to pass. The other politely declined. Du Roy insisted :

" Please go on, sir."

" After you," replied the commissary.

Du Roy bowed and in tones of ironical politeness said :
" It is your turn to go first, sir. I may be said to be at
home here."

Then he gently closed the door behind them with an
air of discretion.

An hour later George Du Roy entered the office of the
Vie Française. Monsieur Walter was already in his room.
He continued his careful direction and supervision of the
newspaper, which had developed enormously and greatly
assisted the ever-widening operations of his bank.

The director looked up.

" Oh, there you are ? What a curious look you have !
Why didn't you come and dine with us ? What have you
been up to ?

Sure of the effect he was about to produce and laying stress
on each word, Duroy announced :

" I have just come from downing the Minister of Foreign
Affairs."

Walter thought that he was jesting.

" Downing ? . . . How ? . . ."

" I am going to make a change in the Cabinet. That's
all. It's quite time we turned out that blackguard."

Old Walter was taken aback and thought that his editor
much be drunk.

" Come, you're talking wildly."

" Not at all. I have just caught Monsieur Laroche-
Mathieu in *flagrant délit* with my wife. The commissary of
police was a witness. Laroche is done for."

Dumbfounded, Walter pushed his glasses right up on to
his forehead.

" You're not joking ? " he asked.

" Certainly not. I'm just going to write an Echo about it."

" But what do you intend to do ? "

" Ruin the scoundrel. He's a rascal, a public malefactor."

Laying his hat on a chair, he added :

" People who cross my path had better look out I never
forgive."

Still bewildered, Walter muttered, " But . . . your wife ? "

" To-morrow I shall apply for a divorce and restore her to the late lamented Forestier."

" You intend to divorce her ? "

" Certainly. They made a fool of me. But I had to pretend to be blind so as to catch them. I've succeeded. I'm master of the situation."

Monsieur Walter did not return to the subject, but he cast a startled glance at Du Roy, thinking to himself :

" By Jove. It's as well to keep on good terms with a fellow like that."

" I'm a free man now," George resumed, " I possess a small fortune. I shall present myself as a candidate in the October elections in my own part of the country where I am well known. I could never attain a position or make myself respected with a woman like that, whom everyone gossiped about. I was a fool to let myself be inveigled and captured by her. But as soon as I knew what she was up to, I kept my eyes on the minx."

He laughed and added :

" That poor old Forestier, who was so sure of himself and so imperturbable was certainly made a fool of, there's no doubt about it. I am now quit of the plague he bequeathed to me. My hands are free. Now I shall go far."

He was seated astride his chair. He repeated, as if in a dream :

" I shall go far."

Old Walter with his glasses still on his forehead, continued to gaze at him and said to himself :

" Yes, he will go far, the rascal."

George rose.

" I am going to draft that Echo. It will have to be done with discretion. But you know, it will be a fearful knock for the Minister. He has gone overboard. He is past saving. The *Vie Française* need not consider him any longer."

Old Walter hesitated a few moments. Then he made up his mind.

" Go ahead," he said. " So much the worse for people who get themselves into scrapes like that."

IX

THREE months had passed. Du Roy had obtained his divorce, and his wife had resumed the name of Forestier. The Walters were leaving for Trouville on the 15th of July, and it was decided to spend a day in the country, before they went away.

A Thursday was fixed, and the party set out at nine in the morning in a large travelling landau, with room for six, and drawn by four post horses.

They were to lunch at St. Germain, in Henry IV's pavilion. Bel-Ami had begged that he might be the only man invited, because he could not endure the presence of the Marquis de Cazolles or the sight of his face. But at the last moment they arranged to pick up the Count de Latour-Yvelin as soon as he was out of bed. He had been warned the night before.

The carriage rolled down the Avenue of the Champs Elysées at a rapid trot ; then crossed the Bois de Boulogne.

It was beautiful summer weather, not too hot. Against the blue sky the swallows described curves, which seemed to be visible even after they had disappeared. The three women occupied the back seat of the landau, the mother between the two girls, while the three men sat with their backs to the horses, Walter between his two guests.

They crossed the Seine, skirted Mont Valérien, reached Bougival, and then followed the river bank as far as Le Pecq.

Count de Latour-Yvelin, a man of ripe age, had long wavy whiskers with floating ends that blew about in the slightest breath of air, and inspired Du Roy to say :

" He gets charming wind effects in his whiskers."

The Count gazed affectionately at Rose, who had been engaged to him for a month.

George was very pale. He looked frequently at Suzanne, who was also pale. Their eyes met, appeared to deliberate with mutual understanding and a secret exchange of ideas, and then to avoid each other. Madame Walter was placidly happy.

Luncheon was a lengthy affair. Before leaving again for Paris, George proposed a stroll on the terrace.

Ranged along the wall, they admired the view and went into raptures over the wide prospect. At the foot of a long slope, in the direction of Maisons-Laffitte flowed the Seine, like a huge serpent lying in the grass. To the right, on top of the hill, the side of the Marly aqueduct stood out against the sky like an enormous, long-legged caterpillar, and Marly itself lay below, hidden in a thick clump of trees. Here and there on the wide plain that lay before them, a village could be discerned. The formal sheets of ornamental water at Le Vésinet showed up in shining patches in the scanty verdure of the little wood. To the left, in the far distance, the pointed steeple of Sartrouville rose in the air.

" There isn't such a view anywhere else in the world," exclaimed Walter. " Switzerland has nothing to equal it."

They strolled on slowly for the sake of the exercise and the view.

George and Suzanne had fallen behind. As soon as they were a few paces away from the others, he said in a low, restrained voice :

" Suzanne, I adore you. I am madly in love with you."

She whispered, " And I with you, Bel-Ami."

He replied, " If I cannot have you for my wife, I shall leave Paris and France."

" Why don't you try asking Papa for me ? " she replied. " Perhaps he would consent."

He made a little gesture of impatience.

" No, I tell you for the tenth time it's useless. I should be forbidden the house and turned off the paper, and we shouldn't even be able to see each other. That would be the pleasant result of a formal request. You have been

promised to the Marquis de Cazolles.   They hope that you'll
end by saying yes.   And so they're waiting."
" Then what had we better do ? " she asked.
He hesitated and cast a side-long glance at her.
" Do you love me enough to do something reckless ? "
" Yes," she replied firmly.
" Something very reckless indeed ? "
" Yes."
" The most reckless thing there is ? "
" Yes."
" And would you also have the courage to defy your
father and mother ? "
" Yes."
" Really and truly ? "
" Yes."
" Well then there is one way, and only one.   The thing
must come from you, and not from me.   You are a spoilt
child, and allowed to say what you like, and no one would
be much surprised at one audacity the more from you.
Listen to me.   This evening when you get home, go first
of all and see your mother, just your mother by herself,
and confess to her that you want to marry me.   She will
be terribly upset and extremely angry . . ."
Suzanne interrupted him.
" Oh, Mamma would be pleased."
" No," he replied promptly.   " You don't know her.
She will be more distressed and more indignant than your
father.   You will see how she will refuse.   But be firm,
do not give way.   You must tell her again and again that
you intend to marry me, me and nobody else.   Will you ? "
" I will."
" After telling your mother, you must say the same thing
to your father, in a very grave and determined manner."
" Yes, yes.   And then ? "
" And then, this is where the thing becomes serious.
If you are resolved, firmly resolved, very, very firmly resolved
to become my wife, my dear, dear little Suzanne, I will
run away with you."
She jumped with joy and nearly clapped her hands.

"Oh, how lovely! An elopement! When will it come off?"

All the old poetry about midnight elopements, post-chaises, inns, all the charming adventures out of books flashed through her mind like an enchanting dream that was about to be fulfilled. She repeated:

"When is our elopement coming off?"

He answered in a very low voice:

"Why . . . this evening . . . to-night."

She asked, trembling:

"And where shall we go?"

"That's my secret. What you have to do is to consider carefully the step you are taking. You must realise that after running away with me you must become my wife. It is the only way, but it is . . . it is very dangerous . . . for you."

"My mind is made up," she declared, "where shall I meet you?"

"Can you get out of the house unaided?"

"Yes, I know how to open the small door."

"Very well. About midnight, after the porter has gone to bed, come and meet me at the Place de la Concorde. I shall be there in a cab, opposite the Ministry of Marine."

"I will come."

"Really and truly?"

"Really and truly."

He seized her hand and pressed it.

"Oh how I love you! How kind and brave you are! Then you don't want to marry Monsieur de Cazolles?"

"Oh no."

"Was your father very angry when you refused him?"

"I should think he was. He wanted to send me back to the convent."

"Then you see that we shall have to be resolute."

"I shall be."

Her head full of the idea of the elopement, she surveyed the wide horizon. She was going farther away than that . . . with Bel-Ami. She was going to elope. She was very proud of it. She had no thought for her reputation or for anything shameful that might befall her. Had

she indeed any idea of such a thing, or any suspicion whatever ?

Madame Walter turned round and exclaimed :

" Come here, child.   What are you doing with Bel-Ami?"

George and Suzanne joined the others.   They talked
about sea bathing at Trouville where the Walters were going.
Then the party drove home by Chatou so as not to return
the way they came.

George was silent.   He was thinking to himself, that if
only the child showed a little boldness he would succeed at
last.   For three months he had been casting around her the
encircling net of his devotion.   He had charmed her, captivated her, subjugated her.   He had made her love him as
he knew how.   With ease he had plucked her trifling,
doll-like soul.

First of all he had induced her to refuse Monsieur de
Cazolles.   Now he had persuaded her to elope with him.
For there was no other way.   He was aware that Madame
Walter would never consent to give him her daughter.   She
still loved him, and would always love him, with unmanage-
able violence.   He held her in check by his calculated
coldness, but he knew her to be devoured by a hopeless,
consuming passion.   He would never be able to prevail upon
her to yield her consent.   She would never allow him to
have Suzanne.   But once the child was away, and in his
power, he would have the whip-hand of the father.

Occupied with these thoughts, he replied briefly to the
remarks addressed to him and did not listen to anything that
was said.   He came to himself as they entered Paris.
Suzanne, too, was dreamy.   The little bells on the horses'
harness rang in her ears, conjuring up broad high-roads, that
ran on into infinity in perpetual moonlight, through dark
forests.   At the wayside inns, the stable boys would change
horses for them in haste, since everyone would guess that
they were being pursued.

When the landau drew up in the courtyard of the house,
Madame Walter pressed George to stay to dinner.   He
declined her invitation and returned home.

After taking some food, he put his papers in order as if

he were going on a long journey. He burned some compromising letters, others he concealed ; and he wrote to some of his friends.

From time to time he looked at the clock, thinking to himself :

" Things must be getting lively at the Walters now."

He was consumed with uneasiness. Suppose he failed. But what had he to fear ? He would get out of it all right. Still, he was playing for a high stake that evening.

Towards eleven o'clock, he went out again and wandered about for a while. Then he took a cab and drove to the Place de la Concorde, drawing up by the arcade in front of the Ministry of Marine. From time to time he struck a match to look at his watch. When he saw that it was close upon midnight, his impatience rose to fever point. Every moment he put his head out of the window to look about him. A remote clock struck twelve ; this was repeated by a nearer one, then by two together, and finally by another in the far distance. When the strokes had died away, he thought to himself.

" It is all over. It's a failure. She won't come now."

Nevertheless he made up his mind to summon up his patience and wait there till daybreak.

He heard the quarter strike, then half-past twelve, then quarter to one. Presently all the clocks chimed one in the same way as they had proclaimed the hour of midnight. He no longer expected her, but he remained there, racking his brains, trying to imagine what had occurred. Suddenly a woman's head appeared at the window and a voice exclaimed :

" Are you there, Bel-Ami ? "

He started and caught his breath.

" Is that you, Suzanne ? "

" Yes, it's I."

He could not turn the handle of the door fast enough, and he cried :

" Ah, it's you, it's you, come in."

She stepped into the cab and collapsed.

He called out to the driver.

" Go on," and the cab rolled away.

She was breathless and speechless.

"Well," he said, "how did it go off ? "

Almost fainting she murmured :

"Oh it was terrible, especially the scene with Mamma."

He was uneasy and gave a nervous start.

"Your mother ? What did she say ? Tell me what she said."

"Oh it was awful. I went to her room and recited my speech to her, which I had made up carefully beforehand. She turned pale and then she exclaimed, 'Never, never !' I burst into tears. I was furious, I swore that I would marry nobody but you. I thought she was going to beat me. She behaved as if she was mad, and vowed that I should be sent back to the convent the very next day. I have never seen her like that before. Then Papa, who had heard all the silly things she was saying, appeared on the scene. He wasn't as angry as Mamma, but he said that you were not a good enough match. Between them they put me into a rage, too, so I screamed louder than they did. And Papa ordered me out of the room with a dramatic air that didn't suit him at all. That was the last straw, and here I am. Where are we going ? "

He had put his arms gently round her, and he listened to her intently with beating heart, while a rankling hatred towards her parents awoke within him. However their daughter was in his power. Now they should see.

"It is too late to take the train to-night," he said, "so we will drive in this cab as far as Sèvres and spend the night there. And to-morrow we will move on to La Roche-Guyon. It is a charming village on the Seine between Mantes and Bonnières."

She murmured, "I haven't brought anything with me, anything at all."

He smiled carelessly :

"We'll see to that when we get there."

The cab rolled through the streets. George took the girl's hand and kissed it lingeringly and reverently. He did not know what to say to her, not being accustomed to platonic love-making.   Suddenly he became aware that she was crying.

He asked in alarm :

" What is the matter, dear little girl ? "

She replied with tears in her voice :

" I'm thinking of poor Mamma who won't be sleeping, although it's so late, if she has discovered that I've run away."

She was right.   Her mother was not asleep.

When Suzanne had left the room, Madame Walter had remained staring at her husband.   Bewildered and aghast she exclaimed :

" Good God, what does it mean ? "

Walter cried in a passion :

" It means that that intriguing scoundrel has turned her head.   It's he who put her up to refusing Cazolles.   It's because he likes the look of her dowry, confound him."

He began furiously pacing the room.

" You encouraged him too, you did ; you flattered him and coaxed him, and couldn't pet him enough.   It was Bel-Ami here and Bel-Ami there from morning till night. Now you are paying for it."

Livid, she murmured :

" I !   I encouraged him ? "

He shouted in her face :

" Yes, of course you did.   You are all crazy about him, vou and that Marelle woman and Suzanne and the rest. Do you think I didn't notice that you couldn't bear to be two days without having him to the house ? "

She drew herself up dramatically :

" I refuse to be spoken to like that.   You forget that I was not dragged up in a shop, like yourself."

At first he remained rooted to the spot, petrified.   Then he ejaculated, " Good God ! " and went out slamming the door.

As soon as she was alone, instinct drove her to look at herself in the mirror as if to see if nothing in her face had changed, so impossible, so monstrous, seemed this thing that had befallen her.   Suzanne in love with Bel-Ami !   And Bel-Ami wanting Suzanne !   No, she must be mistaken ;

it could not be true. The child had a very natural fancy
for a good-looking young man, and had hoped that he would
be given to her for her husband ; her head had been a little
turned. But he ? Surely he could never have been a party
to this. She reflected with the agitation one feels when face
to face with some terrible calamity. No, Bel-Ami could
have known nothing of Suzanne's infatuation.

For a long time she weighed the chances of Du Roy's
guilt or innocence. What a villain he was, if this blow was
his doing. How would it all end ? She foresaw dangers
and torments unending. If he knew nothing about it, the
affair might still blow over. She would take Suzanne
travelling for six months and that would put a stop to it.
But afterwards how would she herself contrive to see him
again ? For she still loved him. Her passion for him had
pierced her like a barbed shaft that can never be plucked out.

To live without him was impossible, she would rather
die. Her agony and uncertainty bewildered her. She felt
a burning pain in her heart. Her thoughts became laboured
and confused. She wore herself out trying to get at the
truth, and was beside herself with doubt. She looked at
the clock ; it was past one.

" I can't go on like this," she said, " I shall go out of my
mind. I must know. I must wake up Suzanne and
question her."

Barefooted, so as to make no noise, she took a candle and
stole to her daughter's room. She opened the door very
gently, entered the room and glanced towards the bed. It
had not been occupied. At first she did not realise what had
happened and supposed that the child was still arguing with
her father. But immediately a frightful suspicion flashed
across her mind and she hastened to her husband, pale and
trembling. She dashed into his room. He was in bed and
still reading.

He asked in alarm :

" Well, what is it ? What is the matter with you ? "

" Have you seen Suzanne ? " she faltered.

" I ? No. Why ? "

" She . . . she's gone. She is not in her room."

He jumped out of bed, thrust his feet into his slippers and without waiting to put on his trousers, and with his shirt flapping around him, rushed to his daughter's room.

As soon as he saw it, he had no doubt whatever. She had run away. He sank into an arm-chair and put the lamp down on the floor beside him.

His wife had joined him.

" Well ? " she gasped.

He had not the strength to answer her, and he no longer felt angry.

" The thing is done," he groaned, " He's got her. We are lost."

She did not understand.

" Lost ? " she repeated.

" Yes indeed. She will simply have to marry him now."

She uttered a cry like an animal.

" Marry him ? Never. You must be mad."

He answered sadly :

" It's no use crying now. He has carried her off and ruined her reputation. The best thing we can do is to give her to him. If we set about it in the right way we shall be able to hush the matter up."

She repeated, shaken with terrible emotion :

" Never. He shall never have Suzanne. I will never consent."

Walter replied dejectedly :

" But he's got her. The thing is done. And he will simply keep her and hide her away until we consent. So to avoid a scandal, the only thing to do is to give in at once."

Torn by an agony that she could not avow, his wife repeated :

" No, no, I will never consent."

He replied exasperated :

" But there's no arguing about it. It's absolutely necessary. What a scoundrel to play us such a trick! . . . But there's a great deal in him all the same. We might have made a better match from a social point of view, but not from the point of view of intelligence and prospects.

He's a man with a future. He will be a Deputy and a Minister of State some day."

Madame Walter declared with frantic energy :

" Never, never will I let him marry Suzanne. Understand me . . . never."

At last he lost his temper, and like a practical man, began to take Bel-Ami's part.

" Be quiet. I tell you it's got to be ; it's absolutely necessary. And who knows ? Perhaps we shall not repent it. With men of that stamp you never know what may happen. You saw how he did for that fool Laroche-Mathieu in three articles, and in what a dignified way, which was not so easy in his situation of injured husband. We shall see. The fact remains that we're fairly caught. We can't get out of it."

She wanted to scream, to roll on the ground, to tear her hair. She repeated, in an exasperated voice :

" He shan't marry her. I won't have it."

Walter rose from his chair, picked up his lamp and replied :

" Why you're just as silly as the rest of your sex. You women are always governed by your emotions. You don't know how to adapt yourselves to circumstances. Women are unreasonable creatures. I tell you that he must marry her. It's imperative."

He shuffled away in his slippers. A comical apparition in his night shirt, he returned noiselessly along the wide corridor of the great, sleeping house to his own room.

Madame Walter remained standing, racked with intolerable pain. Even now she had hardly grasped the situation. She was simply in an agony. Then she felt that she could not remain there, rooted to the spot, till daybreak. She had a violent desire to take refuge in flight, to run on and on, to get away and seek help. She racked her brains to think to whom she could turn. Some man ? She could think of none. A priest ? Yes. A priest ! She would throw herself at his feet, pour everything out to him, confess her sin and her despair. He, at least, would understand that that wretch could not marry Suzanne and would prevent it.

She must get hold of a priest at once. But where could she find one ? Where should she go ? And yet she could not continue like this.

Suddenly before her eyes, like a vision, appeared the calm image of Christ walking on the waves. She saw him as clearly as if she were looking at the picture. Surely he was calling her, saying to her :

"Come to me. Come and kneel at My feet. I will console you and inspire you to do what is right."

She took her candle, left the room and went downstairs to the conservatory. The picture of Christ was at the far end, in a little alcove which was shut off by a glass door, so that the dampness of the soil should not injure the canvas. It formed a kind of chapel in its bower of outlandish plants.

When Madame Walter entered the winter garden, which she had never seen except when brightly lighted, she was struck by its deep darkness. The tropical plants burdened the atmosphere with their heavy fragrance. The doors were closed, and the air of the winter garden, under its glass dome oppressed the lungs and produced a sensation of giddiness and intoxication, half pleasure, half pain, transfusing the body with a vague and enervating voluptuousness.

The unhappy woman moved slowly, affected by the gloom, out of which emerged in the flickering light of her candle weird plants of monstrous aspect, with the appearance of living creatures, fantastically deformed. Her eyes fell on the picture of Christ. She opened the door that separated her from it and threw herself on her knees.

At first she prayed distractedly, faltering out words of love, passionate and despairing invocations. Then the fervour of her appeal abated. She raised her eyes to the face of Christ, and was seized with anguish. In the trembling gleam of the solitary light which faintly illuminated the picture, He bore such a striking resemblance to Bel-Ami that it was no longer the Saviour but her lover who was regarding her, with her lover's eyes, countenance, expression of face and cold, disdainful air.

"Jesus ! Jesus ! Jesus !" she said brokenly. And then the word "George" came to her lips. Suddenly it flashed upon her mind that perhaps, at this very moment, George was embracing her daughter. He was alone, with her, somewhere, in some room. He! Bel-Ami and Suzanne.

She repeated "Jesus! Jesus!" But she was thinking of them . . . of her daughter and of her lover. They were alone in a room . . . and it was night. She saw them. She saw them so clearly that they rose up before her in the place of the picture. They were smiling, they were kissing each other. The room was dark. The bedclothes were turned down. She rose to go to them, to seize her daughter by the hair and snatch her away from his embrace. She wanted to take her by the throat and strangle her, this daughter of hers whom she hated, and who was giving herself to this man. She reached out her hands and touched the canvas. Her hands were on the feet of Christ.

She uttered a loud cry and fell backwards. Her over-turned candle went out.

What happened to her then? For a long time she was haunted by strange and frightful dreams. George and Suzanne continually passed before her eyes, their arms round each other, while Jesus Christ was shedding a benediction upon their vile union. She realised vaguely that she was not in her own room. She wanted to get up and to escape, but she could not stir. A torpor had crept over her, paralysing her limbs and leaving only her mind active though in confusion, tormented by terrible, unreal, fantastic spectres, and lost in a feverish dream, that strange and sometimes fatal dream, which in tropical lands is instilled into the human brain by soporific plants with their grotesque forms and heavy perfumes.

At day-break Madame Walter was taken up unconscious, almost asphyxiated, from where she lay beneath the picture. She was so ill that they feared for her life. She did not regain complete consciousness till the following day. And then she began to weep.

Suzanne's disappearance was explained to the servants by an intimation that she had been sent back to the convent at a moment's notice. And Monsieur Walter replied to a long letter from Du Roy by acceding to his request for his daughter's hand.

Bel-Ami had posted the letter just as he and Suzanne were leaving Paris. He had written it on the evening of his departure. In it he said, in respectful terms, that he had long been in love with Suzanne ; that there had never been any understanding between them, but that as she had come to him of her own free will, and had said that she wanted to be his wife, he thought himself justified in keeping her, and even in hiding her away until he had had a reply from her parents, whose formal consent had for him less value than the wishes of his betrothed.

He asked Monsieur Walter to reply to him *poste restante*, a friend having undertaken to forward the letter.

When he had received Walter's consent he took Suzanne back to Paris and restored her to her parents, but refrained from presenting himself at their house for some time.

George and Suzanne had spent six days on the Seine at La Roche-Guyon. The girl had never enjoyed herself so much in her life. She had played at being a country lass, and as he passed her off as his sister, they lived in a free and innocent intimacy, a kind of lover-like comradeship. He had judged it expedient to respect her. The day after their arrival she bought herself underlinen and clothes such as the peasant women wore, and she spent her time angling, her head covered with a huge straw hat with a wreath of field flowers round it. She thought the country delightful. In the neighbourhood there were an ancient tower and a castle where some fine tapestry was exhibited.

George, in a jersey which he had bought from a local shopkeeper, went on expeditions with Suzanne, either on foot along the steep banks of the river, or in a boat. They kissed each other continually with trembling lips, she all innocence and he on the verge of yielding to temptation. But he was able to control himself, and when he said to her :

"We are going back to Paris to-morrow. Your father has promised me your hand," she replied ingenuously :

"Already ? It has been such fun being your wife."

X

It was dark in the little flat in the Rue de Constantinople. George Du Roy and Clotilde had met on the doorstep and had entered hurriedly. Without giving him time to draw back the blinds she had said to him :

"So you're going to marry Suzanne Walter."

In a gentle voice he admitted it, adding :

"Didn't you know ? "

She stood facing him, in a fury of indignation.

"You're going to marry Suzanne Walter. It's monstrous, monstrous. For three months you have been throwing dust in my eyes. Everyone knew it except me. It was my husband who told me."

Du Roy chuckled a little. At the same time he felt a slight embarrassment. Placing his hat on the corner of the mantelpiece, he seated himself in an arm-chair.

She looked him straight in the face and said in a low, indignant voice :

"Ever since you left your wife you have been planning this match, and you calmly kept me on as a stop-gap. What a cad you are."

"I don't see why," he said. "I had a wife who deceived me. I found her out. I got a divorce and now I'm going to marry again. What more simple ? "

She exclaimed in a trembling voice :

"Oh, what a treacherous brute you are ! "

He smiled again.

"It's always the fools and imbeciles that are the dupes."

But she followed up her train of thought.

"I ought to have got your measure at the very beginning.

But how could I ever have believed that you were as vile as that ? "

He assumed an air of dignity.

" Kindly be careful what you are saying."

His resentment infuriated her.

" What ! You expect me to mince words when I talk to you now. You have treated me disgracefully, ever since I have known you, and now you want to prevent me from telling you so. You deceive everyone, you exploit everyone. You grab pleasure and money everywhere, and yet you expect me to treat you like a decent person."

He rose from his chair and said with trembling lips :

" Be quiet or I'll turn you out."

" You'll turn me out ? " she stammered, " Out of here ? . . . You'll turn me out of here . . . you . . . you ? "

She was speechless, choking with rage. Then suddenly, as if the floodgates of wrath had burst, she broke out :

" Out of here ? You forget, do you, that it's I who have paid for this flat ever since the first day. Yes, I know you took it over from time to time. But who was it who engaged it ? I. Who was it who kept it on ? I. And you want to turn me out of here. Hold your tongue, you good-for-nothing. Do you think I don't know that you robbed Madeleine of half Vaudrec's legacy ? Do you think I don't know that you seduced Suzanne to force her to marry you ? . . ."

He seized her by the shoulders and shook her.

" I won't have you talk of her. I forbid you."

" I know you slept with her," she screamed.

He would have stood anything else, but this lie exasperated him. The home truths she had a moment ago flung in his teeth had made him tremble with rage, but at this slander about the girl who was to be his wife, his hand ached to strike her.

" Hold your tongue and take care. Hold your tongue."

He shook her like a branch from which one shakes the fruit.

With disordered hair, wide open mouth, and wild eyes, she screamed :

" You did sleep with her."

He let go his hold of her and slapped her face so violently that she fell against the wall. But she turned on him again and raising herself on her hands, shrieked once more :

" You did sleep with her."

He rushed at her and holding her down, struck her as if he were hitting a man.

She was suddenly silent, and then began to groan under his blows. But she made no movement. She had hidden her face in the corner of the wall, and was wailing plaintively.

He stopped beating her, rose up and strode up and down the room to regain his self-control. Then an idea occurred to him, he went into the bedroom, filled a basin with cold water and dipped his head in it. Afterwards he washed his hands, and carefully drying his hands, returned to see what she was doing.

She had not stirred. She was lying on the ground, crying softly.

" Have you nearly finished whining ? " he asked.

She made no reply. He remained standing in the middle of the room, a little embarrassed, a little ashamed, with her prostrate at his feet. At last he came to a decision :

" Good-bye," he said, seizing his hat from the mantelpiece. " When you're ready you can give the porter the key. I'm not going to wait for your good pleasure."

He left the flat, closed the door behind him and went to see the porter.

" Madame Du Roy is still in the flat," he said, " but she will be going presently. You can tell the landlord that I've given notice for the first of October. This is the 16th of August, so I'm in time."

He strode rapidly away, for he was in a hurry to make the final purchase of gifts for the bride.

The wedding had been fixed for the twentieth of October, after the Chambers had met. It was to take place in the Madeleine. There had been a great deal of gossip, but no one was acquainted with the real truth. Different stories were circulated. It was whispered that there had been an elopement, but nothing was known for certain.

According to the servants, Madame Walter, who never addressed a word to her future son-in-law, had poisoned herself in a rage the very evening on which the marriage had been arranged, after sending her daughter away to the convent at midnight. She had been found half dead. Certainly she would never recover. She had the air of an old woman now ; her hair was turning quite grey ; and she had plunged into devotion and went to communion every Sunday.

At the beginning of September the *Vie Française* announced that Baron Du Roy de Cantel had been appointed Editor in Chief, while Monsieur Walter retained the title of director. After this the staff was increased by a battalion of well-known writers, paragraphists, political editors, art critics, dramatic critics, all captured, by means of bribes, from the great newspapers, the long-established newspapers of standing and influence.

The sober and respectable journalists, no longer shrugged their shoulders when they spoke of the *Vie Française*. Its rapid and complete success had effaced the scorn with which serious writers had regarded it at the beginning.

The marriage of the editor-in-chief was a social event in which all Paris was interested. For some time George Du Roy and the Walters had excited a great deal of curiosity. All the persons whose names figure in society notes intended to be present.

The ceremony took place on a bright autumn day.

As early as eight in the morning the entire establishment of the Madeleine were engaged in laying a wide carpet on the steps leading down from the high platform of the church to the Rue Royale. Their activities brought the passers-by to a halt and announced to the people of Paris that a great wedding was about to take place. Clerks on their way to office, little work girls, shop boys, stopped to look, with vague ideas about the rich people who spent so much money on their weddings. About ten o'clock the curious began to stand about. They would remain for a few minutes, hoping that the show would soon begin ; then they would go away.

At eleven o'clock, detachments of police arrived and at once began to disperse the groups which were forming every moment.

Soon the first guests appeared, people who wanted to be well-placed to see everything. They took the chairs at the end of the rows on either side of the central aisle. Gradually others arrived, women in gowns of rustling silk, and austere-looking men, nearly all of them bald, with a formal correctness of bearing and exhibiting even more than their customary gravity in this place of worship. The church was slowly filling. A flood of sunshine poured through the great doors, throwing a brightness on the guests in the back rows. In the somewhat gloomy choir the candles on the altar shed a yellow light, which was pale and insignificant compared with the radiance that entered through the wide doorway. The guests bowed and made signs to one another, and gathered together in groups. The literary men, less reverent than the society men, spoke in undertones. Glances were cast at the women.

Norbert de Varenne, in search of a friend, caught sight of Jacques Rival somewhere in the middle of the rows of chairs, and joined him.

"Well," he said, "it's the artful ones who prosper."

Rival, who was never jealous, replied :

"So much the better for him. His fortune is made."

They began to name to each other people they recognised.

"Do you know what has become of his wife?" asked Rival.

The poet smiled.

"Yes and no. I'm told she is living a very retired life somewhere in Montmartre. But . . . there's a but. For some time past I have been reading in *La Plume* political articles which bear a striking resemblance to those by Forestier and Du Roy. They are by one Jean Le Dol, who is a very good-looking and intelligent young fellow of the same species as our friend, and who has made the acquaintance of Madame Forestier. From this I conclude that she has a passion, and will always have a passion, for beginners. She's rich, by the way. Vaudrec and Laroche-Mathieu didn't frequent the house for nothing."

" She has her strong points, has little Madeleine. Very intelligent and very subtle. She must be charming in intimacy. But tell me, how is it that Du Roy is getting married in church after having had a divorce ? "

" He is being married in church," replied Norbert de Varenne, " because according to the Church he wasn't married the first time."

" How so ? "

" Our Bel-Ami, either through indifference or from motives of economy, considered the Town Hall sufficient for his marriage with Madeleine Forestier. He accordingly dispensed with the ecclesiastical benediction, and that, for our Holy Mother Church, constituted simply a condition of concubinage. Consequently he appears before her to-day as a bachelor, and the Church places all her pomp at his disposal, which will cost old Walter a pretty penny."

The murmurs of the assembled throng increased beneath the vaulted roof. Voices were heard speaking almost aloud. People pointed out celebrities, who were passing, delighted to be on view, and carefully maintaining the demeanour they had adopted for public use. They were accustomed to exhibit themselves in this way at all social functions, as indispensable ornaments, artistic gems.

" Tell me, my dear fellow," Rival went on, " You often go to the director's house. Is it true that Madame Walter and Du Roy never speak to each other ? "

" Never. She did not want him to have the child. But he had a hold over the father by reason of certain skeletons that he had discovered, skeletons, it appears, buried in Morocco. So he threatened the old boy with frightful exposures. Walter remembered the case of Laroche-Mathieu and gave in at once. But the mother, pig-headed like all women, swore that she'd never address another word to her son-in-law. They are deuced odd, sitting opposite each other. She has the look of a statue, a statue of Vengeance ; he is very much embarrassed, but he puts a good face on the matter. He has plenty of self-control, has Du Roy."

Brother authors came and shook hands with them. Scraps of political talk were audible. And through the door, rising to the vaulted roof with the sunshine, came, like the vague roar of a distant sea, the murmurs of the crowd collected in front of the church, heard above the more restrained manifestations of the select throng within the building.

At last the beadle rapped on the wooden floor three times with his halberd. All the guests turned round with a prolonged rustling of skirts and a moving of chairs. The bride appeared on her father's arm in the bright light of the west door. She still had the look of a doll, a delightful, fair-complexioned doll, under her wreath of orange-blossom.

She stood still for a few moments on the threshold. When she took her first step into the nave the organ burst forth with a loud crash, proclaiming, through its great metal pipes, the arrival of the bride.

A sweet and charming miniature, she moved with bowed head; without timidity, but stirred by vague emotion. The women smiled and whispered as she passed by. The men murmured :

" Exquisite, adorable ! "

Monsieur Walter walked with an exaggerated air of dignity ; he was a little pale and his glasses were planted perpendicularly on his nose. Behind them went four bridesmaids, all dressed in pink, and all very pretty, who formed the court of the little toy queen. The groomsmen, carefully chosen and all of the same type, moved as if they had been taught their steps by a dancing-master. Madame Walter followed them, on the arm of Rose's father-in-law, the Marquis de Latour-Yvelin, an old gentleman of seventy-two. She could not be said to walk ; she dragged herself along, almost fainting at each forward movement. It seemed as if her feet clung to the flagstones ; her limbs refused to move, while her heart beat in her breast like a wild beast struggling to escape. She had grown thin. Her white hair made her face appear more wan than ever and her cheeks more hollow. She looked straight in front of her, so that she might see no one, and perhaps in an effort to escape from the thoughts that tortured her.

George Du Roy appeared accompanied by an old lady whom nobody knew. He held his head high ; and he, too, looked straight ahead, his eyes steady and hard under their curving lashes. His moustache seemed to bristle. The spectators considered him a fine-looking fellow. He held himself erect, his figure was graceful and well made. His frock-coat fitted him well, and on it like a drop of blood was displayed the little red ribbon of the Legion of Honour.

Then followed the relations. Rose who had been married six weeks, came with Senator Rissolin. Count de Latour-Yvelin escorted Viscountess de Percemur. After them came an odd collection of Du Roy's allies and friends, whom he had introduced to his new family. It consisted of people on the fringe of Parisian society who are prepared to become the intimate friends, or, if convenient, the distant cousins of rich upstarts, a class including aristocrats who have lost caste, money, and reputation, and sometimes gained wives in the process, which is worse. Such were Monsieur de Belvigne, the Marquis de Banjolin, Count and Countess de Ravenel, the Duke de Ramorano, the Prince of Kravalow, the Chevalier Valréali. The Walters's guests included the Prince de Guerche, the Duke and Duchess of Ferracine, the beautiful Marchioness des Dunes. A few of Madame Walter's relations had a respectable, provincial air, in the midst of that horde.

And all the time the organ poured out into the enormous church, through its gleaming pipes, its sonorous and rhythmic peals which proclaim to heaven the joy or the grief of men. The great folding doors were closed and suddenly the church became as dark as if the sun had been shut out.

George was now kneeling beside his bride in the choir, in front of the lighted altar. The new bishop of Tangier, crosier in hand and mitre on head, came in sight, issuing from the sacristy, to unite them in the name of the Almighty. He asked the customary questions, effected the exchange of rings, pronounced the words which bind like chains, and delivered a Christian address to the newly united pair. He spoke at great length, and in pompous terms, of fidelity. He was stout and tall, one of those handsome bishops of majestic portliness. A noise of sobs made several people look round. Madame Walter, her face buried in her hands, was weeping.

She had been forced to yield. What else could she have done? But since the day of her daughter's return, when she had driven her out of her room and refused to kiss her, since the day when she had said, very low, to Du Roy, who was greeting her ceremoniously on his reappearance: "You are the vilest creature I have ever known. Never speak to me again! I shall not reply to you"—she had suffered intolerable, unappeasable torment. She hated Suzanne with a fierce hatred, compounded of mortified passion and rending jealousy, the strange fierce jealousy of mother and mistress, which she could confide to no one, a jealousy which burned like an open wound.

And now there was a bishop marrying these two, her daughter and her lover, in a church, in the presence of two thousand people and with her looking on. And she could say nothing. Could she not prevent it? Could she not cry out:

"But this man is mine. He is my lover. This union which you are blessing, is infamous."

Several women murmured sympathetically:

"How the poor mother feels it!"

The bishop held forth.

"You are among the fortunate of the earth, the rich and the respected. You, sir, whom your talents distinguish above others; you, who write, who teach, who advise, who guide the populace, you have a noble mission to fulfil, a splendid example to set . . ."

Drunk with pride, Du Roy listened to him. It was he, George Du Roy, that a prelate of the Church of Rome was thus addressing. And he was conscious that behind him there was a crowd of people, illustrious people, who had come on his behalf. It seemed to him that there was some force, which thrust him forwards and raised him up. He, the son of two poor peasants at Canteleu was becoming one of the masters of the earth.

He had a sudden vision of his parents serving out drinks to the country folk in the humble wine-shop, at the top of the hill, above the great valley of Rouen. Out of Count de Vaudrec's legacy he had sent them five thousand francs. Presently he would send them fifty thousand, and they would buy a small property and be very happy and content.

The bishop had finished his discourse. A priest in a golden stole was ascending to the altar. And the organ began again to glorify the newly wedded pair.

Sometimes it poured forth swelling waves of sound, sustained and prodigious, so sonorous and mighty that it seemed as if it would burst the roof and diffuse itself into the blue ether. Its vibrations filled the whole church, and set body and soul trembling. Suddenly it grew fainter ; and quick, delicate notes rippled through the air, caressing the ear like a gentle breeze ; little, graceful, trifling, playful melodies, which fluttered like birds. Suddenly this dainty music assumed its former grandeur, and became terrible in its force and fullness, as if a grain of sand had grown into a world.

The sound of human voices succeeded it, floating over the bowed heads. Vardi and Landeck from the Opera were singing. The incense diffused a delicate odour of gum-benjamin, and on the altar the divine sacrifice was consummated. The Saviour, at the summons of His priest, was descending upon earth to consecrate the triumph of Baron George Du Roy.

Kneeling beside Suzanne, Bel-Ami bowed his head. At that moment he felt himself almost a believer, almost of the faith, full of gratitude towards the divinity which had so favoured him, and had treated him with such consideration. And hardly knowing to whom he was addressing himself, he thanked him for his success.

When the service was over, he rose to his feet, offered his arm to his wife, and they proceeded to the sacristy. Then began the interminable march past of the guests.

Beside himself with joy, George imagined himself a king who has just been acclaimed by a nation. He shook hands, uttered meaningless words and greetings and replied to congratulations :

" You are very kind."

All at once he caught sight of Madame de Marelle, and the remembrance of all their kisses, the remembrance of all their embraces, her charm, the sound of her voice, the touch of her lips, instilled into his veins a sudden desire to take possession of her again. She was so pretty, so attractive, with her saucy air and her lively glances.

George thought to himself :

" After all what a charming mistress she was ! "

She drew near, rather timidly, rather diffidently and stretched out her hand to him. He took it in his own and held it. Then he felt the discreet womanly appeal of her hand, the gentle pressure which forgives and forgets. And he returned her clasp, as though to say, " I shall always love you, I am yours."

Their eyes met, smiling, flashing, full of love. And she whispered in her pleasant voice :

" We shall meet soon."

" We shall meet soon," he echoed gaily.

She passed on.

Others were pressing forward. The throng rolled past him like a river until the last guests had expressed their congratulations. George offered his arm to Suzanne to lead her back through the crowded church. All the guests had resumed their places to see them pass out together. He walked with calm and deliberate step, his head held high, his eyes fixed on the great doorway through which the sunlight poured. He felt himself quivering with the chill tremors of intense happiness. His eyes saw no one. He thought only of himself.

On the threshold he caught sight of the crowd that had gathered there ; a dense excited throng, which had come to see him, George Du Roy. All Paris was gazing at him, envying him.

Looking up, he caught sight of the Chamber of Deputies

behind the Place de la Concorde. And it seemed to him that one leap would carry him from the portico of the Madeleine to that of the Palais Bourbon.

Slowly he walked down the lofty flight of steps between two ranks of spectators. But he did not see them. His thoughts were now casting backwards, and before his eyes, dazzled by the brilliant sunshine, floated the image of Madame de Marelle. She was standing in front of the mirror, adjusting her little side curls, which were always untidy when she got out of bed.

THE WORKS OF PIERRE LOTI

ILLUSTRATED *with* PLATES *in* COLOURS *by*
MORTIMER MEMPES, ROMILLY FEDDEN,
A. LAMPLOUGH, JOHN FULLEYLOVE, *etc.*

JERUSALEM (JÉRUSALEM)

Translated by W. P. BAINES

There are many books on the Holy Land, but not
one that has in it anything such as Loti has put into
this nor one that makes Christ seem so real, and yet
all the time the author professes to be an unbeliever.
It has an extraordinary charm and fascination, and
believers and unbelievers alike will appreciate it.

JAPAN (MADAME CHRYSANTHÈME)

Translated by LAURA ENSOR

Loti's wonderful pictorial sense shows to the greatest
advantage in this account of his stay in Japan. From
the time his war boat arrives at Nagasaki until its
departure months after he keeps us enthralled with his
wonderful word pictures of the town and country scenes
and the people of the country. The book is charmingly
illustrated with pictures drawn specially for it.

THE WORKS OF PIERRE LOTI

ILLUSTRATED *with* PLATES *in* COLOURS *by*
MORTIMER MEMPES, ROMILLY FEDDEN,
A. LAMPLOUGH, JOHN FULLEYLOVE, *etc.*

EGYPT (LA MORT DE PHILAE)

Translated by W. P. BAINES

As the author glides over the darkening waters to the half-submerged island of Philae, gradually a comprehension grows upon him of the reasons that made Egypt the first country to awaken from the torpor of barbarism and to build monuments which are the wonder and admiration of the whole modern world.

INDIA (L'INDE, SANS LES ANGLAIS)

Translated by GEORGE A. F. INMAN (OF BOWDEN)

Loti's idea in going to India was to discover if in the Buddhist faith he could find anything to replace the Catholic religion in which he could no longer believe. He visits the ruined temples of the ancient Gods, he listens to the languorous Oriental music on the moonlight nights; he experiences nameless dreads, indescribable terrors. He visits the sacred city of Benares, and watches the rapt worshippers on the banks and the smoke ascending from the funeral pyre of an exquisitely beautiful Indian girl. Finally he visits the high priests of Theosophy who have sought refuge in India away from the tumult of life, and finds what his soul craves for.

THE WORKS OF PIERRE LOTI

ILLUSTRATED *with* PLATES *in* COLOURS *by*
MORTIMER MEMPES, ROMILLY FEDDEN,
A. LAMPLOUGH, JOHN FULLEYLOVE, *etc.*

A TALE OF THE PYRENEES (RAMUNTCHO)

Translated by W. P. BAINES

A love idyll in the setting of the Pyrenees, in the country of the Basques, that ancient and dwindling race which preserves so passionately its native pride, its old piety, and its disdain for things new and strange. The story of Ramuntcho's wooing of the golden-haired daughter of the enemy, and the misfortune that overtook it, is beautifully told, and the descriptions of the local scenery in the different seasons of the year, of the religious festivals, of the great contests in the national game, of the smuggling enterprises are marked by inimitable skill.

A TALE OF BRITTANY (MON FRÈRE YVES)

Translated by W. P. BAINES

This tale of Breton peasant life, with its simple joys and sorrows, is beautifully told. There are grim and sordid scenes at Brest showing the temptations that lie in wait for the sailor as he comes ashore, and the sufferings of the wives living in the seaport, and of course there are characteristic descriptions of the Breton country-side. Parallel with these there are descriptions of life in a warship during its cruise about the world.

THE WORKS OF PIERRE LOTI

ILLUSTRATED *with* PLATES *in* COLOURS *by*
MORTIMER MEMPES, ROMILLY FEDDEN,
A. LAMPLOUGH, JOHN FULLEYLOVE, *etc.*

MOROCCO (AU MAROC)

Translated by W. P. BAINES

Pierre Loti was a member of a diplomatic mission to
the Sultan of Morocco at Fez, and in this book he gives
us an extraordinarily fascinating account of the journey.
The departure of the caravan from Tangier, the encamp-
ments, the nightly arrival of the Mouna, the crossing of
the Oued-M'Cazen in flood, the fantasies and "powder-
play" of the Arab horsemen, the magnificent state entry
into Fez, are described in a succession of vivid pictures of
most brilliant colour.

THE SAHARA (LE ROMAN D'UN SPAHI)

Translated by MARJORIE LAURIE

Loti's sensitive, almost sensuous, and exotic art is
peculiarly fitted for such a subject as "the great sea
without water," and the Spahi on the Senegal, of romantic
passion and seductive smile, "undisciplined but not dis-
solute," whose love adventures range from sordid and
riotous town affairs to his passionate desert romance
with Fatou-Gaye.

THE WORKS OF PIERRE LOTI

ILLUSTRATED *with* PLATES *in* COLOURS *by*
MORTIMER MEMPES, ROMILLY FEDDEN,
A. LAMPLOUGH, JOHN FULLEYLOVE, *etc.*

MADAME PRUNE (LA TROISIÈME JEUNESSE DE MADAME PRUNE)

Translated by S. R. C. PLIMSOLL

In this book Loti describes his second visit to Japan,
and there are many charming pictures in the true Loti
style : pictures of himself seated solitary on black velvet
cushions, while two little Japanese maidens sing and dance
for his sole pleasure : of the lonely wood by the deserted
temple, where he keeps a daily tryst with a Japanese child
love : of the mountain-side where the graves are : of a
quaint fête day : of various tea-houses and of a visit to
Corea and the King's Court there.

SIAM (UN PÈLERIN D'ANGKOR)

Translated by W. P. BAINES

Loti describes with his extraordinary pictorial skill the
journey from Saigon into the interior ; first along the river
Mekong, at the time in flood, then through the thick
forest in the heart of which is buried the ruins of Angkor-
Thom, with its palaces and temples. His pathetic and
sentimental spirit is at home amongst these ruins, which
are all that remain of the proud Empire of the Khmers
which flourished for some 1,500 years.